LaRenna and Krell exchanged simple nods then apprentice and master reformed as lovers: tangled, panting and groping, caressing and tasting in a frenzy of denied desires. The mental experience fulfilled, the physical, which Krell took ravenously, defied description and they reveled in the insensibility of both until LaRenna's passionate internal cries reduced to an aural murmur that parted their mouths. Only then did they indulge in the joy of slow discovery, delighting in the repetition of what felt so true. Afterward, Krell lingered with her, stroking her face, whispering lover's fancy about her beauty until reality and guilt swept in.

"How could I be so stupid?" Krell's face pinched with revulsion as she pushed away.

"What?" Before LaRenna could prop on one arm Krell had risen and was dressing.

"I took something from you that I can never give back." Krell spoke over her shoulder as she tugged on her boots. "I've broken every barrier, crossed every line."

"You took nothing I wasn't willing to give." LaRenna, shivering from the sudden removal of companion warmth, drew into the sleep corner and sat upon the bedrolls.

"You weren't ready to lose your virginity yet, third Kimshee, and you certainly shouldn't have wasted such a precious commodity on the likes of me." Krell couldn't bear even the briefest of glances at LaRenna. She smelled like commitment. The room reeked of commitment as well—the safe, satisfying, stay at home, fresh cut flower joy of two women growing old together. It was nauseating. Krell had to leave and so left, ignoring LaRenna's calls to return so they could discuss things. She was dirty. Krell was dirty. What they had done was insanely wrong. Yes, Kimshees had sex, but they never made love.

Visit

Bella Books

at

BellaBooks.com

or call our toll-free number

1-800-729-4992

NO SISTER OF MINE

by Jeanne G'Fellers

Bella
BOOKS

2005

Bella Books, Inc.
P.O. Box 10543
Tallahassee, FL 32302

Printed in the United States of America on acid-free paper
First Edition

Editor: Anna Chinappi
Cover designer: Sandy Knowles

ISBN 1-59493-017-1

For Mamaw, who was Taelach tall and strong and unconditionally loving of her eldest granddaughter.

Acknowldgements

No Sister of Mine and all the novels in The Silver Kinship series derived from my need to escape. While my reasons for escaping have changed throughout the years, the need still remains as does the drive to tell the stories of those I met during my escapes. These women live in a plane I reach simply by closing my eyes. Theirs is a less than perfect existence—perfection must be horribly boring to write about—but it is a world built upon my wildest fantasies and deepest fears, a creation that would not have come about if it hadn't been for those dear to me, especially my mother. Thanks, Mom, for hiding a copy of this work from those who threatened to destroy it and for encouraging my writing when no one else seemed to care.

Virginia Marion and Kay Bridges have also been instrumental in developing my writing. Without their encouragement and their "You go, girl!" attitude I never would have had the strength to keep churning away at this novel and my college education.

To all those at Bella, including Linda Hill, Becky Arbogast and, of course, my editor Anna Chinappi, I say thank you for putting up with the myriad of questions from a newbie and the ecstatic, girlish squeals of a woman learning her first manuscript has been accepted.

Finally, I would like to express love and gratitude for my partner, my favorite Gunny at ease, the one I love always and all ways—Anna Koetter. Thank you for your unconditional support, for your assistance with child-wrangling, for taking the household helm when my graduate courses take place at night, and for your daily office drudgery that allows me to continue my schooling and writing. And last but certainly not least, thank you for encouraging me to submit *No Sister of Mine* to just one more publisher. You were right, my love, Bella is where it belonged.

Prologue

By the late twenty-third century, numerous stars in the Milky Way were known to have orbiting planets capable of sustaining life. One of these, Sixty-One Cygni, a yellow sun with a planet similar in orbit and mass to Earth, intrigued human researchers and entrepreneurs alike.

Entrepreneurs, given a head start by the unrest between the Earth and Moon/Mars Alliances, won the competition for exploration, establishing a mining colony in the mineral-rich, frozen subsurface of Sixty-One Cygni's sixth planet, which later came to be known as Farstar. A small group of researchers soon followed and began studying the second planet in the system—then known to be inhabited by a humanoid species calling itself the Autlach. When natural disaster struck the colony, the human colonists fled to this planet to await rescue—one which never came. As time passed, they began to intermingle then interbreed with the Autlach, forever changing the genetic makeup of a society, one which was steeped in religious teachings of the deity Raskhallak. The Raskhallak teachings demanded the Autlach follow a strict canon of daily prayer and obedience. A good man ruled his family with an iron hand and taught his sons to be future rulers. His daughters were taught subservience from birth. Any deviation from their duty, any sin (so Raskhallak claimed), evidenced in the birth of an albino child. Fathers flogged their daughters for bearing such a babe; husbands destroyed the evidence, sometimes killing both mother and child to hide their embarrassment.

As heinous as this was, such an event remained rare until the second generation of Human-Autlach hybrids. In that generation, a recessive human gene made itself known, producing a mutation when present in both parents. The resulting daughters—pale, blue-eyed, sterile and telepathic—were everything the russet Autlach were not. Rejected by their families, they found acceptance in each other, forming small clans that kept to the high mountains far above the Autlach.

Centuries of misunderstanding melded into stricter religious doctrine, giving the pale Autlach daughters, now called Taelachs, unwarranted reputation as cruel witches. They were killed at birth unless rescued by a Kimshee—a Taelach sister trained to sense Taelach fetuses through telepathy. Sparse in numbers but determined to survive, the Taelach clung to their existence, eventually rediscovering the history of their origins and with it, the technology that brought humanity to Sixty-One Cygni. This technology also brought the Taelach together under one governing body— The Silver Kinship. Now capable of securing infant sisters from their disinterested birth parents, Kinship numbers skyrocketed almost as quickly as Taelach technology advanced. They were now able to explore Sixty-One Cygni and colonize the worlds surrounding it, bringing about an era of harmony that lasted until the unthinkable happened in a peaceful society—civil war.

A faction bent on the enslavement of the Autlach rebelled against the Kinship, shaking the very foundations of Taelach culture. Amidst the chaos, a new leader rose to power. Young as she was unrelenting in her love for the Kinship, Belsas Exzal took the Kinship's reins, soon squelching the rebellion and sentencing the conspirators to exile on Farstar's prison colony. Cance Creiloff, the leader of the rebellion and former comrade of Belsas Exzal, promised to return, a pledge that grew into vowed revenge as she and the other conspirators were branded with the Taelach symbol for traitor.

So ended the Taelach civil war and began the six-decade reign of Belsas Exzal as Taelach of All. A strong, vibrant leader, Belsas guides the Silver Kinship through a decade and a half of continued problems, including an Autlach uprising against the Kinship and the invasion of Iralian Commitment—an alien reptilian species with the macabre reputation for feasting on living enemy flesh. Now bound together against a common enemy, the Taelach and Autlach form an uneasy alliance—one as vulnerable to old prejudices as it is strengthened by fear.

This tale begins one decade after the Taelach civil war.

Chapter One

Take the child of your resemblance. There is no place for her in the limits of the Autlach existence.

—Taelach saying

―――――――――――

Fizzelle tried to focus on the troubled face that lingered above her own. The pains in her abdomen had subsided, leaving her feeling quite empty inside. "Where's the child?" she muttered. "I want my baby."

"You're too weak." Laiman pulled the blankets to her chin, smoothed her whorlish curls, then looked toward the small, crying bundle nuzzled in the midwife's arms.

Fizzelle's dark eyes glazed with want. "Laiman, the child. Let me see it."

The midwife shook her head a decided no.

"Sleep now, Zelle. I'll tend the baby."

"What's wrong with the babe? Laiman? Why can't I . . ." Her

voice trailed off as he eased the sleep smoker mask over her nose and mouth.

"Forgive me." Laiman's heart broke as her hold loosened then fell away. "But it's easier to forget what you never see."

The midwife clutched the child tight and turned toward the doorway. "They'll be here soon. I'll watch her until they come."

"Wait."

"Laiman, no." She pulled just out of his reach. "Don't make memories."

"They're already made. Now let me see my daughter." He took the baby from her resistant arms and cradled it in his own. "She has her mother's round face and button nose."

"And Taelach hair and eyes," reminded the midwife as she forced the infant from him. "The infant must go. She's one of them."

"But what do I tell Fizzelle? She's longed for another child."

The midwife scowled. Further delay would mean contact, unavoidable conversation with those she detested. "She already has two. One loss won't make that much difference. Mothers have endured this for eons. A little sacrifice won't harm her, or you. Let it go, Laiman. There'll be others—"

Two imposing shadows appeared just outside the door, hesitating to share an embrace before they entered the small birthing chamber. The smaller of the pair approached the now gray-faced midwife and reached a slender hand toward the baby. "A beautiful child." Her whisper was thickly accented. "She will be treasured." With an approving nod to her partner, she pulled the young one into her arms, delighting when a tiny hand grasped her finger and pulled it to a suckling mouth. Eyes reflective with understanding, she spoke something in the Taelach tongue Laiman couldn't comprehend, drew her cloak around the baby, and departed.

Once the first Taelach was safely away, the second, room-dominating figure pulled back her hood, revealing a strong-featured face. White hair came into view, white hair that was cropped razor short save for the two braids that hung from her right temple. She gazed at Laiman, her blue eyes reflective as well, but almost cold in their intent. "Does the child have a name?"

Laiman froze at the demanding voice, staring at its owner.

"The child? Has she been named?"

The midwife broke Laiman's silence. "The mother said a girl was to be named LaRenna."

The Taelach nodded slowly, as if digesting the bit of information. "Then LaRenna it shall be."

Laiman grabbed the arm of the dark-cloaked figure in desperation. "My wife? What do I—" Fear swelled into such consuming anger he shook. "You can't take our child!" The steady stare that met his sent a spine-tingling sensation of calm washing over him. He released his handhold then stepped back, astonished by his sudden inexplicable passivity.

"The child is Taelach," came the sedate explanation from the remaining figure. "She was born with a warrior's spirit and a seer's mind. Could you teach her to use her gifts as we can? She belongs with her own kind. It is for her benefit and safety she becomes one of us." Hood now drawn, the Taelach paused on the birth room threshold, her muscular shoulders leaving room for little else. "Full separation is best. Tell your woman the child is dead." The rhythmic clicking of her boot heels faded into the early morning mists, replaced, only briefly, by a quickly answered infant's bawl of hunger. Taelach babies were taught to cry in silence. Laiman, heavy-hearted, turned back to his wife, wishing he could learn the same.

Chapter Two

Listen to your Raisers. Through their wisdom and experience you will rise above Autlach prejudices.

—Taelach saying

Malley leaned out the window, eager for a better view of the courtyard below. "They're posting! It's about time. Where do you think they'll send us? How about a look, LaRenna?" Malley turned to see her roommate closed-eyed and round-shouldered over the music recorder in her petite lap. The earpieces blocked all outside noise as she hummed with the music. Malley sighed and snatched a pillow from the sleeping corner. It grazed the side of LaRenna's face, knocking an earpiece from her curl-covered head. "Hey! You gonna meditate all day or do we get to see our posts?"

"They're posting? It's still early, isn't it?" LaRenna set the recorder on her chair and joined Malley by the window. "Let's give it a few minutes to clear out."

7

"How crowded can it get? There are only eighty of us up for posting this training term."

"And all but two of us are down there right now." LaRenna glanced at the courtyard. "Besides, Grandmaster Quall is there. You want one of her once-overs?"

Malley's nose wrinkled with disdain. "Not particularly. Quall is still after me because I sneaked out of an Autlach customs seminar."

"You should've stayed." LaRenna's finger spotted one of the closures of her roommate's polished tunic buttons. "It was a damn sight more interesting than that Engineering Maintenance trainer you took in its place."

"That's what you say."

LaRenna gave a cherubic grin only she could manage. "With that class on your records the only thing you'll EVER be doing is scanning cell reading boards. And it'll probably be on a repair dock."

"What's wrong with a repair dock?" Malley's mouth puckered.

"Too tame."

"Tame?" The remark earned LaRenna a sour glare.

"Exactly! No thrill. No challenge."

"I'm sure the Iralians would be more than honored by your presence at the truce line." Malley peered hard at LaRenna. "What's it been now, twenty passes? You'd rather post there I suppose?"

A stray flounce of hair fell across LaRenna's dimpled chin as she shook her head. "Staring down scale backs? Not me. I've a sense of adventure. An explorer vessel is more my style."

"For you, maybe, but not me. Besides, explorer vessels have little call for Kimshees, or"—Malley made a dramatic pause and poked LaRenna's upper arm—"snipers either."

"Sniper?"

"Come on, Renna." Malley chortled. "Everybody knows your perfect kill ratio on your last three plasma bow exams."

"I didn't tell you that."

"Didn't have to. Everyone in your training squad's pissed that you ruined the point curve. And seeing as I'm your roommate . . ." Malley shrugged.

"They should have practiced more."

"Practice my eye! The only thing you've ever practiced hard at is a recorder box. Oh yeah, and bitterwine."

LaRenna crossed her arms. "Not true! I had to work to get a decent score in linguistics and you know it."

"Decent?" Malley snorted indignantly and pulled a hair from the corner of LaRenna's pouting mouth. "You scored fluent in ten Aut dialects."

"So? You have to be good at something. I seem to recall you gliding through engineering courses I barely scored proficiency in. I'll never get pilot qualified at this rate."

"It fascinates me. That's all."

"And bores me." LaRenna's lighter mood seemed to return. "Too many dry numbers and schematics to memorize."

Malley's slowly reacting features started to pull with concern. "Guess we like different things, don't we?"

"Then why have you bunked with me the last three passes? I've kept you in trouble." Malley, with an expression now on the verge of piteous, joined LaRenna and fingered the fringed edge of the blanket roll nearest her. The reason was plain enough, but Malley always proved too reserved to admit it. "I don't know. Maybe because you never let me take myself too seriously."

"What's the use? Life's no fun if you can't see the humor in things." LaRenna winked at her friend, a gesture that sent Malley's heart soaring. "Sometimes, the humor has to be coaxed out. Call it creativity."

Malley lowered her head as an embarrassed chuckle escaped her happy mouth. "Like the time you switched activation agents in Master Riles's lab? I think she failed to see the humor in the test fuel cells foaming and freezing when they were supposed to be charging. I don't remember you laughing about those seven off days you spent on night sentry post as punishment either. Mighty creative of you, Renna."

"You laughed enough for both of us," LaRenna said.

"That's because it took an entire moon cycle for the green discoloration to wear off your hands and arms. Was body art what you had in mind?"

"Bet I'll never be posted on a cell maintenance station." LaRenna punctuated the retort with a smart flick of her tongue. "That'd have to be boring duty. Worse than a stinking repair dock." She checked the courtyard again.

"Quall still down there?" queried Malley in futile hope.

"Of course." LaRenna settled her back against the sill. "She even gives the graduates a hard time. Right now she's doing a number on poor Salu. Isn't she senior level?"

"Think so. I wonder what she did." Malley's voice remained low, as if believing Quall long-eared enough to hear three floors up. "We'd best stay out of sight. Get back from the window."

LaRenna cast her roommate an all too familiar grin. She loved to push things one step further whenever possible, a fact that had landed her at disciplinary hearings on several occasions. "But Malley," she cried with a wave to the courtyard's occupants. "If I lean out a little more I can spit in the center of Quall's head!"

Malley gasped. "You wouldn't?"

LaRenna cleared her throat and pursed her lips. "Watch me."

"Oh no!" Malley's normal monotone disappeared into a shriek. "You're not getting me in deep this time!" She grabbed LaRenna's boot tops, pulling her to the floor. The weapons belt circling LaRenna's curving waist gave a metallic clank as it bounced on the floor tiles.

"Ouch!" LaRenna rubbed her insulted backside. "Would you give me a warning or a cushion?"

"Let me know before you decide to wash Quall's hair and you won't need a cushion for your rump," grumped Malley, offering a pillow.

"Thanks, Mal. What hair? Quall's guardian, remember?"

"And what's wrong with that?" Malley snapped. "Or do you forget what I am?"

"How could I?" A brief, intimate familiarity swept into LaRenna's tone. "Besides, I knew you were when we first met."

"At sixteen?" Malley's hands found their way to her mussed crop of flaxen hair. "I wasn't even quite sure myself at that age."

"Everyone decides in their own time. I'd just decided before we met." LaRenna tousled her roommate's short, unruly locks as she ran her free hand over her own loosely tacked spirals. "You chose well."

Malley reveled in the warmth of her touch. How she loved LaRenna's caresses, infrequent and platonic as they might be. Malley had always been attracted to women like her roommate— their curves, their gentle smell when she bent to kiss them, but with LaRenna her attraction neared obsession. Familiarity and trust led to the mind linking required of Taelach mates, they said. Malley held tight to those words. "Where do you think they'll send us?"

"Who knows?" said LaRenna softly. "But at least we won't be alone."

"Yes, we will." Malley's head now rested fully against LaRenna's shoulder. Should her urges, her emotions be expressed before they were separated? No, the timing just wasn't right.

"You're assigned to a Kimshee your first post."

"That's only temporary." Malley's return sounded almost angry. "Maybe it's me, but I always feel so uneasy when I'm in a room of Auts."

"When were you ever in a room of Auts?" Malley's teeth clenched and released at LaRenna's biting observation. "Most of them accept us these days. They depend on us as much as we do them." LaRenna continued stroking Malley's hair and smiled thoughtfully. Her high-shouldered roommate was demonstrating some of the customary Taelach reservations. Besides, a strong sense of protection was part of a guardian's nature, and Malley's had come to include LaRenna. It was all right that it be extended to her. They had been roommates for quite some time. "Like it or not, we are related to them."

"Yeah, we're mutant cousins." Malley slid down to use LaRenna's thigh as a headrest, affording her the lingering physical contact she longed for.

"That's not our fault."

"They treat you differently if you're Taelach. It's as if they don't trust us." Malley toyed with the holder loops of LaRenna's loose belt. "You're losing weight again. Get much smaller and someone will mistake you for a child."

LaRenna ignored the affectionate concern. Malley knew well enough that she was frequently mistaken for a Taelach youth. "Look at our history. We're like them but nothing like them. Too hu-man—" she stumbled over the pronunciation—"in appearance. Physically too similar to the witches the Autlach's Raskhallak deity warns against. Besides, would you trust a people who obtain their young by taking yours? Even if what they take are your castoffs, your misfits, your cursed?"

"Your gay."

"There're gay Auts."

"Not if they're caught at it." Malley shuddered a bit. "The way they cleanse . . . it's so . . ."

"Fire cleansing's been banned so there's not as many disfigurements as there used to be. Kimshees are helping in that regard." LaRenna sat up a bit taller.

"Only 'cause we forced the Auts into it as part of the treaty."

"Doesn't matter how it came to be, only that Kimshees are opening Aut eyes. A Kimshee's purpose, besides bringing infants to their raisers, is to help us adapt to the Aut and them to us. That's why I chose to become one."

"Well, I certainly couldn't do it."

"Why?" asked LaRenna, though she had no doubt about the answer.

"Too much bad blood." Malley's lean face darkened with contempt. Autlach blood might course through Taelach veins, but it certainly didn't mean they had to be an intricate part of their lives. Malley couldn't understand why a beautiful, bright woman like LaRenna would want to either. Taelachs who never dealt with Autlachs seemed to live much happier lives. "They used to hunt us. Slave us. Burn us alive. Cleanse us en masse. Worse. Many Auts would still have it that way if it weren't for our technology. How can you possibly get past that enough to deal with them on a daily basis?"

12

Malley's bitterness deeply disturbed LaRenna but it was something she knew she'd never change. Like Autlach prejudices, they were ingrained into the Taelach mentality. "I think about the future. I think about the young ones I will get to hold before their own raisers do. I think of how lucky we are that now we no longer have to abduct mothers carrying Taelach sisters to ensure the baby's survival. I think of how the Kinship's numbers are growing because we finally convinced the Autlach to accept us."

"They merely tolerate us because we could blow them from the sky at any moment and they know it." Malley's mouth twitched with scorn. "And so do you."

"I admit it's sometimes a strained relationship, but it's something and more than we've ever had before." LaRenna's fingers unconsciously tightened about Malley's hair until her eyes opened. LaRenna's downward gaze was by far her most serious. "I want to help change things, be part of the peace. That's why I chose to become Kimshee."

"And go through apprenticeship training to do it. You'll never finish your schooling." Malley ran her finger down LaRenna's soft palm. "Do you ever think about them?"

"Kimshee apprentices?"

"No, your birth parents. Don't you ever wonder what they're like or if you have Aut brothers and sisters?"

"Of course I do." LaRenna scratched at her hand. "Who hasn't? But I don't very often. Belsas and Chandrey raised me with love. I feel almost guilty asking for more." She pushed Malley away, rose to her knees, and peeked hopefully at the courtyard. "All clear. Let's check our postings."

"What was it like?" Malley lingered on the floor, still holding LaRenna's hand.

"Being raised by the Taelach of All?" LaRenna settled cross-legged beside her.

"Uh-huh."

"My gahrah is like most of your brooding types, pretty reserved, sometimes unemotional. I never could read her well enough to tell when I had overstepped my bounds."

Malley raised a high arched eyebrow in suspicion. "Really?"

"She'd just smile like nothing happened and find me the most horrid chores to do around the housing compound."

"She never smacked you?"

Shock sprang into LaRenna's long-lashed eyes. "Why, no! Mamma would have exploded if Belsas ever had. When things got intense, Bel would just walk away. I probably would have preferred a thrashing to those chores or Chandrey's lectures. It certainly would've been quicker." LaRenna shook her head as childhood memories encroached her thoughts. "Those lectures made me feel so small."

Malley dropped her handhold to smooth the bedrolls into inspection perfection. "I would have taken chores or words over a belt to the back end any day. Believe me, LaRenna, you would have too."

LaRenna offered her friend a considering stare. Malley's childhood had been impossibly rough, plagued by a pair of raisers who had never gotten along and had taken their problems out on their only child with regular ferocity. No wonder Malley had gone into military schooling at such a young age; it was an escape mechanism. "You make me feel privileged to have been raised by them. Chandrey and Belsas have always been close. That's probably why they waited so long before they took a child to raise. I guess they were making sure of themselves."

"Lucky you." Malley's expression turned dourer than ever. "Dressa and Whellen seemed to think raising me involved intense screaming and yelling. Not that it matters. I survived it."

"And managed to rise above it, Third Engineer Malley Whellen." LaRenna gave Malley's hand a confident squeeze and then tugged her toward the door. "Come on, you overcharged sodium cell." Laughing, she vaulted down the corridor to the floor-level lifts, dragging her reluctant roommate behind. "Let's check our posts."

Chapter Three

Speak not of your Taelach daughters. Their birth is substantiation of your sin.

—*Autlach saying*

In the high plains of southern Vartoch, deep within the Taelach-owned lands opened for Autlach settlement, Sentry Commander Trazar Laiman watched his father polish two names listed on the Death Stone. Unlike the other forgotten names, these two were meticulously kept. "You keep their memory well."

"You'll be going soon, won't you?" His father's hands never wavered from their task.

"My launch leaves in an hour." Trazar ran his palm over the top of the weathered boulder. "I wish I had better memories of M'ma."

Laiman nodded slowly. "You weren't yet six when she died. Mercy barely seven. Neither of you was old enough for many memories. I did what I could to make her seem real."

At the sound of his father's anguish, Trazar offered what comfort he could. "You did well by us."

"I'm proud of my children." But Laiman avoided his eyes. "I sometimes wonder how things would have been if she'd lived. Losing the baby destroyed her so. It wasn't half a moon cycle later that she . . ." Laiman's voice trailed off.

Curiosity topped Trazar's better judgment, driving him to question what no one dare speak of. Minor inconsistencies in what little he had been told indicated his mother's suicide but not his infant sister's fate. "Why did the baby die? Nobody ever told me."

Laiman gave his son a long, pained look. Memories hurt. So did lies. "She was a lot like you in the face, same chin, same jaw line. She even had the same birthmark on her ear. If only . . ."

"If only what? What happened to the baby?" Trazar stopped his father's polishing hand with his own. "What happened?"

"It's a long trip to the launches and two hard days to Langus. You'd best go."

"Answer me!"

Laiman bowed his head, shoulders slouched and arms drawn as if cuddling the lost child. "She was perfect except—" He paused. "Then, despite my efforts, she was gone. No one could have prevented it. It doesn't matter what took her, only that she's gone."

"I wish I'd known her."

"Me, too," mumbled Laiman, pushing away the invisible bundle. "Me, too."

Trazar looked at the sun's place in the afternoon sky, aware of the time but reluctant to leave. "I have to go. I'll send word as soon as my post on Langus grants time."

"Safe journey to you." Laiman wrapped his arms around his son in a gruff embrace. Trazar had matured well. He was a full head taller than Laiman and almost twice as broad in the shoulder which, though not astounding for an Autlach, was unusual for the family's small-statured genetics. Laiman admitted military training could fill one out in such a way, but liked to think a childhood spent in the fresh air of Vartoch's single expansive continent had. "Be careful. Langus can be dangerous."

16

"Not the base, Dah, and that's where I'll be." Trazar turned and walked down the hillside toward the launch stop, his shoulder pack swaying with his pace. He wondered if things were really as his father said, or if possibly . . . ?

Laiman ran his hand over one of the Death Stone's names. The ridged letters stung his fingers with the lie they contained.

LARENNA NELL LAIMAN
BIRTH/DEATH
DAY 4–CYCLE 10–RECORDED PZ4428

Turning back, Laiman watched his son fade from view. He longed to stop him and tell everything, something, anything about that morning twenty-two passes ago. It had been unfortunate, a terrifying event, and if anyone ever found out . . . Laiman shook his head. If anyone found out, the family lineage would be marred for generations. They would be known as producers of Taelachs, of white witches, of the barren, pale-eyed women who'd rather die in the fires than kneel before an Autlach husband. To seed or bear one was unnatural, despite any rumor the Taelach might spread about genetics. If anyone knew, Laiman's descendants would be unmarriable, untrustworthy, barred from holding public or temple positions. No, it was too great a risk to tell Trazar. The midwife's silence had cost the family's savings, and the ties had been cut with the infant's shushed cry. Laiman's hands returned to LaRenna's etched name. The Taelach pair had seemed stable enough. Well off. Not children, but the Taelach never sent children. Nor had he ever heard of them sending anyone besides the customary Kimshee, and worst of all Laiman had recognized the taller one's voice. It was a voice few Auts could forget. Belsas Exzal had spoken to the Autlach people at large on several occasions since the Taelach civil war had ended. Laiman's recognition of the voice had only made things worse. To be known as the sire of the Taelach of All's daughter? No one could ever know. It would be the family's ruin. The secret was his alone to bear and bear it he would, for the rest of his life.

Chapter Four

Your post is your life. Guard it as such.

—Sarian Military Standards of Honor

"It must be there somewhere. You've just overlooked it." Malley fidgeted as LaRenna re-read the courtyard postings.

"For the third time, Mal, it's not damn well there!" LaRenna flung the list at her dorm mate. "You look!"

Malley's fingers drew over the series of names and destinations in hopes of spotting an error. Finding none, she gave LaRenna a nervous, lip-chewing glance. "You're right! What gives—you fail a final or something?"

"Not bloody likely," came the flustered reply. "There must be a mistake. I'd better check with the Master Yeoman. I'm sure she has my posting." LaRenna cast her roommate a circumspect look and their eyes locked in the same dumbfounded manner. What could she possibly have done wrong? Had Quall been aware of her mischief? "I hope she has my posting."

"I'm sure she does." An odd grin splashed over Malley's cheeks, scrunching her broad face as she turned toward the opened dormitory doors. "You check then come back to our room. I'll be packing. I still can't believe I've been posted to Master Engineer Ockson on the Predator. Praise be, my posting is to a Taelach ship. No Auts to deal with and no Kimshees to work under! No offense intended." Malley bubbled with such excitement that LaRenna felt a twinge of jealousy. "Besides, I've no desire to be around the Master Yeoman. Grandmaster Quall lurks around there entirely too much."

"Well, they are life mates." LaRenna sucked her cheeks in dismay. "But I so hope Quall's not around. Last thing I need is the Protocol Master on my back—again. Wish me luck."

"You'll need it if Quall is about."

"Gee thanks, Malley." With that thought weighing her mind, LaRenna jogged toward the Stores building, reciting a little prayer as she went.

Mother Maker take this day and make it work for me.
Your gentle help I'll hold up high for all the world to see.
Your praises I will sing out loud, rejoicing in your light.
Give me the strength to do your work, do what you will as right.

The Stores was a massive facility located in the heart of the training grounds. It was easily ten times larger than the senior dormitory and all the darker, its echoing halls the dirge of many a disobedient student, LaRenna included. The outside columns were carved with the everyday scenes of Sarian life and the walls graced with paintings of Taelach folklore. LaRenna usually stopped to enjoy these captivating pictures but this time passed them without notice. She identified herself to the sentry posted outside the main doors then went down the hall leading to the Yeoman's workroom. The door was ajar.

At her worktable, Wreed Qualls, Master Yeoman, her hair pulled into a neat twist, scribed on a thick bandit-hide scroll. "All the modern forms of recording and communications, and some of the Kinship still insist on the tradition of scrolls," mumbled LaRenna. Some habits died hard.

19

"After six passes under my careful guidance, I would think you would have more presence of mind than to skulk in someone's doorway." Protocol Grandmaster Quall Dawn's commanding voice boomed from a dimly lit corner. LaRenna cringed and took a small step forward. Sometimes even the most consecrated of prayers went unheard.

"Hmm?" The Yeoman squinted her bright, saucer-shaped eyes at the doorway. "Ah, Belsas's daughter. Come in, child. We've been expecting you." The word *we've* soured the remains of LaRenna's breakfast. She swallowed hard.

"There's been a mistake then?"

"Manners, girl!" Quall began to rise. "Remember our ranking before you proceed."

"Apologies, Grandmaster Quall." LaRenna folded her right arm across her chest to her left shoulder and bowed her head in salute.

"Quall," reprimanded the Yeoman. "She's graduate braided. The salute isn't called for among officers of the Kinship in a setting such as this and you know it."

"It is until she officially leaves my training grounds," snapped Quall. The heavy heel of the grandmaster's right boot tapped at a rapid pace, a sign that sent seasoned students fleeing for cover. "At rest Third Kimshee LaRenna Belsas. Have a seat and we'll begin."

LaRenna chose one of the oversized chairs facing the Yeoman's worktable and sat in awkward silence, crossing and uncrossing her legs, wishing that her feet touched the floor. It made her feel like a child in need of discipline and for once, she truly didn't know her crime. Yeoman Wreed picked up on her anxiety and sulked with displeasure. "Quall Dawn!" she exclaimed, pointing to the young officer in front of her. "Look at what you've done! You terrify every cadet to the point they won't come see me unless their life depends on it." Extreme discontent curled the Yeoman's ruby mouth as she peered over her shoulder. "Come out of your hole and sit where we can see you." She turned back to LaRenna with a smile. "She doesn't bite, Third Kimshee. You know how her kind is—all bluff and bellow."

Quall emerged from the corner grim-faced and settled into the chair next to LaRenna's. "I might bite." She sneered and smoothed the generous folds of her instructor's robes. "It's been rumored that I've consumed more than one of my students."

"By the Maker, Quall! I'm warning you to behave yourself." A hide scroll sailed across the room, narrowly missing Quall's close-shorn head. She flinched and sank a little in her chair, a difficult feat for one of such fleshy dimensions.

"All right, Wreed. I was only funning her. It serves a purpose and you know it. My pupils always leave here thoughtful and respectful of their superiors."

LaRenna had never known Grandmaster Quall to back down from anyone—before now. In her wildest dreams, she wouldn't have imagined Quall bowing to the will of someone like the dainty Master Yeoman. Why, she was almost as small as LaRenna was herself!

"I agree with you, Quall." The grudging admission chilled Wreed's otherwise pleasant expression. "But I don't always care for your tactics."

Quall reached a ring-laden hand to pat the Yeoman's forearm. "Point taken, my dear. I'll mind my manners from here on out. Now, let's tell the young woman why she's here."

Wreed shuffled through the mounded scrolls on her worktable. "There was no mistake, Third Kimshee Belsas. You weren't on the posting list for a reason." Smiling at her success, she held up her inkstained hand—"Here it is"—and passed a small signal recorder to LaRenna. "Believe it or not, I do use modern technology on occasion."

LaRenna flipped up the viewer and pushed the replay marker. Surprisingly, the face of one of her raisers, Taelach of All Belsas Exzal, appeared on the thin crystalline screen. LaRenna remembered playing at Belsas's feet when many such messages were sent and, until this moment, had always been envious of the far-off

21

recipient. "LaRenna, my child, I request for you to take a special posting requiring all your abilities and talents. You are to report to First Kimshee Krell Middle on Langus for further details. I believe you are the only one capable of carrying this post to its needed fullness. This is hazardous duty, so you cannot be forced into accepting it. Please advise Grandmaster Quall of your decision. I am forever your proud raiser. Belsas out."

Placing the recorder on the table, LaRenna cast the Master Yeoman an inquisitive look. The message had been exceptionally bare of decision-making information. "What does she mean by hazardous?"

"We can't tell you much." Quall's hand continued its gentle grip on Wreed's slender arm. "They've kept us in the dark as well. But nasty rumors are circulating about doings on Langus. Seems the locals are in a tizzy over the recent base expansion. Talk is of removing it, by force if necessary."

LaRenna's stare proved incredulous. "If it wasn't for the presence of the base, the Iralians would have decimated Langus twenty passes ago! Look what they did to Myeflar." She stood so quickly the force sent scrolls flying from the Yeoman's desk.

"We're aware of what happened during the initial Iralian invasion, Third Kimshee Belsas. Please sit down." The Yeoman hissed recognition of Quall's low chuckle as she retrieved her scattered scrolls. "It's rumored that one of the Branded's been sighted as well."

"But they're all confined inside the prison colony."

"A few occasionally escape into the Jungleland clans," shrugged Quall, still humored by the yeoman's disorganization. "And there are still others who simply disappear. None of them has had the equipment to go off world thus far. Seems someone managed to rig up a launch. Probably smuggled it out of the colony piece by piece."

"Correct." Wreed swatted a scroll at Quall's outstretched hand. "Not a word from you, Quall Marie Dawn. I know where everything on this table is as long as someone doesn't upheave my system. LaRenna, you know as well as we do that the colony is forever having internal problems. I've seen many a good officer corrupted by the black market there. Whoever escaped definitely had high-placed backing."

"And what am I to do about it?" asked LaRenna. "I haven't completed Kimshee training." Her superior's blank expressions showed they knew nothing more. "What's my option if I reject this post?"

Wreed sighed and retook her ink-spattered stylus. "There's a training spot available with the new Kimshee posting at the number four cell charging station on Vartoch."

Quall laughed heartily at LaRenna's long frown. "I've yet to meet a Kimshee who embraces the idea of that post. Your things have been packed for you. The launch for Polmel leaves in an hour. You'll be on Langus in two days."

Chapter Five

Foolish is she who shows the paleness of her face after the sun has risen for she will surely be burned.

—*Taelach proverb*

The faint rays of first dawn were peeking over the horizon when Krell Middle sank her bare toes into the cool white sands of the southern Langus shoreline. This was the ideal time to be out if one was Taelach. The fishing boats had already set out and morning call had yet to be sounded at the base on the hills above the shore, leaving the sands deserted. Once, Krell could become lost in soul searching and reflection in the ocean sounds on mornings like this, but not anymore. The echoes of growth invaded her meditations more and more. Construction progressed around the clock, work lights shining onto the dark, algae-heavy waters, diminishing the splendor of the coming morn.

Shadows from the grassy dunes danced and lengthened in the

starlight. Saria Proper's shadow passed over the sunrise, returning Langus briefly into night. The sand brush cracked against the rough canvas of Krell's duty leggings as she climbed to the top of a small dune near the waterline. Once on top, she pulled a thick stem of grass, placed the salt-laden blade between her teeth, and sat on a boulder perched on the dune's zenith.

They have a legitimate complaint. Krell peered back toward the expanding base. The military had made itself too oppressive a presence for the agrarian mind. The Sarian base had almost tripled in size during the three passes she'd posted there. The rolling farmscapes of Saria Two's only moon were fading into the starkness of a military compound. She wondered how different things would be if the Iralian threat didn't exist.

Meditations complete, the day rapidly approaching, Krell focused on the critical tasks her new apprentice must accomplish. Would an inexperienced Kimshee be able to handle things effectively? Only time would tell. "So, LaRenna Belsas, let's see who you've grown into." Krell pulled a small data recorder from her pocket and flipped up the screen, scrolling until LaRenna's records appeared. Nothing in particular stood out on the first few screens. There were only the standards: limited birth information, early schooling records—the usual. On the fifth screen, a weapons training log, Krell stopped. "Well, I'll be." She mused over what she saw. "If all goes well she'll never have need of that skill." The typical coursework of the Training Grounds appeared next. Above average scores, but nothing overly impressive, besides linguistics. Scores there indicated LaRenna's astounding comprehension of all the Autlach dialects. The optional training proved fascinating as well. Advanced coursework in survival skills often proved the difference between life and death in the Kimshee trade. "Hmmm." Krell read LaRenna's disciplinary summary. "Belsas's girl is every bit the spitfire I remember. Independence is one thing, recklessness quite another. We'll see if she really has the makings of a Kimshee soon enough."

The wake call blared its shrill alarm. Krell closed the recorder and leaned back, extending her arms above her head to remove the kinks. "And the day begins," she sighed, twitching as a particularly deep scar complained about movement. "I'd best get going." Cloak tight against the morning chill, she sprinted toward the Commons, pausing to brush the sand from her feet before she pulled on her boots. "Your recorder," she grumbled, turning back. "It's too damn early to think straight, much less socialize." She snatched the recorder and returned to her run, scaling the rocky incline to the main path in three quick strides. "This Starnes fellow had best show."

Chapter Six

Taelach witch, Taelach witch, cooking in the fire.
Taelach witch, Taelach witch, make the flames dance higher.
Your deadly eyes will burn away and never hurt again.
Taelach witch, Taelach witch, die in Autlach flames.

—Autlach children's rhyme

"Starnes! Bring me another." Brandoff Creiloff narrowed her sapphire blue eyes and pointed to her empty glass.

Starnes stopped sweeping. Scornful of her relentless badgering, he frowned, pulled a dirty rag from his apron pocket, and dabbed at his forehead. "Look, I'm not open yet. Why don't you go upstairs and get some sleep while it's quiet? You could use it."

Her eyes now slitted, Brandoff's pale, leathered face puckered ever so slightly. "You haven't looked in a reflecting board lately have you, portly? Now get me the damn drink!"

Starnes took another wine crystal to the table and poured two glasses, sitting to draw from one while Brandoff guzzled hers in a single swig. "The Regional Patrol will have my hide if they find you here," he pleaded between sips of the sweet brew. "Please, Brandoff, go upstairs."

She slid her wiry bare feet slid into his lap, rubbing them into his groin. "You love the danger of having me down here," she tempted in a low, seductive voice.

Starnes pulled her foot into his palm and began massaging the heel. Only rarely did a Taelach volunteer to have sex with an Autlach but the experience, Starnes had heard, was unforgettable.

"Besides," purred Brandoff, "you're being well paid for your services."

Starnes snickered and gently kissed each toe of the foot he held. His hand inched across her ankle to rub on the lean paleness of her calf. "I don't know if the pay counts for much, but the benefits could certainly be pleasant for us both." He continued his massage, slowly sliding up her leg and underneath her leggings.

Brandoff let a quiet "hmmpfh" and tried to relax into the Autlach's touch. When the sensation proved undesirable, she jerked from his hands and tugged the legging back down. "Enough."

Infuriated, Starnes reached forward and grabbed her streaked hair. "Listen here, you stripe-headed witch, if you don't want it then don't lead me on like that." He recaptured her leg and drew it back into his lap. Brandoff didn't resist but smiled at him, her eyes glimmering amusement as a blinding pain shot down his arms. His hold loosened as he fell, taut with agony, to the floor.

"Cance would kill you if she even thought you'd tried this." Brandoff's upswept grin tensed. "Or maybe I'll just do it myself. You're not necessary to our plan. There are any number of holes we can work from." She glanced away, releasing the painful mind phase that paralyzed him.

Starnes rose, arms cradled to his sides, not heeding the pain, only angered by it. "Don't you threaten me! You know how easy it'd be for me to report you both. All I"—movement in the doorway stalled his speech.

"You must fancy a slow and torturous death, Barman Bane." Cance Creiloff pulled back the heavy cloak hood enveloping her lean face Two long, crescent moon shaped marks twisted down her neck, giving the surrounding flesh a deathlike translucence.

"Dearest Cance." Starnes put on his sweetest smile. "I meant no harm. Your blood sibling's good looks can tend to overwhelm a man is all."

"That so?" Cance sniffed, then glanced to her haggard twin. "What do you think of that, Brannie?"

"No Taelach with half a mind fucks an Aut man," came the derider from the longer haired of the duo, "and your women come to us when they want things done right." Brandoff spread two fingers and licked the space between them. "But Aut men are always good for a laugh or two. Personally, I like seeing their faces when they realize their mistake. But by then"—she bared her teeth, shattering all of Starnes's false concepts—"it's too late for them and damn entertaining for me." Brandoff righted the fallen chair and motioned Cance to sit. "Well?"

"In a moment." Cance blinked hard, flicking her eyes from deep brown to her twin's gem tone. She fixed them on Starnes, sending searing pain that sent him to the floor again. "I believe we . . . were . . . about . . . here. Weren't we, Starnie my boy?"

Starnes's skin prickled as the familiar burning sensation raged through him ten times worse than before. "Pleeaase! I meant no harm. It'll never happen again. NEVER!"

Cance expanded her mind phase to strangle out his pleading. "Don't you just hate a groveler?" She smiled drolly. "Not sure I believe him. How 'bout it, Brandoff? Think he'll behave?"

Brandoff kicked at him, jabbing her toes into his cheek. "He will if he knows what's good for him. Just remember, you bastard, next time I will finish our little game and it won't be your arms I phase the pain into." Brandoff turned away. "Eh, let him go, Cancelynn. He's turning colors."

"As you wish." Cance broke the mind-hold then downed the wine in Starnes's glass. Starnes remained on the floor, relieved, yet gasping for breath.

"Well?" Brandoff questioned again.

"Hold another minute and I'll tell you." Starnes braced for another assault when Cance turned to his direction. "Relax, Starnie." She laughed. "Get your wrap." She produced a banded roll of currency from her waist pouch, tossing it to him as he struggled for footing.

"What's this for?" His throat was parched, sponged dry from the closeness of a likely fatal seduction.

"You're a businessman, aren't you? Go to the Common Stores and get some supplies. We must keep up our professional appearance." Cance undid her heavy cloak and let it fall across her chair back. Her muscled shoulders and upper arms had been hidden under the garment and now held Starnes's regard. He shivered. "Lock up behind you," Cance said then raised a hand for him to wait. "Oh, and Starnes, don't worry. We'll keep an eye on that ailing father of yours while you're away. Wouldn't want anything to happen to the old man. Would we, Brandoff?"

Brandoff headed toward the stairs leading to the second-level living quarters. "Far from it." She piped, "I'll be more than happy to tend him while you're away." She blew Starnes a kiss. "Dah and I will be waiting."

Cance motioned him to the door. "You heard her. Not long and only to the Commons and back." She turned up the crystal, draining the final droplets onto her tongue. "And get some more of this Langus juice while you're out. You keep running low for some reason. NOW GO!"

Starnes locked the door behind him and leaned against it, pressing back his tormentor's proximity as tears welled in his cinnamon eyes. How did he ever get himself in so deep? It had seemed simple at the time. Someone claiming to be with the Kinship had contacted him about temporary lodging for a pair of Taelachs. Taelachs were not welcome at Autlach inns and often appealed to local bar owners for lodging. Despite what others said, he found them to be a warm, friendly, peaceable people, quite charming in their politeness. This time, however, it had turned into a nightmare he couldn't escape. He should have been suspicious when so much money had been offered, but business had been slow. It had simply been too tempting. Now they used his father's illness to control him. "That's all right," Starnes muttered to no one. "It'll end one way or another." He pulled his wrap over his shoulders, using its frayed hemline to clear his eyes before setting out. The Commons were a short walk away and there, he hoped, lay the solution.

"Auts are idiots." Brandoff jumped the stair railing then scrambled to where her twin sat. "No more delays. How'd it go?"

"Like you said, my sister, Autlachs are idiots." Cance kicked off one boot, then the other, then settled confidently back in her seat. "Especially the rural dirt clodders here on Langus. They actually believe I'm going to help them get rid of the Sarian base."

"They bought your 'preserve our farmlands' line then?"

Cance smiled broadly. "Completely and unquestionably. Fear spreads rapidly among the uninformed."

"Yeah." Brandoff's yawn accentuated her growing number of wrinkles. Life on Trimar aged one hard. "Spreads like flame on dry saw grass."

"Exactly. Now get upstairs and rest." Cance cast quick disapproval of her twin's gaunt face. "I'll wait for Starnie."

"Nah, I'm fine. A hit will pick me right up."

"You haven't slept in nine days. A hit won't do you a bit of good. Don't waste it. We may need it later."

"Dammit, Cance. You're too damn tight sometimes." Brandoff's disappointment seemed genuine. "All right then. I'll check the old man on my way up." She clambered up the stairs. Just because she needed sleep didn't mean she couldn't take a small dose as well. Another rush and a little sleep were far preferable to a long rest and a crash. Brandoff patted the pocket containing her inhaler.

"Throw me down some hair dye before you turn in. I'm begin-

31

ning to fade." Brandoff tossed Cance the package then settled into the upstairs apartment but not before inhaling a healthy dose of prock.

In the bar's small kitchen area, Cance filled the basin with warm water. The reflection in the basin's backing caught her attention and she paused, considering it between inhaler puffs. The prock rushed through her, cresting then settling her into numbing alertness. She was wide-awake and angry at the unfamiliar reflection that returned her gaze. She looked nothing like a guardian Taelach should. Her white shock of hair had been allowed to grow out to her shoulders and was the dark shade of an Autlach. *How depressing.* Cance tugged a fading lock. For effect, she blinked hard, allowing her eye lenses to settle back into place. Was this what her birth parents looked like? "Not that it matters," she told the sharp-chinned image that talked back. "They were only Auts."

Cance applied the dye pack's contents then removed the combing stick from the package and pushed the color deep, the excess dripping into the basin and expanding as discolored rings on the water. Her hair completely saturated with color, she quickly rinsed it, then, towel wrapping her head, cast another long look into the reflective backing, eyes drawn to her neck until the ever-present anger spun into fury. "Damn you, Belsas Exzal!" Cance smashed her fist into the backing, denting the metal so it warped her image. "Damn you for the Aut-loving bitch you are! If we'd won the Taelach War, I'd be ruling over the Kinship, you'd be dead, and Chandrey would still be with me. Auts would serve Taelachs and everything would be as it should: MINE!"

Chapter Seven

The Hiding Caves are the essence of survival in troubled times.

—Taelach saying

———————

The journey to Langus served as a sharp cultural awakening for LaRenna. She had never been outside Taelach lands except for necessary travel and that had taken place strictly at night. Taelach children were closely protected by their raisers in fear they would be taken in an ill-fated reunion with their Autlach birth parents. This rarely if ever happened, but the old warnings were still repeated, just as stories of alleged Taelach treacheries were passed down in Autlach families.

The launch stop proved an uneventful place, nothing more than a tiny burrow of a port set in the narrow northern mountain ranges of the Reisfall continent. LaRenna gave the pilot the travel card Master Yeoman Qualls had provided her and stepped aboard the launch. It was far from crowded, but she chose a seat in the rear anyway, pulling her head deep into her cloak. This probably wasn't necessary, for the launch's other occupants were ignoring her presence, but it made her feel a little more at ease.

With a short jolt, the passenger aerolaunch rose and the trip began. LaRenna leaned back in her seat, enjoying the vibrant scenery that had escaped notice on her nocturnal journeys. The launch followed the slow roll of the mountains until it reached the southernmost peaks, then it lurched upward, engines straining to meet the incline of the high passes. When they reached the summit, the pilot paused, allowing his passengers to take in their surroundings as the full wonder of Reisfall's Glory Land made its awe-inspiring appearance on the horizon.

LaRenna had heard dozens of stories about the Glory Land as a child, but not one did it justice. It was an extreme combination of plains and canyon lands, buckling and breathing for thousands of kilometers. At its highest points it bounded with blowing flower grasses and countless wandering Sarian herd beasts. The lowest points hid among the deep canyons, some of which had never been mapped, at least not to the knowledge of the Autlach. There, buried deep within the Hiding Caves, lay the secrets of Taelach self-preservation. Chandrey had taught her how to read the ancient marker signs to locate them. They were the last strongholds the Taelach could flee to in times of peril.

It all passed by too quickly for LaRenna, for she was still lost in thought when Polmel's dark skyline pierced the afternoon haze. At the sight of it, she felt a shot of nauseating anxiety. It was a spiraling, walled shell of civilization that buzzed with the traffic of Sarian commerce. Pollution reeked, the streets were crowded, and the din was deafening. She hated it. Yet, in the scheme of things, it served a vital purpose she had to grudgingly respect.

The launch's maneuvering thrusters fired as they slowly descended to a docking platform. Passengers gathered their belongings and waited to disembark. LaRenna mustered her courage and retrieved her own bag from under the seat. "Well," she whispered with a wary gaze to the platform below. "No one said this was going to be easy."

A jolt signaled touchdown, the landing locks hissing and grinding as they secured to the platform receptors. The doors slid open and smothering humidity flooded the compartment. LaRenna gasped as the heavy air filled her lungs with suffocating pressure. An older Autlach woman in front of her turned back to speak, her forehead beading with moisture. "Polmel's dampness can be unbearable, can't it?" She seemed to take LaRenna's appearance in stride. "Don't concern yourself with your hood, my dear. Everyone in Polmel knows a Taelach when they see one. There's almost as many of your kind here as mine." LaRenna shifted uneasily at the unexpected attention. "You won't be given any trouble while in public."

They stepped off the launch and the woman showed the platform sentry her travel card. LaRenna pulled back her hood for identification, produced her card, and gave it to the sentry as well. He read it then passed it back with a salute to match his begrudged tone. "Have a good trip to Langus, third officer."

"Langus?" The woman had lingered. "Well, young lady, that's where I'm heading as well, at least a day or so." She swiped at the perspiration that ran down her face. "My two youngest sons and their families live in a farming compound on the edge of the Balleye Breaks. I'm heading there for a quick visit on my way to Saria Proper. Beautiful country, the Balleye Breaks, you'll have to visit them sometime during your stay." She walked toward the archway at the platform head. Her left foot dragged along the ground as she moved, giving her an odd limp. After a rather amused glance back at LaRenna's apprehensive face, she beckoned her to come closer. "The port at Polmel is near impossible to navigate if you've never been here. Carry my bag, child, and I'll take us to our platform."

LaRenna gratefully accepted the woman's generosity, relieved to know she wouldn't have to find her way through the honeycomb of walkways and landing platforms alone. She took the extra bag

35

and followed. Keeping up with the old woman proved a challenge as they made their way through the crowds. She wove skillfully in and out of the throngs of populace, despite her obvious infirmity.

By the time they reached the Langus transport, LaRenna was exhausted. The weight of her baggage and cloak had drenched her in perspiration, causing everything she wore to stick to her skin. They stopped by a peddler cart at the edge of a vacant platform. "I'm parched!" declared the Autlach, fanning herself. The cooling halted when she noticed LaRenna. "Gracious me, child, but you're half-drowned! Why don't we get a drink?"

LaRenna nodded her heavy head in agreement.

"I'll get us something before we board. Goodness knows the transport doesn't serve enough to keep an insect alive, much less a pretty young woman such as you. Are you hungry?"

"The heat," LaRenna answered as she shook the hair from her sweating neck. "It's made me half ill."

"Understandable. I'll get us some water and a few bush fruits for later." She addressed the peddler and purchased the items. Taking back her bag, she handed LaRenna a large cup of water. "I didn't let him ice it. The cold will cramp you in this heat." LaRenna looped her bag over her shoulder, drew a folded Autlach bill from her pocket, and gave it to the woman, who took the money and placed it along with two small fruits in LaRenna's cloak pocket. "No, child, don't insult me," she said in a mothering way. "You see, I birthed a Taelach daughter who would be around your age now. I would like to think someone somewhere would show her the same kindness."

LaRenna squeezed the elder Autlach's hand. "Thank you."

"My pleasure," beamed the woman. "I could tell it was your first solo outing. Now, let's board before the last-minute rush." They found the transport sentry and presented their cards again. He gave them each a cabin number as he handed the cards back. "Fourth berth, blue level," mumbled the woman. "Where are you at?"

"Twelfth berth, orange level."

"Well, I guess this is where we part, young Taelach. Thank you for assisting an old lady on her way."

"I hardly think it was me who gave assistance." LaRenna smiled.

The woman shook her head, bouncing the neatly looped gray braid on her neck. "Still, I'm in your debt." Then she paused to ponder their meeting. "We never exchanged names, did we?"

"No, I don't believe we did."

"Well, allow me to introduce myself." She bowed reverently, with a grace the Autlach seldom extended their paler relatives. "I'm Nyla Smalls of the rural Autlach settlements of Saria Three."

LaRenna returned her courtesy. "And I'm Third Level Kimshee LaRenna Belsas most recently of the Training Grounds here on Saria Four."

"Belsas?" Nyla's delicate eyebrows rose in surprise. "As in Belsas Exzal, Taelach of All?"

"Yes, ma'am."

"Taelach Belsas, this definitely has been a pleasure. Your guardian raiser is a quality stateswoman. Her posting on the High Council has done much for Autlach-Taelach relations. I hope you do as well as she has." With that, Nyla Smalls shuffled down the transport corridor and disappeared from sight.

A peculiar sense of emptiness fell over LaRenna when she'd gone. Sighing, she recited her cabin number again and took the level lift to her deck. Berth twelve was a double cabin on the starboard side of the transport. She hung her cloak on one of the pegs above the compartment's luggage area and stowed her bag. The aft seating offered a better view so she took her cup to one of the reclining chairs facing that direction, sitting just as the cabin door slid open.

An Autlach couple entered. The man was overly slim, possessing a face that seemed incapable of expressing any emotion other than disdain. His wife, some five passes younger than LaRenna, possessed an apple-cheeked face still bright with young eagerness though she was very pregnant. She froze in the doorway when she

37

saw their cabin mate. "Flannery," she whined in a high nasal wheeze to ruin the pleasantness her eyes still held. "Do we have to share a cabin with her?" Her arms wrapped protectively around her protruding stomach. "Think of the baby."

"We were lucky to get any cabin on this transport," he replied as he led her to the seat directly across from LaRenna. "You'll just have to live with it. This little half-grown snit won't do you or the baby any harm." The he turned toward LaRenna, revealing the sneer under his wiry mustache. "Will you, girl?"

"Hardly!" LaRenna growled in her deepest voice. Legs curled underneath her body, she scowled out the window, trying to ignore the occasional glares and underhanded comments of her unwanted traveling companions. If this was the type of treatment she could expect, maybe becoming a Kimshee wasn't such a good idea after all. She desperately hoped there were more like Nyla out there.

Chapter Eight

Be wary! You never know who your true enemy is.

—Sarian military saying

The Commons were teeming with business when Krell arrived. Hood high against the day, she crept into the dining plaza, taking a quiet corner table. The spindly Autlach waiter spotted his newest customer and disappeared into the kitchen, returning a moment later carrying a small tray. "It's been a while, Krell. Where have you been keeping yourself?"

Krell pushed back her hood until it bunched behind her ears then peered up, smiling. "At the base more than is good for my sanity, Russ. What's for breakfast?"

"Your usual, brown bread and tea." Russ set a plate on the table then laughed at the crushed expression Krell offered in return. If any one thing gave him pleasure, it was teasing his lankiest customer. "Something wrong?"

"No sweet jams?"

"But of course!" With an exaggerated flourish, he laid a jam pot before her. "I know better than to serve a Taelach bread without sweet jams." Russ's eyes twinkled with merriment. "You're obsessed with sweets, the whole lot of you."

"We are not." Krell tried to appear offended while she layered the jam.

"You never see an Aut spread jam like that."

"It's not that thick," she mumbled between bites. "And I've never seen an Aut spread jam at all."

"It's a good three fingers deep." Russ cringed. "Ugh! How can you eat that?" He stepped back from the table, ready to steer away from such indigestible conversation. "Now, I've worked here enough to know food is never your motive for being here, so what gives? Got a hot date or something?"

Krell had grown accustomed to Russ's teasing and often enjoyed the opportunity to reciprocate, this time sticking her finger in the jam pot and sucking the sugar-covered digit clean just to see him wince.

"Smartass." A snarl parted his mouth just enough to show the slight separation between his front teeth. "You know that makes me want to retch." He snatched up the pot and placed it on a nearby table. "Who's your date?"

"No date, just business." Krell waved him way. "But he won't show if you're hanging around."

"He?" Russ continued his caddish teasing. "Seeing Autlachs are we?"

"Now I'm going to retch." Krell reached for the jam pot.

"All right, I'm going!" Russ thrust his fist to his chest as if stabbed. "I'm heartbroken." He dabbed his face with his apron tail. One of the cooks witnessed his theatrics and bellowed for him to return to work. Bad enough they'd been forced into serving Taelachs, but did the staff have to call attention to the fact?

"Pity for you, Krell, I'm already taken."

"Yeah, I know, to an ugly woman who can't cook." For once

40

Krell could agree with the opposition. Russ was attracting far too much attention. She kept her tone low , hoping he would take the suggestion. "Go away; I have work to do."

"Since when?" he snipped.

"I mean it."

His jovial smile faded. "Serious, aren't you?"

"As I can be. Don't you have some work to do?" The cook leaned back out the window, this time launching a long line of obscenities in Russ's direction.

"At least someone loves me." He gathered the dishes from Krell's table and turned, pouting, toward the kitchen. "More tea, first officer?" Now he was overplaying being prim and solemn. So much so, Krell felt guilty for being short.

"Please, and thank you, Russ."

"Ahh, no harm done." He disappeared inside, returned briefly to refill her mug, and then left her alone.

Krell was beginning to doubt the lead's validity when a heavy man in a faded wrap stepped onto the plaza. He squinted around the square then slowly approached. "You Taelach Middle?"

"See any other Taelachs about?" she replied coolly. "Who're you?"

The man shifted uneasily. "Starnes Bane."

"Well then, Starnes, you're late." Krell pushed the empty chair from the table. "Sit and tell me what you want with the Kinship."

"I gotta be quick." Starnes pulled his wrap tighter across his shoulders and glanced around. "If I don't get back soon they'll come hunting."

"Who?"

"The two Taelachs who are holed up at my place."

Krell eyed him charily. "The only Taelachs registered in this area are myself and a healer."

"Nah, they wouldn't register. These two are strange, cruel to be sure. Twins, too."

A pit formed in Krell's stomach. The vilest Taelach criminals came from undestroyed twins, but only one set was of recent times

41

and they were acknowledged dead. Her voice remained low. "Twins?"

"Yes, alike in the face with odd markings on their necks."

Now Krell was certain. "Markings?"

"Sorta moon shaped. Like this." Starnes held his hand up in a perfect letter C.

Krell nodded and tapped thoughtfully on the table. Belsas Exzal was right, two of the Branded had escaped, and identical looks meant twice the trouble, triple the insanity. "What do you want the Kinship to do about it?"

"Do?" Starnes wheezed. "Do? I want the bitches outta my bar. That's what I want!"

"Tell me more." Krell cast Starnes a slow stare that planted a subtle mind phase to check for lies.

"What else is there to tell?" He shrugged. "They're Taelach, they drink too much, and they're pure evil coming to an ugly head." Then he cocked his head and pointed to Krell. "They both had braids like yours, but one of them cut theirs off and dyed"— Starnes hesitated, reforming his next words in an effort to not offend his only chance at assistance—"its hair, tinted its skin, too, but the dye made it sick before it could accomplish a very dark tint. The other one hasn't tried to change a thing. Hair is real long, sort of a dingy white with a few of those dark streaks your people get as they age. Kinda skinny as well, looks kinda like one of your women," he scowled, "but it sure as hell isn't."

"Taelachs are all women and my type is called guardian, not *it*," snapped Krell. "And if you wish assistance I suggest—"

"You have my apologies," stammered Starnes. "But *it* is a better word than most my people use."

"Point taken. Continue."

"Neither of them is especially tall to be guardian. That's what they are though. They're your kind. You take care of them."

Krell rested her elbow on her boot top. "They're not in the Kinship and they're not supposed to be here. Anything else?"

"Yeah." Starnes wagged a fat finger toward her. "The one who cut off the braids, Cance is her name, wears brown lenses." Having seen Cance both in and out of her Autlach disguise, he preferred the lenses. With them, she couldn't mind-phase him the way she could and did when she wasn't hiding her telltale blue eyes.

"Look Autlach enough for a passing glance?"

"Does a pretty damn good job of it. Got walking and talking male down to an art." Starnes drew back when a couple sat down at the next table. If Cance had the means to pass as Autlach there was no telling who else was involved. "Time's up. You going to help me or not?"

"You know where the Hiring Hall is?"

"Of course," he said. "But the last thing I need is—"

"Silence. In five days, go to the Hiring Hall and ask for someone who can wait tables and clean up. Be sure to talk to the Assistant Hall Master. He'll be expecting you."

"For the love of—"

"You're not listening." Krell showed her impatience by drumming her fingers on the table. "Just do it, and make sure you hire a female."

"Taelach?" he asked hopefully.

"No, Autlach. Her name will be LaRenna. Remember that." Krell rose from the table and peered at Starnes, who flinched involuntarily. "If you want help, this is what you'll do." Krell turned to leave, but halted when the Autlach reached out.

"And what do I tell my unwanted guests about a new employee? Things have been slow."

"You're about to have a boom in business."

This still failed to pacify the barman. "Listen, my father is ill. He's bedfast. They won't let me get him treated."

Krell picked at his head a second time. Again, no deception. "What's wrong with him?"

"Strong's Seizures."

"How long?" Her concern surprised a man used to the unfeeling nature of his current boarders.

"A full moon cycle, maybe a little longer."

43

"Strong's Seizures take two to three cycles untreated to be fatal. Keep him comfortable and I'll send medicine with your help." Then Krell reminded him sternly: "Five days. No more, no less." She threw Russ's payment on the table and walked away.

"Wait," implored Starnes, but Krell was gone, lost in the crowds of the Common Grounds. How does one so large disappear so quickly, he wondered, then lumbered toward the market area to make his purchases.

Russ remained by the kitchen window until they had safely departed. He knew of an individual who rewarded handsomely for such information, provided he could locate them. "Sorry, Krell," he murmured, deep in for the monetary boost heading his direction, "but times are tough and I have children to feed. We all must sacrifice something."

Chapter Nine

Taelachs are cunning creatures. They are never where or what you would expect.

—Autlach warning

Krell searched for fair Taelach hair swimming above the sea of dark Autlach heads ebbing from the passenger transport. *Maybe I'm too far back*, she thought and pushed more to the center of the platform. In her haste, she bumped into a small, hooded figure skirting the crowd, knocking it to the ground. "Apologies, friend." Krell offered an arm in assistance. A delicate, pale hand accepted the gesture and sparkling blue eyes met her own. Krell startled, drawing a quick breath. "Third Kimshee Belsas?"

LaRenna snapped to her feet, dusted herself off, and raised an arm in salute. "Reporting for my post as required. Are you first Kimshee Middle?"

"Yes, uh—" Krell faltered, caught off watch by the unexpected beauty of the slight woman before her. "I'm sorry, but are you sure you're Kimshee? It's generally not a— A little small, aren't you?"

Small? LaRenna thought. *Why, I'll show—*

"My guardian raiser says size isn't what makes one large or small." LaRenna cringed, hoping that hadn't sounded as asinine to her superior as it had to her. She wanted to make a point, not alienate herself.

The tall Kimshee only laughed, pushing a smile into the full mouth topping her square jawline. "Yep, that sounds like Belsas Exzal."

Now LaRenna was startled. "You know my raiser personally, First Kimshee?"

"Know Grandmaster Belsas? Why, I've attended every lecture she's ever given at the Training Grounds and served as her Autlach liaison at several posts as well. Don't tell me you're that bright-eyed child who used to tug on everyone's tunic tails?"

"Guilty as charged, First Kimshee." LaRenna smiled up bashfully. "I remember you now. You took a youth group I was a member of hiking when I was around eleven."

"You're right, and call me Krell. We don't have time for the formalities or any more small talk. Let's go."

They walked quickly across the base. Krell's strides far outpaced those of the shorter Taelach's gait so she slowed to a stride LaRenna could maintain. They stopped here and there along the way, Krell indicating points of interest. It was a vast space, as large as Polmel, as populated but cleaner and more simply arranged. Krell told of the recent expansions and apologized for the living conditions. "If it wasn't so crowded, I would have insisted on private quarters for you. But as it is, and will continue to be, we're fortunate not to be sharing with an entire sentry squadron. I tried to make the lack of space tolerable, cleared out a few shelves and scrounged up an extra clothing cubicle for you."

LaRenna appreciated the concern for her personal comfort. "I'm sure it will be adequate," she said politely, trying not to appear so intimidated by her teacher's sheer size. Krell was exceed-

46

ingly tall, even for a guardian. She was muscular as well but in that lean, graceful way Taelachs were known for. "I really didn't bring that much."

"So I noticed," replied Krell with an admiring glance at the top of LaRenna's generous locks. "But then again, I didn't to my first post either. Here we are." She pointed to the housing compound directly ahead. "We're fourth floor, number four two four."

LaRenna's blue eyes brimmed with doubt. "Everyone shares quarters here?"

"Yes, the Langus base no longer segregates housing areas, officer-enlisted, or Taelach-Autlach," said Krell bluntly, though not indifferent to LaRenna's reluctance to accept what was all so new. "Things go smoothly most days. Not that you'll be around enough to worry about it. You'll be far too busy." She stepped onto the lift, holding it open while LaRenna and a weary Autlach sentry boarded. He leaned against the lift walls, near asleep. Krell nodded acknowledgment to his half-hearted salute then let silence prevail until they reached the fourth level.

"We're home."

Krell turned down the right-hand passageway. LaRenna followed slowly, taking in her new surroundings. The quarters here were indeed cramped, some sentries forced to bunk in cleared storage closets. Krell placed an index finger on the security plate and the hatch to their quarters hissed open. "We'll add you to the identification program tomorrow." She tossed her sandy cape onto its hook then placed a partially filled water urn to heat. "Put your bag in the corner and have a seat."

LaRenna obliged, flopping her spent body into a chair. Her head held an indefinable ache, one she wasn't sure came from exhaustion or from the hunger that twisted her insides. Not that it needed labeling; both needs would be met soon enough. She pulled off her boots and rubbed her swollen feet, flinching as she touched the new Kimshee symbol gracing the upper third of her right foot.

Krell bent close to examine the reddened tattoo. "Marks hurt at first, don't they? Guess that's why most of us get our family ones

47

when we're too small to remember. It'll heal soon enough. Leave your boots off the rest of the evening so it can air. That'll help speed the process." Drawing her eyes upward, she noticed the hunger-wrenched expression on LaRenna's face. "Bet you're starving. I'll run down to the main level galley and bring back something for us both. Why don't you clean up and change while I'm gone?"

LaRenna nodded and watched the First Kimshee depart. She wondered if she truly looked and smelled bad enough to warrant the suggestion of bathing. Krell was probably just thinking of her personal comfort, she assured herself, and removed her travel-grimed uniform.

The warmth of the tub offered to take away some of the journey's stress so LaRenna sank deeply into it, submerging her head to wet her hair, then letting the water float it freely. She took the soaping stone and cleaned head to toe, proclaiming all the while that the mineral-laden waters of Langus would never make her feel clean enough.

The hiss of the hatchway and the unmistakable aroma of nourishment alerted her to her mentor's return. Driven by the smell, she dried quickly, wrapped her head in the same towel, then slid a lightweight service tunic and leggings over her feminine shape.

Krell had moved the worktable to the center of the room, neatly arranged the food on it and was pouring two cups of tea when LaRenna emerged from the bathing chamber.

"Better?" Krell cast her a warm smile.

"Much," replied LaRenna, reclaiming her space at the table. She took the cup Krell offered and sipped, the inside of her mouth puckering from the lack of sweetener.

"Ferntree tea, hope you like it." Krell chuckled when the bitterness caused her mouth to draw in a similar fashion. "Sorry, but I'm out of sweetener at present. It can be hard to obtain at times. I believe sweet root is the only crop Langus doesn't grow." She sat across from LaRenna and lounged back, one elbow on the chair arm, head leaning on her fist, picking at her dinner as she considered LaRenna at length. She was incredibly beautiful, that was a certainty. But, as an adult child of Belsas, she was a far cry from what Krell had expected. Maybe size had caused her surprise. LaRenna was nearly the same height as when Krell had last seen her over ten passes ago. Oh, she'd filled out nicely enough, any Taelach with half a libido would admit to that. LaRenna had taken graceful curves to the extreme, developing an hourglass figure: full chest and pleasing hips sculpted at the center by a narrow waist. Surely, she surmised as LaRenna became aware of the intense gaze she was receiving, their former meetings and pure physical attraction were to blame for the sense of familiarity.

LaRenna finished her meal, flushed her disposable dish down the waste tube, then cleaned and sheathed her boot knife. She yawned deeply then, stifling a burp with the back of her hand, and collapsed in her seat. "Thank you. That was wonderful."

"Starvation is what made it edible. Most anything's preferable to transport rations." Krell chortled as she tossed remains of her meal in the tube. The condition of the eating blade was a direct reflection of one's personal habits in the Taelach culture, so Krell cleaned hers to a gleam. Then, well accustomed to the bitterness, she poured more tea, then asked LaRenna if she desired the same. The soft sounds of someone in a deep slumber were the only reply. Fatigue had won its battle. "Poor girl," whispered Krell, carefully removing the towel from LaRenna's damp ringlets. "The food did you in." She unfolded a platform and bedding roll, then placed the blanket over LaRenna, running her fingers lightly over the young woman's arms. LaRenna's form was solid, forcing Krell to admit error in assuming her career choice had been poor. She was tough—a neat little package of muscle and intelligence, ideal for a Kimshee. Krell now looked forward to their first lessons, but that would simply have to wait until morning.

Krell wrapped in her cloak and crept out the door. Loose ends needed her attention. One of the sentry commanders was about to receive an after-hours visitor. Starnes needed a boost in business and that was precisely what he was going to get.

Chapter Ten

The mind of the masses is a rusted, barnacle-ridden vessel, free of most logical thought, heavy with pack instincts. High surge in either direction divides the pack and the ship capsizes to the lean of the majority, survivors clinging to the bottom side. A direct puncture to the hull and the pack drowns as a whole, leaving no one to bear witness to the captain's sabotage.

—Taelach wisdom

Rain threatened the horizon, dampening the lights in a small valley not far from the Sarian military facilities. An angry but surprisingly quiet crowd had gathered, ears turned to a lone speaker in their midst.

"Brothers!" Cance Creiloff stood on a small boulder. A head over the tallest in attendance and paler than most, she looked a bit out of place but fit in unlike Brandoff, who was necessarily absent. Forced weight gain and male clothing put her above casual suspicion so she stood proudly among the Autlach, detesting their presence, savoring thoughts of their deaths even though she looked like one of them. "The time has come for us to take back what is ours." The scars of her true identity hidden under her tunic collar, Cance looked down on the Autlach congregation. *Simple fools*—she pulled the stiff collar higher—*so easily deceived, so willingly misused. It's a pity really. The challenge is almost nonexistent.* "Some Sarians believe they can take our land and say it is for the benefit of us all. They destroy our fields, ruin the fishing waters, and what do we receive in way of compensation? Nothing!"

Agreeing murmurs wafted through the crowd, Cance's speech increasing to match the fervor.

"We have the right to demand restitution and demand it now!" The murmurs intensified into cries of "justice" and "freedom for our lands," ensuring her of the words' impact. So Cance continued, with a tightly held frown to prevent her true emotions from leaching through.

"It is our right to have enough land and fishing waters to nourish and support our families. Since the military base has expanded its presence on Langus, the average family earnings have decreased nearly thirty percent. Poverty is running amok. They are draining the lifeblood of Langus and denying us the crop room critical for the support of our mother planet. It must stop!" Cance stretched her arms wide. "If we don't, Langus will become as desolate as the Stonemar Plateau on Firewall." The bleak image of the moon's yellow-orange surface produced waves of shocked gasps.

"But what can we do?" wailed a voice.

"You." Cance pointed to the balding man who asked the question. "There is much you can do. I've been informed by others concerned with the disappearance of Langus farms that a charter of demands has been forwarded to the High Council on Saria Three. They have seven days to begin withdrawal of military forces from Langus."

"What if they ignore the demands?" cried a young man in the rear.

"Then we give them a demonstration of our intent." Cance leapt from the boulder and drew closer, beckoning the most interested to approach. "In seven days"—her face remained guarded—"in seven days, if they refuse our demands, we strike! Every compound, post, and yes, even the base itself will feel the impact of our blows." Cance picked up a small boy in the crowd and held the squirming child high, exclaiming: "We do this for our children and our children's children. We do this for ourselves, and we do this for Langus!" Frenzied cries drowned all attempts at speechmaking so Cance joined the celebration, returning the child to his proud mother before adding to the drone.

When the boisterous display had subsided, she continued the oration, shouting until it was sufficiently calm. "Volunteers are needed to help with our strike at the base, brave men who are willing to risk their lives for their people, fearless souls who will go down in history as the ones who freed Langus from the destructive greed of the Sarian military." The words rolled off Cance's tongue far smoother than she had rehearsed. Evil can make a convincing argument when it suits a purpose, and Cance was certainly evil, decades of imprisonment only serving to mold her ambitious mind into one of crazed malefactor. "Do I have volunteers?"

Ten arms waved high in the air, richly delighting the branded Taelach.

"Those of you who've volunteered, meet me by the tree line in five minutes. Everyone else, return to your homes. Do not speak of our plans, not even to each other. The eyes of the Sarian military are everywhere, perhaps among us now." The listeners unconsciously recoiled from one another. "We stand on the shores of freedom, our sails unfurled for a favorable breeze. In seven days it begins."

The crowd dispersed into small groups and drifted toward their respective homes. The remaining handful gathered at the tree line to wash away the evening chill with an oversized wine flask. Cance snatched the container and took a deep swig. "I see some of us are true to the Cause." She looked around the group. "Let's see what we have here. You!" Cance indicated the heavy man now holding the flask. "You ever in the Sarian ranks?"

"Two passes," he said with a boastful squaring of his shoulders.

"Ever post on the base here?"

"No."

Cance grabbed the flask from his hand. "Go home. We don't need anyone who isn't familiar with the layout of the base. Who has worked or posted there?" Four hands went up, the exact number for Cance's purposes. "All but these four leave." She turned to the quartet, casting their wives a scouring glare. She had little use for Autlach women besides occasional physical satisfaction, and none of these appeared adequate for that. "Send your women home. They've no place here."

"We have as much to do with this as anyone!" blared a slack-breasted mother of far too many, ignoring her husband's embarrassed hushing. "These are our lands, too."

Our lands too? Cance suppressed her rising anger. Autlach women had no rights of ownership. They'd been taught their place, something some Taelachs, Cance believed, could learn from. She smiled lightly then addressed the women in a gentle tone. "I understand your wanting to participate, but the strength and mental stamina required for this demonstration is ill-fitting a woman. Return to your homes and children. The less you know the better. The Cause has no wish to confuse the delicate emotions of lovely ladies such as you."

This, accompanied by their husbands' insistence, seemed to pacify the women's concerns and they departed, chattering amongst themselves. Again, Cance drank deeply from the wine, refraining from speech until only her chosen remained. "Let's get down to business. The Langus Cause has asked that the four of you effect a raid on the base."

"Raid?" The longhaired member of the foursome sneered. "Ta' what purpose?"

"A simple one. And one I'll tell you in due time. For now, let's discuss the layout of the base." Cance knelt, motioning the others to do the same. From a hidden pocket she produced a small tube and popped its end, removing a scroll and two light sticks.

"This"—Cance unrolled the scroll, securing its curling ends with the sticks—"this is the key to it all." The lights sputtered to life, their dim, odd green glow spilling across the soil. The men, still squatted, gazed inquiringly at the scroll then their informant. "I presume everyone here has worked a boundary sentry station?"

All four nodded.

"So getting onto the base won't pose a problem. The difficulty will be here." Cance indicated the Main Center's Assembly in the middle of the map.

"Hold on," lamented the man wearing an eye shroud. "That's the most heavily guarded area on the base."

"On this entire blasted moon," agreed the darkly tanned individual to his left. "Langus's central weather, water, and power controls are there."

"Exactly." Cance made a popping sound with her tongue, a habit obtained during lonely days spent in the prison colony's isolation chambers. "So are the main controls to the security matrix. That's what we're after."

"Ah' see," said the longhaired Autlach. "If the main matrix goes down," he said, rolling his R's with the thick accent of the southern Langus farmland, "it goes down moonwide. Plus, we'll have power over the other control centers."

"A drink to the winner!" Cance passed the flask. "When it goes down the Cause can make its move all across Langus."

"I sentried at the Center's Assembly." The fourth member of the group finally spoke, his black eyes squinting to focus in the fading light. "The Assembly is Taelach tech. The entryways are sealed and rigged to detonate if tampered with. You can't get in there."

"They have to be opened for servicing don't they?" Cance had little patience for such stupidity. "If it can be opened for that, then I can get you in there."

"How?" demanded the longhair, his questions clearly establishing him as the group's leader.

Cance pulled up a sleeve and moved into the light, revealing the plasma bow spanning her arm. "With scan decoders and a few of these."

"Whoa! Where did you get that?" The man with the eye shroud stumbled back a pace. "I lost my eye to one of those hair-triggered little bitches."

"And Autlach illegal outside military installations." The tanned man spat, raising a suspicious brow. "How'd you get one?"

"The Cause has their resources." Cance rose to full height and cast the men a significant frown. "I have no problem using Taelach tech when needed. Do any of you?"

Four heads shook adamantly. No one wished to challenge this odd Autlach, especially when he had a bow lashing his arm.

"Very well." Cance grunted. "Back to the bows."

"They're effective but difficult to master," admitted the quiet one. "The Sarian military rarely uses them because they take too long to train on."

"Not this one." Cance waved the device under their noses. "It's been modified to track and fire on a verbal command." She flipped up the palm lever to reveal the blank underbelly. "There's no trigger."

"And no manual aiming makes for a sure shot." Longhair grinned. "Got one for each of us?"

"The Cause has provided funding for four fully charged bows and two scan decoders." Cance mentioned the Cause to remind all of the reasoning behind their actions. She disposed of the lighting sticks by cracking them in half, rolled the map scroll, and slid it into its tube. "Meet me at the Waterlead bar tomorrow evening. I expect to see each of you there, no excuses. You are sworn to this and to me. Failure to carry out your promise will be regarded as betrayal and dealt with accordingly by the Cause." Cance gulped from the flask. "To Langus and her salvation!" The men shouted their concordance and took their own turns at the drink. Supportive or not, believing or otherwise, they knew there was no backing out.

"Return to your homes," Cance told them, adding this harsh

warning: "Tell no one. One slip of the tongue could be the demise of us all." With that, the four scattered and faded into the country-side.

"Excellent work, my enterprising Taelach." A voice buzzed from just inside the tree line.

"It's clear, Talmshone." Cance's mouth contorted in a wicked, loathsome smile. "Come have a drink to our success."

The field grasses rustled with footsteps and a heavily webbed, three-fingered hand wrapped around the wine flask. "The Commitment will be thrilled to hear their plans are developing so nicely." Talmshone wiped the flask opening on his cuff then drained its contents in a single gulp. "Ahh, Sarian wine. 'Tis the only decent thing the Autlach produces, besides a few choice Taelachs such as yourself." He gave Cance a vicious double-lidded wink.

"Flattery, Talmshone, can get you everywhere." But Cance stepped back, so as not to encourage an advance from the scaly Iralian.

"Do not concern yourself with your personal safety." Talmshone flung the empty flask to the wayside. "I fail to find Sarians enticing, Autlach or Taelach. You are both too delicately made and oddly arranged for my satisfaction. Even you guardians."

"Delicate?" Cance took four shots from her inhaler. "Iralians are not exactly my ideal date either. Where's my pay?"

Talmshone placed a band of rolled Autlach bills in Cance's out-stretched palm. He was well aware of her addiction and considered it the unstable link in their alliance. Prock, a native plant of Trimar, was liquefied to produce an inhalable spray. It was widely used among the inhabitants of the penal colony, more so by those escaped or slaved into the icy Junglelands surrounding the prison. Few served their sentence without becoming lifelong addicts.

"This makes us up to date plus expenses." Talmshone waited for Cance to regain composure before he continued. "I would refrain from spending it all in one place, or on one thing."

Cance sniffed, more at the remark than to clear her satiated nasal passages. "Like I'd go anywhere without a generous supply. Remember, I'm due four billion in Iralian funds when the job is done."

"Four billion plus control of Langus. I am familiar with Commitment's agreement. Just do your job." Talmshone bared his pointed teeth in a crooked leer, the Iralian version of a polite smile. "And we shall do ours."

Chapter Eleven

The braided Taelach guardian is a deadly enemy with no remorse for its actions. It will defend both post and family to the bitterest end.

—Autlach saying

The door alarm's aggravating chirp awakened Trazar Laiman from a tantalizing dream. He shivered in his blankets, glanced up at the wall chimes, and yelled to whoever was on the hatchway's reverse side.

"Go away and come back in the morning. It's too frigging late!" He jerked the blankets over his head and tried to recapture the moment. Maybe whoever it was would give up.

A pounding fist brought him up a second time. Just as well; the temptress had faded. "This had better be good." He stumbled into his leggings. "Stipall, you too drunk to remove your gloves to open the hatch again?" Trazar leaned wearily on the wall and hit the hatch release, imagining it was the face of the party on the other side.

"Sentry Commander Laiman?" Krell Middle towered in the hatchway.

"First Kimshee Middle!" Trazar attempted a salute but chose instead to save his dignity and grabbed the waist lacings of his sagging leggings.

"You know who I am then, Commander?"

"Of course I do, First Officer." Trazar made a quick knot in his legging's cording. "This is my second post here and there aren't that many of your kind around."

"Taelachs do stick out in a crowd," admitted Krell in a short laugh. "Apologies for the late hour, Commander, but I have pressing business to discuss with you. May I come in?"

Trazar stepped back. "Pardon the mess. Quarters are becoming unusually tight. Four of us have to share a single's space. Not that officers have such difficulties."

"Sentry, even officers are double bunking these days." Krell removed a pile of clothing from a chair, pulled it into the center of the room, and took a seat, returning the startled glances of the room's other half-awake inhabitants while Trazar pulled on a duty tunic. The others were members of the same squadron so Krell could speak in confidence. "I'll be brief. Sentry Laiman, I need the services of your entire squadron. Their available evening hours, that is."

"Come again?" Trazar was positive lack of sleep was responsible for what he had heard, but it must have been correct because his roommates let sounds somewhere between a snicker and a gasp.

"I know this is an unusual request. You probably won't understand the logic of—"

"Taelach Middle"—Trazar took quick insult when caught off guard in the presence of his men—"you suggesting I don't have the ability to understand a proposal involving my squad?"

"Nothing of the sort." Krell's voice and expression remained neutral. "I'm not entirely convinced of the proposal's logic myself. Nonetheless, this is what I require." She proceeded to explain the proposition in earnest, stopping several times to answer Trazar's questions and clarify his misconceptions. He paced the room, twisting the end of his single battle braid around his index finger while he listened.

"Let me get this straight. You want my men to go to this bar on the lower side every evening until you say otherwise?"

"Correct."

"And I'm not to know why they are doing it?"

"Why is not important," said Krell with a bitter glare that sent Trazar's subordinates diving under the blankets. "All you need to know is what I've told you. The fate of Langus may rely on it."

"Heavens help the day the fate of this moon comes down to a drunken sentry squadron." The request amused him until his eyes gleamed defiantly.

"Believe it or not, Sentry Laiman, it does, and I'll order your men to do this, above your head if necessary."

"I have every intention of doing as you request, First Kimshee Middle!" Trazar bowed with what could easily have been a challenge. "I wasn't ignoring you. I was only concerned for my men's safety. Kinship officers sometimes view Autlach sentries as a disposable commodity."

"I am not one of them. They will be at no risk. Now, do you understand what is to take place?" Krell detested being questioned under any situation, but this particularly addled her. She was tired and surrounded by the dank smell of male sweat. LaRenna's gentle aroma was decidedly more satisfying.

"Basically, you want my squadron to patron the Waterlead every night until further notice." He sniffed. "One question."

"And what is that?" Krell sighed, anxious to leave.

"Who foots the bill? Sentry pay isn't much. Most of my men send home every bit they make so their families can live. I know officers can afford it"—Trazar glimpsed at Krell's rank symbol—"but we enlisted grunts can't."

"And where did you get this ripe bit of information?" retorted Krell. "Three quarters of Taelach officer pay goes to the Kinship's coffers. I subsist on about half what you earn, so don't accuse all officers of having overstuffed money pouches." These Auts would serve their purpose then be gladly dismissed, free to slur her name and identity at leisure. "You'll have the funding on your duty work-table every morning. Give each man enough for two or three drinks plus tips."

"I assume this is to be done out of uniform?" Trazar pushed his tone to the verge of insubordination.

"Of course it is, sentry!" Krell spat. "What good would it do my investigation if they appeared at the Waterlead's door in full dress?" She held a finger to his face. "Also, have them undo their braids or tuck them into a headband one. And lastly, make sure they stagger the times that they arrive and leave. I want the effect of a steady stream of customers, not a raid. Any other questions or comments you wish to make, called for or otherwise?"

"No."

"I will leave you to your bed then. If there are any problems, notify me immediately." Krell ignored the sputtering voices that rose as the door closed behind her. "Auts." It was a Kimshee's job to deal with them on behalf of the Taelach people and Krell generally enjoyed it. But occasionally, like tonight, it could tax the short limits of her patience. She paused in the compound court-yard. It was deserted this time of night and the light breeze between the buildings gave it a desirable, peaceful air. Meditating briefly, she focused away from the frustrating sentry commander and centered on the business at hand, a cross-planetary conference with Belsas Exzal, Taelach of All.

Midmorning in the Taelach lands of Saria Three found Belsas in her sunlit workroom, waiting for Krell's transmission. She stood at a window, watching a bandit beast herd amble by on the open grass-lands below. It was calving season and the gawky newborns struggled to keep a stumbling pace with their mothers. Resembling bison, bandit beasts left a path of bare ground as they grazed, effectively robbing all plant life including seeds, fruit, and roots. Their kilometer-wide paths swathed across the northern plains in every direction. Reseeded and fertilized by their droppings, the land rejuvenated rapidly, the life cycle staying in complete balance.

The door to the workroom opened, admitting Belsas's gentle-natured life mate Chandrey. Her full skirts rustled as she joined her guardian at the window and she laughed lightheartedly at two calves that were engaged in a game of chase. "I never get tired of watching them play. Children are the same no matter the species."

"If life were only that simple for us." Belsas drew Chandrey close to kiss her on her high forehead. "What have you been doing this beautiful morning?"

"Pulling tuft snarls from the flowering beds." Despite a thorough washing, she could still smell the muskiness the dandelion-like weeds had left on her hands. "No news yet?"

"Not as yet. It's late where she is on Langus. First Officer Middle may wait until morning her time to contact us."

"Surely not. Kimshee Middle knows you're waiting for confirmation of LaRenna's arrival." Chandrey stood tiptoe to reward Belsas's kiss with a passionate one to her mouth. Sensing the tension in her mate's face, she frowned, her lips drawing in a similar fashion. "Relax, darling. We'll hear something soon."

Appropriately timed, a plump face, cheeks pink with excitement, appeared in the doorway. "Pardon, Belsas, but a coded transmission is waiting for you."

"Thank you, Rona."

"See!" Chandrey grinned so merrily Belsas couldn't help but chuckle. "I told you we'd hear."

"You're correct as usual, love," Belsas said, entering the access number into the adjacent computer panel and the view screen flared to life. "Well, First Kimshee, did she make it in one piece?" Krell's image was dim on the screen. "Are you having transmission difficulties?"

Krell whispered salutations. "Greetings, Grandmaster Belsas.

Good day, Lady Chandrey. There's no problem here. I have the lights low so they won't wake your daughter. She's travel exhausted, but otherwise fine."

"She near?" asked Chandrey, mindful of the overcrowding on Langus.

"Look for yourself." Krell turned the viewer so LaRenna's outline was visible, her white mass of curls peeking from the blankets.

"Poor baby," fretted Chandrey in her melodious soprano. "She's already asleep. The journey from the Training Grounds to Langus can be so hard."

"She's no baby," reminded Belsas. "LaRenna's fully braided and at a post. But then again," she added with a loving smile to Chandrey, "you always were one to worry over the young ones."

Chandrey's eyes never moved from her daughter's form. "I'm a teacher, Bel, it's in my nature."

Belsas gazed reflectively at her mate then turned back to Krell, who again dominated the screen. "All going as planned there?"

"As well as can be expected. I had a meeting with an Aut by the name of Starnes Bane this morning. The reconnaissance was right, two of the Branded are holed up here."

"Did you find out who?"

Krell murmured the answer in a tone so low Chandrey wasn't sure what she'd said. She was about to ask when Belsas's pallored expression told all she needed know.

"The Creiloff Twins!" The color drained from Chandrey's face.

Belsas collapsed heavily in her worktable chair. "I should have executed them when I had the chance. Why did I believe the reports of their deaths?"

Chandrey followed to rub her guardian's bunched shoulders. "How were you to know they would break the Trimar barricades?" she whispered.

"I knew someone would sooner or later." Belsas spoke no louder. "Others have tried."

"And they've been caught," reminded Krell. "We'll catch these two just the same."

Belsas peered at the viewer to lock determined eyes with Krell.

"Whatever you do, First Kimshee Middle, make sure LaRenna is prepared. She should know exactly what she's getting into."

"You have my word."

But Belsas continued as if she hadn't heard. "You have three days to be certain. If she's not ready, abort the mission. We'll call it a loss and pull all Taelachs off Langus. The High Council has received serious threats. Autlach authorities have foolishly chosen to ignore them, but for me to do so would be imprudent." Sinking back into her seat, Belsas let out a weighty sigh. What was LaRenna getting into?

Chandrey glided across the room to face the viewer close up, her eyes exuding the same concern as Belsas until her hands trembled. "For the love of the Mother Maker," she whispered to Krell, a fair amount of pleading in her voice. "Don't let her fall to them. If they find out who she is"—she glanced over her shoulder at her shaken lover, then back at the screen—"they'll do far worse than just kill her."

Chapter Twelve

The mind phase can be simultaneous in its joy and terror.

—*Taelach wisdom*

Krell woke LaRenna at first dawn. She shook her once, then again, then finally shaking her so hard she almost fell from her chair. "Wake up, LaRenna Belsas." Krell stood over her with a brooding expression. "Planning to sleep away your post on Langus? I've work to do and you've things to learn."

LaRenna's eyes shot open, wide but unfocused as they glanced about the room. Disoriented by the new surroundings, she stood, scratching her head with confusion. "What? Where? Ah, stars!" She stumbled to the facilities and reappeared a moment later, feeling a little fresher and much more alert. "How long was I asleep?" she asked in the midst of a jaw-popping yawn.

"Long enough. Get your boots and cloak on. I don't like waiting." Krell stood by the hatchway, tapping her foot. The younger Taelach wasn't sure how to read her teacher's moods so she acted dutifully and followed Krell out the door.

They exited the housing compound, striding silently out the base's main gates and down the rocky incline to the shoreline, Krell offering cordial assistance at several particularly rough patches of stone. At the bottom, she led the way to her favored dune, drawing into a meditation position atop the boulder as she motioned for LaRenna to settle on the sand before her. "Watch." Krell's eyes closed for meditation.

The spectacle of morning so enthralled LaRenna that she failed to sense the gentle prodding that crept into her mind. It spread throughout her, radiating down her spine in a whispering rush of ecstasy. She shook spasmodically then pushed against the force to find its point of origin: Krell.

So you have practiced the basics of phasing. The shared thought shuddered another wave of joy through LaRenna. *You know there are only two types of mind phase. It would have been cruel to surprise you with pain.*

S-stop, please. A burst of passion accompanied the return. Krell gasped. No student should be capable of such energy! She inhaled, briefly paused in the high, then centered deeper into LaRenna's mind, her hands resting across her apprentice's shoulders.

Show me what you can do.

Leave me alone! LaRenna moaned audibly as the phase hold deepened. She pulled her knees to her chest, tucked her head between her thighs then arched back, trying to wrestle free of her mentor's hold. What was happening to her? This was so much more intense than anything she had experienced with Malley. *Let me go!*

Push me out. Krell expanded even further, sending an almost overwhelming stimulus pulsing through LaRenna's body. *Make me go.* She immediately swept another wave into her apprentice then drew closer, pressing LaRenna against her boot leather. LaRenna resisted, both of them quick to exhale as their minds collided. *That's not enough. Hurt me and I'll go.* Krell pushed beyond the point of a test, far stronger than the normal ability level of a Kimshee LaRenna's age, and into the realm of an almost painful grip.

I can't! LaRenna was petrified, scared of sharing such intense emotions with one she knew so little of, frightened to realize she actually enjoyed the sensuous mental touch.

Krell pressed closer to LaRenna's instinctual core, pulling their physical beings into near oneness as she drew LaRenna into her lap. *There is a fine line between pleasure and pain. Cross it and push me out.* Krell sent another wave of emotion that made LaRenna's entire body shudder uncontrollably, scaring as much as it thrilled. Sheer sexual energy shot back on the link, intensifying the experience even more. Control abandoned, Krell forced the emotion again, this time adding a painful flex to the end of an emotional exchange that far overrode the ethics of her position. LaRenna sobbed and wrapped her hands around her head, both longing to be touched by and detesting the presence that held her.

NO! You're hurting me!

Push me out or I'll do it again. I will not hesitate to hurt you. We have to know what you're capable of.

A frustrated anger began to stir inside LaRenna. If Krell wouldn't go willingly, why she'd . . . she'd . . . *Too much! Get out! I don't want you here!*

You make this far too desirable. Make me go. Undaunted, pleasured to the point of shivering, Krell continued her hold, unprepared for what happened next. LaRenna drew up against her mentor's physical embrace, bunched her shoulders and slammed an ear-ringing mental blast at her teacher that agonized them both. Krell cried out from the internal slap, pushed back defensively, and the phase broke. Neither of them spoke for several minutes while Krell continued to hold her close. LaRenna pulled her head back down and shook as the sensation faded away.

Krell raised her hand to stroke LaRenna's uncombed hair then hesitated and pushed her into the sand. "It was imperative I know what level you phased at."

"I didn't know I was capable of that." LaRenna's whisper was almost inaudible.

"New apprentices seldom are." Krell looked above LaRenna to stare out over the water. "If you don't think you can handle the intensity of my training, you may request another teacher."

LaRenna dared a venomous glance toward her mentor. "No, that won't be necessary. You merely showed me how much I have to learn." She flipped stray strands of hair from her tear-streaked face and stood, knocking the sand from the back of her cloak.

"Your focusing technique is unstable." Krell returned her look with one of sheer hatred. This wasn't right. She was a teacher of Kimshees and, though Kimshee teachers were required to know their apprentices intimately, there could be no love between them. Emotional barriers had to stay in place. Physical barriers were unbreakable. "We'll work on it the next few days, if you choose to remain."

"Few days!" LaRenna turned to observe the way Krell's lucid face darkened. "But Krell, it takes passes to—"

"Address me by title from here on out, Third Kimshee Belsas," interrupted Krell. "You have a natural gift for high-level phasing. We'll polish a few edges while we can. That should be all you require for this post." She handed LaRenna a piece of cording and motioned for her to gather back her hair. "Get it out of your face and keep it that way. You can't work if you can't see." She wondered what Belsas's reaction would be to the bond they had just formed. No matter how wrong it might be, it could not be undone. "You never phased before to any real extent?"

"Once or twice with my roommate Malley, a little play on a few, um, interesting dates maybe, but nothing like this. Why?" she asked, adding when Krell glared at her, "First Kimshee."

Because you pleasure-phase to me with the sensitivity of a long-term lover jumped to Krell's lips, but she clenched them tight, swallowing the words away as "curiosity" escaped her mouth. "New Kimshees typically are incapable of achieving such depth in a test phase." She longed to add a few words about how personally gratifying it had been, but stopped short. The wake call sounded across the base as she spoke, disrupting the exchange. Krell rose as the noise faded. "Follow me."

"First Kimshee Middle?" LaRenna trotted to keep up with Krell's wide gait. "That was so unexpected that I have to ask. How close to . . . to . . ." LaRenna's face scrunched as she struggled for the words. "You seem upset. If I did something wrong when we phased, I apologize."

Krell never slowed, but she noticed, she noticed so very much. LaRenna, who was now almost running to keep up, barely reached midway on Krell's chest, a size difference that made her all the more enticing. Krell hated her for that fact. "I was simply unprepared. It won't happen again."

"Yes, First Kimshee." No matter how LaRenna tried to shake it off, there was a certain level of their contact that remained, a small piece of Krell that lingered on.

Krell's face remained solemn though she was also aware of the bond. A small amount of LaRenna had permanently lodged in her mind and heart, tempting and satisfying her in a way she never thought possible. "After breakfast, you will report to Healer Wileyse at the medical complex."

"But there's nothing wrong with me, First Kimshee."

"Your resulting discomfort is not my concern." Krell paused long enough for LaRenna to catch up. "You're to report directly after breakfast. Wileyse is expecting you."

"Yes, First Kimshee."

There was no further conversation between them during the walk to the galley or through breakfast, leaving LaRenna to wonder if the feelings stirring deep within her were justified. And Krell, fully enwrapped in overwhelming emotions that she must deny, could do no more than sip her tea and look away.

Chapter Thirteen

Beware the Kimshee in disguise.

—Autlach saying

———————

Krell changed seats repeatedly then paced the room until she'd worn ridges in the ornate rug in Wileyse's office. Finally, losing patience completely, she traipsed down the hallway to see if LaRenna was anywhere near presentable. Wileyse met her at the examining room door. "We're all but done, First Kimshee Middle. She is changing as we speak." Wileyse stepped into the corridor, making sure to jerk her heavy skirts free before the door shut on them. "We need to discuss your apprentice for a moment."

"It all went well? Nothing's wrong, is it?"

"Fine, fine. It went well. Not one word of complaint or even a flinch when she was fitted with the lenses, and you know how uncomfortable that can be." Krell nodded for Wileyse to continue.

"Physically, she's strong. It's her mental state I'm concerned about." Wileyse's voice often held an arrogant edge that made others feel they were being talked down to. Unfortunately, they usually were. "Her heart rate and blood pressure are elevated enough to indicate her post is stressing her. I want your assurance she can handle herself or I won't approve her for duty."

Krell hadn't wanted anyone, least of all Healer Wileyse, to know about the phasing experience, but now found it necessary. She sighed. "What you're seeing is the aftereffect of the rough start we had this morning. You see—"

"First Kimshee Krell Middle! Have you completely lost your mind?" Krell startled at the healer's shrill reprimand. "Did you bother to read that woman's records before you tested her?"

"Of course."

"I mean her medical records, you dolt!" A frown pulled the corners of Wileyse's thin, painted mouth.

"Number one, why would I read a student's medical file? They're confidential. Number two, I thought I told you never to—"

"Drop the tough act." Wileyse pushed the high-glossed nail of her index finger into the tip of Krell's nose. "I find it childish, bothersome, and unbecoming of your professional rank. If you had thought to read her medical history, you would have seen she's been capable of high-level phasing since birth."

"Impossible!" Krell swatted away the intruding finger. "The only ones capable of phasing from birth are true females, and none of them are old enough to have completed the Training Grounds."

"Wrong!" Wileyse took great personal satisfaction in the correction. "Wrong! Wrong! WRONG! Your student is one."

"Where's her file?"

They went back to Wileyse's cluttered workroom so Krell could read the fine details of LaRenna's medical history. A single entry at the bottom of one of the screens repeated what the healer had said.

71

SUBJECT DEVELOPING PRIMARY SEXUAL CHARAC-
TERISTICS DISTINCTIVE TO THOSE OF AUTLACH
FEMALE. CAPACITY FOR REPRODUCTION CON-
FIRMED. NEW TAELACH VARIATION DEFINED—TRUE
FEMALE.

Krell handed the recorder back to Wileyse. "So, she was the first."

"Yes, she was." There was a hint of superiority in the healer's tone. "So, I wouldn't phase with her again unless I was up to the level of control it demands. She's vulnerable, hasn't a notion of what she's truly doing, and would be an easy target for someone without discretion." Wileyse's arms were folded across her small, rounded chest and she drummed her fingers knowingly against her bony elbow.

She knows more than you've the capacity, thought Krell as she taunted Wileyse in a low tone. "Are you implying that I can't handle myself?"

"Kimshees are never much for control, discipline, or commitment when it counts." Wileyse's distrust was common among well-off Taelach families. Kimshees were considered a necessary evil, reckless in their manners and morals. They spent far too much time among Autlachs, picking up the worst of their mannerisms.

"Sounds like a comment from a disgruntled ex."

"It is." Wileyse sneered. "One who knows your fear of commitment."

"Commitment wasn't the problem with you, Tatra Wileyse. Your habit of looking down that skinny nose of yours at everyone is what turned me away."

Tatra's slender fingers trembled against her arm. "I do not peer down my nose! What gets me is your need to seek out and sustain friendships with Auts. Aren't your own people good enough?"

"It's my job. It's my post. It's how I was raised. I'm a Kimshee, for the Mother's sake! Try talking to Auts instead of down to them and you might find a friend or two. And if you'd ever stop obsessing over yourself—"

"Obsessing?" The healer chewed her bottom lip while she struggled for just the right retort. She wouldn't give Krell the satisfaction of winning this argument. "I am not obsessed with myself. I'm a healer. Caring for others is what I do. How can I focus on myself when saving a life?"

"It's the afterglow that slays me, Tatra, that smug look that crosses your face when you succeed. You're so damn self-absorbed that I could never obtain a full pleasure phase with you, much less enjoy your mind. It was full of self-satisfaction before I ever phased in. The most important person in your life will always be pampered and spoiled, powdered and painted Tatra Wileyse."

"What a hateful, vengeful bitch you are."

"It's been rumored."

Tatra opened her mouth for another rejoinder when something familiar caught her eye. Krell had that look, that conquering look she always had following good sex. "You didn't?"

Krell happily fed on the healer's shock. "I said it was an intense interaction, didn't I?"

"And intense means?"

Krell raised a brow. "Better than you."

It was more than Tatra could take. "You mean to tell me you found a first phasing with that inexperienced little apprentice Kimshee better than anything we had in a pass and a half together?"

"Take it as you will."

"Of all the—" Tatra quelled her barrage when her Autlach assistant appeared in the open doorway. "WHAT?"

"Healer Wileyse," the young medic whispered his response. "Your patient is ready to depart."

"Thank you." Krell passed the Autlach, who promptly saluted. "Good to see someone around here has a few manners."

Tatra stood in the doorway, hands balled on her knobby hips. "I hope you two are deliriously happy together," she shouted.

Krell spun in the middle of the corridor. "The only thing I'm sorry for, Tatra, is ever thinking you'd be able to let me in! You never understood me or my ways. Who am I kidding, you never even tried." She offered a final heated glare, spun back around, and stomped down the hallway.

"Oh, Krell." Tatra swallowed hard as the Kimshee disappeared around a corner. "In hindsight, it's surprising we lasted as long as we did. They say it takes a Kimshee to understand a Kimshee. Maybe it's true."

"Third Kimshee?" The examining room appeared empty when Krell entered. There was a shuffle and a hand waved from behind the changing screen, fingers wiggling a quick greeting.

"Here, First Kimshee." LaRenna walked from behind the screen and whirled around, her multilayered skirts billowing as she turned.

All the anger Krell felt from the confrontation with Tatra dissipated. LaRenna looked as if she had been born Autlach, necessary if she was to succeed in reconnaissance against other Taelachs. Her eyes were a delicate fawn brown and her skin the sun-kissed warmth of the Langus farmwomen. She wore a fitted white cap-sleeved work frock, brown overskirts, and flat beast-hide slippers. The untamed mop on her head had been bobbed midneck and glistened with red highlights.

LaRenna viewed herself in the reflecting board above the examining room basin and howled dismay. "I look horrible! So, so, monochromatic. Brown! Every inch of me is brown or some variation thereof." Her unhappiness increased with the awareness of Krell's intense stare. "Oh my," cried LaRenna. "Is it really that bad?"

Krell startled then looked away. "Your appearance merely reminded me of the descriptions of an Earth animal I've read about. You look like a wren."

"What?" LaRenna stopped, thinking the word was an attempted play on her name.

"A wren." Krell carefully spelled out the word. "Have you ever read any of the archeology files from the ancient human mining colony on Farstar?"

"Yes, First Kimshee, Belsas is a trained historian. However, I am not familiar with this term. Is wren another word for *plain* or boring in human?"

"No, it's not." Krell bit down to keep from admitting just how pleasant LaRenna's appearance really was. "A wren is a type of animal called a bird. It's small, brown, and covered with something called feathers."

LaRenna groaned. "I resemble a dull, brown animal?"

"Birds are fascinating."

LaRenna ventured another glance at Krell in the reflecting board. "Please tell me more, First Kimshee."

"For one thing, they fly."

"Like the winged rodents on Saria Three?"

"Similar, but to achieve flight, birds use wings, not skin stretched between the front and hind legs. Wrens are much smaller, too." Krell sat on the examining table's edge and leaned forward, cupping her hand for demonstration purposes. "They'd fit in the palm of your hand. That's why I called you one."

LaRenna leaned against the basin as she questioned the analogy. "You are referring to my physical size, First Kimshee?"

"It does concern me."

"It was never a question during my initial training or coursework," the pseudo-Autlach interrupted. "Why would it come into play now?"

"Never mind." Krell stiffened then stood, pacing the room in quick, wide strides. "Practice sliding those lenses back. You'll need speed if you fall into a fight."

After several hard blinks and a bit of impatient instruction from her mentor, LaRenna did as instructed, refocusing through her natural pale blue color to find an intent look and phase from Krell waiting for her. *Not near good enough, girl. You lack control. This isn't school. This is reality. I could have killed you twice over.*

LaRenna was quick to push Krell's presence into a far corner of her mind. *I'm trying, First Kimshee.*

Try harder. Krell gave LaRenna the equivalent of a mental pinch, then dropped her phase. "We'll reduce your endeavors to working with Autlachs," she said despite the want for more. "Most can master control of the Aut mind in a short time. But be warned, their minds are so open that it's easy to overdo it."

"And where do I find an Autlach willing to let me play with his head?"

Krell sighed at LaRenna's naiveté. "Where Auts play, girl. The market. The best time to toy with an Aut's mind is when you're right beside him."

"I don't understand."

"I don't expect you to." Krell tossed LaRenna her cloak. "We're going to the Common Grounds. It's midday, so the place will be teeming with unknowing subjects." And they were off, LaRenna once again running to keep up with her teacher's gait.

Chapter Fourteen

Dearest LaRenna,

*This note was given to Master Yeoman Quall to be forwarded to you.
I pray it reaches you. Nobody will tell me where your posting is. It seems
to be a closely protected secret. Just like you, disappearing without saying
goodbye. You probably love the mystery of it. I hope you find the adven-
tures you are seeking. Remember, I post on the Predator. Please send word
as time allows. I miss you.*

Yours always,

Malley Whellen

Third Engineer

Chapter Fifteen

Identical Taelachs feed off their twin's negative energies, creating a disastrous combination of hatred and insanity.

—common Taelach knowledge

Bane woke with a jerk then stared at the ceiling, wondering how long he had been unconscious. Seizures came so frequently that he'd lost all sense of time. The hour, he surmised, must be evening because voices and the clanking of dishware echoed up the stairwell. The noise was louder than it had been in some time. Business must be good.

He rolled to his side and balanced on one elbow. His tunic was fresh, his bed linens clean, and a tray of warm food lay within easy reach. "Bless Starnes's soul." Bane was humbled by his loss of control. No matter how bad it became, and it was frequently that, his son always tended to his needs. Shaking, he reached for the water glass and drew a sip over his cracked lips, wincing at the pain that accompanied swallowing. He returned the glass to the tray and lay back, startling when another thud on the adjoining room's wall made the water slosh. Footfalls vibrated and a low drawl cursed. Bane sank in his bedroll. If he pretended to be asleep, he might be left alone. Eyes shut tight, he listened to the disjointed ranting that flowed from the next chamber, praying they wouldn't come to include him.

Brandoff stumbled across the room, a near empty wine crystal in her hand. "Stay upstairs, Brandoff. Be quiet, Brandoff. Quit your bellyaching, Brandoff. I'm sick of it!" Brandoff pried her boot knife from the wall, circled, and threw again. Thud! The knife sank to its intricately carved hilt. "Why's it always me who ends up stuck high and away? Always me who's left hanging while Cance makes things happen?" Thud! "Cance doesn't trust me to take care of things. Why couldn't I disguise my appearance, too?" She jumped back to avoid a bad throw that ricocheted off the wall, stepped on the blade's tip to raise the handle, picked up the knife, and threw it once more. Thud!

Cance bounded up the stairway in an angry snit. The throws were audible through the bar's thin floors. "Brandoff! What the fuck are you doing? This bar is packed and I'm trying to conduct a business meeting. I don't have time for your games." Thud! The knife sailed past Cance's head, imbedding in the wall.

"I'm bored outta' my mind. There's nothing for me to do. Let me put my cloak on and come downstairs. I promise to stay out of the way and keep my mouth shut. Come on, Cance!"

Cance jerked the knife from the wall and flung it between her twin's feet. "Not a chance. Hyped and drunk as you are, you'd pounce on anything that bounced or wiggled through the door. I'd have to keep constant watch on you."

Brandoff slid the knife into its sheath then collapsed, weary with boredom, into a chair. "I'll even work the kitchen, Cance. Come on. I'm going crazy up here." Brandoff dropped to the floor, rattling the room again, her hair flying forward as she begged for something to do.

"You want to keep busy?" Cance shoved Brandoff back into the seat. "I'll give you something to do. Wait here." She vaulted down the stairs to return momentarily with a heaping pile of dirty kitchen linens that she shoved into Brandoff's arms. "Knock yourself out."

Brandoff dumped the insulting bundle. "Do I look like your fuckin' Aut drudge?"

Look, Brandoff, Cance pushed the tiniest of phases. *You have your role to play in a couple of days. Be patient. Please. There's a clean set in the washroom. Fold them, start these, and I'll be up in a while to check on you.*

All right. Brandoff's hair fell into limp clumps about her drawn face. *I'll do them, just promise we'll be out of this hole soon. I'm feeling useless.*

Useless? Where would I be without the best pilot in the Sarian system? Brandoff's ability to fly almost any craft, Taelach or Autlach, was the main reason Cance had risked taking her unstable twin from Trimar's snowfields. There was little sibling bonding between them and what existed was often volatile. *I need you, Brannie.*

You do?

'Course I do. "Now, my Kimshee senses tell me the old man is awake. Have him keep you company and help fold those linens." Cance paused on the stair head to peer down at the main dining room's crowded conditions. "Starnes wants to go to the Hiring Hall in the morning and I think maybe he should. I'm no bartender and he barely has time to cook, much less throw together drinks and serve them. Behave yourself, Brandoff. I'll be back."

"Yeah, Cance." Brandoff gathered the linens as the door fell shut. "Bitch, you think you know so much. My knife and I know better and one of these days we're gonna show you just how ignorant you really are." Brandoff carried the linens to the washroom, threw them on the counter and removed the fresh ones from the cleaning unit, grumbling unsavory grievances all the while.

Crammed to capacity with soiled towels, the unit chirped and hummed its cycle signal, needing no further attention. Brandoff balled the sweet-smelling towels in her arms then went to Bane's corner. "Get up, old fool. I know you're faking it." She threw the bundle on his chest. "Fold these while you tell me another of your stories."

Bane opened his eyes. "Should have known better than to try to fool a Taelach." He tried to sit up but the trifling weight of the linens pinned his frail body, laboring his breathing. "Move these," he wheezed, "and you'll get your story."

"A demand from the dying?" Brandoff snorted. "Very well, I'll fold them. Just spare me from boredom."

Weight lifted from his chest, Bane pushed to a reclining position, the effort throwing him into a painful coughing spasm. He sputtered and gurgled, choking on his own fluids.

"Mess yourself and it won't be me who cleans you up!" Brandoff pulled a chair beside him.

"Water," he gasped, "please."

Brandoff grabbed the glass from the tray, dunked her fingers into it, and flicked them in his face. "Drink up." Bane stared at her, too winded to object, far too used to her cruel manipulations to give the pleasure of a reaction. "I guess you want me to hold the glass too, don't you?" She raised his head and held the glass to his lips, allowing him several sips before she jerked it away. "Now, spin me a tale, old man, before I make you the new target for my knife play."

"Did you ever hear the story of the Greatest Gift?"

"No, let me hear it."

"On the edge of the eastern Langus shore there is an island called Vinsite. The seas there are unusually rough. They batter the rocky cliffs and storms frequently bash the small cluster of compounds that lie there.

"A child by the name of Talana lived there with her family."

"Aut or Taelach?" Brandoff continued to fold linens.

"Autlach of course," said Bane irritably. "I know no stories

81

involving Taelachs that you would approve of. Now, it was the Feast of the Making and a terrible storm was raging on the island. Talana's home was warm and a chasa meat roast was cooking over the fire. The table was set with the makings of a wonderful meal, but Talana and her mother weren't interested in it. Instead, they walked to the windows every few minutes, drawing back the drapes to look down the hill toward the sea. Talana repeatedly asked when her father would return. Her mother would say 'soon' and leave it at that.

"Talana's father was a fisherman and sometimes gone for days at a time. He always returned with something for Talana, usually a pretty shell or some other trinket. But this time, because of the Feast, he had promised her a special toy.

"The storm grew angrier and angrier."

"What about the environmental controls?" Brandoff asked

"This was before the Autlach had stable weather control." Bane wheezed heavily. "If you keep interrupting me I'll be too spent to finish."

"Go on then." Brandoff stacked the folded linens at her feet.

"The windows rattled and the wind pulled at the roof. Talana's mother was in tears with worry."

"Typical Aut bitch, crying at everything."

After a glare, Bane continued. "Finally, a faint knock sounded on the door. Talana flew to open it and there stood her father. He was soaking wet, his clothes covered with mud. His boots left puddles as he dragged himself to the fire. Talana's mother wrapped a blanket 'round him and stoked the flames. After some time, he told them what had happened. His ship had been caught outside the docks when the storm blew up. It was impossible to navigate around the barrier rocks in the heavy seas, so they forced the ship to the far side of the island and into the coastal caverns. He had walked across the island in the storm to reach his home. On his way, he had gotten turned about and wandered for hours in the forest.

"Talana's father called her over and told her he had lost the toy in the storm. He held her close and she could feel his warmth and caring. Suddenly, the toy wasn't important. She kissed her father's cheek, hugged him close, and told him his being there was the most special gift he could ever give."

"A children's story?" Brandoff bristled a little. "You waste my time with a fucking children's story?"

"A teaching tale, nothing more." Bane's breathing had become labored. "No insult was intended. I only did as you said."

"So you did." She took the stew plate from the bedside tray and set it in his lap. "Eat something. I can't have my only entertainment kicking off yet."

"Can't," he whispered. "Too tired."

"Must I feed you like an infant, old fool?" Brandoff snatched the plate and spooned a bite into his mouth. "Don't get used to it. I'm feeling generous for some reason." She waited while he struggled to swallow then shoved another at him. "Hurry up. I'm only giving broth. There's nothing to chew."

"No more." Bane fairly mouthed the words. "Water." Brandoff helped him take another drink then eased him back on the pillows.

"The old man is making you soft." Cance stood at the stair head. "Why bother? He's dead when we leave here." She took the stack of linens then looked back to where Bane's wasting body was curled. "Why help him linger? Let him die."

"He occupies my time."

"Not now he doesn't. I need you to complete the modifications on the plasma bows."

"They're finished."

Cance smiled. "Perfect. Check the scan decoders. I'm fairly certain they're synchronized, but you're the expert. Double-check my calculations. And my bow is due a charge. Get it done." Her twin's attention adequately diverted, Cance disappeared down the stairs.

"You have no intention of helping the Cause, do you?" whispered Bane from his pallet. "Why are you really here?"

"Don't worry your feeble head over it, old man. You'll be dead by then. We don't leave witnesses alive. Ever." Brandoff opened one of the decoders and began tinkering with the internal settings.

"I"—Bane winced as a seizure began to flame its way through his skeletal frame—"have children, grandchildren . . ."

Brandoff watched in demented fascination as palsy caused Bane's wasting body to jerk spasmodically. Prock overdosers did the very same thing and Brandoff had done it more than once. The Taelach called it *aelandac*, the death dance. No one had helped her. Cance had only seen that she hadn't choked. Why should she help now? Bane wasn't overdosing, just dying an old man's death and besides, he was Aut. "You wrinkled fool, you just don't understand, do you? Old, young, all of you are worthless imbeciles in desperate need of an end to your pitiful lives." Brandoff walked away, taking his pillow for a quieter knife target and his dinner simply because. "You'll all die and the world will be a better place for it."

Chapter Sixteen

You are my heart, my spirit, the reason for my being . . .

—from Guardian's Song

———————————

Two days passed quickly, Krell and LaRenna's stressful, addicting bond intensifying with every teaching phase. LaRenna's abilities were unlike anything Krell had ever imagined. Already, she phased at or above the level Krell had practiced over sixteen passes to obtain, and Krell was highly regarded in the Kimshee calling.

The sun had long set and they had returned to their shared quarters following a session at the weapons range in which LaRenna had thoroughly smashed Krell's previously untouched accuracy ratio with the plasma bow. Krell seemed angered by the defeat, but was beginning to take such events in stride. Training LaRenna was proving exciting indeed.

"Again." Krell motioned to LaRenna. They were sitting in the sleeping corner, Krell reclining against the stacked bedrolls, LaRenna kneeling before her instructor. Between them the room's only light, a meditation candle, cast a low blue ripple. The mental concentration needed to light and extinguish a flame was intense. Krell had only recently mastered it, which was sooner than most Kimshees. The majority of other Taelachs found it an impossible task, far above the standard levels of control. LaRenna, much to Krell's embarrassment and vexation, took to it with ease.

"Center more into the core of the flame." Krell watched as the candle's glow increased in response to LaRenna's phase. "That's enough. Now snuff it out."

LaRenna pushed a smothering phase pulse over the luminary and it died with a puff of smoke to make her smile. The grin faded when she noticed Krell's eyes on her. "First Kimshee?"

"You still lack control," she mumbled for lack of any other complaint. "But all in all you have improved."

Another grin fluttered briefly across LaRenna's face in response to a rare compliment.

Don't be smug. Krell's sudden presence doused LaRenna's rising ego. *You are anything but prepared for the worst.*

"Ouch!" Krell rewarded her student's vocal cry with a second then a third mental pinch.

Use your mind.

My phase conversing is getting better, too.

Overconfidence will be the end of you. Krell's inner being reached again but this time LaRenna was ready, successfully pushing her mentor's presence a comfortable distance from her own. *Merely pushing your opponent away will only delay your death.* Krell moved in again, shoving against her apprentice's mental barrier until LaRenna's resistance began to weaken. *Come on. Give me a challenge.*

Back off. The energy within LaRenna's body faded then rapidly rose again, wavering with anticipation of her teacher's next move. *I know I puzzle you. I know you've never met another mind like mine.*

Quit your babbling. An annoyed grunt rose from Krell. *Scared of me, aren't you, girl? So scared that you can't sit still!* A quick roll in response to LaRenna's angry, concentrated energy thrust and Krell expanded her energy, circling it, embracing LaRenna until she moaned with sweet agony.

No fair! LaRenna gasped.

Nothing is fair in a fight. Krell's presence now pulled hard at her apprentice, tearing pleasure into a thousand bits of pain that washed through LaRenna's body. *Fight me or feel the heat of your too easy compliance.* LaRenna's physical being convulsed in time with the energy exchange. Despite the agony, she reached out, striking Krell on the chin. *Don't use your body to fight me, girl. I am much too big for that. Your physical size will work against you in a phase battle. Use that mind you have such confidence in.* Krell sent pulse after pulse into LaRenna's flailing being. *Fight me as I know you can. FOCUS!* The responding blast of energy brought tears to Krell's eyes. *Is . . . is that the best you can do? I told you to hurt me, dammit, so do it!*

"That did hurt you, First Kimshee." LaRenna's fist ricocheted off Krell's shoulder. "I could feel it."

Krell phased a cutting slap to her insolent apprentice. *Who're you to decide what hurts me? I'm experienced, girl. I've earned my rank through survival. Your best is nothing to me. I can take ten times that on my worst day.* Krell readily deflected LaRenna's next blow then responded mentally, launching an energy pulse that should have brought the strongest apprentice to her knees.

Mother's mercy! LaRenna did indeed crumple, but not in the way her mentor expected. She collapsed against Krell and they fell to the floor LaRenna had polished only that morning, chest-to-chest, mouth-to-mouth. LaRenna looked up to find Krell studying her intensely, with a reckless possession that refused further starvation. A simple nod was exchanged then apprentice and master were reformed as lovers: tangled, panting and groping, caressing and tasting in a frenzy of denied desires. The mental experience fulfilled, the physical, which Krell took ravenously, defied description and they reveled in the insensibility of both until LaRenna's passionate internal cries reduced to an aural murmur that parted their mouths. Only then did they indulge in the joy of slow discovery, delighting in the repetition of what felt so true. Afterward, Krell lingered with her, stroking her face, whispering lover's fancy about her beauty until reality and guilt swept in.

"How could I be so stupid?" Krell's face pinched with revulsion as she pushed away.

"What?" Before LaRenna could prop on one arm Krell had risen and was dressing.

"I took something from you that I can never give back." Krell spoke over her shoulder as she tugged on her boots. "I've broken every barrier, crossed every line."

"You took nothing I wasn't willing to give." LaRenna, shivering from the sudden removal of companion warmth, drew into the sleep corner and sat upon the bedrolls.

"You weren't ready to lose your virginity yet, Third Kimshee, and you certainly shouldn't have wasted such a precious commodity on the likes of me." Krell couldn't bear even the briefest of glances at LaRenna. She smelled like commitment. The room reeked of commitment as well—the safe, satisfying, stay-at-home, fresh-cut-flower joy of two women growing old together. It was nauseating. Krell had to leave and so left, ignoring LaRenna's calls to return so they could discuss things. She was dirty. Krell was dirty. What they had done was insanely wrong. Yes, Kimshees had sex, but they never made love.

The Kimshee lifestyle's lonely reality descended on LaRenna as the evening wore on. She bathed, attempted meditation, and then lay in her bedding, back to the wall, hands wrapping her knees as she forced back the lingering flurries of pleasure. Yes, Kimshees had sex, mind-blowing mental sex, but they seldom indulged in the physical act and they most certainly never, under any circumstances, despite what the soul might cry for, made love, not even with another Kimshee.

Chapter Seventeen

The size of your enemy is no indication of their strength or capabilities.

—from the Sarian Military Standards

The Hiring Hall was a squat stone structure situated in the oldest part of the Common Grounds. Narrow streets and alleyways circled it, making unseen access possible. Krell and LaRenna edged down one of the darkened gaps between buildings, twice stepping over a snoring patron of overzealous indulgence. The hall's rear entrance was unlocked in anticipation of their arrival. They slid inside and Krell lightly rapped on one of the inner doors.

"Enter." A low, rumbling bass pierced the predawn stillness.

Krell pushed the door open, bent slightly to enter, took LaRenna by the shoulder, and led her in. "You will keep manners with me and those who help our mission," she said, then bolted the door behind them. "Morning, Firman. How's life treating you?"

"Viciously, thanks for asking." A broad-bodied Autlach sat at the worktable in the room's center. He held his close-cut salt-and-pepper head at a peculiar angle, unsuccessful at evading the swimming sensation that lingered from previous night's activities.

"Looks like whatever you bit last night is biting you back this morning." Krell's head grazed the ceiling, sending plaster residue flying. "Blast it! How I hate old Aut buildings."

Firman let out a throaty chuckle and pointed at LaRenna. "This her?" He eyed LaRenna thoughtfully as he sucked tea from the black bush of a mustache hiding his mouth. "Does her hood come off or is it permanently attached to her cute little head?"

"Behave, will you? You're being facetious." Krell pulled LaRenna to the front and flicked back her hood. "Third Kimshee LaRenna Belsas, meet Firman Middle, my brother."

"Belsas?" Firman's mug suspended midway to his mouth. He looked at LaRenna again, then to his sibling, questioning surprise pushing his eyebrows almost into his hairline. "Well, well, what a notion. My sis is training the Taelach of All's kid." His brows slowly found their way back home and he smiled lightly. "So, how goes the phase training?"

"Firman!"

"Sorry, Krell, but you now how it is for us single types. We take our joys where we find them." He motioned for LaRenna to sit. "Pull up a seat, pretty lady, and tell me how much this too-tall, short-patienced, over-stubborn guardian Kimshee has corrupted you so far." He never took his rich brown eyes off her as he pushed his near empty mug to the table edge. "Be a good sibling, Krell, and pour us all a mug."

"I will when you quit ogling my apprentice." Krell laughed, aware his suggestive behavior was an act. Firman was actually a gentle giant of a man with a huge soft spot for the ladies, Autlach or Taelach. Krell took his mug to the cook corner and filled it along with two others from a steaming ewer of premixed tea. "Third Kimshee," she said between pours, "sit."

But LaRenna remained standing, bewildered and disbelieving.

Krell had never mentioned any of this. "Brother?" she repeated. "Your Autlach brother?"

"One of three, actually," said Firman, "and it is just like her not to mention us before now." He glared at his sibling. "Shame on you, Krell. Don't start your newest relationship with deception. Makes for a bad omen."

"The girl is my apprentice, nothing more."

"Yeah, right." Firman turned back around. "Please, sweet flower," he said in a soothing tone. "Please sit. And don't be angry with her. She never admits to things that are glaringly obvious to everyone else." He glanced at his sibling. "Isn't that right, Krell?"

Krell set a mug before each of them and joined her brother on one of the worktable's undersized benches. LaRenna's short legs fit the seat height perfectly. Krell's, on the other hand, stuck up awkwardly and uncomfortably, her knees almost hitting her chest. The sight made LaRenna smile.

"It was never imperative you know my history," Krell began in a voice to freeze the tea in their mugs. "But I suppose now you have the right. Firman is my brother, one of three. I was raised Autlach." She fell into brief silence, hoping the words would placate the rage LaRenna's thoughts had been broadcasting all morning. "I wasn't taken in by the Kinship until I was fourteen passes old. Up til then my life revolved around being the youngest child of a mountain herbalist on Stockrim."

"You were raised Aut?" inquired LaRenna, deliberate in her deletion of Krell's title.

"The Kinship didn't know I existed. We lived outside either of the moon's major colonies and Father kept very much to himself. I was discovered when a Taelach healer came to purchase some rare medicinal herbs he'd grown."

Firman nodded agreement. "Mother died the day after Krell was born. We kept to the hills because Father couldn't bear the thought of losing Krell too."

"So that's why you chose to be Kimshee." LaRenna kept her

surprise contained and stared blankly across the room. "You wanted to be close to your raising, your roots."

"She's smart as well as beautiful, Krell." Firman beamed. "How'd you manage that?"

"For the millionth time, she's my apprentice!"

Firman jiggled his expanding midline. "And I have women flocking to me for my physique."

"Firman!"

"That's my name." Their candor made LaRenna squirm uneasily. She drew a swallow from her mug and concentrated on counting the floor tiles.

"I believe our talk has made your lady self-conscious." Firman patted LaRenna's arm. "Just as well we refrain from the more vivid details of your relationship. It's almost first dawn." He gathered four recorders from the table's corner, juggling them back and forth as he grabbed for his mug. "I'll be back for you in a while, LaRenna. Say your good-byes, Krell, and kiss her once for me."

"Why, I oughta—!" exclaimed Krell. "If it were true I'd say you were jealous."

"It is and I am." The slamming door echoed his sentiment.

"Be wary of my brother, girl." Krell glanced over her shoulder. "He's the type that'll look up your skirts if given half a chance."

"Must run in the family."

Krell stiffened then returned the mugs to the cooking corner. "Your being on post does not give you license to drop protocol, nor does last night's setback." Krell paused until LaRenna dropped the glare on her mentor's back. "Firman will see that you meet up with Starnes. Accomplish your post and nothing more. If at all possible, I need you need to meet me on the beach at first dawn. I'll be waiting."

"Yes, First Officer."

"Have Starnes make the excuse of sending you to the Commons so you can get out unquestioned."

"That early?"

"Don't question, just do. The Wine Stores are open then. Have him send you there." Krell's long fingers gripped the tabletop. Could looking at LaRenna be avoided? "You have the medicines?"

"Stitched in my skirt hem where you had me put them." *Look at me.* The phase bounced off Krell's mental barrier and back to its sender.

"As soon as you know what's being planned, get out."

"First Kimshee, we've been over this a hundred times." LaRenna squirmed with agitation.

"Make it a hundred and one then." Krell spun from the corner and opened the door in such a rush LaRenna fell back onto a bench. "You will be reassigned as soon as you complete your post."

"I haven't requested reassignment."

"I have for you." Krell's response echoed down the street. LaRenna watched from the narrow window, launching phase call after unanswered phase call until she was certain the distance between them was too great. Then the same pit of emptiness she had felt with Nyla Smalls returned in magnitude. "You're a big girl. Deal with it." LaRenna collapsed back onto the bench and sulked into her mug.

It wasn't long before Firman returned. "Well, let's go," he said in a level tone. He balanced a large stack of paper files on his arm. "Better use the facilities first, if you've need. There's not one in the waiting area. Jobless Auts are notoriously messy, so we closed the one up front."

LaRenna took his advice and made use of the small water closet off the workroom, glancing in the worn reflecting board to smooth her hair before she rejoined him. Firman handed her a local work card as soon as she emerged. "According to this, you're quite the barmaid. Hope your man shows up early or someone else will want to hire you." He eyed her head to toe, rating her appearance with an approving if not somewhat enchanted smile and a nod. "Nice."

"Beg your pardon?" LaRenna wondered if her mentor's warning had some merit after all.

"Nice disguise job. If I didn't know better, I'd swear you were Autlach. Makes me wonder whatcha' look like Taelach."

"I'm a smaller version of Krell."

"Nope. I don't believe my guardian sibling could pull off wearing skirts." Firman drew his hands down in two straight lines. "No figure." With a flamboyant wave of his arm, he held the door wide for her. "After you."

"Thank you."

"Anytime." He smacked her firmly on the backside as she passed. "Anytime at all."

LaRenna whirled about. "Must you?"

"I have a reputation to uphold." Firman gave her another playful swat. "Besides, you'd better get used to it. There's not a barmaid alive that hasn't had to endure the occasional swat or pinch to the hindquarters." With a persistent grin that challenged even the sourest of thoughts, he waved her out the back entrance. "What's it all coming down to when a man can't tease his own kin?"

"Me, linked to you?" asked LaRenna. "Not possible unless you are referring to the First Officer."

"First officer?" Firman chuckled "No need for formality around me, LaRenna. Krell is simply Krell—big, moody, and from what I can tell so deeply infatuated with you that life must be damn near impossible."

"I'm being transferred after this post at her request."

Firman stopped chuckling to regard LaRenna with a gentle expression. "This is serious then." He clasped her hand and held it tight. "The key to Krell is learning to read in opposites. Has she been sending you mixed messages?"

LaRenna appreciated the warmth and opportunity to discuss what had been plaguing her mind. "No, the messages have been clear enough since last night."

"What happened?"

Certain of the friendship of her mentor's brother, LaRenna began to speak without hesitation, sharing both the joy and injury what had taken place the night before. "Krell hates me now, positively loathes me! I'm certain of it."

"Do you feel the same?"

"Yes! No! Aw, Mother's mercy, Firman. I don't know top from bottom right now. I have never wanted and abhorred someone so badly in all my life." Firman pulled her into a hug. No phase was needed to know his intentions. There was genuine concern, friendship, and sincerity behind this giant man and his comical grin.

"You two have it bad for each other, don't you?"

"Just because we did what we did doesn't mean we love each other."

"Two Kimshees making physical love? I know enough about Taelach customs to know what goes on, and that just doesn't happen." He kissed her forehead then held her at arm's length. "Jolly and Trishvor will like you."

"And they are?"

"Krell's and my brothers of course." The Autlach released his hold and strode to his worktable. "Be patient with Krell. Things will work out."

"I doubt it. We can barely be in the same room together."

"That'll pass." Firman winked at her. "Wait and see." He waved her toward the door. "Time you got into character and made your way around front, but take your time about it. Give me a chance to get up front before you appear. A woman in the Hiring Hall line's going to cause a stir." Firman let the door smack LaRenna's rear the third time.

Alone again and becoming oddly used to it, LaRenna circled the hall, stopping where the alley and narrow stone street came together. The line leading into the hall was immense, stretching from the entrance to cross several adjacent storefronts. The owners of those shops complained about the blockage, but it did little good in a time when so many were searching for employment. LaRenna took a spot at the end of the line and tried to be patient. Heads turned her way—eager, dark-faced leers followed by the low rumble of voices. One impudent older man in well-worn coveralls and heavy boots stepped out of line to approach her.

"Need work?"

"That's why I'm here."

"Can't your man take care of you?"

"I don't have a man." The last word rolled off her tongue with particular distaste. Autlach society treated its women as helpless creatures, incapable of independence or thought. Sadly, the majority of Autlach females believed it to be true, a fact that disheartened the equality-minded Taelach.

"No man?" The older man laughed uproariously. "The likes of you? No man?" His whistle gained the attention of the dwindling few unaware of LaRenna's presence. "Lookee here! She's searching for work. Says she doesn't have a man to keep her!"

"What is she," yelled someone near the head of the line, "one of them snow-headed witches?"

"She's no Taelach. This one's Autlach through and through." He whistled again, this time directing it toward LaRenna. "And what a woman she is."

All movement had ceased in that section of the Commons. LaRenna, thrown off guard, closed her eyes for a brief moment, wishing she were somewhere, anywhere else but there. Firman had warned she would make a scene, but she hadn't imagined this. Several more whistles and select lewd comments were thrown her direction, adding to her anxiety.

"Over here!"

"I'll put you to work!"

LaRenna opened her Autlach eyes and forced an amused expression on her face. If she couldn't pull this off, fooling two of her own kind would be impossible. "Why, gentlemen," she purred, tailoring her accent to the regional dialect. "What would I want with a man who doesn't have work? I'd be no better off than I am now."

The cocky Autlach slapped his knee in a resounding laugh. "She's got us there. This one's witty, she is." Every male in the crowd roared their agreement. Several women shopping in the area left disgusted, visioning what kind of work a woman could hope to find at the Hiring Hall and what she would have to do to gain it. The man choked off his laugh and took a step closer, something approaching greed shimmering in his eyes. "Seriously girl, why you here?"

"Work."

"Mean it, don't you?" His sun-creased face wavered from humored to suggestive while maintaining its smile. "I know an easy way for someone of your looks to make a bundle." Several men winked at each other while still others began fumbling in their belt pouches.

"I know what you're getting at," replied LaRenna. "And I am far out of the price range of the unemployed."

"Miss a few meals," squeaked an elderly male voice, "and you'll do it for almost nothing!" The crowd burst with laughter again and began to throw an increasingly vulgar display her direction.

"What's going on?" Firman Middle filled the main door of the Hiring Hall. LaRenna hadn't realized that while a good two heads shy of Krell's height, he was far broader in the shoulder. "I'm running a business, not a gambling hut." He looked directly at LaRenna. "Or a brothel. If you men want to work, get in line and shut up. Woman, go sell yourself elsewhere. You're disrupting my day."

LaRenna pushed out of her place in line. "I came for work, just like the others." Their dialogue had been carefully scripted to gain her entrance.

"You've got a live one here, Hallmaster Middle!" shouted one of the waiting men.

"I see that," replied Firman, his thumbs looping his wide belt as he sauntered to where LaRenna stood. "Want work, do you?"

"Yes."

"It doesn't come easy these days." His expansive fingers twisted into her hair, the touch reminding him how much finer Taelach hair tended to be compared to Autlach. "Everyone here needs work. What makes you so special, besides the obvious?"

"I'm good at what I do."

"That so?" Firman pulled her head back until it was directly under his then gave her the slightest wink of assurance. "And what work do you do, woman?"

"Whatever pays the most."

"Really?" Firman gave those closest his most enlightened smile. "And just what would you do to get work? The hall doesn't generally provide employment leads to women. Females of decent upbringing are properly supported by their men and would never be seen here. You know what this will cost."

"I'll do whatever it takes. I have to eat," whispered LaRenna, intent on her role. "I have to support myself."

"Well, if you want it that badly . . ." Firman fairly swooned with counterfeit excitement. He wrapped his hand fully around her upper arm and half-dragged her toward the hall. LaRenna dug in her heels as she was jerked along. She didn't want to appear too eager for what the others thought awaited her.

"Not fair!" protested the Autlach who had started the ruckus. "We can't whore ourselves to get in your good graces."

"You could try," said Firman with a grin. "But the answer would be no and your friends would never let you live it down." Successful in diverting the crowd's attention, Firman slammed shut the hall door. He lay against it as he wiped his brow. "You're good, too good," he told LaRenna. "You all but got yourself mobbed out there. Aut men aren't used to a woman commanding attention. It either excites them or pisses them off, neither of which you want when you're that outnumbered."

"Got me in here without anyone the wiser, didn't it?"

"That it did, but will it get you past the Hallmaster still clothed?" He took her arm again, not quite so roughly this time, and led her to the double doors on the foyer's far side. "Ready?"

"In a second." LaRenna closed her eyes tight then refocused on Firman through glass-blue eyes. "Now."

"Taelach eyes." He shivered. "They can be so cold." He slammed his free hand against the doors, flinging them open with a bang. "Look what I found outside, Hallmaster Tynnes." He shoved LaRenna into the room. "This one wants work."

"Hello there." The Hallmaster peered over the recorder in his grubby hands. "Only one way for a woman to get work out of my hall. She willing?"

Firman stroked the back of LaRenna's head, half for effect and half to offer silent support. His other hand still gripped her securely. "She said she'd do whatever it took."

"Is that so?" Tynnes scratched beneath the greasy knots making up his hair. "Come here, woman, and we'll, um, discuss your qualifications."

Firman released his hold and she walked around the worktable, careful to keep her gaze from the Hallmaster's. When she drew near, Tynnes clutched her about the waist, pulling her into his lap. "My, my, but you're a pretty one. I'm going to enjoy this immensely."

"I figured you'd like her," agreed Firman. "I know I do."

"Out!" The Hallmaster pointed to the double doors. "I need to interview this young woman." He pushed his nose in LaRenna's shoulder and breathed deep. "Sweet."

"I found her, Tynnes!" Firman rounded the table in a single fluid stride. He was not going to allow his superior one second alone with his sibling's love interest. Damn the pretense. Damn the outcome. "I should get a turn, too."

"Very well." Tynnes sneered. "When I'm finished, she's yours." He undid two snaps of LaRenna's frock and set his face deep into her cleavage as his hand inched up her skirts. She cast Firman a look of expanding terror and revulsion. The lead Hallmaster was disgusting, both physically and mentally; his smell, combined with the pressure of his excitement against her leg, was enough to make her vomit.

Firman's expression became anxious. "Do it," he mouthed, his skin crawling at the thought of Tynnes's filthy touch.

"Tynnes," LaRenna cooed in the Hallmaster's ear. "I'll do whatever it takes for work. The better the job, the more I'll do." She massaged his bony shoulders and tickled his neck. His skin prickled in response.

"I can see you will," he mumbled and pulled her into a greedy, full-mouthed kiss. Then he pushed back to stroke her downcast face with a greasy finger. "Look at me," he demanded, digging his fingers into her side until she squirmed in his lap. "Look at me, woman."

"Whatever you want." LaRenna focused a deep stare on him and smiled, delighting in the way his expression shot from ecstasy to repulsion.

"WITCH!" Tynnes jerked his hands back and stood, throwing LaRenna to the floor. She never lost eye contact as she fell, pushing pain phase enough for him to grab at his head. His mind was open, defenseless to the attack. So open, it made her glad Krell had forced her to practice. A loss of control would prove deadly right now and she wanted to temporarily disable, not permanently handicap the smelly little man. When she pushed a little harder, the Hallmaster collapsed in his chair.

"Did you kill him?" Firman rushed to his employer's side.

LaRenna scrambled to her feet and wiped Tynnes's slime-ridden kiss from her mouth. "Of course not, I only phased him unconscious. He'll be out most of the day but when he does wake, he'll be satisfied. I gave him a wonderful delusion of what happened." She ran her fingernail over his neck, leaving a thin scratch.

"Why'd you do that?"

"Effect. Adding the physical to the mental heightens the memory's effectiveness."

"Oh." Firman jerked the Hallmaster upright and threw him over one broad shoulder. "LaRenna, remind me never to piss you off. You've too much of a mind." Tynnes' lack of hygiene forced a crinkle into Firman's nose. He pushed the offending Autlach as far from his face as possible and carried him through the small door at the back of the workroom.

"Where are you taking him?"

"To his bed." Firman stepped into the bedchamber, tossed Tynnes onto the unmade platform, and partially undressed him. "For effect," he assured her, then closed the door and drew a long breath. "Only thing worse smelling than Tynnes," he declared, "is his room. It hasn't been cleaned once in the seven passes I have worked here."

"Neither has his mouth," replied LaRenna as she snapped her top. "Maybe I should plant the suggestion of bathing in his mind." Tynnes's dirty hands had smirched the laced edging of the frock. She rubbed at the stains and glanced up at Firman. "What's next?"

"I process some of those waiting in line and you stay out of sight until this Starnes arrives."

"Where do you want me?"

Firman grinned and pointed to the corner door.

"Oh, no." LaRenna cringed at the suggestion. "Not in there. Anywhere but there."

"Sorry, kiddo, but the crowd will get restless if there are further delays in processing. All the other rooms are in use."

"What about your personal quarters?" she pleaded.

"You have to go through the main waiting area to get there." Firman shrugged. "And anyone who saw you come in will be expecting you to be entertaining the Hallmaster." He pointed to the door again. "In there."

"Only for my post would I even think of doing this!" LaRenna held her nose and stepped into the doorway quarters, Firman giving her a little shove forward before he pulled the door shut. The room was acrid with sweat and urine.

"Have fun." The door muffled his voice but failed to buffer his amusement. LaRenna cleared the garbage from a chair, turned it backward, and straddled the seat. The high back was the exact height for a chin rest when she crossed her arms on the top so she draped over it, trying to ignore Tynnes's snores. The noise and smell must not have been too offensive because suddenly Firman was shaking her awake. LaRenna stretched and wiped her mouth. She'd been dozing hard.

"Hard night last night?" Firman indicated her sprawled position. Her skirts were pushed into a mid-thigh wad. "Not very lady-like, especially in skirts."

"I've always detested skirts. They're impractical, especially for a Kimshee."

"That's almost refreshing to hear. Personally, I have always fancied the definition leggings bring to the female form. Wish more of you wore them."

"Krell was right about you." She laughed. "You're too fresh for your own good."

"Oh, I'm basically harmless. I like to make a game of flirting and looking. Call it a hobby."

"Obsession."

"All right then, obsession. Point being, I talk a lot more than I'll ever do. I've had very few serious female companions in my lifetime and would have committed to any of them in a minute. Seems they felt differently." Firman's confession tugged LaRenna's heartstrings. Now she saw him as Krell did, a deeply caring and compassionate hulk of a man who longed for a steady relationship. The antics disguised his loneliness.

"You'll find what you're looking for someday," said LaRenna.

"Maybe so, but I'm getting a little long in passes for high hopes."

"You're as old or young as you choose to be. If I were Aut, I'd be after you in a minute."

"Girl?" Firman cast her a surprised but appreciative look. "I'm old enough to be your father."

"There's something to be said for maturity. The best wines have age on them, don't they?"

Firman squared his shoulders. "You don't find the mid-age girth distracting?"

"Your sister is beginning to develop one too, in case you haven't noticed." LaRenna smiled. "Though, I don't think Krell would admit it."

"No, she wouldn't," replied Firman. Spirits lifted, he resumed his affectionate teasing. "Just wait until I tell her you actually slept with the Hallmaster."

"Why should she care?"

"Because guardians are a jealous lot when it comes to their women."

"You aren't going to give up on that idea, are you?" She wondered if the stench of Tynnes's breath would linger on her until she next saw Krell.

"Nope, I'm the eternal optimist." Firman cast her one of his comical smiles. "Anyone ever tell you you're small for a Taelach?"

"Everyone tells me that!" LaRenna groaned.

" 'Cause it's true." Firman grabbed her under the arms in a dizzying lift. "I used to do this to Krell. Stars, was that ever a long time ago. You're lighter though. Don't you ever eat?"

"More than I should." She laughed.

"Can't prove it by me." He carried her into the workroom, setting her by the double doors. "Time for you to make your appearance in the waiting area."

LaRenna blinked to regain her Autlach appearance as Firman waved her through the door. "If anyone asks, Tynnes is taking a rest, recovering from his encounter with you." He couldn't resist the urge. "You wore the man out, you trashy wench."

"Like you said, Assistant Hallmaster Middle, I'm good." LaRenna said this loud enough to carry into the waiting area.

"Play it up, why don't you?" He chuckled then shoved her gruffly from the room. "If we desire your services again, I'll call for you." Firman flicked up LaRenna's calf-length skirts for the benefit of the room's occupants. She brushed the folds back into place and glared at him.

"I gave you what you wanted. Now give me what I came for—work."

"If something comes in calling for your special qualifications, you'll be called." Firman pushed her into a chair. "Until then, sit down and keep your mouth shut."

Firman left her sitting among a group of Autlach males. Aware of the stares she was receiving, she folded her hands primly in her lap and gazed out the window. Let them look. She had nothing to prove.

Firman soon returned. "Come here, woman. I've a position for you."

One of the waiting men confronted him. "Didn't you get enough last time? I've been in here all day every day for half a cycle and haven't been called for a job yet." His scathing glower was meant more for LaRenna than the Hallmaster. "Then this, this, whore comes in here, spreads her legs for you and gets a job within minutes."

"You would too if you had the right assets and the gumption to use them," replied Firman, nodding toward LaRenna's generous proportions. "I've got three more positions to fill after I finish with the girl. You'll be out of here within the hour if you can do one thing."

"What's that—screw you myself?"

"No, smartass, sit down and shut up!" Firman's bass voice rattled the decaying building. Aggravated but mindful he might be thrown from the hall, the man returned to his seat, growling under his breath when LaRenna flicked the back of her skirts at him.

"See ya later."

"Trollop," he mumbled.

"That's employed trollop to you." Firman jerked her away before she could say more.

"Don't overdo it." He shut and barred the door behind her. "LaRenna, let me introduce you to Starnes Bane, owner of the Waterlead."

Starnes frowned. "This little girl, this child is what the Kinship sends to stop their renegades?"

"Things are not always as they appear, Barman Bane." LaRenna bowed a short greeting. "Rest assured, I'm qualified for this post. The Kinship would not have sent someone who isn't."

"Hmph." Starnes snorted. "I don't think one Autlach barmaid will have any impact."

"Probably not." LaRenna blinked hard. "But a Kimshee will."

Starnes's double chin dropped to his chest so fast it coaxed a laugh from Firman. "Amazing what a good dye job can do, isn't it?" The big Autlach chuckled.

"I'd never of known."

"That's the intent," said LaRenna. "I have to appear real enough so another Taelach won't suspect me." She noted a marked change in Starnes's attitude since she had revealed her identity. He seemed to stand a little straighter, with renewed confidence. Were things really so bad? "Anything new happen since you met with Taelach Middle?"

"My father has taken a turn for the worse. He can't eat anymore."

"I've medicine with me. We'll begin treatment this evening."

Starnes's tension reduced even more, permitting him to accomplish a short smile. "We've got to get back. If I'm gone too long, Cance will come hunting."

LaRenna nodded then gave Firman a quick hug about the waist. "Thanks for the help."

"Anytime," he said, cupping his hand to her ear. "After all," he whispered, "we'll be seeing each other often." He gave her another swift swat and unbarred the door. "Carefully, my friends. Much depends on your success."

They departed the Hiring Hall from the rear, away from the prying eyes of the mouthy and unemployed. Starnes was only slightly taller than LaRenna, but his hurried pace forced her to jog. They made their way across the Commons and through a small ramshackle housing area. On the far side, he stopped and pointed ahead to a shabby two-story building just as old if not older than the Hiring Hall. "There it is."

"Needs work."

"Work?" exclaimed Starnes. "It needs to be leveled. I hate it." He scratched his side and shrugged disconcertedly. "But I guess it's a living."

"Better than the Hiring Hall, I'm sure."

Starnes grinned at her. "I suppose it is. So, you going to cover those gorgeous blue eyes of yours or not?"

"Yeah, right now." LaRenna closed her eyes to replace the lenses. "Better?" She didn't want to admit she had forgotten about their removal.

He still grinned at her.

"Something else wrong?"

"No." Starnes's smile spread all the way to his outward-turned ears. "Can I ask you something?"

LaRenna nodded, though she knew the question he was about to ask.

"Sorta short for a Taelach, aren't you?"

Chapter Eighteen

He who aids the Taelach shall become as soulless as the blue-eyed witch, his misdeeds punished in the cleansing fires.

—from the text of The Raskhallak Stipulations

"I expected you to bring back a barman, Starnes, not a waif still smelling of the farm." Cance watched LaRenna clean a corner table. "Was the selection at the Hiring Hall that pitiful or have you that desperate a need? Brandoff was perfectly willing to—"

"No, Cance, quite the opposite. She was the best the Hall had to offer skillwise." Starnes averted her eyes as he restocked the bar. Cance rattled her empty glass against the counter until he slid a filled decanter to her.

"Good boy, Starnie, you're learning." She swiveled and lounged against the heavy glass counter to watch their new employee. "Best qualified, eh? I'll be the judge of that. You, girl, let me see your worker's card. I want to know your job history."

LaRenna rose until she could see the other Taelach through the maze of chair bottoms and table bases. Cance stared back at her, mouth pursed as LaRenna whiningly objected. "Barman Starnes has seen the card."

"I don't give a damn what Barman Starnes has or hasn't seen of you, though I suspect he already has seen quite a bit. He may be the owner, but I manage this establishment and I require your card. Bring it here." LaRenna pulled the card from her skirt pocket and grudgingly offered it to Cance, who snatched with a scowl. "You want to work here, girl, you do as you're told. Get it?"

"Yeah." LaRenna turned back to her work.

"Hold on! Did I say you were excused?" Cance caught LaRenna's leg with her foot, nearly causing her to fall. As it was, LaRenna fell to one knee, bashing her forehead on the nearest chair back. Cance laughed uproariously at the sight. "Clumsy! Stand straight and tell me where you've worked."

"It's on the card." LaRenna rubbed at the small knot rising on her brow. It wasn't a serious bump but enough to bruise her pride.

"Humor me."

LaRenna rolled her eyes as she recited the list contained in the card's small writing. Krell had been correct in insisting she memorize it. Cance was thorough. "I've worked at the Base Ender, the Downsider, and the Planetrise."

"Uh-huh." Cance read the card's front then flipped it over and eyed LaRenna expectantly. "Tell me about your background."

True to her disguise, LaRenna questioned Cance again, in a tone more whining than before. "Is this really necessary? Everything I'm saying is on the card. The Hiring Hall has verified it."

"You'll answer." Cance's Taelach drawl began leaching through. "Or find yourself whoring to get back into the hall."

"If you must know, I'm from one of the farming compounds west of here. My father was in charge of the community stores, so I helped there until I took out on my own. Anything else?"

"By the look of you I'm sure you were thrown out, but I've no more questions. Not for now. Get back to work." Cance flung the work card to the floor and poured a glass from the fresh crystal, watching with wistful interest as LaRenna bent to retrieve the card. The low cut of LaRenna's frock was the reason she'd tossed it to the floor to begin with. "Finish up, girl, we open in less than an hour."

Starnes had completed stocking the shelves. "Father needs tending. I'm taking him some food before business starts up." He turned toward the kitchen.

"He stinks." Cance's crinkled her nose. "Clean him up."

LaRenna was bent over yet another table, wiping the base. When Starnes returned from the kitchen, he came close to inspect her work. "Who taught you to clean? Not like that, girl. Like this." He placed the tray on the table and crouched to scrub the base himself. "Don't just stand there. Get down here and watch the right way to do this." LaRenna hunkered beside him with an inquisitive look on her face. She knew the job was adequate and wondered why he chose to criticize her so. "Medicine," he whispered when she was close enough. "Please." She glanced to see if they were still being observed. Cance's back was to them.

LaRenna flipped up the hem of her skirt and popped two of the stitches. The medicine packet fell into her palm. "Here." She slid the pack into his hand. "Half now, the rest in four hours."

Starnes placed the packet in his vest pocket and stood. "That's better, girl. Finish them last two tables then get something to eat. You can't work half the night with nothing in you." He left her to finish the task.

When she'd finished, LaRenna removed her apron and washed her hands in the kitchen basin. A variety of aromatic roast meats and breads were keeping warm on the steam table, a difficult choice, as Starnes was an excellent cook. She chose a slice of each then carried her plate and a neglected sweet jam pot to the dining area. Cance leisurely observed all the while, expressing mild surprise when LaRenna walked behind the bar counter, chose a dusty crystal from a high shelf, and took it to a table.

"Drinking the profits with our dinner, are we?" Cance tossed LaRenna a clean glass.

"It doesn't look like bitterwine is a popular choice. It won't be missed."

"Bitterwine and sweet jam, interesting combination." Cance stared piercingly at her, wishing her lenses were back so she could edge into the barmaid's mind. "Where did you say you were from again?"

"West of here, near the Lanslotchin valley." LaRenna spread a thick layer of jam on her bread and poured a shot of wine. Cance's brows knitted with suspicion.

"Then where the hell did you pick up that habit?"

Only then did LaRenna realize her mistake. Sweet jams on bread was a decidedly Taelach habit. Her mind raced for a second then she smiled. This was easy to explain away. "We had a Taelach teacher who divided her time between my parents' farm compound and three others. When she was teaching at ours, she usually boarded with my family. I guess that's where I picked up my affection for jam."

"Oh?" Cance remained unconvinced.

"She shared a room with me and my two older sisters. Always brought loads of sweets. Now that I think about it, I probably picked up a few other small Taelach habits I don't realize."

"Like the capability to form a complete sentence?" said Cance in hopes of argument. "Farm brats seldom learn that skill. You people spend far too much time with your animals to be very intelligent."

"My father believed in education, even for his girls to a certain level. I had an excellent teacher." LaRenna shoved a large cut of meat into her mouth. She couldn't make another mistake if she kept it full.

"So you read and write?"

"Mmmhm."

"A Taelach taught you?"

LaRenna nodded.

"Hmph. Autlach children need Autlach teachers. Taelachs disrupt the natural cycle when they put their noses where they don't belong."

LaRenna swallowed, quickly shoved another bite into her mouth then shrugged, hoping the answer would suffice.

To her dismay Cance rose from her stool to take a seat at the same table, a casual, almost flirtatious smile crossing her face as she approached. "Too much sun will make you wrinkle before you should. It'd be a pity to see such a pretty young woman go to waste."

LaRenna feigned ignorance. "Really? I always stayed this way from fieldwork. Never heard it was harmful, only healthy."

"Move to the northern highlands and you'll lose that color." Cance held out her palm. It was pale, but not outside Autlach possibility and nowhere near as washed as LaRenna's natural tone. "That's where I'm from. You can't go outside there during the winter cycles. Too cold."

LaRenna let the poor explanation stand and downed a shot of bitterwine. The dark drink had a syrupy consistency that repulsed most, Cance included. "I don't know many who actually care for bitterwine these days. It's a drink for the old." LaRenna smiled and drained a second shot, clinking the glass twice as she set it down, which brought yet another puzzled look to Cance's face. "You remind me of someone."

"I do?"

"I'm not sure, but somebody I know does that when they drink shots." Cance peered at the empty glass. "I wish I could remember. Ah, no matter." The thought faded into insignificance as Starnes shuffled down the stairs.

He watched them for a second then turned to LaRenna, unable to mask his confusion. "I . . . uh . . . hurry up with your dinner, girl. We open in minutes."

"Leave her be, Starnes." Cance caressed LaRenna's forearm.

"She's kept me company. Bright girl to be working here." She pointed toward him with the other hand. "You found her at the Hiring Hall?"

"Times are tough," said LaRenna to prevent a fatal error on Starnes's part. "You take what you can get."

"I suppose." But Cance still wondered. This girl was capable of far more than waiting tables, that was for certain. "I'm going upstairs to work, but I wish to speak with you a moment first, Starnes. Come here." She dismissed LaRenna to the kitchen area, allowing him to slide into her still warm seat.

"I don't want to find out you've told the help of our little arrangement." Cance's hand now rested on Starnes's arm, gripping until her nails left marks. "If I do, I'll make you watch as I kill your father."

"I haven't breathed a word."

"Keep it that way." Cance grabbed the crystal from the bar and climbed the stairs, stopping midflight to restate the warning. "I'll be down later. Behave." She leered down at LaRenna as she emerged from the kitchen. "Both of you."

When she was gone, LaRenna drew to a chair beside Starnes. "It's nothing I can't handle."

"You haven't met the other one yet," he whispered. "Brandoff's a true Raskhallak curse."

"Everyone has a weakness." LaRenna peered up the stairwell. "I'll find theirs and use it against them." Kimshee determination darkened her disguise. "I swear it'll bring them both down."

Chapter Nineteen

Do not judge another's post as simple until you have spent time at it.
—instructor's wisdom from the Taelach Training Grounds

The Waterlead bustled with a crowd larger than LaRenna had anticipated. Not only did the sentry squadron patron the bar as ordered, but they brought friends, most of whom lingered well into the night. Trazar Laiman was among them, assuring his men's sobriety with his presence. LaRenna dashed between tables, delivering drinks and platters around the dining area. The job was difficult, trying to the mind and the body but flowed smoothly once she had established a rhythm. When one table ordered, she delivered their drinks and approached the next, then delivered any food the first table had ordered, delivered drinks to the second, approached the third and so on throughout the evening.

"Trazar?" One of the sentries leaned back to address his commander at the next table. With no uniforms to show affiliation, rank and title were not to be mentioned. "Do you have relatives on Langus?"

"Not that I'm aware of. Why?"

The sentry pointed to where LaRenna was squeezing between the crammed tables. "The little vamp slinging drinks looks a lot like you. I just wanted to make sure she wasn't your cousin or something before I hit on her."

"Nah, the girls in my family are stocky built. She's too tall and slender to be my relation."

"She doesn't look tall to me," stated a lankier sentry at the same table. "And she may not be heavy, but she's very well-rounded. Figures like hers are few and far between. Sure you're not related? She's got the same mark on her left ear."

Trazar peered up from his drink. "She can't. It's a family trait. My sister and father have one, too."

"So does the barmaid. Call her over and see for yourself."

Trazar raised his hand for service. LaRenna dropped a round to a nearby group then approached his table. "Need another?" The question sounded tired. Her feet ached and the fresh Kimshee symbol throbbed from the rub of her shoe. Besides, she was slightly abashed by the way Trazar looked at her. He looked friendly enough, somewhat familiar, but she hadn't the faintest notion why.

"No." He leaned forward to view her left side. "My friends were curious about the diamond-shaped mark on your ear."

LaRenna rubbed at the mark. "What about it?"

"Is it a scar, a birthmark?"

"Birthmark. Why?"

"You have any relations living in Vartoch's southern mountains?"

"I've never been to Vartoch and I doubt I have family there. I'm local." LaRenna smoothed her hair over the questioning mark. "Now, unless you have an order, I really must get to work."

"Hold on," said another at the table. "I'm local, too. I would remember someone like you and I've never seen you before."

"Guess you never knew where to look," retorted LaRenna with the slightest of grins. "I was raised in a farming compound just west of here."

"Farm girl, huh?" Trazar returned her grin. He had many distant farming relations and was positive his next question would clear the air. "What's your name, sweetheart?"

"LaRenna."

Trazar choked on his wine. "LaRenna?" He gasped. The Death Stone's cold image flew to mind. Hadn't his father said the baby was born with the same mark? "Are you sure?"

"About my own name? Yes. Excuse me, but I am busy." A corner table whistled for her attention. She took Trazar's empty glass and turned.

"Wait." Trazar grabbed her hand. "How old are you?"

"None of your business." She struggled against his touch. "Let go."

Trazar realized the strength of his grip and released, but his eyes remained transfixed on her face. Shades of Mercy were present in this young woman, as was his father's jaw line. Could it be? Surely it was coincidence, a strange one for sure, but it couldn't possibly be more. "I'm sorry, it's just—"

"You gonna flirt all night or do your job?" LaRenna startled and turned to find Cance behind her. "The corner table demands your immediate attention. They're friends of mine so their drinks are on the house." She looked at Trazar. "Keep your hands off the staff or I'll kick your ass out."

"I meant no harm to the girl," he replied.

"Sure you didn't." Cance escorted LaRenna from the table, making rude accusations concerning her propositioning the customers until they reached the table. She took a chair beside a long-haired man. "Service leaves something to be desired." She elbowed Longhair in the ribs."Nice to look at though, isn't it?" The Autlach gave a polite laugh and whispered something in one of the lesser-known dialects to one of his comrades. Cance and LaRenna both understood the lewd comment, but neither dared react.

115

"Bring us two wine crystals to sip from." Cance's attention reverted to LaRenna. "And me a dish of the roast you were eating earlier."

"What else?" An unrolled scroll map on the table had caught LaRenna's attention, so she lingered, trying to interpret the diagram without being seen.

"Yeah." Cance sniffed. "Make it a crystal and a plate for each of us." When LaRenna hesitated, Cance lashed out, pinching her leg through her skirts. "Slow barmaids have a bad habit of losing fingers and a lot more around me." Cance twisted tighter before letting go. "Understand?"

"Yes, sir." LaRenna rubbed her thigh. "You've made it painfully clear." She flounced her skirts and hurried toward the kitchen. It wouldn't do any good to challenge Cance's cruelty now. Too much relied on her role. Besides, she had seen all she needed of the map. It was of a Center's Assembly, specifically the sentry stations in the vicinity thereof.

Safe in the kitchen, she examined her purpling thigh then spooned five servings of the meats, arranging them on a large tray. She laid the bulky load on the back counter then tapped Starnes on the shoulder. "Five crystals and a single glass."

"Five?" Starnes had been wiping the counter with a damp towel. "Who ordered so much and did they show their money?"

"Cance says they're on the house."

"Figures." He helped her center the crystals on the tray. "She could outdrink a water demon." He balanced the load on her shoulder then set the single glass in the center. "Want me to carry it?"

"I can manage." LaRenna grunted from the demand on her tired muscles but held the tray steady. "Where's Brandoff?"

"Upstairs. Cance won't let her down during business hours. Seems she don't know how to behave in public, is the more off of the pair—if you can believe that." Starnes glanced to where Cance sat. "Better get over there."

"On my way." LaRenna slowly made her way through the

116

tables. She balanced the tray on her hip and distributed the order, ignoring Cance's attempts at flirting. The single glass she saved for last, creating an excuse to see Trazar.

"I didn't mean to startle you before and I certainly didn't mean to get you in trouble," he said before she could turn away. "Is the manager always so rough?" A short nod in Cance's general direction showed his distrust. "I saw him give you that pinch. Are you hurt? Why do you put up with it?"

"Don't worry over me. I'll survive. There's not much honest work available for a woman. Everyone knows that. I took the only decent thing offered me." LaRenna tried to pull away again, but Trazar held his solid grip.

"Don't you have family?" He looked into her face.

LaRenna relaxed and squeezed his hand. No phase was needed to know Trazar's intentions were noble. "None that will claim me."

"Man?"

"The same."

Trazar squeezed her palm before letting go. "If you need anything, anything at all, let me know."

"Thank you." From any other man the words would have sounded hollow, an attempt to wedge into her life and bed, but for some unexplainable reason, she could believe them from him. She smiled back. "I'll try to remember that."

Trazar winked and waved her away. "You'll get in trouble if I monopolize any more of your time." He watched as she went about serving the other tables, positive they were related though the rationale still evaded him.

"I think our valiant leader is sweet on the barmaid," one of his sentries teased.

"That's not it." Trazar sipped his wine. "I know I'm related to her, and I think I know how. But how do I prove it?"

"See, I told you," said the sentry who'd noticed the similarity.

"Think I'm a little sweet on her myself!" exclaimed another, a little too brash and tipsy for Trazar's liking. "I'm going to wait around til closing and see if she has plans for the night."

"You do"—Trazar turned to face him—"and you'll find yourself rotated to night duty for a pass. Leave her alone." Glass to his lips, he mumbled his suspicions to the crimson contents, the words disappearing on the wine's surface. "I've got to find out more about her."

Chapter Twenty

New lovers are seldom discreet. The desire is simply irresistible.

—*Taelach saying*

_____

Starnes locked the doors behind the last customer, grabbed a handful of empty glassware, and carried it to the counter. LaRenna was close behind him, her arms laden with plates. She heaped them in the kitchen basin and returned, yawning, to the dining room.

"I laid you out a pallet in the storeroom." Bane repeated her yawn. "Get some rest. We'll finish this later."

LaRenna shook her head and pulled him close. "Let me clean up now," she whispered, "then send me to the wine stores at first dawn."

"Why would I?"

"Shhhh." LaRenna placed her hand over his mouth. "Listen,

send me with a list and payment. Everyone knows the best supply is available in the morning. Say you had a regular customer request one of those odd fruit wines they produce on Saria Four. It's an excuse for me to leave." He mumbled something against her palm and nodded just as Cance stepped from the small bathroom located beside the bar. LaRenna dropped her hand and returned to work.

"I told the girl to go ahead and clean up." Starnes thrust a wadded Autlach bill into LaRenna's hand. "A regular customer requested a regional wine I charge premium for. The girl can get it at first dawn otherwise they'll be out. Stocks always run low on odd lots."

"Why don't you go?" Despite a short rest, Cance looked tired. Prock gradually shifted one's brain wave patterns, ruining all attempts at restful sleep.

"I have to tend Father," Starnes stammered. "Let her do it. That's what we hired her for, isn't it?"

"I suppose." Disgust added to Cance's tired expression. "Clean up the privy first. It's rank. There's not a man alive who can hit his target after a couple of drinks." She yawned and motioned for Starnes. "Come on, Starnie, let's get some sleep."

"In a minute." Starnes gathered another stack of glasses. Cance, never to be disobeyed, lunged forward and hooked his collar.

"No, now. Let the girl do the work. That's what we hired her for. Isn't that what you said?" She pulled him to the stairwell, Cance slowing long enough to give LaRenna one last thoughtful glance. "Be quiet in your cleaning, girl. Don't wake us breaking dishes. Hurry to the Stores and back to your bed. Use the funds Starnes provided you and bring back a receipt—and the change. I'll check on things later in the morning."

"Yes, sir." LaRenna watched Cance force Starnes up the stairs and into the upper level. Being alone was easier, but the quiet proved lulling. To stay alert, she proceeded to scrub every inch of the bar, paying close attention to the table and chair bottoms Starnes seemed so concerned about. She was drying the last of the glassware when traces of morning began trickling through the bar's high windows. Energies renewed by dawn's radiance, she tossed the towel onto the bar and grabbed her wrap. Krell was waiting.

"There she goes." The twins stood in the dark of an upstairs window, Cance cleaning under her nails with her blade. "Follow her, Brannie." She waved the knife toward the street below. "Make sure she goes directly to the Stores and back. There's something about her I don't trust."

"Anything to get out of here a while." Brandoff slid down the banister, scurried out the rear entrance, and trailed LaRenna through the narrow streets leading to the Commons, becoming suspicious only when LaRenna failed to turn down the lane leading to the Wine Stores. LaRenna, looking back only once or twice, took a back alley to the perimeter of the Commons then trotted straight down a pathway leading to the beach.

"You scheming little tramp. Cance was right about you." From a crevice in the path's rock outcropping, Brandoff could see everything that took place on the sand below.

Krell was waiting where she'd promised. "Everything going as planned?" LaRenna nodded but said nothing. "Third Kimshee Belsas?" asked Krell as gently as she dared. "Have you slept since we parted?"

"No, First Kimshee," she mumbled. "I've worked straight through."

Krell looked above her apprentice's head toward the water. LaRenna looked exhausted, but the sight of her caused Krell's very being to ache. "Starnes was supposed to aid in your cover, not drive you. Was it worth your while?"

"Yeah, it was." LaRenna smiled and stretched. "The tips were nice."

"You know I don't mean the money, Belsas." Krell resisted the urge to ruffle her companion's chestnut curls. "I meant—"

"I know." LaRenna yawned. "They're planning something concerning the Center's Assembly."

"Success so soon?" Krell seemed truly impressed. Most posts of this nature took several days, if not cycles, to gather any useful information. "Any idea what?"

"Not yet." LaRenna stifled another yawn into her cloak. "I'll try again tonight."

"Slide your lenses back so your eyes can rest." Krell's breath steamed in the morning air. "It'll keep you alert."

LaRenna slapped away the phase that waited for her. *I'm not too tired for a fight if that is what you're wanting, First Kimshee.*

Just a test. Krell dropped the phase after another rejected probe. "If that is all there is to report then return to your post, Third Officer."

"Yes, First Kimshee."

"Return here tomorrow for another report."

"Yes First Kimshee."

"Til tomorrow then."

"Tomorrow, First Kimshee."

Brandoff shoved her chilled hands in her pockets. She could kill LaRenna before she returned to the Waterlead, but there'd be no sport in it. Besides, Cance would want to question the girl. Brandoff sighed. Questions, questions, and more questions. Cance would want to know anything and everything about the infernal girl. But after that—the sigh turned into a chuckle. After that, the fun began. Brandoff retreated from the crevice and to the Commons, anxious to update her sibling.

When LaRenna turned to depart, Krell suddenly grasped her around the waist, spinning her around and pulling her close. She peered at the pathway, uneasy, inexplicably tense as she scanned the length of the trail above them.

"Someone up there?" LaRenna looked over her shoulder to the path. Krell, now intent on the dark cliffs behind them, squinted and listened, the only sound the slow break of waves.

"First Officer?" LaRenna chirped anxiously. "Krell?"

"Shhh." The noise came out sterner than Krell intended. "I thought I saw something." She pulled LaRenna within the depths of her cloak then continued to scan the path, her racing heartbeat causing LaRenna's neck hairs to stiffen.

Krell, stop. You're smothering me.

After a moment, Krell relaxed her grip. She searched the path a final time then stepped back, not entirely convinced the danger had passed but unable to put a finger on the reason. "I must be seeing grass shadows. There's nothing up there."

LaRenna turned for her own search. "It could have been a rock goat. They're up and grazing this time of morning. But, whatever it was, I think it's gone. Besides, it's almost second dawn. I'd better get to the wine stores."

Krell pulled LaRenna's wrap snug then dropped her hand, embarrassed by such an affectionate display. "Be careful."

"I will." LaRenna began to turn away but halted when Krell touched her shoulder.

"Pull out if there are any problems." Krell released her touch one finger at a time, as if each would be the last. "I'll be ready should you need me."

"I know you will." LaRenna scrambled up the rocky bank to the pathway, stopping at the crest to look back. Krell cut an alluring figure in the morning light. She stood on a boulder, one hand resting on her narrow hip. The ocean breeze caught the tail of her cloak, slapping it about. Krell snapped it back and looked up, reaching out and up with her hand. LaRenna, tingling with the relevance of the moment, held out her hand as if to accept Krell's, pulled it to her chest, and offered her palm back to Krell, who completed the exchange by pulling back her arm and placing her hand on her chest. Drawing two into one, the exchange was a symbol long used by the Taelach to signal the pain of separation.

After a final glance, LaRenna turned back to her assignment. She replaced the Autlach lenses and climbed the hill to the Commons, ready to complete her post so she could return to this curious life she was beginning.

Brandoff was well ahead of her, blowing in the back door of the Waterlead, blaring the news, but not before downing half a crystal.

Cance was waiting in the main dining room, also well into the drink, her face twisting with deceit as she lashed on a plasma bow. "We had a visitor while you were gone." Cance pointed to the body lying haphazardly across a table. It was Russ, Krell's favorite waiter from the dining plaza. Blood trickled from his nose and his lifeless face retained the maddening effects of the relentless mind-picking pain phase that had murdered him. Cance pulled his head up to give his face an open-handed smack, jerking loose a handful of hair before dropping it forward. "And he had some very interesting things to tell me."

Chapter Twenty-one

Never rest in the den of your enemy. Keep your mind and body alert, or comfort may overtake you, blocking all means of escape.

—Kimshee training wisdom

The Waterlead appeared deserted when LaRenna elbowed through the rear door. Her arms were laden with stock, the weight and awkward size of which forced her to take short, shuffling steps across the kitchen. Exhausted, she placed the boxes on the counter and collapsed on a high stool. Every fiber of her being screamed for the comfort of the bed. She undid her cloak and let it fall to the floor then, using the countertop for leverage, she pulled up, laid the change and receipt behind the bar, and stumbled to the storeroom, sleep engulfing her before she could do more than unroll the bedding.

Brandoff and Cance waited an hour before they crept downstairs, the quiet assuring them LaRenna was comfortably napping. As a final caution, Cance slid the storeroom door open and peeped in. LaRenna was indeed asleep.

"Well?" Brandoff was loud to the point of impertinence, bouncing thirstily, fists clenching and unclenching.

Cance pulled her head back. "Would you be quiet?"

"Yeah, yeah. So, she sleeping or not?"

"Yes, and soundly. She didn't even stir at your screeching. Will you calm down? You get worked up over the damnedest things."

"Shut up, Cance. You know I've been bored." Brandoff's plasma bow emitted a low whine that brought matching smiles from the twins. "Ready when you are."

They pushed into the storeroom, silent as they took positions at either end of their intended victim. Cance nodded, gave a silent count of three, and watched as Brandoff sank her foot deep into LaRenna's lower back. LaRenna wailed as a sudden nightmare invaded her much-deserved rest. She pushed up just as Brandoff landed another kick to her spine. The second blow careened her forward, smashed her head and knees into the wall, then bounced her back, bringing her face to face with her attackers.

"You!"

Brandoff pressed her bow into LaRenna's temple, index and middle fingers spread to act as sights. "Don't give me an excuse to kill you," she said. "You've no wish to die prematurely of less than natural causes, do you—sister Taelach?"

LaRenna drew into the corner, choking back the fear and nausea that surged in her throat. "Taelach?" she gasped. "I'm not—"

Brandoff swung out with her bowed arm, the blow so vicious it tore open LaRenna's jaw line. "Save it, bitch! I saw you and your lover on the beach this morning."

Cance laughed at Brandoff's graphic interpretation of what had happened. Brandoff somehow managed to reduce their final exchange to the point it sounded like some meaningless coupling with a prostitute, but LaRenna wasn't ashamed. It was a simple, pure gesture and nothing could taint it.

"Now then, my pretty sister." Cance swiped at the blood that had splattered her tunic. "I'm sure you know what these are and what they signify." She displayed the telltale burn scars of the Branded.

LaRenna only nodded, hoping her silence would buy the time to slide her lenses back. Her phase was her only weapon so she must act now. Brandoff's reply was just as swift, her finger sights pressing hard into LaRenna's temple. "Don't think so!" She grabbed LaRenna's hair and pulled, forcing her eyes open. Brandoff focused on her and a sharp wave of excruciating heat raged down LaRenna's back, so hot she bit her tongue to keep from crying out. It burned until she shook, steaming her insides, hurting like nothing she had ever felt, but she knew it was not beneath her own developing capabilities. A simple refocus of the energy direction sent the same wave spiraling back on Brandoff, loosening her grasp. LaRenna took advantage of the situation, jerking Brandoff off balance, sending her face-first into the floor.

ENOUGH! Cance threw a pain phase that was far above Brandoff's. LaRenna grabbed the sides of her head as the sensation swallowed her. This power she knew nothing of and could not fight effectively. Every joint in her body was on fire! She choked then screamed, praying for it to stop or kill her at once.

"Hurts, doesn't it?" Cance forced LaRenna's eyes open. "Your phasing is intense for your age. Your mentor taught you well, but you've never been in a real fight, have you, precious?" LaRenna stared up blankly. What good would it do to admit to such weakness? Cance took the silence as confirmation, clutching LaRenna's face as thought pierced the pain. *Shame on the Kinship for sending such a child. Though, I do bow to your superior acting skills. Your size threw me off for a while as well. Never seen a grown sister as small as you. You're quite different, little girl. I'm intrigued.* Cance released the mind hold, grip still firm on LaRenna's head as the rest of her body sank to the floor.

"Sorry, little Aut sucker." Brandoff regained her footing. "Phase-burn me will you? Let's get rid of those lenses so I can show her what kind of phase I really prefer."

"Yes, indeed." Cance forced another phase, not a painful one this time but a sickening pulse of unwanted pleasure. LaRenna slapped at the phase but it held, twisting her stomach even tighter. *You've pissed off my twin, pretty one. Not a smart move.* She glanced at her double. "Little thing's a fair shot. Bloodied you up nicely."

"She's not half as good as I am." Brandoff grabbed LaRenna, pulled to full height, and jammed one knee deep into her stomach, the blow throwing her back into Cance's arms. The force crunched ribs, jarring inward workings until LaRenna gagged, startling Cance into breaking her phase and tossing her to the floor. LaRenna barely made it to her knees before she lost control, her searing gut in spasms as she expelled mouthful after mouthful of bile-tasting spew.

"Now look what you've done, Brannie," Cance teased. "The barmaid has a mess to clean." Cance kept back and allowed their prisoner to empty her stomach onto the floor, sure the punishment was unfitting the crime but unwilling to censure Brandoff. When the retching subsided, LaRenna crumpled to her side, finding momentary peace until Cance pulled her to a chair in the dining room's center.

Cance handed a roll of hide binding to Brandoff. "Truss her good but not too tight. Remember what happened to that Aut girl you took to on the way here."

"How was I to know she'd die from that?" Brandoff, ignoring Cance's reminder that far more than strangled limbs had killed that child, secured LaRenna's hands and feet, double-checking for fit. "Pity." She forced up LaRenna's lacerated chin until their eyes met. "Such a delicious little thing to rough up so. Do us all a favor, beautiful, be a good girl and cooperate from here on out. Don't make me hit you again."

Cance's fingers lightly brushed LaRenna's hair. "My twin has a fetish for small ladies." The touch sent chills down LaRenna's spine. "Too bad for you."

Brandoff moved closer, her mouth cold on their prisoner's ear. "And too good for me." She locked LaRenna's head in her elbow then wrapped the other arm over her forehead, pulling upward so her brows drew up. "You phase me and I'll be forced to snap your sexy neck before we get to have any fun."

"She's smarter than that, Brannie." Cance pinched LaRenna's cheek then used her thumb and index finger to hold her left eye still, the other hand pushing back the lid until the edge of the brown lens became visible. "I won't have you sliding these into place when I ask questions," Cance explained. "You're just stubborn enough require a phase to ensure honesty." She grasped the lens between her nails. "And I will get answers."

"True answers." Brandoff braced against the chair back and Cance yanked the lens from LaRenna's left eye. LaRenna gasped but said nothing, even when her captor's nails scraped the sensitive whites of her eyes.

"Now the other." Cance repeated the procedure, LaRenna coughing from the stomach acid that bubbled in her mouth. Her eyes burned, her sniffing proving uncontrollable as bloody tears trickled from the corners of her swelling lids. Brandoff loosened the hold on her forehead to suck at the salty streaks.

"She's juicing ripe, Cance. Can we now?"

"Work then play." Cance patted the bar counter. "Bring her here and we'll pull off her slippers. I want to see her markings."

"By the time you're finished there won't be much worth having." Brandoff tossed LaRenna onto the bar and stretched her across the top, all the while observant of her languid state. LaRenna wasn't unconscious but rather listening, waiting for her chance to escape, all of which changed with Brandoff's next words. "What'd you say to giving her a puff? Won't be near as fun if she's comatose."

"She does look out of it," her twin agreed. "A half-dose should do wonders." And Cance shoved an inhaler into her sedate captive's nostril.

"No!" LaRenna returned to life, kicking and screaming, launching four rapid phases at her captors that paralyzed Brandoff but only angered Cance. The mind battle that ensued was frenzied, Cance regaining control only after several physical blows to LaRenna's midsection. As LaRenna lay gasping, Cance sat on her arms, pinned her head, and shoved the inhaler deep. "Don't want to take you too far up. I want you and that sharp little mind of yours aware of everything that happens." She pinched LaRenna's nose and mouth shut, forcing the vapor into her sinuses. "Enjoy the trip." Cance climbed from the bar and removed one of LaRenna's slippers. LaRenna struggled against her touch, launching a scratching phase at her captors until the prock began to surge. It was the strangest sensation, drawing her to an instant orgasmic peak then plummeting her into a distorted awareness. Colors were brighter, realer, fascinating in their complexity. Why, she could see them clearly despite her eyes! She was aware her cover was blown, but didn't care as long as the pleasure continued. It was thrilling, but so very wrong, going as quick as it came to leave her violently angry. She was rabid, screaming obscenities and twisting in attempted escape.

Cance clenched her bare foot even tighter. "Just our luck! She's a prock virgin, Brannie. Look how it's hitting her. Things are perfect. Perfect! Couldn't be better if we'd planned them this way!"

"How's that?" Brandoff, still shaking from the phase fight, had taken a seat by LaRenna's head.

"Read these." Cance held up LaRenna's foot. Brandoff read the markings then leaned forward, bare inches from LaRenna's face. "Hello there, third Kimshee daughter of Belsas Exzal. I'm Brandoff Creiloff, one of the thousand-odd sisters your bitch of a guardian raiser had heat-branded like common herd animals and banished to Trimar's ice caves. What you're feeling now is just a taste of what we've endured. Prock keeps you awake so you aren't killed or enslaved in the Junglelands. It's an eat or be eaten existence on Trimar." Brandoff licked her lips. "And I've learned to be very hungry." LaRenna could smell soured wine on Brandoff's breath, feel her unkempt hair brushing her shoulder. It was disgusting and so distorted Brandoff's actual image that LaRenna couldn't concentrate enough for a phase.

"I know who you are," she sputtered, in a voice far weaker than she intended. "You're murderers without souls or morals—a smudge on the glorious Mother's golden skirts."

"Temper, temper," Brandoff replied. "We just met. Don't be so quick to judge me and I'll try to keep from doing the same." She forced her mouth onto LaRenna's. No one but Krell had ever kissed her like that. It was bitter. Vulgar. It made her desperate and she withdrew against the counter, biting Brandoff's bottom lip until it bled.

"You provoked that one. Let her up and I bet she'd flatten you again." Cance was overjoyed by the reaction, even though it only served to make Brandoff's crude advances even more insistent. Brandoff pulled back from the embrace, undid LaRenna's belt, and jerked it loose, snapping the doubled leather very near LaRenna's ear, which startled her so completely Brandoff repeated the crack.

"Look at her scare. This is going to be the best I've had in ages."

LaRenna bucked against her restraints with renewed vigor. Maybe if she fought hard enough they would cease the games and fight her fairly. Training and instinct both said death would be easy compared to this torment, a sacrifice in the name of duty. But Cance knew all this and intended to squelch the notion, grabbing her feet even tighter and rotating her right ankle. "Stop wiggling or I'll break it."

"Let me go!" LaRenna jerked her knees to her chest then kicked out, throwing Cance into the wall. The force slid LaRenna down the smooth counter, straight into Brandoff's stout arm and boot knife.

"I'll save us all trouble and kill you where you lie. You'll serve my purposes alive or dead." Metal scraped LaRenna's throat, a convincing and almost welcomed reminder her life might soon be over. But the attack had to be met, so LaRenna reached out with her mind, found Brandoff, and ripped into the guardian's rage, feeding it with pain until Brandoff began pressing the knife.

"DON'T!" Cance gasped. "She wants you to kill her!" She

131

knocked the dagger from Brandoff's grip then fell back wheezing. "I . . . want . . . her . . . alive!" Cance bent at the waist as her air returned. "She's a ticket to safe . . . passage if there are . . . any problems."

Brandoff rubbed the hand Cance had slapped. "Huh?"

"Belsas won't let anything happen to her brat. Besides, the bitch took what was mine and now I have something to even the score." Cance, aroused as she was perturbed by such resistance, snatched LaRenna's legs into the air, twisting her slender right ankle out of place. "Realize now, I do what I say, every time."

LaRenna cringed as her legs were dropped back on the bar. The prock swept away the pain and she soared again. It was engaging, intense, beautiful, until it dropped her, this time spinning her just short of unconsciousness.

Cance pulled her to a sitting position. "Speak up, girl. What did you tell your contact?" Silence echoed as the twins waited for an answer not forthcoming. LaRenna was limp, unable to answer even if she wanted. Cance shook her and restated the question. "The map, did you tell your lover about it?"

LaRenna's high peaked once more into fury. She opened one eye then rolled it back as she spewed the only answer that made sense in such insanity. "Fuck you."

Brandoff waltzed behind the bar and began to massage LaRenna's trembling shoulders, sliding beneath her top to fondle her breasts. "Did you hear that, Cance? She's begging us to do her. Come on, I'm about to burst. Maybe she likes two on one. Prock does that, you know."

"I heard her. Just won't learn, will she?" Cance took LaRenna's hands and began to rub the palms. "Last chance, my sweet, tell me what I need to hear."

"No." Determination and finality clenched LaRenna's mouth closed. No matter what they did or how they drugged her, she would never betray her post.

"Your choice." Cance twisted the little finger of LaRenna's left hand until it snapped. "I'll break you one bone at a time if need be. That's two. Wanna go for three?"

A single pained sob escaped LaRenna's mouth, then she clamped down again, rankling her captors all the more. Their patience drawn to the limit, they nodded agreement on the next punishing tactic. LaRenna was forced back on the bar and stretched prone, her eyes blindfolded, her leg bindings divided and secured at opposite ends of a wall rack, her arms lashed at agonizing distention to the counter's pass-through overhang. Brandoff undressed then straddled their captive, her bare knees pressing into LaRenna's tender sides. Teeth bared in carnal foreboding, she pulled briefly at LaRenna's skirts then paused to take four quick shots from her inhaler. "Your lover has nothing on me, girl. I'll leave you screaming for more." Brandoff's grin turned malicious. "Well, I promise to have you screaming."

"Tell us about the map." Cance tempted amnesty one last time. "I won't let her hurt you if you do. Don't"—she pulled at LaRenna's top—"and I'll help her." The room remained quiet until Cance sighed, sealing LaRenna's fate. "The prock didn't work. I should have expected as much from a Kimshee. It's part of the training. Have at 'er, Brannie. She won't talk no matter what we do."

Screams formed in the deepest part of LaRenna's being and escaped in rafter-shaking amplitude throughout the Waterlead. She fought valiantly, dizzying height after dizzying height; writhing, biting, and scratching until Brandoff finally reared back and struck her hard. Even then reality hung on one miserable minute more, withholding the peace of insensibility until one memory became indelible. Cance removed the blindfold and looked deep into her as she slipped away.

"You're mine by oath." Cance's expression was trancelike, contented by the memory of someone else. "Belsas will never win you from me, Chandrey. Never."

Chapter Twenty-two

My promises are deep and true. Forever I am yours.

—from Guardian's Song

Belsas paced her workroom. "I trust you with my only child and this is what happens? How could you, Krell?" She stared intensely at Krell's apprehensive projection. "This is simply inappropriate."

Chandrey shook her head. "LaRenna is a braided Kimshee on post. She's an adult capable of making her own choices. You've reminded me of that several times as of late, Bel."

"But they've only known each other a few days."

"You thought her competent enough to assign undercover, didn't you?" intervened Chandrey. "Krell suits her. They'll be good together. Besides, Krell thought enough to ask you first. That has to mean something." Chandrey smiled at Krell. The more she could do to soften Belsas's bluntness, the better. "Krell stuck to tradition in an age that doesn't call for it. That in itself speaks volumes."

"I understand the unusual nature of this call," began Krell. "But LaRenna and I have formed a unique bond, one that I would like to pursue at length."

"Like the one you pursued with Tatra Wileyse?" retorted Belsas.

"How do . . . ?" Krell had quite forgotten that Tatra had told everyone, anyone who would listen, that they were going to oath. "I never offered to fully bond with Healer Wileyse and we certainly never oathed."

"Tatra's raisers are old friends of ours," Belsas replied. "According to them, the two of you were very close not to be oathed. Sharing a bed, I believe."

"For a while I suppose, but I, we never—"

"A pass and a half is what I heard." Belsas rocked on her heels. "Couldn't make a commitment in a pass and a half, but now you want to make a serious go of things with someone you've known three days?"

"Well, I—"

"Kimshees are not known for stability in their personal life." Belsas's fiery tone increased. "You're willing to give up apprentices and take reassignment for LaRenna?"

"LaRenna is Kimshee, too, Grandmaster Belsas, and very mature." Stubbornness sparkled in Krell's eyes. "I know that this means I can no longer train her and that reassignment will be necessary for me. I am also aware of the implications on my career, but I feel it is important, no, necessary for LaRenna and me to find out just how deep this bond of ours can go."

"If all this is true," Belsas inquired, "how could you let her take this post?"

"She accepted the post before they met," Chandrey interjected.

"They began bonding before she went undercover. Krell could have stopped all this simply by calling us sooner." Belsas turned back to the screen. "Why didn't you, Krell? Her welfare fell on you until she posted. If there was anything questionable about her readiness, if there was a chance your bonding could have interfered with your judgment of her readiness, then it was irresponsible of you to send her on."

Krell folded her arms across her chest. "The post means everything to her. She thinks it will prove her capabilities. I couldn't very well deny her the opportunity with her thinking so."

"Her wants matter little, First Kimshee. I am speaking of her readiness. She was your charge until she posted!" Belsas's face was fiercely red. "And you denied your bond call to let her meet danger? ALONE?"

"Belsas, dear." Chandrey's soft soprano was calm yet demanding. "You're not angry with Krell for allowing LaRenna to take post. You're furious at yourself for sending your daughter against the Creiloff twins." The name sent sharp chills down her spine, catching hard at the scars creasing her back. "Look at this objectively."

"I am!"

"No, you're not." Chandrey leaned across the worktable, hands extended, palm up, toward her guardian. "You're angry at yourself. You decided correctly that LaRenna was the best suited for the post, so you sent her to Langus. It was a good decision at the time."

Belsas sagged against the worktable. "If I had known for certain the Creiloff twins were involved in the unrest on Langus, I'd never have sent her. Those two and their supporters have been thorns in the Kinship's side for far too long."

"Eventually, they will become too elderly to be much of a bother, just as we will." Chandrey patted Belsas's hand.

"Belsas." Krell spoke in the low, rambling drawl guardians used when discussing personal matters. "This was her first post. It would have been selfish to deny her the right to prove herself. Surely you can understand that."

Belsas drummed her fingers under Chandrey's touch. "Maybe you're right."

"Generally I am," Chandrey teased. "About what this time?"

"This situation. LaRenna is such a free spirit that perhaps she needs a steady mate." Krell breathed an audible sigh. "Maybe you can tame her quick mouth, Krell."

"There's nothing wrong with stating your mind," retorted Chandrey. "Krell, you do know she's physically different, don't you?"

"I am aware LaRenna's true female, if that's what you are referring to," replied Krell. "Her capacity to have children has increased her phasing abilities to amazing heights. She's a powerful mind. She just needs to refine her skills."

"I'm glad she's able to explore her potential with you." Chandrey squeezed Belsas's hand. "If she's anything like her gahrah, she'll learn fast."

"I'm sure she will. I believe her determination derives from her mamma?"

Belsas shoved a precautionary hand into her pocket. "As does her trickster side. Word to the wise: always check your clothing before sending it to be cleaned. The fabric maintainers at the Training Grounds once came across a note Chandrey had left in my pocket. They still refer to me as, well, I'd rather not repeat it, but the name has stuck to this day."

Ringing laughter filled rooms on both Langus and Saria Three. "And it still fits you." Chandrey's eyes danced merrily. "Think of it, Bel, we could be grandparents, not grandraisers, grandparents!"

"Don't rush them." Belsas chuckled. "They aren't oathed yet and besides, LaRenna is young."

Chandrey refused to let pessimism douse her spirit. "LaRenna is only one pass younger than I was when we oathed."

"Times were different, Chandrey, and Krell is five passes older than I was. That makes her a full seventeen older than LaRenna."

"I just turned thirty-nine." Krell had become sensitive to the subject of LaRenna's age, quite possibly defensive. There didn't seem to be any difference when they were together; Krell only knew the rightness of it. "I don't believe it's of any significance in our relationship. LaRenna is decades older in her phasing."

"Well spoken, First Kimshee Middle." Belsas carefully studied the other guardian's expression. Whatever Krell may have lacked in reputation she made up for in determination, a trait Belsas admired. "I still think she's a tad young for all this and she may not appreciate any of what we've said here, but Krell is to my liking." Belsas raised her hands in submission. "I suppose it's serendipity. If LaRenna agrees then you have my blessing."

"Mine, too!" Chandrey piped. "Blessed be the day she met you, Krell."

"Chandrey, please!" Belsas poured a shot of bitterwine from a worktable crystal and held it up in toast. "Happiness to you both."

"Thank you." Krell found LaRenna very similar to Chandrey at that moment. "I can see where LaRenna gets her energy."

"It doesn't decrease with age," mumbled Belsas through her glass.

"I also see where she developed her fondness for bitterwine." Krell's mouth drew at sight of the thick black concoction.

Belsas grunted, downed the shot, and set the glass back on the table with two quick clinks of its bottom. "Few truly appreciate the taste of bitterwine."

"I'm not one of them." Chandrey shared Krell's grimace. "Blech!"

"It's an acquired taste," said Belsas.

"Very!" exclaimed the others in unison.

"I'll be glad when LaRenna returns. She appreciates fine drink." Belsas turned when a loud knock interrupted their light-hearted discussion. Rona stood in the doorway.

"New reports have come in, Grandmaster Belsas. You should take a look at them."

"Lay them on the table. I'll get to them in a while."

"No, Belsas, read them now!" Rona thrust a recorder into her hand.

"All right." Belsas, puzzled by her assistant's odd behavior, flicked the recorder on and read the report while Rona waited. "Is there a fast frigate in orbit?" Belsas handed back the recorder.

"The *Predator* is in the orbital docks for routine maintenance," replied Rona.

"Bel, what is it?" queried Chandrey.

Belsas raised a hand for her to wait. "Have it readied. We'll launch up after the Council meeting late tonight." Belsas turned to Krell. "Is it possible for you to contact LaRenna today?"

"It would be extremely dangerous." Krell's heart skipped one beat then another.

"Wait until morning then. When you see her next, take her and Healer Wileyse directly into orbit. I want all Taelachs off Langus. That's an order." Belsas's arms opened to receive Chandrey. "The Iralians are massing on the truce line. At last estimate, the largest of their ships, the *Blackmore*, will cross the line tomorrow morning."

Fear contorted Chandrey's slender hands into pale knots. She watched Rona exit the room then flew into her mate's arms, trembling with mother instincts for her child. "Tomorrow is the deadline for the High Council to concede to the demands of the Langus Cause!" she cried. "What's going to happen?"

"Nothing good, I'm certain. We must go to Langus to thwart whatever is unfolding. Our people, the Sarian system demands it." Belsas made a quick, severe gesture to Krell. "LaRenna's post did not cover this variable and is hereby withdrawn. Retrieve her at first dawn. The post's risks far outweigh any reward."

"My brother is here, too." Krell's eyes were wide to the upcoming events. "Let me arrange for him to transport off with us, please."

"I'd forgotten you were Aut raised. Do what you need, just be in orbit with LaRenna when we arrive. Belsas out." She shut off the screen and looked grimly down at her lover. Chandrey was in need of her reassurance, but duty also called, and, after a moment's soothing the call became overwhelming. "Help me into my dress uniform, Chandresslandra." Belsas pushed away. "The Council will be waiting."

Chapter Twenty-three

The only good Taelach is a dead, burned, and ash-scattered Taelach.

—Autlach quote

"Why do I always get the grunt work?" Brandoff carted LaRenna's limp body up to the living quarters. Cance followed behind, whistling, LaRenna's slippers and skirts tucked under her arm.

" 'Cause you beat her half to death, that's why." Cance puckered to resume the tune then paused, her mouth flattening in brief contention. "She would've responded better if you hadn't kneed her so early on. Next time, I question her alone."

"She won't tell you shit and you know it. You just want a chance to coo over her without me there to laugh." Brandoff dropped LaRenna close to where Bane lay, frightening him into noiselessness so that Brandoff promptly admonished, "You're not asleep, old man."

Cance tossed the clothing into an empty corner then touched

her twin's blackened eye, somewhat gladdened LaRenna hadn't made things too easy. It showed strength. Cance adored conquering strength. "Have a look at yourself. She made a proper mess of you." Brandoff peered in the room's wall-mounted reflecting board. Cance stood behind. LaRenna had gouged long scratches on their faces and a bite ring was clearly visible between the brands on Cance's neck. She fingered it gingerly, as if recapturing the moment. "What a woman! Fought the whole way through, prock high and all. Imagine what she'd be like if she was willing. Wild is my bet, how 'bout it, Brannie?"

"Yeah, I gotta give her credit for linger ability"—Brandoff's mouth points stretched a little higher—"and delectability. One of the best I ever had—until she passed out. A little while longer would have exhausted me enough for sleep."

"I'm there now." Cance cleaned her scratches with a cloth. "Someone her age, even a Kimshee, shouldn't have that sense of control. It took everything I had to phase her into submission. Gave me a headache." Cance surveyed Brandoff's ruffled appearance then passed the cloth. "Here, doctor yourself then lace back up. You're leaving nothing to the imagination."

Brandoff snorted and took the cloth. "Eh, I'm fine." She spied her sibling's disapproving reflection. "And if you think differently, take a snort to clear your senses." She broke her gaze to glance around the room. "You seen Starnes since we came up? He didn't sneak out, did he?"

"If you'd use that head for more than a prock port you'd know where he's at. He's hiding in the washroom, scared senseless. Typical Aut, no mind control whatsoever. I hear everything he's fretting over." Cance stepped over LaRenna's sprawled figure and jerked open the washroom door. "Get out here, Starnie."

Starnes timidly exited his hiding place holding a small, neatly folded stack of linens. "Just prepping up some clean towels for tonight." He kept his gaze down. The perfect squares fell from his arms when he saw LaRenna. He gulped and took a backward step. He'd known they'd hurt her, but surely they hadn't . . .

"Is she—no!" Black char wafted through the air as he collapsed to the floor. Cance stood over him, bow poised to repeat Brandoff's attack.

"She's not dead, but you'll be if you don't listen. We had a visitor while you slept, little man. Said he saw you and a Taelach from the base cozying up at the Food Plaza, the same one Brandoff saw your new barmaid with this morning. You turned us in, you sorry little—"

"No, I promised. We had a deal!" Starnes held up his hand to ward off the second plasma arrow that scorched through his shoulder. He squealed and drew into a fetal position, sure another blast would be his end.

"I hate being lied to." Cance ground her heel into his shoulder. "You knew she was Taelach and you knew we found her out, so why didn't you run while we were using her?" Cance aimed between his eyes. "My patience is gone, Starnie!"

"He didn't leave because of me." Bane sat up in his bed. "I'm the reason. Now let him be."

Brandoff sniffed at the dutiful dedication. "I say we kill them both. They've outlived their usefulness." She aimed at Bane and smiled. "Shame to do away with such an entertaining storyteller." The bow whined readiness and Brandoff waved goodbye, finger flexed on the weapon's manual trigger.

"Stop!"

Brandoff downloaded and looked at Cance, who pointed to the lower level. Someone was knocking on the Waterlead's front doors. "I'll go tell whoever's there that we're closed today—family tragedy." Cance laughed at what she said. "Singe the first one who opens their yap." Tunic collar high, sleeves unrolled to cover her bow, Cance blinked to replace her Autlach lenses and trudged down the stairs.

"Sorry." She cracked open the door. "Family emergency. We're closed this evening."

"Wait!" Trazar Laiman stuck his foot against the doorjamb. "I'm looking for LaRenna. Is she here?"

"Nope. She took off at closing last night with some stocky man in baggy coveralls. No telling where she is." Cance tried to push Trazar's foot from the door, but he held his stance.

"I see." The man Cance referred to was one of Trazar's sentries and second to him in the squadron's command. They had walked back to the housing compound together so he knew LaRenna wasn't around. "You don't know when she'll be back?"

"She won't be."

"She quit?" Trazar's unshaven cheeks sank.

"No." Frustration crept into Cance's tone. "I fired her for propositioning the customers. Once a whore, always a whore."

"Oh." Trazar masked his face into disinterest. He pulled his foot from the jamb, thanked Cance, and strolled toward the Commons. When the Waterlead's doors swung shut, he back-tracked to hunker under an overgrown shrub near the main entrance. He had been lied to more than once in the course of that short conversation and intended to find out why.

"Damn Aut men." Cance climbed the stairs two at a time. "Always after a piece." LaRenna stirred when her footfalls neared the top. "She awake?"

"Sort of." Brandoff snapped at LaRenna's bare legs with one of Starnes's discarded towels. "I had to shove a rag in her mouth to stop her confounded moaning." Brandoff aimed again at Bane. "Now, where was I?" She turned to Starnes. "Here?" Then she bounced back to his father. "Or maybe here?"

"If you must kill one of them then make it Starnie," said Cance. "We'll pour our own drinks tonight."

"No!" pleaded Bane from his bed. "I'm already dying. Spare him and take me."

"You served as a military medic, old man. I need you to treat this one's wounds. Here, look her over." Cance pulled LaRenna within his reach. Her underskirts bunched at the waist as she was moved, revealing a series of bloody streaks that stretched down her inner thighs. Seeing them, Cance glowered at Brandoff. "You idiot! Look at this! I told you not to be so rough. Dammit, you could have killed her!"

"I wasn't that rough!" protested Brandoff, sounding more insulted than concerned. "And I didn't do anything to cause that, not when I laid her, leastways. It must be from the knee to the stomach." Apathetic at best, she aimed squarely at Starnes. "This is becoming tiresome. Any last words for your dah?"

"NO!" called Bane. "Murder him and I won't treat the woman. She'll bleed to death where she lies."

"The old fool isn't so foolish after all." Brandoff's high had worn until she squinted. "Well, Cancelynn?"

"Tie Starnes while I get some bandages for the not-so-foolish one to use," she replied. "We can't have our trophy dying before we have the opportunity to show her off." She turned to Bane. "Aren't we making a speedy recovery? Brought you medicine, didn't she?"

"Does it matter?" Bane frowned, brushed the hair from LaRenna's face, and quickly evaluated the extent of her most obvious injuries. "I need some hard liquor."

"Sounds good to me but I suggest you try wine first." Brandoff secured Starnes's arms behind his back. "Your stomach is probably weak."

"He doesn't want to drink it, you half-wit!" Cance replied angrily. "He needs to cleanse the girl's cuts. Go get some."

"Uh!" Brandoff stomped down the stairs. "Do this, Brandoff. Now, Brandoff. Who the fuck named you Mother Maker?"

"I'm self-appointed so hurry before I choose to end that sorry excuse you call a life!" Cance watched Brandoff's tangled mop of hair disappear then turned back to Bane, hesitant to hear his diagnosis. He'd removed the cloth from LaRenna's mouth and was smoothing out the remains of her skirts. She groaned, fighting him weakly as he rebuttoned her shredded top.

"What did you do to this child? I heard her scream until her voice went."

"More than I intended." Cance stooped by LaRenna's side. "She fought everything we did. Things became heated. Is she bleeding badly?"

Bane pushed on LaRenna's torso until the touch provoked a

loud cry. "I don't believe she is, but a fair number of her ribs are broken. We'll need to bind them."

"Anything else?"

"Yes," he replied. "Keep your maniac twin away from her. One more hard blow could drive one of those loose ribs into something vital. Remember that if you want her to live."

"Oh, I do," assured Cance. "And not just so I can use her like I already have. I like her spirit." She pointed to the dried clots. "What about this?"

"Normal female cycle."

Cance startled then stared at him. "Taelachs don't have cycles. We're sterile. Everyone knows that."

"This one does. I've outlived two wives and have four daughters. That's enough experience to know what the normal cycle smells and looks like."

"Can you stop it?" Brandoff stood at the top of the stairs, a bottle of clear liquor and two wine crystals in her arms.

"Do you lose your senses every time you fuck while laced?" Cance absently fingered LaRenna's hair. "Of course you can't stop it. It's a natural function." She smiled down at LaRenna. "You're more valuable than ever, my beloved. You're breedable. Just imagine what they'll pay to get you back—if I give you back at all."

Brandoff handed Bane the liquor and took the crystals to the room's only chair, settling into it and glaring at the object of Cance's affection. Bane poured a little of the spirits on a cloth and gently cleansed the bloody patches on LaRenna's face until she became alert enough to object. She coughed and gasped as the alcohol burned her open flesh, making her painfully aware of her broken ribs, her foot, her hurt all over.

"Where am I?" The question was no more than a rustle in her throat.

"With me, bitch." Brandoff had dosed while downstairs. LaRenna struggled to find the location of her voice, found Cance first, and swung out with all her might, collapsing back against Bane when her ribs shifted within her.

Keep still. Cance's mental tone was as soft as the pain-relieving phase LaRenna immediately threw from her mind. *Very well, my love.* Cance pushed away. "Hurt if you insist, just let us treat you."

Bane held her head firmly to finish cleaning the worst from her face and neck. "Shhh," he whispered when she protested. "Let me clean you up a little." Then he took her hand and carefully examined the broken finger. "What else did you find necessary to break on this child?"

"Just her ankle." Brandoff sounded proud of the way LaRenna winced in response. "Cance did it and her finger. I'm the one who busted her ribs. In just one blow, I might add."

Bane remained unimpressed. "Good for you. I'm sure you're proud of your conquest over such a superior-sized enemy."

Brandoff flung her boot knife into the wall above Bane's head, skimming brittle white hairs from his scalp. "Bite your tongue, old man, or you won't have one to chew."

Bane ignored the threat. "I need splinting material for the finger and ankle." LaRenna lay perfectly still in his arms, listening. She was too weak for an effective phase and too winded from her recent movement for anything more.

Cance nodded then disappeared into the next room, returning momentarily with a small bundle. "This should be enough. I even found a needle and gutting thread for that gash Brandoff left in her jaw."

"It does need stitching." Bane felt increasingly weak from the exertion but kept his pace. He had to look after LaRenna. She had, after all, done the same for him. "First the ribs. Sit her up and we'll wrap them." He pulled Brandoff's knife from the wall and began to slice the light coverlet on his bed into long strips.

"I hope you plan on returning that." Cance drew onto the floor beside LaRenna.

"I have an option?" Bane raised his head to look at her. "My only concern is for my son and the girl. Sit her up." He handed the knife to Cance, handle first, who returned it to Brandoff.

Cance looped under LaRenna's arms and pulled her to a sitting position.

"Gently!" snapped Bane.

"That's as gentle as I get!" Cance snapped back. "Now what?"

"Help me wrap these strips around her gut. Snug but not too tight. She has to be able to breathe." LaRenna's expression pulled Cance's attention from the task.

"Your eyes deceive you."

"Do they suggest loathing?" asked LaRenna.

"No, my love, fascination. You are trying to figure me out."

"Only so I can kill you."

"Such anger so soon in the relationship?" Cance laughed. "It's far too early for that. Relax, LaRenna, and let us treat you."

"Why, so you can prock-lace me again?"

"Smartmouth." Cance appreciated the argument. "You have an appealing edge to you." She wrapped LaRenna in a hug, placing a pair of light kisses to the side of her head before LaRenna could wriggle away. "Next?" She looked at Bane.

"Set her finger." Bane closed his eyes in concentration on his long ago training. "Feel to see if the fracture is at the joint." Cance grasped the injured hand and pressed on the finger. LaRenna squirmed but couldn't pull away.

"It's the joint."

"Good. It will be easier to set. Pop it into place and splint it."

"Sorry, m'lady," Cance soothed with a light touch to LaRenna's face. "But this is going to hurt." LaRenna yelped as the finger popped back into place.

"You bawl like a kicked animal, you stupid cunt." Brandoff laughed between pulls from one of the crystals. "I think I heard that same sound when we were downstairs. Remember what I was doing when you made it? I do. I was—"

"Stop it." LaRenna shook violently against Cance, quaking with rage and fear she could not contain. "She's too bad off for your ranting."

"Why should I care? She's nothing more than a toy for us, or can't you see that anymore?"

"She's a hostage I plan to keep alive as long as necessary. I won't have her dropping off because of your blasted mouth. Her heart all but jumped from her chest when she heard your voice." Cance wondered how much of the shaking was actually from the mental attack and how much was Brandoff's doing. "She's terrified of you."

"It's the prock," retorted Brandoff. "She's crashing."

As the panic subsided and her mind cleared, LaRenna discerned a sick sense of pride exuding from Brandoff's warped mind. Brandoff honestly enjoyed the pain she inflicted on others. It soothed away some of the agony of her own complicated life. Like the drug she was so reliant on, it made her forget. Cance's emotions were evident too, differing from Brandoff's though just as intense. They were a disturbing mix of obsessive affection and erotic desires directed toward LaRenna. She found pleasure in hurting others, but not for the same reasons as Brandoff. Pain was a weapon, a means of effective discipline, a teaching tool. She even used it in the name of love.

"Forgive my sister's shortcomings."

LaRenna knocked Cance's reassuring touch away. "Why should you care what she does to me? You did it, too."

"A danger of the post you took, young Kimshee." Cance splinted LaRenna's finger. "And may I remind you that I held my pleasures to the traditional way between Kimshees."

"That was not pleasure."

"Really? Then what would you call it?"

LaRenna remained silent for a moment. "Rape." The word tasted a thousand times filthier than Tynnes's single kiss. "It was rape."

"Oh, I believe you've been misinformed. This seems to be an ongoing problem with my lovers. It might prove necessary to leave you alone with my twin when you are better healed. What she does is far and away more the definition of rape than what I enjoy. Maybe then you'll change your description of the pleasures I offer." Cance put an end to the conversation by moving to LaRenna's ankle. "All right, old man. Let's finish up."

"Undo the bindings first." Bane slid into Cance's former position, his open mind projecting tender sympathies for LaRenna, scathing hatred for those holding them hostage. "She can't go anywhere in her condition. You've both seen to that." Cance flashed him a scowl but conceded to his wish. LaRenna moaned and shook as the renewed circulation caused the foot to burn and throb.

"We can't set her ankle while she's shaking," said Bane. "Let me give her some wine to dull the pain."

"No. She's lost too much blood."

"She's well on her way into shock as it is," he objected.

Cance clicked her tongue. "Very well. But give her wine, not liquor. I don't want her heaving with broken ribs. Brandoff, bring that second crystal over here. Quietly, mind you."

"Why should I?" Brandoff's voice rose to a level she hoped would add to LaRenna's agony. "If she goes into shock, she goes into shock. What does it matter? I got what I wanted once, and I'll do it again later." Her eyes slitted in direct defiance of Cance's wishes. "Hopefully, it'll kill her."

Cance crossed the room in two powerful strides, wrenched the chair from under her sister, and tossed it down the stairs, where it splintered against the Waterlead's doors. "Are you touched or just plain stupid? This happens every time I let you get your jollies. Damn prock fiend, you've lost all concept of reality!" Cance snatched one of the crystals, flinging it into the wall when she found it empty. It shattered above Starnes, showering him in a rain of fine shards. "Belsas's daughter has to stay alive! She's the ultimate trophy of our triumph."

Brandoff pulled her knife as she rose. "Sister or not, I will cut you wide if you ever do that again." She then leaned against the wall, eyes fixed on her Autlach-disguised double. "You want the girl because she reminds you of Chandrey. All of Langus heard you cry her name downstairs. She's not a trophy to you. Your first life mate renounced you so you want another. Face it, Cancelynn Creiloff, you're not fucking guardian enough to hold on to one."

LaRenna craned her trembling head at Chandrey's mention,

149

only to be pushed back prone by Bane's steady hand. "Don't," he whispered. "This isn't the time."

"Never mention that name! Its beauty is wasted in your stinking mouth." Cance thrust the second crystal at Bane and hovered over LaRenna, her downward stare as longing as it was vexed. "Yes, girl, I know her. I was her life mate once upon a time. She'd still be mine if it hadn't been for Belsas. Who knows, I might have been your guardian raiser if things had turned out differently." Cance watched Bane fill his empty water glass with wine and hold it to LaRenna's lips. "You act so much like her that it brought back memories. You're very much her daughter. There is the same spark of disobedience in you both. I'll simply have to remove it from you as well." Bane drew LaRenna away from Cance's gaze and encouraged her to drink deeply of the wine.

Brandoff sheathed her blade and turned toward the stairs. "Since you insist on giving the last of my wine to the whore, I'm going down for more." Brandoff waited for Cance to answer, but Cance's attention was still fixated on LaRenna. "Cance?"

"Yeah, whatever." She dismissed Brandoff with a wave then knelt by LaRenna's side to hold the glass. Cance's seasoned face had softened with memory. "How is Chandrey? Does she still have that beautiful silver mane I fell in love with?"

So this was the reason Chandrey refused to speak of the Taelach civil war. "Belsas says she looks better than ever." LaRenna stared at Cance, challenging her with the words.

Cance merely sniffed. "I'm sure she does." She turned the glass up, forcing LaRenna to gulp. "Ease the pain before we set your ankle." Her tone was quite tender, trying to love that which she could only rule over. "Is your hair the same color as Chandrey's? Are the curls natural?" Cance delicately fingered LaRenna's spirals until she jerked away in disgust. "In time, precious, you'll learn to appreciate me just as Chandrey once did. I had her very well trained. You'll be the same picture of obedience after a few lessons."

"Cance!" Brandoff had gotten no farther than the stair head. "She's not Chandrey!"

"I know that," said Cance. "But she will serve me just as well, if not better. I believe I'll keep her for myself. What of it, woman? Are you oathed to that Krell you called out for downstairs?"

"No." LaRenna spoke as loudly as her pained ribs would allow. "But I would never—" Bane placed his hand over her mouth. He stared pleadingly at her and shook his head.

"No matter." Cance passed the glass back to Bane. "I won't oath with you until I see you in your true Taelach form. I'll strip the dye from both our heads as soon as we leave Langus. By then, I'm sure you'll be more considerate of me." Cance glanced back at Brandoff. "You getting more wine or not? I'm thirsty."

"I'm going. I'm going!" Brandoff flew down the stairs and stepped behind the bar, where she vented her frustration by throwing several empty crystals against a nearby wall.

Upstairs, Bane helped LaRenna drain a second and third glass in rapid succession. The wine absorbed quickly in her empty stomach, making her visibly lightheaded as it interacted with the remaining drug in her system. "I think she's had enough," said Bane when she had choked down most of a fourth. "Let's set it."

Cance positioned at the twisted ankle and held it firm. "You got her?"

"I may not be able to hold her still if she struggles."

"Starnes!" Cance bellowed. "Get your ass over here and lay across her legs. That'll keep her down." She snickered. "Stars, that'd keep me down." Starnes made his way slowly across the floor, cutting himself several times on shards of broken crystal. He reached his father's side and drew his considerable girth across LaRenna's upper thighs. "Brace yourselves," Cance warned and pulled the joint back into position. LaRenna screamed as bone scraped bone. The cry was audible physically and mentally, broadcasting over the immediate area to produce ringing pain in Cance's fine-tuned Kimshee mind.

"She's shocky." Bane wiped the cold sweat streaking LaRenna's face and grabbed her wrist to check her pulse. "Hurry this before it stops her heart. She's still not completely down from the prock."

"Again then." The joint slid into place with a resounding pop

151

that forced an even louder mental shriek. Cance had to shake off the call's effect and Brandoff could be heard below, cursing for the sound to stop. Cance bellowed for silence then turned to Bane with a face drawn by the sound's complexity. "How the fuck did she get this finely tuned at her age? I've killed centenarian sisters with less of a mind."

LaRenna spasmed in Bane's arms, ending the cry. He checked her pulse again and sighed.

"She's in shock. Put something under her legs before you splint the foot." Cance took the pillows from the bedding platform and placed them under LaRenna's feet.

"The joint moved, but it still doesn't look right." Cance's mind burned to the point where she drew from her inhaler to relieve the fire.

"There's too much damage." Bane drew a blanket from his bed. "She needs a Healer's touch." He tapped Starnes's shoulder and motioned him to move from LaRenna's legs, lest she lose what little circulation remained to the injured one. His dark face was pasty gray and a chilling sweat dripped from his temples as he rolled to the side. Bane smoothed the blanket over LaRenna then reached two fingers to his son's neck. "Not you too, boy."

Trazar circled the Waterlead in the long cast of the evening shadows. The rear entrance was almost in his grasp when movement caught the corner of his eye. He retreated, flattening against the building. The shadow failed to notice him and continued its twisting lope to the door. In the dull reflection Saria Proper cast on its moon, Trazar managed a fleeting glimpse of the suspicious individual's legs. The feet were unshod, heavy-clawed, and four-toed. They could be nothing other than Iralian.

Chapter Twenty-four

Dreams are the mind's gateway to reality.

—*Taelach wisdom*

"What the—?" Krell pushed back the blanket to grab her ankle. Various aches had awakened her during the night but none as severe as what she felt now. Her sides throbbed, her jaw stung, and her abdomen—Krell wrapped her arms around her knees, pulling them to her stomach. The entirety of her lower abdomen felt raw. Clutching her belly, she stumbled to the bathing chamber, barely making it before the pain overwhelmed her. She laid her forehead against the smooth stone of the toilet, gasping for breath between retchings. How unlike her to ache for no reason. How unlike her to be so nauseous. How unlike her to be—Krell swallowed hard. How unlike her to be so worried, but she couldn't help it. "LaRenna." Krell sank to the floor, afraid to move farther. She stayed in this position, sweating against the cool floor tile until first dawn approached, forcing her into motion.

On the far side of the Commons, Trazar scaled the Waterlead's external supports, inching his way across a horizontal crosspiece until he could see into the second level. The same man who'd turned him away was bent over one of two prone figures. An elderly man sat beside the other.

Cance knotted the final loop stitched into LaRenna's chin, clipped the thread, and leaned back to examine her handiwork. "Think it'll scar?" she asked Bane. "I'll scar Brandoff if she left one."

"Your stitches are clean and her nose set well." Bane tempered his approval. "The scar won't show to any extent as long as infection doesn't set in." He returned his attention to the remains of his son's shoulder. "There." Bane drooped against the wall behind his pallet.

"Hey, Cance!" Brandoff stumbled into the living area, her hand wrapping a near empty crystal. "Look who finally showed." She stepped aside and Talmshone loped to where Cance stooped. The trio of fingers on his left hand looped a crystal of Starnes's finest.

"My my, what a pitiful collection you have accumulated, Cance." His smile revealed row upon row of razor-tipped teeth, which he flashed at the wide-eyed Autlach men. "Why are they still breathing?"

"The older one's been nursing our backup plan." Cance kissed LaRenna's hand, placed it by her side, then rose to Talmshone's level and returned his crooked smile. "The girl here is—"

"Your sibling has provided a sufficient update," interrupted Talmshone. "So this is the Taelach of All's only child." He lifted the edge of LaRenna's blanket and shook his head. "You two definitely know how to amuse yourselves." Then puzzlement creased the Iralian's eye ridges. "She is Taelach, is she not? Her size is rather disconcerting."

"Military brat of a military bitch." Cance glowered suspiciously at the Iralian. "And don't get any bright ideas. You haven't paid me enough for that privilege. She's mine so leave her alone." Cance jerked the blanket from his hand and smoothed it back in place. LaRenna stirred when she was touched, opening her eyes to see who was tending her.

"Iralian," she whispered. "I should have known."

"Seems your lady has regained her senses." Talmshone's animalistic grin softened with his laugh. "Since her condition has stabilized, shall we return to the lower level and discuss business over more Sarian finery?"

"I suppose it's safe." Cance eyed her captives, casting each a separate but equally threatening glare.

"After you, then." Talmshone spoke with the grand eloquence all Iralians possessed, an effective ruse for the savagery they were capable of. He held the door open for Cance and Brandoff then followed them down the stairs, looking back briefly to bare his teeth again at Starnes and Bane.

Trazar waited until things were quiet then rattled the window casing. The noise caught Starnes's attention, drawing him toward the sound. Seeing Trazar, he sighed, mouthed a brief prayer to one of the lesser Autlach deities then shook his father. "Dah, the window! Quick!"

"By stars," Bane declared when he woke. "Help has arrived." He crawled to the window, held fast to the ledge, and unfastened the lock.

The window groaned when Trazar slid it open. Once inside, he rushed to LaRenna's side. "Hey, you," he said. "I've been looking for you. Your employer said you ran off with one of my sentries, but I thought better." LaRenna peered up at him, her delicate blue eyes standing out against the dark bruises on her face. Trazar's mouth opened and closed in dumbfounded surprise. "Taelach!" he whispered. "You're Taelach!"

"You shouldn't be here," she began.

"Family helps family," he replied deftly, making a quick check of her physical condition as he shushed her objections. "We're related," he assured her. "I'll explain how later. Right now, we need to get you and the others out of here." He turned to Starnes. "Sentry Commander Trazar Laiman of Vartoch at your service."

"Great," sighed Starnes. "Another one for the slaughter."

"My son's pain has clouded his manners, Commander Laiman." Bane frowned at his offspring. "I'm Asabane Tackwell and this is my youngest boy, Starnes. We're grateful for any assistance you can offer." His keen eye immediately recognized the resemblance in LaRenna's and Trazar's faces and he smiled, warmed by the commitment of family. "Brother and sister, aren't you?"

"Yes, we are," Trazar replied, half to Bane and half to his disbelieving sibling. "Trust me." He looked about the room, trying to determine the best escape route. "Any suggestions?"

"There are no other exits besides the ones downstairs," supplied Bane. "But sometimes," he added, "the best course of action is simply to wait. You could drop them individually as they come upstairs."

"They may not come up that way." Starnes proved as pessimistic as usual.

"I'll take the chance," snapped Trazar. "We have the element of surprise on our side." He slid his arms under LaRenna's shoulders and knees. "I need to move you out of harm's way." Trazar carried her into the adjoining room, placing her on Starnes's sleeping platform. "I didn't mean to hurt you."

"I know," she said between gritted teeth. "You did what was necessary."

"Hang on, little sister." Trazar patted her head. "You'll be safe soon."

Starnes came next. Trazar assisted him into a chair despite his vocal preference for the padded lounger by the door. "I want you all as far back as possible." Last, he assisted Bane to a spot on the floor next to LaRenna, placing his hand on top of hers. "Watch her, please. She's in a lot of pain."

"She'll be fine." Bane pulled a small dagger from beneath

Starnes's bed. "I'd been saving this for just such an occasion, but I hadn't had the strength to get to it until now." He offered it to Trazar, who refused the gesture by brandishing a double-edged serrated blade from his boot sheath.

"Already got one." He used the knife to free Starnes, carefully removing the barman's leg tie in a solid piece he could reuse.

"Give the knife to me." LaRenna held out her free hand.

"You're in no condition," said Trazar and nodded to Bane, who placed the blade in his back waistband.

"Neither is he," she began, but Trazar placed a finger to his mouth. There were footsteps on the stairwell. He slid into the front room and shut off the light, exerting enough force to shear the switch.

Brandoff stepped through before she noticed the darkness. "What the—CANCE!" Trazar twisted Brandoff's arm behind her and covered her eyes, thwarting any phase. He pushed her head-first into the doorjamb, giving her head quick cracks until she crumpled to the floor. Trazar jerked up as she fell, snapping her shoulder from its socket. He rolled her out of the way and slammed the door in Cance's face.

"Open up!"

"Allow me." Talmshone stood behind her. He punched through the door's metal casing, grasping and twisting for the shorn handle. Trazar thrust his blade through the Iralian's palm before he could pull back. Talmshone roared in pain and withdrew. "It appears we underestimated the abilities of our captives." His voice remained placid, but a blood-red brilliance swirled in his reptilian eyes.

"Move it!" Cance blazed a plasma streak that blasted the door from its hinges then pushed into the room. "Dammit! I can't see! Brandoff! Where the fuck are you?"

"Here!" Brandoff pulled up on all fours. Cance followed her voice to find her twin, dull illumination spilling across them as Talmshone cut on the stairwell lighting.

"Behind you!" He looked up to see Trazar's shadow wrap the binding around Cance's neck, her knees buckling as he severed her airflow. Brandoff, blood staining her white hair crimson, threw her knife at their attacker. Trazar ducked the blade and returned the throw with his own, his hold on Cance never loosening as the blade sank deep into Brandoff's chest. She clutched at the blade handle then reached toward Cance, falling at her feet.

"An assassin is afoot!" Talmshone flung Trazar against the opposite wall, but he failed to break the sentry's grasp on Cance's neck. She was dragged along, unable to fight his hold, not to launch a phase, not to cry out. Her universe wavered and blackened. Brandoff beckoned. They could be together, of similar mind when the physical reality had ceased, neither fighting the complexities that had kept them separated in life.

"Release her!" Talmshone crashed his fist into Trazar's face, throwing him back again. This time the chokehold broke, the binding sliding from Cance's neck before eternity and Brandoff won. Talmshone pulled her to the side, clearing the path between himself and the sentry commander. "You wish to fight?" He waved a talon at Trazar. "Fight another man, not a Taelach. I will shred you with my bare hands."

"I've skinned Iralian snakes before and welcome the chance to do so again!" Trazar lunged at Brandoff's neglected knife. Talmshone reached the blade first and sank it through Trazar's extended hand, pinning him to the floor.

"Tit for tat." Talmshone extended his wounded palm as evidence. "Slice me and I slice you back."

"My turn next." Cance aimed between Trazar's eyes. "I'm going to send you to a hell so deep your own whoring mother won't be able to reach you!" Cance squeezed the palm trigger, anticipating a glorious ending to Brandoff's killer. Nothing happened.

"Damn you, Brannie!" Cance discarded the weapon and all tender thoughts of Brandoff. "You never listened to a fuckin' thing I said. This bow was to be charged two days ago!" Cance jerked the weapon from Brandoff's arm, lashed it on, and aimed again between Trazar's eyes. "Don't think you'll get that lucky twice."

"Cance, stop." Talmshone blocked the distance between them. "Think about what you are doing."

"Outta my way. This is a family matter. Justified restitution. I'll shoot you too if you don't back off."

Talmshone refused to move. "Yes, it is indeed a family matter. Have you noticed the resemblance between this Autlach and the young Taelach you seem to hold dear?"

"I don't care if they're brother and sister. He dies!"

"My point exactly. They are siblings," he said. "If you will look closely you can just see the crimps of his service braid. The man is military."

"So what? You're wasting time. Move!"

"Your eyesight won't allow you to pilot, so who is going to pilot the launch we plan to escape in?"

"Brandoff wi—" Cance stopped as Talmshone's logic sank in. "Can he pilot?"

Talmshone pushed Cance's bow aside and jerked Trazar's ponytail loose from its band. "I believe so." He pulled a strand tight. "These are not curls. They are from an eight-plat half hitch. He is pilot qualified."

"You win." Cance downloaded her bow, then retrieved the cording Trazar had used. "Behave yourself, sentry, or I'll vent my frustrations on your delicious sister."

Talmshone took the cord and bound Trazar's wrists before he removed the imbedded knife. "Get up. We have business to attend to." He belted the blade then pushed Trazar toward the second room. "I suppose your friends got to about here." Talmshone peeked around the corner and gave his captives a toothsome grin. "Correct. They are indeed present. I believe this completes the reunion."

Cance squinted. "They're untied." She spun on one heel, kicking Starnes in the face. The blow threw him from the chair and he fell, howling, onto his blackened shoulder. "Was it you who brought in the sentry?" Her next kick was for Bane. The old man reeled back but remained upright and silent. "Or, was it you somehow, old man?"

"It wasn't either of us." Bane's mouth bled heavily. "Kick the girl like that and it'll kill her."

"She won't be kicked. I have other plans for her." Cance sank to the floor and pressed her knees into LaRenna's sides in the same controlling move Brandoff had done on the bar. "The more I think it over, girl, the surer I am it was you. After all, he is your brother." Cance leaned forward. "Smart girl, getting your Aut brother to off Brandoff. She was becoming quite the pain where you're concerned. He merely saved me the inconvenience. Problem is, now I'm all alone." Her mouth curled into something near a pout. "And I really, really hate being alone." Cance twisted the end of LaRenna's hair around her finger, each twirl further diverting her anger to desire. "It's time we talk of commitment. Oath to me now and I'll show you things you've only dreamed of. You will rule Langus with me, be my heart's only desire." Cance kissed her forehead and drew her chin up until their eyes met. "I really am a gentle creature when given the respect I deserve. What say you, my sweet little sister? Shall we speak the words?"

"You're no sister of mine!" LaRenna spat in her captor's face.

Cance reared back to punish the misbehavior but stopped short of it, humor smoothing her callused features. "You know," she said, wiping away the spittle, "I would have done the very same thing. We'd be a good pair, you and I."

"No." LaRenna shook her head. "We're nothing alike. I would never forsake the Kinship."

Cance fell forward, so close her chest pushed painfully into LaRenna's ribs. Her face was devoid of emotion. It was Brandoff's cold look and Brandoff's voice hissing in her ear, Brandoff's form pressing her down and pulling her head back by the hair. "You will keep a well-mannered tongue and learn when and where not to speak. You're my property. Do you hear that? Mine!" Cance forced rough kisses on LaRenna's face and neck until LaRenna wriggled free enough to slap her.

"You might as well kill me, you branded bitch," she wailed. "Because I will never, NEVER be yours in any way. Not of my own free will. No amount of violence or drug can convince me anything about you is right." LaRenna spat at Cance again. "Slow death is preferable to spending one more second with you. Fuck off!"

"I believe the young woman dislikes your company." Talmshone glanced through the window at the approaching first dawn. "Time grows short. We must keep our schedule."

"Screw you and your schedules! It's time I teach my new bride about obedience!" Cance tore off LaRenna's blanket and remaining underskirts. "This is what happens when you mouth off, girl. I command respect and I will get it each and every time." LaRenna mustered her strength to roll from beneath Cance, landing, gasping, a few inches away. Cance grabbed her, dragging her back to the pallet. "A filthy mouth prompts filthy actions. Take your punishment and learn from it."

"NOOO!" LaRenna fought to keep the second assault from occurring. She kicked with her good leg, trying to throw Cance's phaseless blows off balance. Trazar fought against Talmshone, desperate to come to his sister's aid. The Iralian pinned him to his seat with a solid hand to his shoulder then did the same to Bane, gripping the old man's shoulder so tight it audibly cracked. A mere turn of his flaring red eyes kept Starnes at bay.

"I do not condone this unfortunate incident, gentlemen," he said. "But if you interfere, Cance will kill you all out of pure rage and I will be without transportation home."

"Damn you!" Cance pressed her hand to LaRenna's throat. "When will you learn?" LaRenna growled her response, striking Cance with her splinted hand. Cance grabbed her outstretched arm and pulled, sending searing pain down LaRenna's side. "Very well, a proper lesson it shall be." She pulled a second and third time. "Rule one, the harder you fight, the rougher I become." LaRenna screeched as Cance repeated the process with her other arm. "Shut up, LaRenna Cances."

161

"I'll never be known as yours!"

Cance twisted LaRenna's right breast. "I said shut your fuckin' hole!"

"Never!"

Cance released the bruising pinch, doubled her fist, and smashed it into LaRenna's abdomen. LaRenna's eyes rolled back, but she still wriggled to get free.

"Stop it!" cried Trazar. "You're killing her!"

"She just wishes I would." Cance bashed LaRenna again. "Isn't this how you Auts treat your wives? Or is it this?" Cance brought her knee up, ramming it into LaRenna's crotch until she ceased moving. "Rule two, LaRenna, always, always obey me."

"No one should be treated like that." Bane pulled the hidden dagger, plunging it into Cance's shoulder. "The lady said no!"

Talmshone plucked him up by the scruff of the neck and held him suspended midair. "Now where were you hiding that?"

Cance sprang up, took a controlled breath, and removed the imbedded blade. "It takes more than that to stop me, old man." She peered down at LaRenna, whose breaths had become ragged. "Lesson complete, my love." Cance traced LaRenna's side with her toe. "Time we made things official." She laid her hand onto her shoulder, then to LaRenna's right shoulder, leaving a perfect red palm print. "There." Cance cleaned the blade and passed it to Talmshone, who belted it beside Brandoff's blade. "That'll lay my claim until I have my symbol inked on you."

"No . . ." LaRenna never opened her eyes.

"She even defies you in catatonia," observed Talmshone. "What about the Autlach senior?" He held Bane out a second time. "I am not a cloak hook."

"Break the fucker in half." Cance watched as the Iralian squeezed Bane's frail neck until it cracked.

"Done." Talmshone tossed the remains into a corner. "Next?"

"I'll take care of Starnes." Cance centered an intense stare on the cringing barman, anger and frustration venting into her phase. Its powerful broadcast caused LaRenna to shriek, Starnes screeching discord with her cry. Cance pared the phase until it excluded her fairer hostage then held it, toying Starnes's mind into insanity. He rocked back and forth, babbling incoherently.

"You are going to leave him in that manner?" asked Talmshone.

"Does it bother you, scaly?" Cance grinned at him as she drew her blade across Starnes's throat. "I'm done. Let's go."

"Not yet." Talmshone's disapproving expression lingered. "How are we moving the girl?"

"*We're* not." Cance undid Trazar's bindings. "Get your sister ready to move. Attempt to run or engage me, Commander, and I'll do all the nasty things I can think of to her. TWICE!"

Trazar moved to LaRenna's side. "She needs clothes."

Talmshone rifled through Starnes's clothing cubicle, pulling out a knit sleep shirt. "This will have to do. There are no clean leggings."

"They wouldn't fit anyway," said Cance. "Put it on her." She tossed a strip of torn underskirt to Talmshone. "Bandage your hand." She tore two more strips and folded a panel of the remaining material into a tight roll. "Hurry up, sentry. We haven't got all day!" Cance tossed the rags to Trazar. "Put that roll where it'll catch her bleeding. Sick enough it's all over my knee, but I won't have her staining up my craft."

"We are more likely to succeed if we proceed separately." Talmshone descended the stairs. "I am going."

"So are we." Cance passed Trazar a blanket that he wrapped around LaRenna and scooped her up. "Stick to the side streets and go directly to the terminal. Anyone stops us, we're taking your sister to a healer. I'll have my bow in your back the entire way. Slip up and I'll set you both ablaze."

Trazar nodded and stepped into the crisp morning air. First dawn was fading.

Talmshone waved back at Cance. "I shall meet you there." He drifted into the shadows, leaving little in the way of tracks.

Cance pulled back the blanket, kissed LaRenna on the forehead, then pushed Trazar forward, steering him toward a lesser-

163

traveled street. "Good thing you dropped in," she told him as they walked. "Now I have both a pilot *and* a porter."

"Lucky you." Trazar trudged ahead, protecting LaRenna from jarring movements while ignoring Cance's insults. "You've given it your all," he whispered in his sister's ear again and again. "Whatever you do, don't stop now, Renna. Don't stop now."

Chapter Twenty-five

Taelach vengeance is slow in coming but smothering and complete upon arrival.

—*Autlach saying*

Krell paced the dozen odd lengths between the nearest dune and where Firman and Tatra stood, her angst growing with every turn. Twice, she had heard LaRenna's voice on the morning breeze. Twice, Krell's companions had heard nothing.

"Where is she?" Tatra peered up at Firman through her wind-blown hair. Krell's concerns, usually the point of irritation, were beginning to develop merit. "She's long overdue. The *Predator* won't wait forever."

"It'll wait until we get there," snapped Krell. "Who's going to pilot the launch, you?" Her nausea still lingered. "Come on, LaRenna."

Firman placed his hand on her shoulder. "Be patient, sis."

"I shouldn't have let her go. She's in trouble. I know it. I feel it."

"LaRenna can handle herself. She proved that at the Hiring Hall. Have faith. Give her until full sunrise." They stood in silence until the sounds of fighting rose from the base.

Krell turned toward the sound. "Time's up, Firman. Take Tatra to the launch. I'm going after LaRenna." She dropped her bag and LaRenna's beside Firman's and dashed up the stone embankment toward the Commons.

"Wonderful, just wonderful!" Tatra stamped her foot. "A ship's coming for us and Krell takes off for Mother knows where."

Firman grumbled under his breath and looked toward the Commons. "You know the way to the launch, don't you?"

"Of course I do! What kind of a fool do you think I am?"

"You really want an honest answer to that?" He pushed the luggage toward her and scrambled up the path.

"Where are you going?" she cried. "Who's going to carry the bags? Krell told you to take me to the launch."

"Krell is my sibling, not my superior. Carry the bags yourself. I'm going to help find LaRenna."

"Uh!" Tatra stood, hands on her hips, swearing at Firman as he disappeared into the ocean fog. "Nobody ever thinks about my needs." She gathered the baggage and made her way to an easier side trail that led to the Commons, her spiked heels sinking in the sand as she walked. "I hate the Middle family," she sobbed. "I hate Kimshees and most of all, I hate playing porter to someone else's stinking luggage!"

Firman caught up with Krell halfway across the Commons. She ran the main streets, cloak and braids streaming behind her. "Don't try to stop me," she called back. "I promised to watch out for her."

"I couldn't stop you if I tried." Firman dodged a wide-eyed, basket-toting Autlach woman who crossed his path. "I want to help." They ran until the Waterlead came into view.

"Here." Krell slapped a small blaster into his hand.

"That's my Krell," teased Firman, the seriousness of the situation momentarily lost in his panting jester's grin, "Always ready. We going to going to walk right in there?"

"We are. Take the back?"

"You bet." He edged around the building, signaling when he was in position. Krell waved back and approached the main entrance, mumbling suspicions when she found the front door unlocked. Cautiously, bowed arm in a firing posture, she pushed it open.

The main dining room was scattered with overturned tables and chairs. Firman burst in from the kitchen area as Krell fingered a large smear of blood and fluids on the bar counter. "I don't like this, Fir." She held up her hand. "She's been hurt."

"Don't jump to conclusions," he replied. "LaRenna may be the one who caused that spot. There's nobody in the back, but the storeroom is a wreck. Stinks like someone's been sick." Firman watched his sibling touch the marks clawed into the counter's pass-through end. "Probably just the scars of a drunken brawl. Did you check the downstairs facilities?"

"Not yet."

"I'll do it." He stepped inside the small room and quickly retreated. "Come look." Krell stepped in and out in the same manner, her mouth covered to ward off the stench.

"Know him?" asked Firman through pinched nostrils.

Krell nodded then exhaled to keep her gut reactions at bay. "His name's Russ. He waited tables at the Food Plaza. Wonder how he's involved." Krell considered the possible relationship for a few seconds then gave up with a shrug. "We need to check upstairs. Back me up?"

"Yeah, just a sec." Firman picked up a small hide belt from the floor. "Isn't this LaRenna's?"

"I'm afraid it is. Merciful Mother, what've they done to her?"

Firman startled at the fear in Krell's voice. This wasn't the woman he knew. Krell was solid and unyielding, a dedicated military officer and Kimshee. She never showed her deeper emotions, especially in times of distress—or did she? Was LaRenna already that imbedded in Krell's mentality? "If I know LaRenna, she's probably at the beach as we speak, cursing you for leaving her alone with Tatra." He followed Krell up the treads, grimacing when he saw the charred door.

Krell checked the rear of the apartment while Firman examined the body in the front room. He was covering it with a blanket when Krell reentered with the remains of LaRenna's bloodstained underskirt.

"This one's Taelach," he said. "I think it's one of the Creiloff— What is it, Krell?"

"LaRenna's." Krell held out the scraps.

"It's not."

"It is."

"You don't know that for certain."

"I took it off her night before last. Dear Mother, what have I done?" Krell sank to the floor, cuddling LaRenna's belongings. "I told her I'd be there if she needed me. I promised. How could I be so stupid?" She shook remorsefully, clinging even tighter to the cloth, the meager remains of LaRenna.

"She's not dead, Krell." The words sounded so forced he began again. "She's alive. We'll find her. Wait and see."

"Where do I begin?" Krell sniffed hard then held up the underskirt. "There's so much blood. It's everywhere. She's hurt. I can feel it. I knew it last night. Oh, Firman, what have I done?"

"Faith, Krell. Have faith." Firman took the clothing from his sibling's shaking hands and drew Krell's pale palms into his dark ones. "Remember when you lost Mother's amulet?"

"Yeah," she mumbled.

"Remember how Father gave it to you for your tenth birthday?"

"Yeah."

"How long did you have to look for it before you found it?"

"Over two passes," Krell whispered between sobs.

"You never gave up searching, did you?" Firman squeezed her hands. "Answer me. Did you?"

"No."

"The amulet meant so much you never thought to quit," he continued. "Do you care about LaRenna half as much as that fool piece of jewelry?"

"I was going to give that fool piece of jewelry to her when I saw her next. Life won't be worth living without her. Oh, Firman, what have I done?"

"You've done nothing but love. We'll find her. How hard can it be?"

"Firman, I—"

"Don't Firman me, Krelleesha Tanchana Middle." Firman's tone reminded Krell of their father, to whom Firman bore a striking resemblance. "She's waiting for you. You heard her cries. She needs our help. As long as there's a chance she's alive, we'll search for her."

Krell's somber eyes focused on him. "We?"

"Think I'd let you go it alone?"

She shook her head. "I'm a blubbering idiot, Fir. You're always around when I need you most."

"That's what big brothers are for, help and aggravation." He caught Krell's head and knuckle-scrubbed the top. "We better get to the launch. I left Tatra to carry the bags."

"You didn't!" Krell chuckled at the thought of the thin-framed healer juggling substantial baggage.

"Yes, I did." Firman assisted her rise. "It's good to see a smile on your face, even a small one. Now, let's go."

The firefight continued around the Center's Assembly. Cance's select four had successfully taken control of the facility's perimeter and were maintaining their ground, waiting for the scan decoder to work its magic on the hatchway's encrypted codes.

"Hurry up!" The tanned Autlach drew flat against one of the building's decorative pillars. He wished nothing more than to be with his family. This wasn't his idea of a glorious victory, and martyrdom now seemed pointless. "Do it now! The entire base will be on us in a minute."

"Two markings left. Hold your position." Longhair watched as one then the other locking number fell into place. A yellow light signaled the hatch's release, allowing him to avoid the volley of blaster fire that rained on their position. Once inside, he took his bearings and located the master control panel. "All right, here we go. Blue means water supplies, gold sanitation tube ways, brown, green. Where's the confounded black key locks?" They sat to the side of the main panel array, protected by a heavy glass case. He smashed the cover with a padded elbow, setting off a blaring base-wide alarm. The small hardwire box Cance had entrusted him with hooked easily to the locks and repeated the same repetitious jumble of numbers. One by one, they clicked into place.

"Atmospheric Purge System activated. Secondary authorization required for this action." The Assembly's computer spoke in the rhythmic feminine alto typical of Taelach-installed systems. The hardwire box clicked in response, this time a much shorter series of numbers flashing across its screen.

"No!" screamed Longhair. "The security grid, not atmospheric controls!"

"Security matrix controls are designated by yellow key locks, black is for atmospheric controls only." The reply came as the final number unencrypted. "Atmospheric purge system on line. Deionization to begin in five minutes."

"Raskhallak's wrath and hell's glory, what have I done?" Longhair pounded the control panel. "Shut it down!"

"Off moon authorization from two remote locations is required for that action. Four minutes thirty seconds remaining." Longhair started throwing random key locks. "Environmental purge sequence automatically disables all other systems," replied the computer. "No further action is necessary. Four minutes ten seconds remaining. Immediate evacuation of all remaining personnel is required at this time."

The same countdown that sounded in the Center's Assembly echoed across all of Langus. Firman and Krell skidded to a stop, mortified when they heard the announcement.

"No!"

"Get us out of here, Krell!"

"LaRenna!"

"Cance wouldn't stay on a moon on its way to a purge," shouted Firman, "and neither should we!" He jerked her arm until she resumed running. They reached the Taelach-designated platforms a few seconds later, running straight into Tatra.

"Open this thing!" She tugged at the doors of planetary launch.

Krell entered her access code, released the door latch, and followed the others inside. Firman secured the hatch while Krell began the preflight functions necessary to disengage the landing locks.

"Let's go!" Tatra's primped face twisted with terror.

"Sit down and hold on! It's fixing to get bumpy!" warned Krell and the engines roared to life. She throttled the craft upward, bounding it into flight with a violent rock that sent Tatra careening to the floor. Firman pulled her up, planted her in the seat next to his, and secured her safety harness.

"When Krell says hold on, she means it." Tatra nodded and held fast to her seat, the first time Firman had ever seen her without a showy comeback.

They entered the lower levels of the Langus atmosphere as the countdown ended. Violent sulfurous thunderheads could be seen forming to the south, blue-green streaks of lightning cracking through them. Tatra turned to watch in gruesome fascination, her mouth opening and closing in awe. Firman jeered at her indiscretion and jerked her back around. "I once heard a story about a woman who died when she looked back to witness the destruction of a city. Best not tempt fate."

171

"Sounds like one of Krell's stories from the ancient human colony." Tatra glowered at him but remained facing forward.

"It is one of my stories, Tatra. It's about a man named Lot and his wife who turned to a pillar of salt for being sick-minded enough to watch the death of others." Krell rotated the pilot's seat. "We're clear of Langus. The *Predator* has signaled. It'll be here within the hour. Not a word from either of you about LaRenna not being with us. I'll tell her raisers myself. It's my duty." Krell glanced around the craft in search of their baggage. If nothing else, LaRenna's personal effects might provide some comfort. "Where's our stuff?"

"I think we left it on the platform," replied Firman.

"Oh." Krell turned back to the controls and sank back in her seat, crying softly. It wasn't that the material items mattered, but they had been tangible. They were all she had possessed of LaRenna and now they, too, were gone.

Chapter Twenty-six

Necessity can make competitors into coconspirators.

—*Taelach wisdom*

Third Engineer Malley Whellen stood at her station, reading the updates on the Iralian fleet's position. Master Engineer Freena Ockson, her lengthy braids looped neatly behind one ear, pushed past her, rushing here and there in final preparations for battle. "Anything new, Whellen?" Ockson was elbow deep in fine-tuning the *Predator's* forward shield array.

"We seem to be faring well," replied Malley. "The largest of the Iralian ships has been crippled. It's retreated behind the boundary line."

"Thanks be to the Mother for that small miracle," said Ockson wistfully. "I was hoping for something good to tell Grandmaster Exzal. You schooled with her daughter, didn't you?"

"Yes, Master Ockson, I did."

"Pity to lose one so young."

"What?" Malley spun around.

"Hadn't you heard? She was posted on Langus."

"Oh my." Malley fell hard against the wall. Ockson assisted her to a seat at the deck's massive worktable.

"I wouldn't have told you if I had known it would affect you so, child." Ockson looked sympathetically at Malley. "You knew her well?"

"We roomed together for over three passes." Malley's stomach churned. "I never got to tell her goodbye at the Training Grounds."

"You have my deepest sympathies. I'm sure she was a good friend." Ockson helped Malley into a seat. "Was your relationship with—" The deck lift doors slid open and both engineers came to attention, Malley sniffling as Belsas came on deck.

"Grandmaster Exzal!" Ockson held a tight salute Belsas quickly returned. "There is good news to report. The *Blackmore* has been heavily damaged. She's retreated her position."

"That is good to hear. At rest, Engineers. Return to your duties." Belsas took the worktable's lead chair, letting the others situate themselves before speaking. Malley, as required, stepped back to her workstation but kept an ear to the discussion.

"Let me introduce my companions," said Belsas with a wide sweep of her arm. "You know my life mate, Chandrey Belsas." Ockson and Chandrey exchanged brief pleasantries. "Beside her is First Kimshee Krell Middle and, uh—"

Firman leaned across the table to shake Ockson's hand. "Guess I'm literally the odd man out here," he chuckled. "I'm Firman Middle, Assistant Hiring Hallmaster at what used to be South Coast Langus. It's a pleasure."

"Odd staff if I do say so, Belsas." Ockson smiled wryly at her old friend. "This is my assistant, Third Engineer Malley Whellen." Ockson patted the remaining seat at the table. "Sit, Whellen. You'll fall over if you lean this direction any farther. Program your station screen to read at the table."

"Thank you, Master Ockson." Malley took her seat and kept her eyes focused on the screen.

Krell sat back. "Malley Whellen? The name is familiar."

"It should be, Krell," said Chandrey. "Malley is LaRenna's best friend from the Training Grounds. How are you, Malley?"

"Devastated to hear about LaRenna," Malley replied faintly. "I'll miss her."

"She's not dead!" Krell pounded the table. "She's very much alive. It's just a matter of time until we find her."

"Please excuse First Kimshee Middle's shortness," said Belsas. "Krell Middle is LaRenna's intended. That's why she and her brother are here. The *Predator* is going to lead the search for my daughter and those holding her captive."

"Where do we begin?" asked Ockson, surprised the news had failed to relieve Malley. "There are an endless number of places they could be headed."

"Sarian space wouldn't be safe for them." Krell pondered the envious glare she was receiving from Malley. "There was an Iralian in the group. We should begin by scanning for lone launches headed toward the system's edge."

"Whellen, initiate the necessary program. I'll take the updates myself." Ockson input a string of commands into her terminal. "Seems we have the Iralians on the defensive. Twelve ships destroyed. Ten theirs, two ours."

"Either of them Taelach?" asked Belsas.

Firman raised his brows. "Does them being Autlach make the loss any less significant?" he asked.

"No, it doesn't," replied Belsas. "Any losses at all are too many. I do, however, need to know the status of my own forces."

"Neither of them were Taelach vessels." Ockson reviewed the crew manifests of the fallen ships. "But there were two Taelach officers serving on one and a Kimshee in transport on the other."

"Master Ockson, I think I've found something." Malley pushed away from the table. Ockson read her findings and clasped Malley's back in congratulations. "Excellent work. Why don't you transfer this to the wall viewer and share your discovery."

Malley activated the wall screen behind the worktable and stood to one side. "At any time there are twenty thousand or more planetary launches in use." Everyone nodded at what was common knowledge. "That would typically make tracing one almost impossible."

"Get on with it, Third Officer," said Krell. "Time is wasting."

"However," Malley's voice rose against the disruption, "all non-military traffic was suspended yesterday. That left only twenty-one launch flights on record. Only four of those are currently en route." Malley tapped the wall controls, bringing up a large diagram of the Sarian system. Five distinct dots appeared on the display—four blue, the other a fiery orange. Malley indicated the four blue ones. "These are the authorized launch flights, and this"—Malley pointed directly to the swift moving orange marker—"is a rogue."

"It's moving too quickly to be a planetary launch," observed Chandrey.

"Not if it's been fitted with hyperburners," countered Firman. "Is it a full launch or personal two-passenger?"

"Two-seater by my estimate," Malley replied.

"Then it's not what we're looking for." Belsas slapped the table in frustration. "Damn!"

"Hold on." Firman leaned to his sibling. "Think Cance might've outfitted it like the old land launch we tinkered with when we were kids?"

"It's possible," said Krell. "Very possible. Where is the craft headed, Whellen?"

"At present course, it will reach the *Blackmore's* pre-retreat coordinates in three hours."

"Point of origin?"

"The tracking beacon has been deactivated, but its flight path suggests Langus."

All eyes were on Krell and Firman. "What are you two brewing?" Chandrey prayed she was reading their expressions correctly.

"We once had an old two-passenger land launch," explained

176

Firman. "We rebuilt it when we were youths, ripped out the cargo area behind the standard seats and installed additional seating. Why couldn't Cance have done the same to a planetary launch? It's faster than a standard four-seater, especially if you add boosters."

Belsas clenched her fists by her side as she rose. "Ockson," she said officiously, "have your crew set an intercept course. We've found LaRenna."

Chapter Twenty-seven

The Mother Maker has her own way of righting any wrong.

—Taelach reasoning

"Watch it!" Cance centered more firmly in her seat. The screen before her was smeared with blood, the impact point between her shoulder and the front console when the launch had lurched forward.

"You want I should hit the next one?" Trazar dragged his tunic cuff across the smear so he could read the launch's status. "I'd be more than happy to oblige. Your body would add to the rubble."

"Watch your mouth, sentry, or I'll pop your sister's lip for your insolence."

Trazar leaned back in his seat and gripped the flight stick a little tighter. The coordinates Cance had required him to program into the flight program were coming up, so he concentrated on the heading, jerking the craft as another slab of floating debris crossed their path.

"What the fuck are you doing?" Cance pulled from the side bulkhead. "I thought you were pilot qualified."

"I am!" bellowed Trazar, struggling to maintain control of the craft. "We've come across some kind of wreckage."

Talmshone, taut muscles braced against the rocking, peered out the side viewport. His breath fogged the window. "Battle remains," he sighed. "Iralian vessels. Are we near the proper coordinates?"

"All but." Trazar glanced at the console screen. Saria Four cast an impressive blue and green reflection off the launch's transparent metallic windows. It had none of the gray pollution bands of the Autlach home world, save for the smudge surrounding the port city of Polmel.

"Where's the ship, Talmshone?" Cance flicked her dagger from palm to palm. "Where's the *Blackmore?*" She turned full around, looking expectantly at the Iralian as she pointed the blade like a finger.

"Obviously delayed," he answered in the most unfazed of voices. Suddenly, the launch gave a violent heave that cracked Cance's chin on the seat back. LaRenna winced as her own jaw bounced hard against her chest.

"Dammit!" Cance slid back around to cuff Trazar's upper arm. "Keep this thing under control. That's not a request."

"Then buckle in!" Trazar ducked a second blow meant for his face. "I'm not responsible for the ride being rough!"

"Dodge me, will you? I warned you about having a smart mouth." Cance gave LaRenna's bobbed hair a cruel yank. LaRenna squealed then caught the side of Cance's hand and bit down.

"OW!" Cance jerked back to examine the line of cuts. "So you want to bite, little girl?" Her expression was half-amused, half-wanton. "I'll teach you all about it as soon as we dock. I promise to make it a lesson you'll never, ever forget." She sucked at the wound and sat back, incensed as she watched Saria Four spin. "Ungrateful whore. I should have let Brandoff screw you to death. You'll learn soon enough, or die in ignorance."

Trazar stifled a cheer for his sister's diligence as he slowed the launch. "We're at the coordinates."

"They're not here!" Cance's smile reversed to a livid scowl directed at Talmshone. "Where the fuck are they?"

"How should I know?" Talmshone was beginning to lose the ominous calm he normally maintained. "I have been out of contact with the Commitment for over a Sarian cycle. Steady communications would have been impractical."

Trazar cringed as he eyed the lowering charge indicators. If he alone had been captive, he would have said nothing and simply let the launch and his problems burn in Saria Four's atmosphere. But he wasn't, and if LaRenna could fight he would do the same. "We don't have the fuel to stay here long. What do you want me to do?"

"Take orbit." Cance clicked her tongue. "Now the damned fuel's low. Nothing seems to be going as you assured me it would. You didn't double-cross me, did you, lizard man?"

"Lizard man?" Talmshone blinked at his accomplice through angry red eyes. "May I remind you that we are in the same proverbial boat."

"Then we wait." Cance leaned forward to check the launch's main data banks. Tapped into Taelach military channels, they were an excellent means of information provided one knew the correct access codes. The lower-level codes were often changed but were easily circumvented, a skill Cance had learned from Brandoff. "Your boys aren't faring well at all, Talmshone. In fact, they're taking quite a thrashing. Give me the *Blackmore's* frequency so I can check its position."

"Iralian transmissions are encrypted and shielded." He surveyed the wreckage for identifying markings. "You can neither read or track them."

"Yeah, right." But Cance was at a loss for what to do without further codes. "What's the Kinship's high-security call sign for the *Blackmore*, girl?"

"I don't know," whispered LaRenna. Even the quietest of conversations blasted inside her head.

"Sure you do." Cance pressed her dagger to LaRenna's throat. "The *Blackmore* is head of the Commitment's Eyonnic fleet, has been since I served. An active Kimshee knows the codes. Think hard."

"No."

"Tch, tch. Such disrespect so close to ignominious defeat. I suggest you give Cance what she requires." Talmshone cast LaRenna an intolerant smile. "Her fuse is burning sparse and so is mine." He pressed his rough-scaled face against the side of hers, the skin cool in comparison to his pungent breath. "I do admire your bravery, LaRenna. Iralian justice would reward your courageous behavior with painless death followed by the grandest of banquets in your honor. But regrettably, we are not in Iralian space and I have not indulged in fresh meat for an extended period." The Iralian spread his gargantuan hand across her knees, flexing his fingers a minimal amount to demonstrate their sheer power, digging his talons into her flesh to prove his point. "You are still quite young and tender, my dear, and so very tempting to my hungry midsection that I will happily make a meal of you if you do not concede."

"Give them what they want, LaRenna." Trazar glanced over his shoulder long enough to see fear leaching through the stubbornness in his sister's pale eyes. As brave as she might be, she must comply. "He'll hurt you in ways Cance never could."

"4 breakbar 72 matka 112 call over kol 6."

"Got it." Cance entered the codes with a light skim of the symbol board. "Now we know how to get information from her."

"Indeed we do." The Iralian removed his hand, but continued to hold his face tightly against hers. "I will not repeat my demonstration a second time." LaRenna stared straight ahead, breathing heavily. "There is nothing left for me to lose and a full stomach to gain. Do you comprehend what I am saying, young female?"

"Yes." Sweat dripped from LaRenna's temples, stinging the

scrapes in her eyes. She was afraid of him in an infinitely different way from Cance and rightly so. Iralians were known for consuming their prisoners piece by piece while keeping them barely alive. An honorary banquet was just that, with the dead the centerpiece and main course.

"Excellent." Talmshone lounged back and picked at his yellowed teeth with a talon. "There is a time to be noble," he observed, "and a time to think of survival. The difficulty is deciding which applies to the situation at hand. I believe you made the wise choice, young LaRenna. My stomach growls with disappointment, but my mind approves."

As Talmshone spoke, the launch's database finally produced the information Cance requested. She read it repeatedly, smacking at the screen a little harder with each run through. "No, no, dammit. No! NO!"

"Is there a problem, dearest Cance?" Talmshone sounded particularly smug with himself.

"Damn right there is, you double-dealing water serpent." Cance aimed her bow at him. "The *Blackmore* has retreated behind the truce line. I'm stranded!"

"I believe that should be plural, Taelach." Talmshone's eyes whirled with anger so red they flared purple. He blinked once, then again, then pointed toward the humming bow. "You can fire on me if you see fit." He shrugged indifferently. "But, consider this before you do. You miss, you will blow a hole in the launch and we all suffer. Hit your mark, and I will most assuredly rip your arm off before you can trigger a second." Taelach stared at Iralian, each anticipating the other's next action.

Cance's prock levels had receded to the extent that she shook. "Or, I could do you like I did Starnes."

"You try and I will once again remove part of your anatomy, most likely your head." They stared at each other for several more tense moments, Cance's tongue giving periodic clicks of aggravation.

LaRenna opened a weak link to her brother, sending a tickle down his spine. *Maybe they'll kill each other.*

Wouldn't that be poetic justice? Trazar picked up on the mental touch and embraced it, hoping LaRenna could hear his thoughts. *Keep still no matter what happens.*

I hear you, she replied. *Where am I going to go? I'm trussed up like a roast for the spit.*

That's what we'll both be if Talmshone gets hungry enough.

Not funny, Trazar.

It wasn't meant to be. Now rest your head. This must take incredible effort.

You have latent empathic abilities I can tap into, so it's not too difficult. But Trazar pushed for honesty. *Okay, okay. My head is splitting.*

I should say it is.

Was that a joke?

Yeah, a really bad one. You have a prock hangover. I've seen it in sentries returning from post on Trimar. They have to try it just once before they go. Idiots. They had a choice. Close the link, little sister, and save your strength. As their mental tie broke, a low chuckle began to rise from Cance. She lowered her bow and broke out in a hysterical laugh that prompted an even more aggressive stare from Talmshone.

"Would you look at us?" she cackled. "We're at each other's throats when the answer is right here with us." She crawled halfway across the seat, grabbed LaRenna's face, forcing a full, passionate kiss into her mouth. "I would have enjoyed a small bite with that, lover." Cance's mouth curved in perverse teasing. "Talmshone, we forgot our backup."

"You intend to part with your woman?" Talmshone inquired as he watched Cance draw a generous recharge from her inhaler.

"They'll think I am." Cance nodded toward Trazar between puffs. "But that won't be what they get."

Talmshone's leer turned gruesome. "Apologies regarding my earlier indiscretions. It appears you do indeed have matters well in hand."

"Always did." Cance pushed a momentary phase into LaRenna. *You're mine, LaRenna, from now until forever. Accept the love I give. I'm your sole protector from the universe. I'm the only one who cares.*

Cance sighed with the phase's release and held the inhaler to LaRenna's face. "Want a hit to celebrate, my sweet? No? Well, we'll just save it for your next lesson." Victory permeated her drawl. "Sentry, open communications with Saria Four. We have a deal to make."

The *Predator* was a mere hour away when the transmission arrived. Belsas and Chandrey were already on the battle deck waiting when Krell and Firman stormed in. "Anything yet?" asked Krell.

"No. Communications is stalling until we can pinpoint their exact location." Belsas waved them to empty seats adjacent the viewer. "It shouldn't be long."

The lift hatch opened again and Ockson, Malley in tow, rushed onto the deck. "Whellen," huffed the master Engineer, skidding into a chair, "cut on the viewer and inform the main that we're ready."

Chandrey grasped Belsas's hand. "Don't worry, pet." Belsas smiled tenderly at her. "Cance can't harm you from this distance."

"Yes she can." Chandrey's voice trembled. "She has LaRenna."

"A temporary condition I plan on remedying." They settled into their respective seats but remained closely linked under the table, Chandrey's slender fingers disappearing in Belsas's supporting grip.

Ockson tapped the table. "We're ready."

All eyes focused on the wall screen as Cance Creiloff's belligerent sneer came into focus. Two long scratches jagged across her face and her bottom lip was swollen. "Hello, Belsas." Her voice fairly oozed hollow sweetness. Chandrey shuddered and jumped at the sound, finding herself more shaken than she had anticipated. "Good to see you, too, Chandrey." Cance laughed. "How are you, darling? You look well. Miss me?"

"No games." Belsas drew forward, partially shielding Chandrey from view. "What are your terms?"

"Not so fast, old girl. I have a question for you first." Cance sighed at the sight of Chandrey's flowing hair. The desire was still there, as sickeningly overpowering as the need for control that accompanied it. "Some things never change, do they, Chandrey my love? The mere sight of you still drives me wild." Cance held up her hand as if to stop the flood of emotions unleashed by the sight of LaRenna's gentler raiser. "No, no, there's no time to express what I've been holding back all these passes. Maybe later. Preferably face to face. Right now, I have business to discuss with your sorry bitch of a guardian. So, Belsas, history comes to haunt the historian. How does it feel to be on the receiving end for a change?"

"I'm not playing your games this time, Cance." Belsas could feel Chandrey's grasp increasing, slick with sweat, underneath the table. "Bring her back."

"Bring who back?" Cance winked at Chandrey.

"You know who. What's your price?"

"Wellll . . ." Cance dragged the word to its fullest. "How about safe passage for three out of Sarian space?"

"You're charged with mass murder," replied Belsas. "I can't grant passage with that on your head and you know it."

"Belsas." Bitterness replaced Cance's sugary tone. "They were only Auts. I was doing the Kinship a favor. The least you can do is promise passage."

"No, I can't."

Cance's mouth began to twitch. "You can do anything you damn well please, you puckered excuse for a Taelach. Now give me what I need and I'll consider your request."

"I'll give you passage back to Trimar until you stand judgment. The Iralian comes straight into custody. Brandoff is dead, so I know nothing of your third member. Tell me who it is and I may grant them passage to Trimar."

Cance avoided the last remark. "What Iralian?"

"We found a single four-toe track at the Waterlead." Krell joined the conversation.

"Who's your overgrown lackey, Belsas?"

"One of my assistants. Listen, Cance, I—"

"I . . . don't . . . think . . . so." The words inched out in slow, stabbing pulses, Cance's smile broadening with each syllable. "You're Krell, aren't you? You're the one she cries for every time I do her. I've heard your name so many times it disgusts me. Brandoff gave her a beating over it and she still wouldn't shut up. You better talk some sense into that high and mighty leader of yours, otherwise, you'll never see your fresh-tasting little girl again. I demand safe passage for myself and two others through all Sarian space. No deals. No exceptions."

"You've already stated your—"

Cance cut Krell short. "Don't interrupt me, Kimshee. I wasn't finished. These are the only terms I will accept. In return, I'll give back what's left of your woman."

"Cance Creiloff," bellowed Belsas, "if you've done as much as touched one hair on her head, so help me I'll—"

"You'll what?" Cance was openly amused by the threat. "I have her. She's mine to do with as I please. Not only have I touched every hair on her entire body, I've kissed, fondled, and made sweet, sweet, delicious love to them. She's perfect, just like Chandrey. She still has a thing or two to learn about ownership, but she's a smart girl and I'm a willing teacher. Why, I've even gone as far as to blood-mark her. What are you going to do about it, Belsas, blow me from the sky? I have your precious daughter with me. Go ahead, I dare you!"

"All your talk means nothing if she's dead," said Krell after a moment's silence. "Let us see her."

"Take my word for it. I don't have to prove a damn thing, you Kimshee slut."

"Then we must presume she's dead." Krell's heart broke at the prospect. "No deals."

"You're letting a mere first Kimshee do your negotiating, Belsas?" Cance laughed haughtily. "You must be getting feeble-minded in your old age. Chandrey, how could you choose such a rusted-up creature over me? I've aged decidedly better than that and so have you."

"You've aged like the sorry addict you've become." Chandrey spoke with a strength she never knew she possessed. "What Krell says stands. Show us LaRenna. Let us talk to her or I'll personally issue the order to destroy you."

"My, my, my, but haven't we gotten feisty over time. Belsas must not beat you enough. Now I know where LaRenna gets the idea she's equal to a guardian. I slapped it out of you and I'll slap it out of her." This unfamiliar side of Chandrey disturbed Cance, rattling her intentions until she briefly yielded. "I must be getting sentimental. All right, Chandresslandra, you want her, you got her." Cance adjusted the launch's recorder lens to view the rear seating. Talmshone, his talons at Trazar's throat to ensure silence, leaned against the far bulkhead, clear of the recorder's range. Just because they knew of his presence did not mean he wanted to make an appearance. Cance kissed LaRenna then moved back, one hand on LaRenna's head to remind all watching just who maintained dominance. "Say hello to the folks at home, lover. Tell them what a wonderful time we're having."

LaRenna pulled her head to her chest so her hair concealed the marks on her face. She couldn't bear the thought of anyone she loved seeing her in this condition.

"LaRenna, look up." Krell's voice was a ray of light in the dark depths of her fragile soul. She glanced up briefly, then looked away, hopelessly embarrassed. "LaRenna?" Krell's voice sent another wave flowing into LaRenna's heart. She raised her head a little more, trying to focus on the launch's small viewer.

"Krell?"

"Yes, LaRenna, it's me. Are you okay?"

"I'm tired." Her response was truly that.

"I know you are. Be brave. You'll be home soon."

"Home?" The concept sounded foreign. LaRenna pulled her head up fully, straining to see the image that accompanied the caring voice. She had to see Krell.

"Precious Renna." Krell's pain had been more than illusion. "Be strong. We'll get you home soon."

Cance jerked the lens forward. "You've seen her, now do we have a deal or—" The screen died into a spotty feed of static.

"Get them back!" screamed Belsas.

Ockson pecked feverishly at the terminal. "It's not on our end. They must be having power difficulties."

As quickly as it went blank, the screen burst back to life. The transmission was hazy, but Cance's frenzy was crystal clear. "Belsas Exzal, you fucker! You tracked us by our sig . . . we're going down! You'll never see her . . . if she survives this, I swear I'll . . . before you can reach her!" The reception dimmed and crackled as the launch's power supply diverted to emergency systems.

"What's happening?" Krell couldn't breathe. LaRenna was everywhere in her mind.

KKKRRREELLL!

Ockson pounded away at her board, desperate to gather as much information as possible before the launch dropped from orbit. "The Iralians left a tracer charge. It homed in on the launch's transmission signal. They had no intention of retrieving their spy."

Krell cried out as the pleading cry grew louder, shrieking against the mental blast echoing in her skull. *KRRREEELLLLL!*

"LARENNA! NO!" she cried.

"My baby!" Chandrey fell forward across the table, arms outstretched to catch her falling child. "LaRenna!"

Cance's obscene ranting was reduced to a single string of erratic syllables that were barely decipherable among the frantic cries on the *Predator*. "You— Crash— Help— Die—" Then, it stopped, Krell's mental tirade halting abruptly as well.

"LaRenna, no darlin', no."

"Krell, I'm sorry." Firman grabbed her arm to stop her fall.

She pushed him away. "No. This is all wrong. I just found her again. I just told her. No!"

"Krell—" She knocked his compassionate hand away.

"No!"

"Krell?"

"She's not dead." She had managed to regain control. "I feel her. I hear her heartbeat."

"Oh, Krelleesha," he sighed. The denial was familiar. Their father had experienced much the same reaction when their mother passed away. Krell didn't remember, but he did. The death hadn't sunk into him for several cycles, leaving the family's well-being solely in a young Firman's lap until their father had regained his faculties.

There were no tears in Belsas's battle-hardened eyes. "Whellen, you were LaRenna's friend. Please contact my compound on Saria Three and notify them of our loss."

"Yes, Grandmaster." Malley, preferring to grieve in silence, slowly withdrew from the room.

Belsas's hands were icy on Chandrey's slumped shoulders. "Ockson, have your crew prepare a recovery detail. I'll assist. We must bring my daughter home to rest."

"It's the least I could do, Belsas." Ockson silently followed Malley out the lift doors.

Last, Belsas addressed Krell in a no less officious tone. "You're needed on the recovery detail as well. LaRenna was your intended. You must travel to Saria Three with the body so you can witness the death rites."

"I'll go to the surface," she replied. "But it won't be to recover a corpse." Krell peered at Saria Four. It wasn't such a big place, most of the landmass on the Reisfall continent, the remainder scattered on dozens of small islands. LaRenna was on the continent, Krell was certain, unconscious but breathing, dreaming of nothing but Krell's impending rescue. The dream link would help, be a beacon for Krell to follow. And Krell had to follow, for where LaRenna was so was Krell, bound by desire and heart, dependence of mind and body. She shoved off Firman's helping hands, and rose to stand before Belsas, her face hardened with resolve. "No, there will be no funeral fires, no memorial, no ashes scattered. LaRenna is alive and I have every intention of finding her."

Chapter Twenty-eight

The storms of life are oftentimes longer and rougher than any nature can create.

—Taelach wisdom

———————————

Thunder rumbled at a distance, lightning flaring the clouds into brilliance. A drizzle began to fall, pooling then trickling water into the launch's twisted remains, where a pencil-thin stream dripped onto Trazar's face and into his nose, waking him with a chilled, choking start. Disoriented, head pounding from the hard crack it had received, he wondered why the safety straps felt so tight. He shifted position and his splintered left armrest fell past his head to clang on the ceiling. The ceiling? Trazar became aware of his location. The launch had toppled bottom up in the crash, leaving its passengers dangling upside down.

He rested his feet on the launch's metal framework then disengaged his harness. Rolling out of the seat, he crouched for a minute in his topsy-turvy setting. When his head cleared, he checked the other passengers.

Cance was nowhere to be seen. Her console was smashed beyond repair and the clear aluminum window in front of her seat was missing. Talmshone was unconscious and bleeding profusely from his side. A metal support rod had broken loose during the crash and run him almost through. LaRenna hung limp in her restraints, her hands brushing the ceiling. The pressure of the straps had restricted her airflow to the point her skin was tinged blue. Trazar carefully unlatched her harness and pulled her into his arms.

Her right foot was pinned beneath Cance's seat. Trazar turned her so her calf and knee were aligned with the break, then lowered her slowly until her shoulders rested on the ceiling.

"My leg," she mumbled.

"It's the same one as before." He pushed against the seat. "Let me look." Trazar gently touched the splint. The ankle had popped back out of joint, this time penetrating her flesh. The bones of her calf were knocked from alignment and pushed black against her skin. Her heel hung from the bone in fleshy strips. Blood streaked the entirety of her leg.

"Bad, isn't it?" she asked. The foot was numb, making the extremity seem curiously detached.

"No worse than before," declared Trazar. "We just need to get it loose." He began scrounging for something to use as a pry bar.

"How about that hatch brace?" inquired LaRenna. "It's cracked at both ends."

"Excellent idea." Trazar crawled to the door. The piece fit perfectly under the chair frame, allowing him to free her tattered limb. He eased it out and examined the wounds, his dour expression not lost to his sister's sore but observant eyes. "I'm going to remove the splint."

"I believe it's beyond the splint." LaRenna winced at the sight of her mangled leg. "No worse than before, eh? Liar. It's all but gone. But you said that for my benefit, didn't you? Thanks, Trazar.

A little fantasy is what I need at this moment." Then her face took an odd, highly anxious twist, her concern now more for him than herself. "Mother's mercy, look at you!" She pressed his forehead. "No tales this time, Commander. Your head hurt? You've quite a knot coming up."

"My skull is shattering with every throb of my heart," he moaned, grinning then withdrawing when her expression turned longer. "Don't worry about me. It's just one of many bumps to the head I've endured in my life. It'll add nicely to what the lizard gave me." He pulled away when she touched the tender nodule again. "Now that hurts, LaRenna. Hands off. So, as long as we're comparing injuries, how are the ribs?"

"Don't ask." She returned his theatrical moan, but something in the sound told Trazar little acting was involved. "Whatever our ills, I think we both fared better than Talmshone." They glanced at the inversed Iralian, whose breathing had slowed to a wheeze.

"We couldn't help him now if we tried." Trazar was, at most, distantly sympathetic.

"I've never seen his kind before." LaRenna was intrigued by the Iralian's resemblance to many common Sarian reptiles.

"Pray you never do again. They're ruthless. They teach sentries to kill themselves if they become captive."

"Taelachs, too." She broke her curious gaze. "Better than becoming a meal one limb at a time." Then LaRenna abruptly tensed and scanned the cockpit, her joy over survival doused by promised lessons. "Where is she?"

"Cance? Thrown from the launch would be my guess. Serves her right for not strapping in." His assuring words did nothing to ease her mind. "Would you feel better if I took a look?"

"Please." LaRenna's hands felt her marked face. The mental wounds would be much slower in healing. "I'm not sure I can fight her off again. How Chandrey survived being oathed to such a beast I'll never know."

"You're stronger than you think." Trazar clenched his fist. "And this time she'll have to go through me to get to you."

192

"Be careful."

He took the hatch brace and scooted to the open front window. The wind was picking up. "Stay away from the opening. I'll be back soon."

"Hurry, Trazar." LaRenna shivered. "A storm's coming."

"Call if you need me." The ground surrounding the crash was layered with charred wreckage and twisted metal. Cursing the deluge that began to fall, he flipped over the lighter pieces with the brace, looking for any sign of Cance. Nothing crossed his path in the immediate area of the launch, so he expanded his search pattern, scattering wreckage further in his quest. During one of the lightning bursts, the unmistakable glint of Taelach weaponry caught his eye. Trazar approached it warily, the brace raised club-like above his head.

Cance lay facedown in the mud. Her plasma bow had entangled in a shrub's upper limbs, grotesquely stretching her arm when she fell. Trazar was now glad he had been unable to land safely. He used the brace to free Cance's arm and flip her over. Her eyes fluttered then opened. "LaRenna." Her face contorted in agony. "Did she survive?"

"No thanks to you." Trazar raised the brace.

"Bring her to me."

"Never."

"Make it my last request."

"I wouldn't put her through that." Trazar lifted Cance's arm and let it drop. There was no muscle reaction, no response. She was paralyzed from high neck down, her body functions failing one after another. "You deserve to die like this, like some dumb beast with its head up and mouth open in wonder of the rain. Drowning suits you."

"Bring me LaRenna." Cance spat out the rain that ran into her mouth. "I want to die in my beauty's arms, in the warmth of her phase."

"You don't deserve such pleasure. Mine will be the last face you see, last voice you hear."

Trazar brushed the mud from her cragged face. "Where's your inhaler? I'll grant you that small salvation."

"My cloak pocket," she mumbled between gurgling breaths. "Mother praise you for this."

"Your blessed Mother has nothing to do with it. You damned yourself long ago." Trazar jerked her muddy cloak free of her body and rifled through the pocket. "I don't want you howling when the end comes. It'll scare LaRenna."

"Then hurry up," said Cance in a strangely helpless, girl-child's voice. "I'm just short of it now."

"It's not here." Trazar smoothed her cloak over her body. "Must have blown off in the crash. What else can I do to make you comfortable?"

"Bring my woman!" Cance's chest began to tighten. "She must know how much I love her."

"Love?" He tried to shush her cries with his hand. "That was love?"

"As I only know and can give. Where's your compassion, man? This is my dying wish. She's mine. Bring her now!"

"No. Quiet yourself."

"I will not!" The tightness had become crippling, pushing Cance into the dirt. "If you won't bring her, then strike me and end it. Do it now! You know you want to," she gasped. "There's a joy in taking another's life, a high greater than prock, more satisfying than forcing yourself on another." She stared at him a moment, then summoning up the last of her strength, bellowed at him, "Do it, Trazar! I won't be silent until you do."

"I know the high." He held the brace above his head. "It's a gruesome, sickening feeling, a whisper for more. I sense it now. But I'll not do it for that reason. Not for pleasure or vengeance. Not because you warrant it." The brace pierced Cance's chest. She arched, flexed into the blow then collapsed, Chandrey's then LaRenna's name escaping in her final breath.

"There must be peace. She has to know you're gone." He withdrew the brace, cleaning it against the grass. "May the Taelach

Mother forgive me." He took Cance's knife then scurried back to the launch, pulling a large piece of debris over the open window to deflect some of the deluge. "Miss me?"

LaRenna opened her eyes. "Did you find her?"

Trazar nodded his wet head in her face, glad he could respond in a way that would provide relief. "She's dead."

"Not soon enough." LaRenna closed her eyes again, covering them with her hands as tears began to fall. Unsure of what else to do, Trazar pulled her to him. She fell against him when she was touched, shuddering violently, mumbling incoherently. Eventually, and as the pain in her sides became great, her quiet sobs eased then ceased all together. "I'm sorry," she mumbled, clearing her eyes.

"Better? At least a little?" He brushed the hair from her face.

"Somewhat. I—I'm sorry I broke down like that. I don't know what came over me."

"It's called trauma, LaRenna, and no one, even a Kimshee, is above its effect." The emergency lights flickered as wind began to rock the overturned launch. "We'd best wrap your foot before the lighting gives out." Trazar settled her into a corner, then took Cance's dagger, using it to slice off portions of Talmshone's trousers. "Don't think he'll be needing these and we need the rags."

"Guess not." LaRenna smiled at him for the first time since the night they met. It was a mere speck of a turn, but a vast improvement over her earlier state.

"You smile like your older sister Mercy."

"I do?"

"Yep." Trazar undid her splint. "You're an aunt."

"Really? Tell me about our family." LaRenna appreciated the distraction. "Are our parents still alive?"

Trazar fumbled through the launch's emergency stores. "Dah is, though I'm not sure how he'll handle the news of you."

"What do you mean?"

He placed a small medical kit and two blankets by her side. "Your name is listed on the Death Stone above our farming com-

195

pound. Everyone thinks you died at birth." Trazar held the hatch brace to her shin. "I'm going to immobilize your leg."

"He listed me as dead because I'm Taelach, didn't he?" LaRenna could tell by her older brother's sullen manner she was correct.

He gazed at her then shrugged, his reply flat and somewhat embarrassed. "On Vartoch it's commonplace to list Taelach children as deceased. Most Autlachs where I'm from have an outdated view of the Taelach, LaRenna. Bearing one mars a family's reputation. Your people are still very much feared." He returned to the emergency stores case and handed her a bottle of water and ration pack. "Here, you need the strength."

"What about you?"

"I want to finish this first." Trazar turned his attention to her injured leg. He irrigated open wounds with liquid antibiotic from the medical kit, expressing mild surprise when LaRenna failed to react to the cold liquid's bubbling action. Next, he wrapped the ankle in a rolled bandage and positioned the brace on the underside of her leg. LaRenna watched with detached interest as he shredded one of the Iralian's trouser legs into binding strips and used them to secure the brace.

"All done." Trazar patted her good leg, understanding when she unconsciously jerked away. "You didn't feel a thing I did, did you?"

"No. And I know that's not good."

Trazar nodded then separated the ration pack her hands couldn't manage. "Eat something."

"You, too."

"All right already!" Trazar laughed. "Geez, you act like my sister or something."

"I'm not only your sister," she reminded him, her head at a subtle tilt that suggested teasing. "Sentry Commander Laiman, I am also your superior officer. So eat. That's an order."

"Yes, ma'am." Trazar saluted her and took a bite of dried meat. "This is really bad. It's old."

196

"Tough, too." LaRenna choked down a half-chewed bite and shoved the rations away. "I can't eat this. It hurts my jaw."

"Then eat your fruit preserves and crackers. They're still reasonably edible." He traded her meat for his tin of Taelach sweet rations. "Now I'm going to pull a little rank. Your big brother says to shut up and eat, so you'd better mind."

LaRenna stuck her tongue out in her typical mild defiance but did as he asked, finishing the first tin and half of the second by the time he had worked through one meat pack.

"Take this." She pushed the tin at him. "I can't eat anything else."

"Drink your water." Trazar cleaned out the second tin. "Then try to rest. Your eyes are burning in your head."

She slid down, stretched as much as she dared, and peered up at their awkward quarters.

"You know," she yawned, "it's a curious sensation to lie on the ceiling and look up at the floor."

"Even more so to wake up hanging from the floor." Trazar laughed again, happy see her outlook improving. "So tell me, are you and First Kimshee Middle oathed?"

LaRenna was puzzled by the query. "Why, you know Krell?"

"We're acquainted." Trazar thought of the late-night visit to his quarters. In hindsight, maybe he shouldn't have been quite so callous.

"No, we're not oathed." LaRenna let the subject drop as she searched for a position that didn't make her ache.

"Hold on." Trazar unfolded a blanket over her and lay beside her, his arm extended as a pillow. "Get as close as you can. It'll be cold by morning with this rain. We'll both need the heat." She gave him a brief, uncomfortable look then moved close. He spread the second blanket over them both, wrapping his pillowing arm around her until his hand rested palm down on her hair.

"Where's my cloak?" she asked with a fevered shiver.

"Long left behind, I'm afraid." The emergency lighting flickered then died, shrouding the launch in darkness. LaRenna began to shake again, not from cold or illness, but from the fiendish memories that leached in with the night. Trazar stroked her hair to remind her of his presence. "Remember what Krell told you. You're not alone. You're safe."

"Thank you." LaRenna relaxed into her brother's hold and listened to the rain. If it would only wash away some of the pain, some of the deep stains the twins had left on her.

Chapter Twenty-nine

Your deepest instincts should always take precedence over the doubts your mind projects.

—*Sarian Military Standards*

Chandrey knotted the deep blue mourning sash around her narrow waist and draped the excess fabric down her right side. Belsas's sash, though just as large, fit when worn across her shoulder and tucked into belt-line as was the traditional guardian manner. "It was kind of Ockson to provide us with sashing from the ship's stores." Chandrey joined her lover on the overstuffed divan in their temporary quarters. Belsas had remained silent since they had left the battle deck and now sat, staring blankly ahead.

"Bel?" Chandrey smoothed at the bottom section of hair Belsas had removed from her braid. She'd kept it in the same complicated plat for so many passes that the strands refused anything but a return to their accustomed position. Chandrey's hair had rejected the new styling as well, frizzing uncontrollably at the same site. "Bel?" she inquired more gently of her lover. "You all right?"

Belsas looked joylessly up then away. "I'm fine. Have a headache is all."

"Don't shut me out. You have to be feeling something."

"I'm not."

"Yes, you are. Talk to me."

Belsas scowled. "I told you my head hurts."

"I'll do no such thing. Tell me what's going through your mind."

"I told you, nothing!"

"Liar!" exclaimed Chandrey. "Our only child just died the most horrific of deaths and you have no sadness?"

"What do you want me to say?" Belsas slammed her hand against the divan's cushions. "How sorry I am? How it breaks my heart she's gone?"

"If it helps."

"Helps what? Bring LaRenna back?" Belsas ripped her braid from Chandrey's hand and rose from the divan. "She's dead. No amount of grieving on my part will change that."

"Heartless wretch." Chandrey returned Belsas's cold gaze. "Did you ever think that I might need you to grieve with me—that maybe what you are feeling needs to be shared? Am I alone in this?"

"Damnation, Chandrey, I told you twice now that I feel nothing. NOTHING! Nothing except dead inside."

"There are no regrets, remorse, nothing you wish you'd said to her before the crash? Nothing?" Chandrey's pale face turned an anguished pink. "I don't believe you."

"What do you want from me?" Belsas held her arms wide. "Tears? Guardians don't cry. It's unbecoming. The Taelach of All can't have emotions. She must be detached. The post won't allow for anything less."

"What of Belsas Exzal?" sighed Chandrey. "Is she incapable of emotions now as well? Does her post control her so completely?"

"My personal feelings run second to my post. They always have. I can have no regrets, no remorse, no doubts over what I have done in the line of duty."

Chandrey's skirt's twisted when she rose with a force echoed by her angry tone. "Well, I can! You sent my baby, my LaRenna, my only child to face the Creiloff twins, knowing what they did to me during the war. I hate you for that, almighty, unfeeling Taelach of All and I'll never, ever forgive you for it!" Chandrey stormed from the room. She had stood by Belsas and supported all her decisions for nearly thirty passes. Now, the one time she truly needed her guardian to be there for her, only her, Belsas shunned her. Chandrey kept a stoic appearance until she reached the deck's corner set meditation lounge. There, in the room's dim light, she knelt at the Mother Maker's small shrine and wept, begging her creator for the strength to understand and forgive.

On the battle deck, Krell threw her mourning sash to the floor. "She's not dead. I know it. Why won't any of you listen to me? She's hurt. She needs me. She needs us!" Krell turned toward Firman. "You believe me. Don't you?"

"Try to be realistic," he replied. "She was in poor condition before the crash happened. There was no way she could have survived."

"Here!" Krell retrieved the sash from the deck. "You're so damned convinced, you wear it!"

Firman removed the sash from her clenched fist and laid it on the worktable. "I know you loved her, Krell—"

"Love, not loved," she sputtered. "You don't speak of the living in the past tense. It's bad manners." Krell ran her palm over the picture of Saria Four spanning the wall viewer. "Where do you think we should begin looking? Listfeindale? The lower Reisfall ranges?"

"They'll have tracked the crash to a hundred-kilometer radius within the hour," he sighed.

The level lift doors slid open with an airy swoosh, admitting

Tatra. She glided across the room to give Krell a compassionate embrace. "I am so sorry. She was such a sweet girl."

"She's not dead, Tatra. She's down there." Krell tapped the view-screen, intent on the picture.

The Healer glanced at Firman. He shrugged and shook his head in similar bewilderment. "Denial," he whispered.

"There's nothing to deny!" exclaimed Krell, pushing Tatra away. "LaRenna is very much alive. I know it. I feel it in my heart."

"You're positive she's alive?" A physician's analytical tone seeped into Tatra's alto. Her concern for Krell now extended beyond the usual grief counseling and into her actual mental status. "How do you know? All indications are to the contrary."

Krell gazed at her in astonishment. "She's near. Can't you feel her? I hear her voice. Smell her scent. She's close, Tatra. Getting her back is all I can think of."

"Do you dream of her?"

"Every time I close my eyes." Krell's expression darkened. "Mostly nightmares as of late."

"Tell me about them."

Krell stepped back when she noticed the detached clinical expression on Tatra's face. "I don't need any of your psycho-analytical jargon trying to convince me I've lost my senses. I know she's alive. I know it!"

"Chances are she isn't." Tatra glanced again to Firman. "You have to face facts."

"Facts?" Krell's denying expression shifted into indignation. "You physicians think you're above error. You know what you can do with your facts, Healer Wileyse?" Krell overturned one of the worktable chairs in a lunge that shoved Tatra against the wall. "You can shove them and that self-serving, know-it-all analysis up your bony ass!"

"Krell, release me—please. Your personal pain doesn't give you the right to attack another." Tatra chewed at her bottom lip. "I only wish to help."

"Back off, Krell." Firman laid a hand on his sister's shoulder. She shrugged him off and shoved Tatra into the wall again.

"Pain? Woman, you've no idea the pain she's endured!"

"Krell, NO!" Firman jerked back with all his might, tumbling them both over the worktable. Tatra retreated to the corner nearest the lift and watched, gasping as Firman turned his sibling's anger. "Come on, Krell, it won't be the first time I've dropped you a peg."

"And it won't be the first time I've kicked your fool ass either!" Krell swung at him, stumbling forward with the effort. Firman grabbed her arm as she moved, twisting it high on her back.

"If that's the best you can do then I'm disappointed. LaRenna could have done better than that."

"You bastard!" Krell wrapped her foot around his ankle and jerked hard, careening him to the floor. Firman pulled her down as he fell then rolled on top, neatly pinning her with his knees.

"Stupid move, Kimshee. LaRenna would've known better." Firman pushed his knees deep into Krell's back, encouraging the string of curses she threw at him. "Come on Taelach, you too weak to fend off a mere Aut? How do you expect to care for a mate when you can't whip me?" Firman hauled Krell's head back by the hair then bent close. "If this is the best you can do," he whispered in her ear, "then maybe she's better off dead."

Krell bent with uncontrollable wrath, throwing Firman off her back. "You sorry son of a bitch, I told you she's not dead!" She grabbed him by the scruff of the neck and swung him headlong into the viewer's control board. The impact scattered an arcing electrical spray across the room. "She's alive!"

"She's dead and you know it!"

"NO!" Krell grabbed him again, throwing him across the worktable and into a far chair. "Had enough, old man?"

"Not on your life. This is just getting interesting." Firman reached across the table, snagging Krell's tunic. "Come here, kid. Let me knock a little reality into that thick skull of yours." He ducked a punch and landed his fist squarely in Krell's face, sending her sliding back across the table. "Your woman is gone. Deal with it."

Krell quickly shook off the blow. "You'll have to do much more than that to convince me she's anything but alive." Her sweet right toppled him to the floor.

"Whoa!" A grin crinkled the skin surrounding Firman's stinging eye. "It's about time you put some energy into it. Put that much effort into finding LaRenna and you just might get her back."

"What?" Krell stumbled back and dropped her arms.

"You heard me." Firman threw his arm around his sibling in a bear-grip hug. "I haven't put up with your crazy notions for thirty-nine passes without learning they have an annoying habit of being true." He shoved Krell to the floor and collapsed on top of her, his deep laugh shaking the floor. "Come on. Hit me again. I haven't tussled with you in ages."

Krell chuckled and lightly punched his arm. "So, you're going to help me?"

"You know it."

"Have you lost your minds?" Tatra exited her corner to face them, one hand on her hip, the other shaking a critical finger. "You try to kill each other one minute then laugh together the next? I don't understand!"

"You wouldn't." Krell clouted Firman's back. "You don't have a sibling."

"Think of it this way, Tatra." Firman scrubbed affectionately at Krell's head. "She was going to blow regardless. Would you rather have been tossed around?"

"Certainly not," warbled the healer. "I'm no fighter."

"That's obvious," he snickered with a wink her direction. "You're all bone, no flesh. That crash would have snapped a twig like you."

Tatra gaped. "You mean to tell me you think she's alive, too? Ockson said she was in a bad way before the launch ever went down."

"Ockson is a fool who'd never seen LaRenna before today," interjected Krell.

"True," agreed Firman. "I've seen her work. That little

Kimshee left more than one mark on Cance's face. If Krell's convinced she's alive then I am, too." He patted Krell on the shoulder and winked at Tatra. "Hey skinny, did Ockson say when the search teams were setting out?"

"They're assembling in an hour on landing deck two and I am not skinny." Tatra ran a lean hand down her side in demonstration. "My proportions are perfect for my framework." She gave each of them a disbelieving glance then sighed. "Guess I'll be going as well."

"Why?" asked Krell. "Belsas didn't call for you to join the teams."

"I know, but if you have to insist so solidly that LaRenna is alive then I'll have to give you the benefit of the doubt." Tatra stepped onto the level lift then turned back, holding the door long enough to return Firman's wink. "I'll see you in an hour."

Firman elbowed Krell's ribs as the lift door slid shut. "You see that? She's flirting with me. Me!"

"She does have her moments." Krell's eyes were back on the viewer. "Enjoy them. They're few and far between."

"Well, she needs more of them." Firman scrambled to catch the next lift. "I think they make her unbearably attractive."

Chapter Thirty

Sister sister close your mouth
And dare not make a sound
The Taelach hunt is drawing near
Don't let yourself be found

Help the children cover up
Cloak their silver hair
Take the back way through the caves
We can flee from there

Sister sister close your mouth
And dare not make a sound
If Autlachs find us
Taelach blood will spill upon the ground

—old Taelach teaching rhyme

Several seconds of cold waking fear passed before LaRenna remembered her surroundings. She took a slow breath and rolled back to warm against her brother only to find him gone. "Trazar?" He didn't reply. Easing up, she quickly silenced her fears and crept to the open window, stopping when a familiar shape caught her eye.

It was Cance's inhaler, conveniently within reach. She picked it up and held it before her face. One puff and her pain would be bearable. The reaction would be better this time. Her system had acclimated and she would be able to enjoy the full effect. One hit, that was all. It would calm her, soothe away the agony. She'd never let it get to the addictive level of her attackers. Just one.

Go ahead, my beauty. Numb away the hurt. Cance's echoing whisper knotted LaRenna's insides. *One won't hurt. Go on. You need it and so do I.*

"No!" LaRenna tossed the inhaler outside. Cance's specter faded along with it but didn't disappear entirely. She still held a place in the darkest corner of LaRenna's subconscious. "No dead procker is going to run my life! Get outta my head!" She shook off a chill then leaned out of the launch in search of her brother, desperate for his presence. "Trazar?"

"Just a minute." He had slid out and to the rear of the craft to relieve himself, hoping to return to her side before she awoke. He had wanted to spare her the fear he now detected in her voice. "You okay?"

LaRenna glanced at the inhaler. It lay in a puddle, contents leaking harmlessly into the ground. "My leg feels huge."

Trazar trotted over as he retied his waist lacings. In a single fluid movement, he scooped her out of the launch. "Best get you out of there, little sis. By Talmshone's odor, he's dead."

LaRenna crinkled her nose as she became aware of the stench. Trazar laughed at her expression then held her up to view the crash site.

The launch had smashed into the canyon's rock face and tumbled end-over-end until it had reached a flat area near the sandy bottom. The stream of the night before was now a raging river of mud and debris. "We were lucky to have survived. Your faithful Mother was watching over us yesterday."

"About time she took a moment for me. My belief was wearing thin." LaRenna held on to Trazar's tunic as he settled her onto a long metal panel. "Think they'll have trouble finding us down here?"

"Doesn't matter. We can't stay." Trazar pointed toward the churning waters, the surrounding area, then the sky. "We crashed onto a wet weather riverbed. Look at those clouds. It's going to rain again."

"I know. The storm scent is stronger than Talmshone's."

"Another soaking like last night's and this entire canyon floor will be underwater." Trazar checked her bandages and loosened the strips securing the brace. He said nothing of the red marks stretching up her leg. "How are your rib bindings?"

"Better than my bladder." She moaned. "Could you help me find a place I can balance before I explode? The water sound is almost too much."

"Why didn't you say something earlier?" Trazar gathered her in his arms and carried her to the launch's rear. There she balanced on one leg, a disgusted and almost jealous look on her face.

"Sometimes I think life would be easier if Taelachs were physically male."

"Then you wouldn't be my sister." Trazar turned politely away. "Besides, you are what you are for a reason." He ducked into the launch to gather their supplies. "Call me when you're through." Trazar pulled the Iralian's cloak free of his body and bundled a few things into it, his hand throbbing with every stretch of his fingers. The cut should have received a few stitches but would heal decently enough without them.

"Is there a clean rag about?" called LaRenna. Trazar opened the bundle and removed the remaining piece of Talmshone's trouser leg for her use.

"Here you go." He backed toward her, his arm extended

behind. LaRenna thanked him and swiftly tended to her personal needs.

"Don't go. I'm almost finished." She pulled the nightshirt straight and hobbled over to him, grabbing his shoulder for support. "I'm ready."

"No you're not. We can't have you barefoot in the mud." A drizzle began to fall as Trazar carried her back to the metal sheet. He set her gently down then scrambled to the shrubs at the water's edge before Cance's remains washed away. Her took her belt, bow, and boots, tucking them under his arm as he returned to his sister's side.

"They'll be big but they should keep your feet dry." He pulled a boot over her good foot, lashing the gaping top shut with a strip of the twisted belt leather. The second boot refused to slide over her misshapen ankle. "I'll fix that." Trazar split the hide shaft and peeled it apart to the sole. "Now you'll stay dry." He carefully wrapped the open boot about her foot and secured the top as tightly as he dared.

"We ready then?" She eyed the rising water.

"Almost." Trazar draped the Iralian's cloak over her and snapped the neck closed. Its padded shoulders fell nearly to LaRenna's elbows, giving her the appearance of a girl playing dress-up. "You're certainly small to be Taelach."

"Like I haven't heard that before."

"Don't get me wrong. There's nothing wrong with your size." Trazar fastened the front of her wrap. "In fact, I'm glad you're small. It would be hard to carry you otherwise." He shoved their meager supplies into his pockets and tossed her the plasma bow. "Is it usable?"

LaRenna examined the weapon then handed it back to him. "The power housing has a hairline crack. The charge could reverse if it's fired."

Trazar immediately disposed of the weapon. He knew little of Taelach-style weaponry but enough to be wary of the weapon's potential for radiation poisoning. "Won't it leak if the housing is busted?"

"There's a safety cage around the core tank but I'd rather be safe than sorry." LaRenna shivered again and sneezed. "I think the weather is getting to me. Let's go."

At the suggestion, a torrential downpour began to blanket the area. Trazar pulled her close and hurried away from the rising waters. The going was slick, every direction they took ending in an incline too steep to climb without the use of hands.

"I think we may be trapped down here." He brushed the wet hair from her face. "How's your swimming?"

"Taelachs don't swim," she replied through her stuffed nose. "We sink well though."

Trazar took the ill-timed jest seriously. "We get out of here, I'll teach you." He lowered her to the forking branches of a squat tree and stared up the mud-caked slopes. "I can't carry you in my arms and scale these walls. You'll have to ride on my back. Feel up to it?"

"Do I have a choice?" LaRenna wiped at the tickling stream that dripped off her chin.

"No." Trazar bent to her level so she could wrap her arms and good leg around him. He stood up slowly, shrugged to redistribute her weight, then shifted to take the brace into consideration. "Here we go."

LaRenna twisted her hands into his tunic and leaned into his ear. "When we get to the top, head north. The Taelach Training Grounds are in that direction."

"You've been to Saria Four before?" Trazar latched on to a protruding rock and began his ascent.

"Schooled here." She stifled another sneeze into his back. "We're in the Glory Lands."

"*Glorious* is not the term I would use. Does it always rain like this?"

"Just in the spring." LaRenna gritted her teeth as her leg skidded across a projecting stone.

"Sorry." Trazar continued their dangerous climb. Behind them, the water had risen until it lapped several inches deep inside the launch. LaRenna looked over her shoulder and shuddered.

Sharing her fear, Trazar picked up his pace, climbing stone to stone. When they reached a fair-sized outcropping, he set her against the stone face so they could rest.

"You all right?" He squeezed the water from his tunic.

"Freezing." LaRenna followed his lead, wringing some of the moisture from her weighted cloak. Her hands were streaked in color. The thorough soaking was removing the semi-permanent dye from her skin, returning her to Taelach paleness. She rubbed at one hand with the tail of her wrap and held it, palm forward, to her brother.

"You're washing away!" He pushed back her hood and repeated his surprise. Her face was streaked in the same fashion as her hands. He jerked his tunic cuff over his wrist and rubbed at her skin, LaRenna flinching when he mashed the tender bruises spotting her face.

She pushed his hand away. "Stop it. You're pinching my nose."

"Be still. I'm almost through." Trazar scrubbed all the dye from her face except in the immediate vicinity of her stitches. "So that's what my sister looks like."

"Minus the dark hair and bruises." LaRenna rubbed her nose.

"A little more rain and the hair color will be gone, too," he replied. "The dye's streaking down your neck." Thunder shook the canyon walls, pelting the roof of their temporary roost with a shower of small pebbles. "We'd better climb out of here before we end up in a landslide." Trazar kicked away several rocks that had landed near his feet.

LaRenna's death grip properly entangled in his tunic, he shimmied up the outcrop's ironstone covering. A gusting wind began to blow, slathering them mercilessly with mud and small, biting stones. Trazar cursed their luck and strained to pull higher. Below, the launch bobbed in the current.

"I can't go much farther in this wind." Trazar blinked the water from his eyes. "Start looking for a spot we can wait this out."

LaRenna looked upward then released her hand long enough to point to their upper right. "What about there?"

"No matter what it is, it'll have to do." Trazar began climbing in that direction. The climb seemed easier the nearer they came to the opening, as if a rough ladder had been carved into the canyon wall.

"Wait a second!" LaRenna touched the eroded symbols etched between the handholds.

"What does it say?" A violent gust blasted away any answer she may have given and LaRenna clutched his tunic as he scaled the last ten meters to safety. Trazar crawled several lengths into the opening before she would consider loosening her grip and then still held a handful of his dripping tunic.

"Crazy climb, wasn't it?" Trazar peeled her loose then dumped the water from his boots. "What were those symbols?"

"They're Taelach markings of a safe haven." LaRenna gazed around their new surroundings. "This is a Hiding Cave."

"Hiding Cave?" He looked up in the same dumbfounded manner.

"A place to which Taelachs can flee in times of crisis."

Trazar stopped what he was doing. "Why would your people need something like this with all your technology?"

"We've had them since the time of the Hunts." LaRenna briefly explained the Kinship's history to her brother. He listened with locked interest, gaining new understanding and respect of how survival had influenced Taelach culture.

"Amazing," he muttered when she paused. "Autlach teachers never teach any older history."

"They should." LaRenna rasped. "Taelachs learn their own and Autlach history in detail."

"Let's get out of this wind." Trazar helped her hobble into a dark interior chamber and propped her against the wall.

"There should be a light panel here somewhere." LaRenna leaned against the damp stone as Trazar felt for the main panel. His hand grasped something that wiggled like a switch, so he jerked it down, flooding the chamber in a low, pleasing light.

"Got it. Now what are these?" He pointed to the corrosion-proof crates stacked in the room's center.

"Stores. Open them. They should have everything we need."

Trazar unlatched one of the heavy lids and shuffled through the box's contents. "Want some dry clothes?"

"Please!" LaRenna appreciated the thought of being warm again. "I'm frozen through and through."

Trazar gathered a knit tunic, leggings, and underclothing for her. "Will these do?"

"Perfect as long as they're dry." She managed to fumble out of her wet garments without assistance and slid into renewed comfort. Trazar dug back into the crate and pulled out two bedrolls before moving to the next one. It was full of charged lighting rods. Trazar stacked several near the rolls. A third crate provided extensive food stores that he set aside for later.

"Now if we had a little heat to burn off the dampness," he mumbled, "we'd be set."

LaRenna's keen hearing picked up her brother's lament. "Throw the orange breaker beside the one for the lights. Maybe the heating cells still have—" A violent cough brought her sliding toward the floor. Trazar caught her before she landed and carried her near the room's large central vent, where he remained at her side, afraid to move until she assured him heat would help the cough.

The heating system sprang to life with a rusted clank. "There. That should do it." Trazar returned to the crates. "Any of these contain medical supplies?"

"Try the small ones."

He carried one of the smaller crates to where she sat. "Let me change and I'll tend your foot." He resumed his search in the clothing crate, complaining about the selection as he looked. "Skirts and leggings for lanky-limbed women. Don't your people have something for those of lesser height?"

"Not really." She smiled. "Not even children's clothing fits me right. I have to have everything cut to fit. Roll a smaller pair of leggings at the waist and leg bottoms and hold them up with a belt. That's what I do."

Trazar did as she suggested and slid a heavy tunic over the top.

The combination fit loosely once he'd rolled the sleeves. "Did I give you anything for your feet?"

"Nope." She sniffled. "It would be appreciated as would some assistance with my boots."

Two sets of warm footlings and bedroll in hand, Trazar joined her on the floor. He unrolled the bedding and helped her onto it. "Rest yourself while I warm our feet." He slid the leather from her shriveled toes and rubbed the sole of her good foot.

"Oh, thank you." LaRenna stretched into the warming massage. "I was beginning to think it as dead as the other one."

"You still can't feel it?" Trazar moved to the injured leg and removed the brace and bandages. The skin had turned an almost blue-black from toes to heel. Dark drainage coated the arch, crusting into rot-smelling clots on the bandages. "LaRenna," he stammered. "This is in desperate need of a healer. It's infected."

LaRenna propped on her elbows to look for herself. "See what's in the medical crates." She stared at the dying flesh. The foot seemed so detached that the thought of removing it didn't matter. It was useless anyway.

Trazar removed several small packs from the crate. "Your people aren't much for pain medications, are they?"

"We rely on each other for relief. Phasing is faster and more effective than any drug."

"I was afraid of that."

"Why?" LaRenna began to pull her foot away. Trazar shook his head and gripped her leg just above the knee.

"No you don't. The bottom is abscessing. If I don't open it and clean out the infection, it'll spread to your blood." He slid forward until his own legs wrapped around her injured one, his thigh muscles tensing to immobilize the limb. LaRenna squirmed with discomfort as he doused the foot in antibiotic cleanser. "You feel that?"

"Cold."

Trazar opened two surgical packs then washed his hands in the cleansing solution. "Lie back and be very, very still."

LaRenna lay back, her eyes tight in anticipation. She focused on a relaxing meditation chant to ward away the pain, repeating it as Trazar opened the abscess with a small scalpel. The chant was lost, replaced by a low moan when he squeezed the infection into squares of sterile packing surrounding the abscess. A brief reprieve as he changed the packing allowed her to begin again, harder and faster than before. Trazar glanced sympathetically at her pain-riddled face while he swabbed underneath the skin with a medicine-soaked piece of packing. Eventually, she began launching obscenities at him, the words growing louder and harsher with her gasping breaths.

"Go ahead if it helps." His grip became all the harder. "It has to be done."

"Then get it over with!" She restrained her instinct to phase him limp. "Dear Mother take me so it'll stop!"

"There." He removed the last of the packing. "You're not dead and there's nothing left but to stitch it up." He inserted a threaded wire just beneath her skin and loosely closed the wound, providing plenty of room for proper drainage, LaRenna continuing to mumble obscenities the entire time. "I don't know much Taelach, sister, but I do know when I'm being sworn at in any language. You should be ashamed."

"I take no credit for what I say in pain or passion," she growled, her teeth clenched.

"I'll remember that." Trazar placed a light bandage over the incision site. "It's finished. I don't believe I ever heard such colorful metaphors from a woman's mouth. Where'd you learn those words?"

"Auts."

"That so?" Trazar wasn't sure whether to be insulted or amused. "What about the Taelach swears I heard? I'm fairly sure one of them concerned my mother, who, by the way, is your mother, too."

"I told you I take no credit, but I do apologize. Just, please, leave my leg alone. It's throbbing into my hip." She thought of the inhaler.

"I'll leave it alone for a while." He brought her a water bottle from the food stores. "Forgive me?"

"There's nothing to forgive." LaRenna accepted his gesture, pulling from the bottle to coat her throat. Trazar waited until she'd finished then held up several tins and airtight packs for her approval. "They're marked in Taelach. You'll have to translate if you want a decent meal."

"Open everything except the green-topped pack. That's pickled sponge fish." LaRenna wrinkled her nose. "Disgusting stuff."

"I'll take your word for it." Trazar opened the tins with his dagger and set them before her. "You'll have to use your fingers. I can't find any tableware."

"Fork tines and spoons are Autlach conveniences," she said, amazed by how little most Autlachs really knew about their closest cousins. "We only use them around Auts. At home we use our knives. I thought everyone knew that."

"Not everyone," he countered, embarrassed. "Don't you eat soups and stews?"

"Sure. We drink them from a sipper bowl then use our knives to retrieve what sticks in the bottom."

"Now I know why even the youngest Taelach children carry blades."

"That, and old fears." LaRenna took the dagger from him and pointed at the array. "Dig us some preserved black bread from the crate and I'll dish you up whatever you want." Trazar found the bag and handed her one of the small precut slices.

"I'll take some of whatever that is in the oblong tin."

LaRenna deftly layered a piece on the bread. "Here, it's roast bandit beast."

"I've never seen bandit beast cooked that way." Trazar took a small bite. "The color is odd."

"It's been cooked in rangleberries. Hence the bluish color."

"Oh."

They made quick work of that tin and four more of various Taelach staples. Trazar ate ravenously. LaRenna merely picked, more to keep him company than for her appetite. She was coughing more deeply as the day progressed, every hack grabbing at her sides.

He was tossing away the empty containers when a series of coughs cut her breathing short. "I believe the rain has left you with pneumonia." Trazar helped her settle onto the bedroll when the worst was over.

"I'm afraid so." Truth was, she had felt the fluid building long before their rain-soaked ascent. Brandoff's kick had caused her to inhale some of her own vomit, setting in an opportunistic infection of a type Taelachs seldom incurred.

"You're burning up." He retrieved several bedrolls from the crates and stacked them into a reclining wedge for her comfort. "Sleep. That's an order, not from a superior, but from an older, wiser brother."

"You'll get no objection from me, on any count." LaRenna closed her eyes and drifted off. Trazar sat with her a while then took an armful of light rods to the main cavern entrance, spacing them at regular intervals across the mouth. It was a feeble signal at best but the most he could hope for as long as the rain persisted.

Trazar held his hand into the rain as he pondered the dramatic twist his life had taken. LaRenna filled an ever-present void in his life. The pure coincidence of their meeting made him wonder if it had always been part of the Taelach Maker's grand plan. LaRenna relied on him. That, he decided, was why he had been placed here. By helping her, he would help bridge the gap between the Taelach and Autlach, proving that families could exist in harmony no matter their makeup. He wouldn't fail. LaRenna couldn't die.

Chapter Thirty-One

We cannot choose whom we love. The heart acts independently of the greater senses when making such attachments.

—*Elder wisdom*

"Where's your mourning sash?" Chandrey asked Krell as the recovery teams assembled on the landing deck. She knew Ockson had provided the guardian with one and was disappointed it was not draped across her shoulder.

"I threw it away," replied Krell. "It's not necessary."

"Not necessary?" stammered Chandrey. "How can you honor her memory without it? You can't free her ashes to the winds. It's a sacrilege!"

"She's not dead," insisted Krell. "Firman, Tatra, and I intend to find her."

"How—" Chandrey quelled her words when Belsas called the confused deck to order.

"You've all been given your duty assignments." The Taelach of All spoke reverently from the top step of a maintenance riser. "The crash site has been tracked to the Glory Lands. The area is currently blanketed in heavy storms, resulting in the widespread canyon flooding typical of this season. A base camp will be set up at the search area's center. All teams will report to me on a daily basis. There are to be no heroics. This is a recovery operation only. Teams from the Training Grounds will canvass the outer perimeter of the search area. Are there any questions?" Shuffling feet and shifting equipment echoed on the otherwise silent deck. "Very well, all crews are to report to their designated launches."

When the teams scattered, Krell dashed away before Chandrey could ask more questions. Firman and Tatra caught up with her at the launch. They were garbed in heavy climbing gear, Tatra with a small medical pack strapped to her waist. "Here." She tossed Krell a rolled jumpsuit. "That should fit."

"Thanks." Krell slid the suit on. Despite the size, it was still short in the leg. She snorted at the accustomed ill fit and tucked the leg bottoms into her boots.

"Don't feel bad." Firman tugged his jumpsuit down. "She made sure mine was short, too."

"She could never pick clothes for anyone but herself," said Krell.

Firman leaned close and pointed to Tatra's backside as she disappeared into the launch. "I've never seen a climbing suit filled out quite so nicely, how 'bout you?"

"I've always appreciated the way she seems poured into her clothes," whispered Krell. "Her mouth is what scared me away."

"I heard that!" called a voice from inside the launch.

"See?" Krell chuckled as she forced a frown. "All sense of appreciation is lost."

"Not mine," beamed Firman.

"I heard that, too!"

"Good!" he yelled. "Your ears should be burning 'cause the rest of you is flaming hot already."

Krell found their developing relationship amusing. Tatra had never been one to deal with Autlachs more than necessary and Firman was one to love a challenge. They made an interesting pair.

"You going to hold on this time?" he asked when Krell had barred the hatchway.

"Oh, shut up." Tatra turned up her nose.

"You first, if you can." Firman winked at his sibling when she passed. Krell smiled back knowing Wileyse had finally met her match.

They waited their turn for liftoff and took their place in the convoy. The imbedded storms made landing a tricky affair but all crafts were successful. It was late afternoon on the surface, so the teams were dispatched to do preliminary searches while daylight remained.

"There's so much to cover." Tatra surveyed the narrow canyon they'd been assigned. "Where do we begin?"

"Not here." Krell looked toward the western horizon. "Belsas gave us this area because she wants me close to camp."

"There might be something down there." Firman leaned over the canyon edge, watching the bottom rage with muddy turbulence. Chills cascaded down his spine at the thought of LaRenna being washed away, unsteadying his stance until Tatra grabbed his arm, pulling him from the edge.

"Careful, you'll slip."

"Didn't know you cared," he crooned.

"I don't." She dropped her hand. "Just wanted to spare myself any unnecessary work."

"When you two are through," interrupted Krell before Firman could form a comeback, "I think we should look west."

Firman consulted their map and shook his head. "That leads us outside the search parameters. Are you sure you want to cross Belsas?"

"LaRenna is in that direction. I'm sure of it." Krell led the way across the rough terrain. The others followed, dedicated though reluctant, puzzled by her fixed sense of direction.

They walked due west of their starting point, circumventing large standing puddles and deep-mudded bandit beast wallows. Krell kept the lead, homing in on some invisible beacon. All thoughts faded from her mind save one—LaRenna. That one image forced Krell blindly onward. LaRenna was in pain and that's all that mattered.

"Krell!" Firman pointed to the nearly set sun. "It's getting late. We should return to camp."

"No, I'm going on. It'll take most of the morning to get this far again."

"We'll take a land launch."

"It may be too muddy for touchdown. You saw how far the planetary launches sank when we landed." Krell looked at the clouds stacking on the horizon. "I can't leave. Take Tatra back if you want. I'm going to keep moving until it's too dark to see."

"We can't leave you out here alone." His jaw set in a stern lock. "Come back to camp and dry off. You'll catch your death."

"LaRenna already has." Krell's voice took an ominous tone that caused Firman to stare.

"How do you know she's sick?" Tatra had heard most of the conversation and now drew close, hand returning to Firman's arm as she listened. Full-sense telepathy between Taelach lovers wasn't unheard of, but all recorded cases involved pairs who had been together for decades.

"I just do. She's very ill, Tatra. Her chest hurts." Krell drew a ragged breath. "Her foot too, but in a different way."

Firman turned to the healer. "She for real?"

"I believe so," whispered Tatra. "There aren't many pairs who can phase like this. Where is she, Krell?"

"She's asleep, and hot, so very hot." Krell's eyes rolled back.

"A fever." Tatra's nod confirmed Firman's analysis.

"She still a prisoner?" queried Tatra.

"No, I don't think she is."

"She alone then?"

"No, someone she knows and trusts is caring for her."

"Who?" pushed Tatra. "Who's she with?"

"That's all I can sense. I'm still too far away." Krell's eyes opened. "You two get back to camp. I'll go it alone from here."

"Are you kidding?" Firman's hand pressed reassuringly into his sibling's. "We haven't come all this way to be scared by the dark. Have we, Tatra?"

"Nope." She smiled up at them. "We're not turning back now. Show us the way, Krell. We'll follow you to her and help bring her back."

The downpours continued through the evening and night, providing little relief to the search teams. All but Krell's group returned at sunset, no one noticing the missing trio until Belsas called for their report.

Fearing that flash floods might have swept them away, a morning search was organized for the narrow canyon they had been assigned. Belsas knew Krell wouldn't have taken her crew into danger so she assumed they had begun an independent search. Their punishment when they returned would be severe, decided Belsas, especially for Krell. How dare she not stay close when LaRenna's body could be recovered at any time?

Things went no better for the independent threesome. They stopped when the rain became too fierce for movement, seeking refuge under a group of low shrubs. Firman and Tatra cuddled up for warmth as well as companionship, leaving Krell to think.

LaRenna's mental presence was so vivid that they shared the same feverish dreams. The images came in waves, initially revolving around LaRenna's family, friends, and childhood. Krell found these to be pleasant, insightful glances at LaRenna's past. But as the night progressed and her fever rose, the mental pictures became disillusioned and increasingly violent. Surreal visions of the Creiloff twins' depraved behavior pierced their shared nightmare until it twisted Krell into hysterical fury.

"Krell!" Firman shook his sibling. She was on her side, taut and wheezing against the cold ground. "Krell!" His second cry brought her screaming awake.

"What's wrong?" Tatra rubbed her eyes.

"I'm not sure." Firman comforted Krell as best he could, speaking quiet reassurances as she clutched the slick grass beneath her. "She's scared near senseless." He drew close to absorb the tremors wracking his sibling. "Is it LaRenna? Krell? Krell?"

"They took her." Krell sobbed against him.

"Slow down." Tatra took a position on Krell's other side, her slender hand clasping Krell's. "You're hyperventilating. Slow breaths—one—two. That's it."

"Who took her?" Firman asked as Krell began to regain control. "Took her where?"

"The bar on Langus. The Creiloff twins. Cance's scratches." Words couldn't describe the horror Krell was feeling—LaRenna's horror. No wonder LaRenna had been reluctant to look up when they had spoken. She had been ashamed of something totally beyond her control.

"They raped her," grieved Tatra, close to terror herself. "It must have happened on Langus before we escaped."

Krell could only nod. "I could feel her fighting. They forced her at the same time. Tortured her, drugged her, procked her, tied her to the counter. I could see it through her eyes—feel the pain. She wished they would kill her so it would stop."

"But they didn't." Firman pulled Krell to his shoulder. "You couldn't have stopped it, Krelleesha. There was no way you could have known."

"I could have prevented it from happening at all." She collapsed into his embrace. "Brandoff followed her the morning we met on the beach. She watched us. I thought I saw someone on the pathway, but dismissed it as stress. I should have stopped her from going back."

"Could haves and should haves aren't important at this point," said Tatra. "All that matters is that you understand what she experienced and that you help her get past it."

"How could I not? I feel I suffered with her." Krell still shook. "They ravaged her, took everything she was, and all she could think about was how it would hurt me. She cried for me. Prayed for me. Screamed for me! And I wasn't there!" Krell's voice rose as the angst began to twist once more.

"Don't work yourself up again." Firman tightened his hold. "Stay near me. If you have another episode like that, I want you to be close enough so I can knock it out of you."

Unable to complain, Krell relaxed against him, quickly falling into the same dreamless sleep as LaRenna. Firman chuckled as his sister began to snore.

"She still snores."

"And hogs the bed." Tatra looked about for a dry piece of ground. "Where do I sleep now?"

"I snore, too. Gotta problem with that?" Firman extended his arm. "Come on. I have room for one more." She accepted his offer and soon both Taelachs were sleeping soundly against him. "Look at you," he sighed, his chin resting against Tatra's flaxen hair. "Two women and no one about to brag to. You're getting soft in your old age, Firman Middle."

In the Hiding Cave, Trazar held his own sister in much the same way. He cooled her face with damp cloths, trying to calm the scourging memories that penetrated her delirium. She became restless and irritated, fighting against him as he removed her blankets to help combat the fever.

LaRenna howled and moaned for Krell, begging her to make "them" stop hurting her. The pleading proved so sorrowful it made Trazar mindful of the fact his sister might not fully recover from her assault, physically or mentally. "You've been through more in the last quarter-cycle than one person should endure in a lifetime." He wiped down her brow again. "But you're strong, LaRenna, so keep fighting."

Eventually, her nightmares ended, allowing her to drift into a deep slumber. Trazar placed a fresh cloth on her head then went to the cave entrance to replace the nearly extinguished marker lights. "I don't know why I bother," he grumbled while spacing the fresh rods. "They probably aren't visible more than ten or twelve paces in this fool rain."

The rampant canyon flood was audible in the cave mouth. Staring through the darkness, Trazar was positive the launch had washed downstream any number of kilometers. That alone reduced their chances of discovery. Now their rescuers would have to search the entire flood path for them. Trazar prayed they wouldn't be assumed drowned and the search abandoned.

"Trazar!" LaRenna's weak voice brought him running to her side. He laid her back on the bedroll and replaced the cloth on her red-hot face. "I woke up and you weren't here and—"

"I was changing the marker lights," he soothed, aware her fears were being fed by her fever.

"Still raining?" She reached for the water bottle he had placed beside her.

"Yes." Trazar took it, cradled her neck, and held it to her mouth. "Drink. It's good for the fever." She swallowed several times then gagged, fighting to inhale against the pain.

"When won't my damn ribs hurt anymore?" She gasped when the air returned.

"Soon. Try to sleep." He retrieved an unused bedroll and spread it beside hers, LaRenna watching silently from her angled headrest. She had so much she wanted to share with Trazar, but conversation was just too difficult.

Trazar covered up and lay facing her. "You'll be okay. They'll find us tomorrow. Wait and see." LaRenna smiled and reached out to him. He clasped her hand and curled his fingers around hers.

"Please tomorrow," she whispered, " 'cause I'm so tired."

Chapter Thirty-two

Raw and hard the wind does blow
Bleak into the caves
The springtime floods they wash away
The ones the Autlach slays

—Taelach poetry

"First an entire team goes rogue, now this!" Belsas puzzled over the two bodies lying underneath the awning of the morgue tent. She knew they had been part of a recovery team but not the circumstances of their deaths. "What happened?"

Chandrey gave a cheerless look to the cadet who had recovered the bodies from one of the flooded canyons. "They drowned, didn't they?"

"No ma'am," replied the flare-jawed young guardian. "This one's skull had been crushed." The cadet indicated one of the shrouded bodies. "The other one has a broken neck. They were dead before they hit the water."

"Is it possible they were caught in a landslide?" asked Chandrey.

The cadet pointed to the boot toe not covered by the shrouds. "There's no mud, dirt, rocks, or anything else matted into their clothes. No other pre-death injuries we could detect. There would have been if they'd been caught in a slide."

"In other words," said Belsas, "you believe they met with foul play?"

"It appears so, Grandmaster."

"And one sister from the party is still missing?"

"Yes, ma'am."

"You're dismissed." Belsas moved to stand beside Chandrey. "Murder on a recovery operation? Chandrey, I swear if—"

"Grandmaster Belsas?" The cadet scrambled back to where they stood. "Another thing you might find interesting."

"That is?"

"One of them was found without her boots and leggings."

Chandrey waited until the cadet shuffled off a second time then turned to Belsas, astonished. "Without clothes?"

"Odd." Belsas considered the two dead Taelachs, edging back one shroud then the other for analysis. "Very odd indeed. What would someone want with boots and leggings from a dead sister?"

"Could they have washed off in the flood?" asked Chandrey.

"It's possible," replied Belsas. "In fact, it's probably what happened." The morning breezes tugged at the back of their cloaks, flicking off some of the water that had collected along the hemlines. Scents of fresh tea and hot bread mingled in the air, prompting their stomachs into growls of discontent.

"Too little dinner the night before makes the gut angry in the morn." Chandrey placed a hand over her stomach. It growled even louder.

"I don't think you'll quiet it by any means except filling it." Belsas chuckled. "You haven't eaten enough as of late."

"I haven't had the spirit," she replied after a moment's silence.

"It's not the spirit that requires food, my dear. It's the body." Belsas took her by the arm and led the way to the cook tent.

"The spirit needs nourishment, too," said Chandrey as they walked. "Mine's been starving."

Belsas stopped midstep to face her. "I haven't been there much lately, have I?"

Chandrey looked down and away to shield her sad face from her lover. "You've been on post day and night since—"

"Well, I'm not now." Belsas lifted her, holding her suspended at arm's length.

"What are you doing?" exclaimed Chandrey in midspin above Belsas's head.

"I'm giving both our spirits something to nibble on."

"Everybody's watching!"

"So? Since when is it wrong for a guardian to show her lady a little affection?" Belsas spun her around one more time then set her lightly down. "Let's grab a quick breakfast and take it back to our launch. It seems ages since we last talked."

"Or anything else," Chandrey snipped as they entered the canopy where the morning meal was being served.

"That too can be remedied, my dear woman." Belsas held open the tent flap. They waited their turn in the serving line then, food in hand, walked back to their launch.

It was a simple but nourishing meal, the Training Grounds having provided a generous supply of fresh fruits for their consumption.

"You'll have to thank Yeoman Qualls for her thoughtfulness." Chandrey finished off a slice of peeled green melon. The succulent round fruit was her favorite, and she took it whenever it was offered, which was never often enough for her tastes. Belsas had chosen two of the small, pale-fleshed vine plums to accompany her bread and tea.

"I will, as soon as all of this is over."

Chandrey clasped her mug. "When? When will it be over?

We've searched two days for some sign of a crash site. I would give anything for one clue, something, any piece that would let us put LaRenna to rest."

Shhhh. Belsas pushed a calming pleasure phase. *I know this is hard and Mother knows I haven't been any help. You should have been my priority from the beginning.* A second, stronger phase followed the first, bringing a sensual glow to Chandrey's worried face.

We're in mourning.

Mourning, yes, Chandresslandra Belsas. Dead, no. I need you desperately right now and I think you need me, too. Belsas set their mugs to the side then pulled Chandrey close, kissing her ear and her neck before dropping to one knee to kiss her upturned palm. Shivering at the incredible sensation the touch created, Chandrey allowed herself to be pulled across Belsas's lap then lowered to the launch's floor, welcoming the surrounding warmth their pleasure phase offered. Each knew exactly what the other enjoyed, what the other needed. Thirty passes together had made the physical manipulations of lovemaking unnecessary for satisfaction, but Belsas sometimes asked for them, as she did now, smiling down at Chandrey through the joy that encased them. Chandrey swatted Belsas's dangling braids from her face until they finally tickled out an uncontrollable sneeze at the peak of their lovemaking.

"I'm sorry." Chandrey wiped the moisture from Belsas's face. Belsas's nose wrinkled when it was touched and she returned the sneeze.

"Confounded rain," she griped. "It's given everyone the sniffles." Belsas tried to hold back another, but caught Chandrey full in the face. "Oops."

"You meant to do that." Chandrey laughed as she cleaned her face on Belsas's tunic. "Get off me, you beast. You've made a proper mess of my skirts."

"Are you complaining?" Belsas pulled a rolled jumpsuit from their baggage. "Forget the skirts and put this on. It will be easier to manage in the mud."

"You know I don't wear trousers."

Belsas held out the jumper insistently. "Times are changing. LaRenna wore them whenever she could."

"LaRenna was Kimshee. They always do things out of the norm."

"Make an exception. We're heading out."

Chandrey removed her skirts and shouldered the oversized coveralls. The garment was cut for Belsas and hung loosely. She rolled the legs and sleeves until they fit then retied the mourning sash about her middle. "Where to? I thought you were staying in camp?"

"Sometimes," replied Belsas softly, "even the Taelach of All has to bend the rules a little. It makes little sense for me to sit here waiting until someone else finds my daughter. Krell didn't."

"Krell refuses to wear a sash," retorted Chandrey.

Belsas cocked her head. "Maybe Krell senses something we can't. LaRenna's talents are still developing."

"*Were* developing," cried Chandrey despairingly. "I refuse to raise my hopes otherwise."

"Nonetheless, we're going to start our search where Krell's group was looking when they disappeared. We'll follow them."

"We need a third for a team." Chandrey tacked up her hair with a long-toothed comb from her bag. "How about Malley Whellen? She seems good on her feet."

Belsas grinned at her. "You read my mind." They exited the launch, pausing long enough to put on their cloaks and exchange a quick kiss. Belsas jumped across the scattered puddles with an energetic bounce Chandrey hadn't seen in some time. She joined her lover's play, springing across the water spots easily, but without the same level of long-legged grace.

They crossed the encampment until they reached the stores tent. Belsas spoke momentarily with the sentry then ducked inside while Chandrey waited. She quickly emerged with ropes, three plasma bows, and recharge packs. "I'll find Whellen. Why don't you get us some rations?" Belsas passed Chandrey a bow and charger. "Meet me back here as soon as you're ready."

"Who're you leaving in command?" Chandrey knotted her bow's ties.

"I'll bring Protocol Master Quall in to supervise until we return. She runs a tight operation."

"What about the two dead and one missing on team four?"

Belsas appreciated the forethought. "I'll have the other teams keep an eye out for the missing third. It was probably an unfortunate accident. However, I'll have all teams go armed from this point." She bent down to give Chandrey another quick kiss on the forehead. "Hurry now. Time is wasting."

Chandrey watched as Belsas disappeared into the main communications tent, then turned toward her next task, shaking her head. Surely Belsas wasn't hanging on to the same delusions as Krell. Cance had been worse than anyone remembered. The crash had been too sudden. LaRenna was dead, plain and simple. No amount of denial would ever change that.

Chapter Thirty-three

Discovery of love lost is the most powerful of healing agents.

—*Taelach wisdom*

Tatra stood on the edge of the fifth canyon they had encountered that morning. The hole appeared much as the others—a brown, rock-laden gash, oozing with muddy churn. She couldn't understand how Krell could be so adamant this was where LaRenna was. It was identical to everything else they had seen. She raked her boots over a sharp stone to remove the mud then turned back to where Krell and Firman stood. "Found our location yet?"

Krell glanced over the map and shrugged. "Still looking."

"It's not shown." Firman caught the scroll's edge when a wind gust pulled it from his grasp.

"Not all the canyons are," replied Krell. "The Kinship generally doesn't record the ones containing Hiding Caves. Their locations are passed down orally."

"Secrets, secrets." There was an inordinate amount of whimsy in Firman's voice. "The Kinship is full of them."

Tatra smoothed back her hair. "If we recorded them, they'd be ransacked for supplies. You know how Auts are."

"Hey!" Firman caught her by the sleeve. "What do I look like?"

"I wasn't referring to you in particular." Tatra's attempt to cover her blunder only made things worse. "It's just that as a whole, Autlachs can't be trusted."

"Cruel-hearted woman." Firman stared at her. "I thought we might have something special happening between us and now open bigotry from you!"

"Wait . . . I . . . Krell, help me!"

"Don't bother." Firman shrugged her off and stormed over to where their packs rested. He picked up Krell's and his own, setting them neatly on a rain-washed boulder. Tatra's he used as a footrest, grinding it into the mud with a vindictive twist of his heels.

"You stepped in it." Krell's eyes never left the map. "You can clean it off of your boots—and your pack."

"Go talk to him," begged Tatra as Krell stowed the map. "Tell him I didn't mean it that way."

"Didn't you?" She turned away. "You explain yourself. I don't have to understand you anymore, not that I ever could." She watched as Tatra tried, in her own lofty-headed way, to explain away what was said.

Krell. LaRenna's voice was clear.

LaRenna, darlin', where are you? The question rolled so explosively through Krell that she couldn't differentiate between speech and thought.

Krell.

Tell me where you are and I'll come to you.

Close. The impression of a dark opening formed in Krell's mind. It was one of the Hiding Caves but which one? There were dozens spread across the Glory Land, three or four in each unmarked canyon.

Which one, LaRenna? Which one? More images came clear: rising floodwaters, cliffs, the marker for a Hiding Cave, then nothing. *Show me where you are.* Still nothing. *LaRenna!*

Krell. LaRenna's voice was incredibly weak. *Down . . . down.*

Down? Krell's mind became void of LaRenna's presence. *Down where? Help me find you. LaRenna?* The mental tie reestablished, but barely. *Hold on my precious bird. My wren. I'm coming Wren bird. Hold on!*

I love y . . . LaRenna was gone, leaving the distinct sense of a deep, coma-like sleep . . . no thoughts, no pain, just sleep, sleep necessary to keep her frail body alive.

"I love you, too." Krell opened her eyes to find Firman and Tatra staring with well-founded concern.

"You were screaming." Firman gripped his sibling's shoulder. Krell looked around him to the canyon edge.

"She's down there, Fir, in a Hiding Cave."

"We know." Tatra shuddered. "Everyone on Saria Four knows."

"Was I that loud?"

"And then some," answered Firman. "We'll begin looking as soon as this fog lifts a little."

Krell ignored him and walked to the canyon brim. "No time. She needs me now." She looked to the left then right, then disappeared into the fog, moving in a northeasterly direction. But the farther she went, the emptier she felt. "Wrong." She reversed course, concentrating on LaRenna's presence until Tatra and Firman came back into view.

"What's she doing?" Tatra stepped forward.

"I've no idea," replied Firman. "But don't get in her way."

"But what if she goes off the side?"

"There's nothing on her mind right now except LaRenna. Block her path and it may be you who goes off the side." Firman drew Tatra back by the collar. "Let her be."

"But she's babbling!" Tatra pulled loose and rushed forward. Firman snagged her before she had gone three steps, threw her face-first into the mud, and settled his girth across her back. She swore at him, kicking and arching as his knees forced her deeper into the muck.

"Never trust an Aut." Firman smiled smugly down. "We'll get you every time you turn your back."

Tatra hurled a handful of mud over her shoulder, splattering it on his tunic. "Get off me, you moron! Krell's almost out of sight again!"

"Moron?" Firman admonished her insult with a curt laugh. "Who's got a dry seat?" He drew his finger across the mud then her nose, leaving a streak. "I've wanted to do that since I met you, you self-centered, egotistical tease."

Tatra flailed all the more, throwing clay every direction, more landing in her own face than on him. "You're crushing me just like you crushed my bag! GET OFF!"

"Why should I?" He flicked another glob in her face. "You'll take off after Krell again if I do. Leave her be, Tatra. I've a hunch she'll be back when she needs us." Firman bounced a couple of times, pushing her deeper into the slop. "Yep, you're definitely more comfortable than that rock."

"Yeah, yeah." After a moment Tatra ceased her thrashing and peered cautiously over her shoulder. "Firman?" she said. "You finished?"

"You going to chase Krell?"

"No."

"Promise?"

"Firman!"

"Just making sure." Firman took her hand and carefully lifted her from the mud. "Truce?"

"I suppose." She flicked a clump of dirt from his chin. "You're different than any Aut I've ever met."

"Oh, we're all alike are we?" he teased, withdrawing his grin when she scowled at him. "I'm kidding, Tatra. No, I'm not like most Auts." He wrapped his arm around her shoulder, pulling her into a hug. "Above all else, dear woman, I want to be your friend."

"What if I want to go slow?"

"We go slow."

"Really slow?"

"It's a friendship, Tat."

"Just the same—"

"Hush." Firman covered her mouth with his fingers. "You're overanalyzing." She quieted to his request, smiled, and hugged him back.

"FIRMAN!" Krell barreled out of the fog. "I've found her. I've found her!"

"Where?" Tatra stepped away from Firman but continued to grip his warm hand.

"Thousand paces from here, about twenty or so down."

"You can't see that far in this soup." Firman's fingers closed around Tatra's. "You sure?"

"Positive. There's a Hiding Cave down there and someone's burning marker lights in the mouth. Come on!"

Trazar was cleaning LaRenna's fevered face when he heard the first skittering of pebbles in the cave entrance. He dashed to the archway where their chamber joined the main corridor and peered around the corner, dagger in hand. One, two, and then three silhouettes slid down a rope into the cave mouth. He couldn't see them clearly against the glow of markers, but he could recognize two figures as Taelach from the reflections off their hair.

"LaRenna!" The largest of the shadows called out in a definitive Taelach drawl. Trazar sheathed his dagger and stepped out.

"She's in here!" The figure blew by him at alarming speed followed closely by a mud-splattered second. The third approached with slower, calmer strides and extended his hand.

"I'm Firman Middle. The two whirlwinds that just blew past you are First Kimshee Krell Middle and Healer Tatra Wileyse."

Firman clasped Trazar's shoulder. "Who did you say you were again?"

"Sentry Commander Trazar Laiman." Trazar's attention was fixed on those tending his sister. "You said one of them is a healer?"

"The skinny one. I'll have her check your hand later. The other one's been looking for LaRenna for days."

"I know her," replied Trazar. "First Officer Middle posted on Langus, same as I." He watched Tatra examine LaRenna's foot. She checked the bandages to ensure the drainage ran clear and gave Krell a satisfied nod. Then she adjusted the finger splint and began to untie the bindings on her ribcage.

"They're broken," called Trazar.

"I know." Tatra glanced over her shoulder at him. "I'm loosening them to promote her breathing. Did you tend to her foot?"

"I did what I could."

"Good work," she replied. "You saved it from amputation."

"What about the ankle? I didn't know what to do about it."

"It's past full repair, but thanks to you she'll still have it." Tatra smiled sympathetically at Krell, knowing the information was painful. "A brace will help. She'll adjust." LaRenna's low fluidic cough prompted Tatra to hold her ear to her chest. She listened and gave several experimental thumps but no amount of physician's training was able to disguise the diagnosis when she looked up. "She has pneumonia."

"Fix it," said Krell.

"I can't. Not here. There's not a remedy in my pack or in a Hiding Cave's medical stores. Taelachs just don't get illnesses of this nature." Tatra glanced up at Firman. "We'll have to send one of you to the Training Grounds medical compound for what I need."

"Can't we carry her there?" suggested Trazar.

"No." Krell cradled LaRenna's head. "She wouldn't make it off the cliffs and wouldn't last the time it took to go for medicines. She's dying. Tatra, for love of the Mother, please help her."

Tatra placed her hand over Krell's. "There's little I can do. She's simply too weak. Draining the fluid from her lungs might make her more comfortable, but"—she looked to Firman—"it's out of our hands."

"No, it's not." Krell couldn't hold back her tears. "There is something I can do and you know it."

"No!" Tatra's eyes grew large. "It's far too early."

"I'll do it with or without your help. I can't let her slip away from me again." Krell removed the cloth from LaRenna's forehead. "Hold on, wren bird. I'll be there soon."

LaRenna's eyes briefly fluttered in response.

"Krell?"

"Yes, I'm here. Open your eyes for me."

LaRenna's lids slowly parted.

"Krell."

"There you are, wren bird. I've been looking for you. You know what I'm going to do, don't you?"

LaRenna turned her face away.

"No."

Krell eased LaRenna's face around until she looked up again. "I'm not going to argue with you, darlin'. Just know that I love you and I'll be with you in a little while."

"I'm not strong enough to fight anymore."

"Close those eyes, wren bird, before they close themselves. I'll be out here making ready while you rest up for me."

No, let me go. LaRenna's heavy lids collapsed together despite her resistance.

I'm far too stubborn for that. Stop wasting your energy by arguing. Krell pushed a light pleasure phase that forced LaRenna back to sleep.

"Krell, you can't!" wailed Tatra. "A soul phase between new lovers is unheard of. It'll kill you both."

"Life won't be worth living if I lose her." LaRenna began to convulse in Krell's arms, gasping short wheezing breaths that returned little air to her inflamed lungs. "Please, Tatra, it has to be now."

"Firman?" Tatra turned to him. "We can't let this happen."

"The decision isn't yours to make." He pulled her to him. "If their faith in each other is strong enough, it will work. If not, then at least they'll be together. Help Krell into the soul phase then let things happen as they may."

Tatra sighed a deep, tearful breath, then looked back to examine the determination in Krell's face. She was in deep meditative prayer, preparing her mind and body for what was LaRenna's last hope. Such dedication, such self-sacrifice could not be ignored. Firman turned Tatra's face to his and nodded, releasing her of all guilt, any notion of another choice. "Your help is crucial."

"Why do I always find myself a part of the Middle clan's impossibilities?" She sighed. "All right, let's do it." Tatra set about preparing a space in an adjoining room.

Firman enlisted Trazar's assistance in removing all the store crates from the space, explaining the precarious situation to his fellow Autlach as they added the supplies to those of the front chamber. "That's the gist." Firman wiped his brow. "They both survive or they both die."

"And if Krell doesn't attempt the soul phase?" asked Trazar.

"This far away from the proper medicines, if Krell doesn't try this, LaRenna will die for sure."

Tatra passed them sweepers and ushered them back into the room. "Give that floor a good raking. I want it as clean as possible."

"How clean can one get a cave floor?" Firman leered in her direction.

Tatra winked at him. "Just do it and stop overanalyzing everything I say." She giggled at her own retort then returned to the main chamber and the expanded mound of crates. "How do you want things arranged in there, Krell?" She rifled through the contents of the nearest box.

Krell sat cross-legged on LaRenna's bedroll. "Stack the bedding as high and as thick as you can. I want her comfortable."

"Anything else?" She heaped bedding and pillows beside the door.

"No, just that. Please hurry, she's slipping away." The urgency of Krell's request startled everyone into doubling their pace. They unfolded sleep platforms into a double thick, triple width frame and spread an abundance of rolls on top. Tatra disassembled two rolls and laid the blankets to the side for use as top covers. The men piled pillows high at one end of the arrangement.

"Not that way, you lugs, surround the—ah, let me do it." She snatched the pillows and tossed them around the perimeter of the platform, creating the effect of a padded nest. "Done. Go get Krell."

Firman turned just as his sibling appeared in the doorway, LaRenna cradled in her arms. She faced Trazar, letting LaRenna's warm thoughts speak for her. "I'll do everything I can for your sister, Trazar Laiman."

"I never told—"

Krell nodded toward LaRenna. "She did, in her fever dreams. You and Firman must leave. There's nothing else you can do."

Trazar departed after a quick kiss to his sister's forehead, but Firman lingered momentarily. "See you when you return, Krell Tanchana." He pressed the lost amulet into Krell's palm. "Tatra gave it to me," he whispered. "Said she had a copy made when you two were together and gave you back the dummy. She was wearing it when we fled Langus. Now you have everything you were missing. Don't lose yourself." Without another word, he walked away and closed the door. Tatra stood by the bedside while Krell eased LaRenna into its softness then slid the amulet over her head. The healer checked all the bandages then eased LaRenna out of her sweat-drenched clothing and under a light blanket. Krell undressed as well, then took a spot next to LaRenna.

"You ready then?" Tatra asked.

Krell snuggled into LaRenna and nodded. Tatra placed their arms above the blanket then lashed LaRenna's right to Krell's left, immediately above the wrist. "The binding of arms symbolizes the joining of your spirits before, during, and after the soul phase takes place." Tatra's expression lost some of its reverence. "Never thought I'd be putting you to bed with another woman."

"Never thought I'd be letting you. Take care of Firman for me, will you?"

"You can do it yourself when you return." Tatra patted Krell's arm and turned to her medical pack. She opened a small packet of powders into a vial of sterile water, capped it tightly, and shook it vigorously. It reacted chemically, producing an orange smoke that threatened to burst the container. Rag to her face, Tatra released the top of the jittering vial and a thick vapor spewed into the room—a Taelach pain reliever used in large areas where the injured outnumbered those capable of phasing relief. In the chamber's confined space, the effect was compounded, making Krell lightheaded in the first few breaths. Tatra mumbled something unintelligible through the cloth then looked down, removing the cloth to repeat what she'd said. "Bring her back in your soul phase, Krell. We need you both." She covered her mouth again before the sweet-smelling gas could overtake her and backed out of the room.

In the relaxed depths of the drugged haze, Krell pushed a heavy pleasure phase, praying LaRenna had enough remaining strength to accept it. She did. Pure light energy encased them both, bringing them together in a form beyond the physical. Where one ended, the other began. LaRenna's pain was Krell's, Krell's strength LaRenna's. They drifted somewhere between life and death as LaRenna's body began to fail. Krell breathed for them both, sustaining LaRenna's existence. Concepts of time and space, Autlach and Taelach faded from their reality. All that remained was their one spirit, their one being, one voice, one heart. They were soul phased.

Chapter Thirty-four

Painful memories, though deeply suppressed, are never truly forgotten.

—Taelach wisdom

They floated between realities, Krell's entire being wrapping LaRenna's, shielding her from the consuming cold of Death.

Wren bird? Krell's thoughts rang inside their common existence, warming them both. LaRenna pushed at the black as she struggled to respond.

Krell?

Darlin' mine, let me hold you safe while we fight this.

I . . . I can't see you.

I'm all around you. We're soul phased. Can't you feel me?

Silence. *I hurt.*

I'm here, Wren bird. Let me take away some of the pain. Give me the weight in your chest.

No, you'll hurt too . . . I won't lose you, can't lose you.

And I won't lose you either. Give me the weight. LaRenna's smothering pain became manageable. *Better, sweetheart?*

No. You hurt now.

I'm fine. We've divided the pain. Push away from the blackness. Give it a phase to force it out.

Silence. A weaker, pleading call. *Kkrreell.*

Darlin', what's wrong?

They won't leave me alone . . . the more I fight, the stronger they become . . . help me.

They?

They're crushing me.

I'm taking some of the weight from you. Breathe, LaRenna, breathe. Again, the pain released. *Better?*

Yes . . . Silence. *No.*

Wren bird?

Not again.

LaRenna?

Silence.

LARENNA, SPEAK TO ME!

LaRenna managed a tiny hollow hole of a whisper. *Why, Krell, why?*

Share with me, Renna. I'll make them go.

It's too much.

No! Let me in!

Silence, deafening silence punctuated by a single sob.

LARENNA! HOLD ON!

Krell's grip slipped and LaRenna began to fade. Instinctively, she focused a phase that reached far beyond the limits of their joining. Krell's energy entered LaRenna's mind, braced for a struggle but unprepared for what she found—vivid images of the Creiloff twins that had been imbedded by the prock. Their images overwhelmed LaRenna's psyche, crowding her until little of her strength remained.

Cance's image lashed out first. *She's gone, guardian, gone. Leave her with us. She's ours. We've ruined her for all others.*

243

NO! Krell replied as she searched for any sign of LaRenna. *I feel her presence.*

Back off, bitch. Brandoff's specter joined the fray. *She's ours! Cut your losses before we take you, too.*

You're dead, continued Krell as her search became frantic. *You're both dead.*

We live in her mind, in her fears. Cance swept forward, blocking Krell's path. *She sustains us in her nightmares. We've scarred her. She can't escape our touch.*

Krell swung out to strike Cance, but her blow passed through the image and she fell forward, beyond Cance and onto the ground near where LaRenna's injured psyche lay. *Renna, they're not real. They can't harm you anymore. Renna! Listen to me!*

Cance's image stepped up again, blocking the distance between the lovers. *Stupid whore, do you honestly think she can hear you now? She's too weak.*

LARENNA! They're dead. Krell reached through Cance to touch LaRenna's arm. *I can't help if you won't listen. Please, Wren bird, please!*

LaRenna shifted but wouldn't look up. *Krel . . . no . . . save yourself . . . go.*

Brandoff drifted behind her twin's image to stand beside LaRenna. *She doesn't want you. The choice is yours, join her in service to us, or die alone.*

Renna! I won't leave you. I can't live without you. Fight them baby, make them leave you alone. They're in YOUR head. It's up to you.

But how? I'm so tired.

See? Brandoff bent to stroke LaRenna's hair. *She's given up. Prock does that, you know, makes you more willing, submissive even when it hurts. And believe me, guardian, we make it HURT.*

Krell shivered but held fast. *LaRenna, darlin', heart of my own, I will not stand here and argue with specters. You belong to me, beside me, with me. Me and only me. No matter what anyone else has done or said, you're mine. If you won't fight them, I must remain here with you. My place is by your side. Better to die beside you than live without you.* She lay beside LaRenna and curled around her, demonstrating her defiance.

Immediately, the twins' images solidified. Brandoff grasped Krell by the hair and pulled her head back. *Let's find out just how strong you are.*

She's yours. Cance descended on LaRenna. *I've a lesson to teach.*

No, Krell. LaRenna opened her eyes. *Don't let her.*

Krell resisted the urge to cry out in pain as Brandoff pushed her to the edge. *You stay. I stay. You are my intended and I will remain by your side. If this is the fate you choose, so be it.*

Krell, no. LaRenna struggled to free herself of Cance's hold, but Cance pinned her shoulders to the ground.

Shut up, LaRenna Cances.

LaRenna rallied the last of her strength. *I'm not yours. You can't have my guardian and you can't have me.* LaRenna heaved Cance from her, sending her sprawling on the ground a distance away. *Krell, help me. I need you. I want you and only you!*

Wren bird! Krell called out above Cance's angry scream. *Fight with me?*

With you, for you, because of you.

This is the LaRenna I know! Krell laughed bitterly and turned, grabbing Brandoff by the hair.

Stronger than you thought, aren't I?

Brandoff screeched and fell back as her image became transparent once again. *Cance!*

Idiot! Cance turned from her fading twin to glare at LaRenna. *You're a worthless slut, LaRenna, and too weak to get rid of me. Submit now before I teach you both a lesson.* She rotated on one leg and kicked out, trying to knock LaRenna off balance.

Krell blocked her attempt, grabbing Cance's foot, flipping her face-first into the ground. *You won't touch her again.*

Fucker! Cance rose quickly, in a rage that caused LaRenna to doubt her newfound strength. LaRenna looked up at Krell, at her expression, at the love and determination in her eyes. This was real. Krell was real. The twins were dead, images of something that had painfully passed. They only had power if she allowed it.

She took Krell's hand and turned toward Cance. *No! I'm not helpless. Begone!*

Cance flew forward to strike but drew back when LaRenna shook her head. *No more.*

Cance's image flashed briefly but solidly. *Such strength is arousing, little girl. Be careful how you wield it.*

Go away! You are no more than a figment of my imagination—a memory, nothing more!

Bitch! Whore! Brandoff's image pushed around her twin, unsteady and flickering as she spat at LaRenna. *You know what you are deep inside. You can't cast us out forever. We'll be there. You know we will. You can't fight us alone.*

She's not alone. Krell drew LaRenna into her arms. *We're soul phasers, as she lives so do I.*

LaRenna grew within the unconditional love Krell expressed for her. She had the strength to survive, to overcome. Reality waited—a reality infinitely better than the madness present in Brandoff's continued existence. *You're dead! You have no power over me.* With those words, Brandoff's image disappeared.

I won't go so quickly, said Cance, stepping over the spot where her twin had stood. *I continue to eat at you even as we fight. You can't defeat me. I'll always be picking away at you. Piece by piece, I will consume your sanity.*

I say it again—she's not alone. Krell squeezed LaRenna's hand and they kicked out as one, slamming Cance into the wall LaRenna had created with her emerging power.

I AM NO LONGER AFRAID OF YOU, CANCE CREILOFF! The energy of LaRenna's voice resounded through Cance's image, reducing it to translucence. *YOU TOOK NOTHING THAT KRELL HASN'T ALREADY REPLACED. BEGONE AND NEVER RETURN. YOU ARE DEAD! I AM FREE OF YOU!*

Cance shriveled, her image dripping away in stench-filled puddles of decay. *I'll be back, my lady, maybe not this cycle or this pass, but I'll be back. My love for you runs too deep. There are still lessons to be taught. I'll be back, and when I do, I'll take you with me, straight back to the hell you created in your own mind!* With a final burst of flaming hatred, she was gone and there was silence.

Firman roused when the first rumbles of the aerolaunch bounced throughout the Hiding Cave. At first, he thought a new intense storm had unleashed itself and he cursed the weather patterns of the wet season. But the noise grew steadily louder rather than trailing off like thunder should, causing him to sit up and listen. Trazar was also up, concentrating on the sound.

"Cyclone?" asked Firman.

"Too mechanical," replied Trazar. "Has to be a launch of some kind. It is! An aerolaunch! The positioning thrusters just fired. They've found us!"

"What's all the noise?" Tatra stumbled from her bedroll.

"Aerolaunch," explained Trazar. "Have you checked them yet?"

"No, just woke myself. I'll look in on them now." Tatra peeked into the other chamber then pulled back, a befuddled expression pasted on her slender face. "They're gone!"

"Merciful Mother!" Firman howled from close behind her. "I prayed all night that this would work."

Tatra turned to him near panic. "You don't understand! They're gone! Not there! Vanished!"

"What?" Both Autlachs pushed in to see for themselves. The room was empty, save for the bedding they had stacked the day before.

Krell had awakened long before dawn, feeling more alive and filled with purpose than she remembered. Unlashing their arms, she eased from the bed and into a tunic, then snuck barelegged into the main chamber. With silent Kimshee agility, she retrieved two changes of clothing and a generous supply of sterile wraps. She toted her load to the cave's thermal pools, diverted some of the waters into a tub, uncrated several towels and a soaping stone, then hurried back to the bed to waken LaRenna. LaRenna objected to being rousted from the comfort of their bed but stopped complaining when Krell informed her it was for a much-needed bath.

The water's pressure on her fragile ribs phased away, LaRenna soaked, her bad foot draped over the side so the stitches would stay dry. Krell sat on the edge to help her wash. LaRenna was beginning to resemble her former self. Her bruises were fading at an accelerated rate, cuts weren't nearly as angry, and a glimmer of playful spirit shone as gold flecks in her eyes. She teased Krell, splashing her to the point she climbed into the tub without bothering to undress. "It's the driest place to be with you flinging water about." Krell laughed, shaking off a faceful of moisture.

"While you're in here, you might as well help me wash my hair," replied LaRenna. "It always feels better when someone else does it. Besides, it hurts to stretch. And take that tunic off, sweetheart, it smells of sweat now that it's wet."

Krell stood up to remove the waterlogged tunic. "That's not it," she teased, drawing behind LaRenna. "You just wanted me out of my clothes."

"Worked, didn't it?" LaRenna passed back the soaping stone and enjoyed the feel of Krell's gentle hands massaging her scalp. The chore done and the soap rinsed away, LaRenna leaned back and let Krell's tender caresses extend down her neck and body. Krell was infinitely patient and very attentive to her fears.

In the midst of the peace and gentle passion, Krell began to recite the Oath, placing her cheek against LaRenna's as she spoke. "I take you for my life mate, no, my soul mate, the fellow raiser of any daughters we should take as our own. I will defend you from the harms of the world by hand, sword, and bow. Your stores will always be filled and your spirit free from the concerns of Autlach oppression. I vow this to you as your guardian, your lover, your life mate."

LaRenna smiled, kissed Krell's cheek, then replied, "And I take you for my soul mate, my guardian, fellow raiser of any daughters we should take as our own. I will work beside you to benefit both clan and family. I accept the security you offer and in return promise to keep the hearth lit. I promise this as your lover and life mate."

They were wrapped in each others arms, making plans for the

future when Krell first heard the roar of the aerolaunch. "Hear that?"

"Hmmm?" LaRenna roused from her contented daydream. "Yeah, I do. Sounds like a launch."

"An aerolaunch! Our ride home is here." Krell wiped away the spots that hadn't soaked from LaRenna's skin and lifted her carefully to the tub's wide lip. LaRenna toweled off as much as she could. Krell helped, but it was half-hearted, more to dissolve the scent of their passions than to remove dirt.

"It won't do any good." LaRenna draped her towel over her dripping white curls. "One look at the expression on your face will have everyone thinking we're in love or something."

"Is it a look of satisfaction?" Krell jumped from the tub. " 'Cause that's what it is." She threw on fresh underclothes, a sleeveless service jumpsuit, and her familiar rag-toed boots. "Brought you a jumper, too." Krell wrapped LaRenna's ribs with expertise. "No Kimshee I know would be caught dead in skirts."

LaRenna peered up hesitantly. "You don't mind?"

"Why should I mind? It's your body, not mine." Krell cocked a brow. "I'm just happy you choose to share it with me. Besides, I know what's under anything you decide to wear."

"Flirt!"

"Yeah, and you like it that way." Krell fastened the front of LaRenna's jumper and scooped her into the air. "Let's find them before they catch us back here." Krell carried her into the main cavern as their companions emerged from the side chamber and Belsas and Chandrey appeared in the main archway. LaRenna looked at her raisers in dismay and pointed to their blue mourning sashes.

"Who died?"

"No one!" Chandrey ripped away the sash as she rushed to embrace her daughter. "No one at all."

Chapter Thirty-five

If you are not certain the enemy you leave behind is dead, go back and slit his throat a second time.

—*Sarian military wisdom*

A joyful reunion took place that morning. LaRenna told of her harrowing experience, sparing her raisers the more garish details of her captivity. Krell remained by her side the entire time, admiring her lover's sensitivity. LaRenna was quite sympathetic to her raisers' need to comfort her, even allowing Chandrey to fuss over her without complaint.

"Your leg, child, it's in ribbons. And why is the bandage in such disarray? What of infection?"

"I'm fine, Mamma," said LaRenna. "Krell hasn't had a chance to rewrap it this morning. We were in a hurry when we heard the launch. If someone will get the supplies, she can do it right now." Trazar quickly moved a medical crate to Krell's side.

Chandrey smoothed her daughter's jumper. "Your hair is wet, too. Were you bathing?"

"Yes, Mamma, I was long overdue. Yes, my hair will grow back in time. And yes, you can comb it out like you did when I young."

"She didn't say those things to you, Renna," Belsas exclaimed.

"Not aloud she didn't. I heard her think them. I still lack the ability to block out a loved one's thoughts. I didn't mean to hear her. Honest."

"It doesn't matter." Chandrey carefully pulled her pocket comb through her daughter's hair. "We'll just have to watch what we think until you master your abilities."

Krell sent a shiver of delighted energy through LaRenna's body. "The way her talents seem to be developing, that shouldn't take long." She reached into the crate and brought out a large roll of gauze. "If you were only able to heal that quickly, love, I'd have you dancing inside a moon cycle."

"I'm afraid that won't happen for some time." Tatra began removing the soiled bandages. "LaRenna knows she will have to wear a brace."

"Couldn't the specialists help?" Belsas absently projected a picture of her daughter running as a child then shed the thought. "I'm sorry, LaRenna. You're so hurt. The thought just flew into my head. It was your fifth claiming anniversary and we'd taken you—"

"On a picnic. I remember." LaRenna tucked away her sadness and faced her guardian raiser with a bright expression. "We'll have to do that again some day, minus the chase games."

"Yes. Yes, we will." Belsas gestured to Tatra. "What of the foot, Healer Wileyse?"

"The specialists will help somewhat," she replied. "But the joint has been shattered and most of the ligaments, tendons, and well, basically everything is a mess. Surgery will give her some mobility but nothing will repair all the damage." She glanced at Firman, pleading with him for the right words. He raised his eyebrows and nodded slowly, prompting her to say something encouraging. "LaRenna's strong, Grandmaster Belsas. She's survived the unthinkable. This shouldn't prove too much of a challenge for her, especially with Krell's help." Firman grinned and motioned her to join him on one of the crates.

"Very good," he whispered as she sat next to him. "That was quite compassionate."

"Thank you." Her reply purred in his ear. "I just need a reminder every now and then."

"I'll see what I can do."

Chandrey watched them from the corner of her eye, putting to rest any concerns she had about the healer's past with Krell. There was closeness between LaRenna and Krell that eclipsed the normal levels of Taelach commitment. They seemed to communicate without phase or words—Krell offering assistance just before it was needed, flinching when LaRenna caught her broken finger on the cuff of her jumper though she hadn't seen it happen.

"Look at them, Bel," said Chandrey. "LaRenna's never looked so happy and Krell, well, this is the first time I've seen her sit still for more than a few minutes."

"I'm content." Krell tweaked LaRenna's healthy foot. "Your daughter keeps me on my toes plenty enough."

"And she always will," assured Belsas with a sly smile to Chandrey. "Her foot may slow her some, but I doubt it will stop her. Have either of you made plans for after she heals?"

"As a matter of fact, we have." Krell cast an inquiring look that LaRenna returned with a nod to proceed freely. "We would like to become teacher qualified for the Training Grounds. I have the service time and LaRenna, well, her abilities will speak for themselves soon enough."

Belsas seemed distressed by the idea. "Don't know if that will work. Can't have a third officer teaching at the Grounds. It wouldn't sit well with the other faculty." Then her sullen face lightened to a grin. "But if someone was willing to accept a disability discharge and a position as a civilian instructor—"

"If it means I can teach others with my talent, I'll gladly take it!"

252

LaRenna settled back in the comforting knowledge her future with Krell was secured. *Happy, love?* she broadcast on their open link.

Krell's reply twinkled with satisfaction. *Infinitely.*

"I believe the soul phase has changed you both," said Chandrey, observant of their unspoken exchange. "I've known one other souled couple. They were close, but you two seem more so."

Belsas confirmed Chandrey's notion. "I see it, too. That closeness is the very thing that saved your life, isn't it, daughter?"

"Yes." LaRenna offered Krell a fluttering mental caress. "Krell breathed for me when I couldn't, risked everything, life itself, to save me. I live now because of and for her."

"Rightly so." Chandrey paused to clear her throat. "Thank you, Krell, for your unshakable belief when things were at their worst, and thank you again, Sentry Commander Laiman." Trazar blushed at the continued attention. "If it hadn't been for your keen family instincts, she never would have survived until she was found. This truly is a day of celebration."

"I can think of one here who isn't celebrating yet." Belsas nodded toward the cave entrance.

"Oh no!" Chandrey's hands flew to her mouth. "I completely forgot. LaRenna, Malley is here."

"Malley!" exclaimed LaRenna, ecstatic at the prospect of seeing her dear friend again.

"Wait a minute, Renna," said Chandrey. "Malley was crushed to learn Krell was in your life. There is true caring in her heart. Go lightly."

Krell kissed LaRenna's forehead and stood. "She's right, wren bird. I sensed it when I first met Malley. I'd best make myself busy elsewhere while you speak with Malley. Is that okay with you?"

LaRenna's reply bubbled pure gratitude. "Thank you, darling. I think it would be best at that. Why don't you bundle some blankets for my journey home?"

"I'll be as close as the next room. Call if you need me."

Chandrey watched Krell retreat from the chamber. "She's considerate of you, LaRenna. That's an admirable trait I think we all should take as an example. Bel?"

"Commander Laiman?" inquired Belsas. "Would you relieve Third Engineer Whellen?"

"Gladly, Grandmaster Belsas." Trazar disappeared through the archway.

Chandrey ushered the others from the room, leaving LaRenna to wait. A minute later, Malley appeared at the chamber entrance. Her eyes lit when LaRenna came into view and she rushed to LaRenna's side, laying her head in her lap. LaRenna rubbed at her shorn head, soaking in the pent-up emotions an overwhelmed Malley unconsciously projected. "Sweet Malley, you worried for me, too, didn't you?"

Malley reached up to caress her face. "I never heard from you after you posted. Then they told me you were dead. My heart broke when I thought you were gone."

"I only got your note the evening before I had to go under-cover. There wasn't time for a reply. You were in my thoughts and prayers, same as always."

Malley rose and stumbled back. "You mean you were too busy with your new lover to reply." She rejected LaRenna's extended hand to pace the room. "I thought we had a future. Then, then you take up with the first guardian who comes along. Your Kimshee teacher at that! How could you?"

"You're a dear friend, Malley, my best friend. I never knew you felt more."

"Never knew?" Malley's voice trembled. "How could I have made my intentions plainer? We were lovers!"

"We were one-time phase lovers, Malley," reminded LaRenna. "And then we were both wine-laced. You never mentioned or pur-sued it again after that so I assumed you weren't interested. You even saw others socially."

Malley's eyes tinged with jealousy. "Only because you did!"

LaRenna laid her hands to her face. "Malley, you're my closest friend and I love you very, very much, just—"

"Not in that way. I'm always late when it comes to you, aren't I?" Malley shook and sobbed. "Damn you! Damn you! You never could do anything in a small way!"

"Malley, I—"

"Are you oathed?" Malley stopped pacing to stare at her, repeating the question when LaRenna didn't answer immediately. "ARE—YOU—OATHED?"

"Yes, we are." LaRenna wished nothing more than to wipe the tears from her friend's eyes. She didn't regret her choice, only the pain it caused Malley. "I never meant to hurt you."

A low, smooth voice interrupted the dialogue. "Moving reunion but frankly, I am too tired to concern myself with the ins and outs of a Taelach love triangle." Talmshone stood in the entrance, holding a blaster in his trembling hands. "Salutations, young mistress LaRenna, it appears you are on the path to recovery. If you desire to stay that way, you and your companion will remain silent. And keep your phase fired eyes tuned elsewhere. I guarantee I can land a blast in the time it takes you to accomplish a phase. Do you comprehend?"

LaRenna drew back. "NO! You—you died in the floods. Trazar said he saw the launch sink. You're dead!"

"Iralians are capable of holding their breath for many hours. As for your brother—" Talmshone snorted. "The Commander never knew what hit him. For that matter"—he sucked a morsel from between his teeth—"neither did the tender young officer material I dined on yesterday. Now, do you wish to sustain their fate or are you going to cooperate?"

Persuaded by the Iralian's gruesome reference, they complied, Malley drawing close to LaRenna in instinctual guardian protectiveness. Talmshone appeared disheveled and in intense pain. He cradled his bandaged right hand to his side, keeping pressure on the swollen rip in his abdomen. His overshirt was caked with blood and mud and his leggings, a pair of Training Ground issue, strained with every flex of his double-muscled thighs. He looked over Malley's braid markings, grinning subtly when he found what he sought.

"It appears I am in need of your services, guardian engineer. I require a pilot and you so conveniently happen to be one."

"No!" Malley drew up in challenge, standing directly between the Iralian and LaRenna. "I wouldn't run a herd beast out of here for you, much less an aerolaunch!"

"You will." Talmshone took sidesteps until LaRenna was in his sights. "You will or I kill her."

LaRenna clutched Malley's legs. "Don't do it. He'll kill us both regardless."

Talmshone stepped forward and dug the blaster into LaRenna's ribcage until she gasped. "I am out of time and patience. Engineer, pick up your lady love and head to the launch before I burn a hole in her lovely white skin."

"The others will hear you if you open fire." Malley activated her bow.

"Gauge it down and remove it, Taelach, or you both perish before one person gets through the door." He jabbed the blaster into LaRenna again, jarring fragile ribs even more. She winced and clutched Malley's legs tighter as she broadcast the predicament to her life mate.

Krell doubled over in pain. "Iralian."

"What?" Firman was nearest to her, flirting shamelessly with Tatra.

"IRALIAN!" She barreled toward the entrance. "You're not taking her again!" The door shattered from the battering ram force and Krell tumbled out, rolling clear of Talmshone's shots.

"Damn telepaths!" The Iralian backed from the room, dragging Malley and LaRenna along as a shield. In pure unadulterated frustration, he reached out and yanked a fistful of hair from LaRenna's head. "Transmit that to your lover, Kimshee whore!" Malley tried to shield her from the attack, but Talmshone rewarded the effort by smacking Malley's ear with his blaster butt.

Belsas and the others burst into the chamber. "Top Centurion Talmshone of the Siddeaunchlun tribe, the Commitment's most notorious spy." Belsas's stare was cold.

"I thought this had the making of one of your escapades. The Commitment really stuck you this time, didn't they?"

"Belsas Exzal, Taelach supreme, you grace me with your presence." Talmshone bowed but never took his fury-red eyes off Belsas. He held up the handful he'd jerked from LaRenna's scalp. "You see the level of violence your pestering child has reduced me to?" He shook the fist at Belsas. "I have asked her and her guardian friend to accompany me. We are taking the aerolaunch to the nearest planetary port. I am anxious to see my mates and young."

"You'll never get off Saria Four alive." Belsas and Krell took small steps forward until Talmshone warded them off with a line of blasts that smoked the ground just short of their toes.

"One more pace and I will separate you both at the knee."

They stood their ground. "Take me instead," said Belsas. "I'll pilot you out of here, grant you safe passage, and see you get home."

"I am no fool." Talmshone clutched his side as pain faded his green hide to gray-yellow. "If I allow the Taelach of All to accompany me, I will never reach Iralian space. The Kinship will have us shot down before they allow you to fall into the Commitment's hands. No, your daughter is the logical choice."

"I'll have you shot down carrying her as well." Belsas felt numb.

"The Taelach species possesses too much empathy for that to happen. The youngsters go with me." Talmshone backed into the corridor, pulling his prisoners along.

"Renna." Malley drew close to LaRenna's head.

Malley? LaRenna established a mental link. *I—*

Remember, LaRenna. Malley blocked the channel. There was more to LaRenna than Malley remembered, a new substance, a new completion that came in addition to her love for Krell and, in that brief accepting moment, Malley knew it must be protected. *No matter what happens to us, I love you and I always will. You need your energy to phase, so shut the link.*

But—

Do as I ask. Now shut the link.

I love you, too, Malley Whellen. LaRenna closed the channel and braced for the upcoming battle.

Talmshone forced them toward the open doors of the launch, watching those who followed from a distance. Trazar lay in their path, bleeding from the back of the head.

LaRenna probed her brother's condition, rejoicing when she found him conscious. She broke the channel when Malley stepped onto the aerolaunch's extended docking ramp. LaRenna squeezed Malley's hand then sent a crippling pain phase into Talmshone. He shook his head slowly, resisting the temptation to scratch away the aggravating sensation.

"Stop it, Taelach. You do nothing but make me angrier." LaRenna increased the phase, blurring Talmshone's vision. "STOP IT!" He rushed forward, prepared to crush LaRenna's skull. Trazar grabbed his legs when he came within reach and jerked hard, sprawling him forward.

Malley hurled LaRenna into the seats on the launch's far side then kicked back, knocking the blaster from Talmshone's hand. The weapon spiraled off the ramp.

"Bitches, all of you!" He sprang to his feet. "I will kill every last one of you and consume your worthless hearts purely for the pleasure of it!" Malley lunged at him, shoving him toward the edge. He grasped her belt and lifted her over his head, tossing her into Trazar. The force threw them backward, slamming them against the cavern wall.

"Malley! Trazar! No!" LaRenna cried in horror as they fell. In that terrified moment, her phase dropped and Talmshone, leering dreadfully, reached for her.

"Even Kimshee apprentices are all pilot briefed, I do believe." He pulled her into the crushing crook of his arm. "You cannot phase without oxygen, young one." His lock tightened until her eyes rolled back. "I should have done this long ago. It is much tidier than Cance's methods."

"Don't harm her!" bellowed Krell. "She's never flown an aero-launch."

"Then I will drop her from the ramp unless a more qualified individual agrees to be of assistance." Talmshone dragged her to the edge and let her flailing legs dangle into the void. "I am waiting."

"Let her have footing and air," said Krell. "And I'll go with you."

"Remove your bow and walk my direction, guardian."

Talmshone loosened his grip slightly, allowing LaRenna to take a single breath. She dangled from his arm, a bare toe length above the ramp. "I will let her breathe when you are safely in the pilot's position."

Phase him. LaRenna's inner voice was almost nonexistent. *Pain phase him!*

Not until you're on solid ground. Krell slowly entered the launch. "I've done what you asked. Let her down." Talmshone dropped LaRenna on the ramp for a moment, letting her take several deep breaths before he put her in a head lock again, this time with a grip loose enough for her take partial breaths. "Get used to it, girl. My arm and sparing breaths are your fate until we are safely in Iralian space."

LaRenna pushed into his hold, sliding her head down until she could bite his arm. When she did, Talmshone dropped his grip, knocking her off the ramp. Her hands somehow found his ankle as she fell and she gripped it for dear life. Everything spun as she fought to for a hold. She hurt without solace, her stretched ribs searing, her foot an anchor dragging her down. A chorus of cries flew through her head. Had she made them or heard them? Her fingers slid across the Iralian's slick scales, fruitless in their struggle to find a hold. Talmshone reached for her as she fell free, his fingers slipping through hers. Time seemed to slow as she fell. She could see everyone's faces so clearly. Talmshone's gray-yellow shaded a surprised pink. Krell lunged for her. Belsas and Firman ran headlong for her, their faces a mixture of disbelief and helplessness. Tatra clutched Chandrey's arm, pulling her from the cliff edge. Their voices circled her as she tumbled.

"Girl, what are you doing?"

"My baby!"

"Hold on, LaRenna!"

"Renna!"

They jumbled together until she couldn't tell one from the other. Only Krell's strong voice cut the panic. It was telepathic, a booming broadcast of a single command. *Put me where you'll land. NOW! LARENNA! NOW!*

"KKKKRRRREEEELLLLL!" Abruptly, the scream stopped.

"No!" Chandrey collapsed back into Tatra.

Belsas and Firman continued their forward sweep, plowing into Talmshone and throwing him into the launch doors. *You killed her!* Belsas forced a vengeful pain phase at him as he struggled to his feet. *You murdered my child!*

Talmshone shrugged off the phase. "Fight me fairly, Belsas, and quit hiding behind that excuse for a phase. Your daughter had a better command of it than you. Her phase could have stopped me. Yours is an insect—small, annoying, and crushable."

Belsas stepped forward to push harder. "My phase may not be as intense as LaRenna's but I am not alone in my efforts." Talmshone fell back as Chandrey released her anger in the violent spasms that she centered on his spine.

"You took my only child!" She ignored his pleas for mercy and pushed all her energy at him.

"Taelach laws do not allow for death for a single murder." Talmshone cowered in the back of the launch. "You cannot execute me for it! It is forbidden by the Kinship!"

Tatra steadied Chandrey as she lent her own mind to the punishment. "You didn't kill just one. Over one million died on Langus. That gives Belsas the right to pass immediate judgment."

Talmshone howled and stumbled back onto the ramp, scraping the scales from his face as he tried to wipe away the pain. "Mercy! In your Mother Maker's name, have mercy!"

Firman caught the Iralian's tunic front. "I sincerely wish I could push the death phase into you myself, but I'll leave that honor to Krell." He looked into the launch's pilot seat. "Where'd she go?"

Belsas stepped into the launch, never turning from the phase holding Talmshone frozen. Krell was indeed gone. "You threw her over the side as well!" Belsas's anger now burned out of control. "I hereby find you guilty of mass murder, sabotage, and other crimes too numerous to mention. You are sentenced to immediate death by pain phase."

Their combined phases strangled out his objections, collapsing him onto the ramp. Tatra and Chandrey slowly approached, their phases growing heavier as they drew near. Talmshone peered up at them, searching for some sign of sympathy. Finding none, he fumbled in his tunic pocket and pulled a small folding knife, which he drew across his neck, slicing two of the three main veins. The move caught his executioners by surprise, distracting them into dropping their phases.

"Taelach justice is swift." Blood gurgled up and out Talmshone's mouth. "But the Iralian can take that from you, too. I take my own life before I lose it to you." The knife fell from his hand and he slumped forward.

Belsas flipped him over. "He's gone. Iralians consider it an honor to commit suicide in the line of duty. It'll make a martyr out of him." She took Chandrey's arm, leading her away from the scene. "Healer Wileyse, please tend to Commander Laiman while I call for a launch to take Engineer Whellen's remains to the Training Grounds. Firman, would you please begin searching for any sign of Krell and LaRenna? Mother, please let them be alive. We have seen more than enough death as of late."

"A search won't be necessary." Firman stood at the ramp edge. A smile spanned his face, one that was wider than his mustache could ever cover. "You'll have to see for yourselves. Words can't describe this." The others joined him on the ramp and laughed joyfully at what they saw.

Krell was waist deep in the mud, LaRenna in her arms. They

were locked in an exuberant, full-mouth kiss, aware they were being watched but not caring in the least.

Krell?

Yeah, wren bird?

Good catch.

Thanks, but you deserve the credit for teleporting me here.

Nah, it was mainly you. Your idea after all. How did you know I could do it?

Faith and prayer, LaRenna. It was the Mother's way of showing you what a precious gift you have.

Gift?

Yes, lover. Krell winked. *Who but you could move me like that?*

Oh, Krell.

What? My humor fails you?

No, it's just that, well, make me a promise?

Anything, sweetheart, just name it.

Promise you'll always be there to catch me when I fall?

LaRenna Krells, from this day forward, I will be constantly by your side. Come fire, flood, famine, or freeze, I will always be as close as your touch. That is my new Oath to you. I will never leave you again, not for a minute.

And Krell never did, not by choice, not even for a minute.

262

Chapter Thirty-six

Love is a powerful healer, capable of more than science can imagine or reason.

—Taelach wisdom

"Krell, darling, wake up." LaRenna licked her dry lips. It had taken almost a full day for Tatra and the surgical crews to repair her numerous injuries. Krell had been in attendance during the surgeries, refusing to leave LaRenna's side while she slept. It was late now and they were alone. Tatra had removed most of the external sensors, leaving but two to measure her patient's vital signs.

LaRenna looked around the room then closed her eyes, squeezing back the tears. She was thankful for her life, for her new future, but her heart ached—ached for Malley. Why hadn't she sensed Malley's devotion?

"Don't blame yourself." LaRenna opened her eyes to see Krell looking at her. "You aren't responsible for what happened."

"I just wish I'd known." LaRenna allowed Krell to brush away her tears.

"What would it have changed?" Krell kissed LaRenna's forehead. "Malley kept it hidden and your talents weren't strong enough to pick up on such a subtlety."

"I should have—" began LaRenna, but Krell shook her head.

"Things happen for a reason and I'm sure we'll understand this in time."

"I hope." LaRenna laid her head against Krell's shoulder, lost in thought until Krell kissed her again.

"Well, now that I'm awake, how are you feeling physically? I can't tell much without an open channel from you."

"I closed it when I woke. You don't want to sense what I feel. The meds have worn off."

"Then let me help you." They reopened the link so Krell could offer relief. "I'll get Tatra."

Tatra appeared in the suite's doorway as they spoke, wearing a grin as broad as one of Firman's. "I'm here. Just waiting for you two to wake."

"You should be resting yourself," said LaRenna, managing a smile. "What's up?"

"First off," replied Tatra, "your brother will be fine. His pelvis and one leg are broken but should mend completely. If we can keep him off his feet that is."

"He's near?" asked Krell.

"Across the hall sleeping, but that's not why I'm here."

"Oh?" said Krell.

"I did a few postsurgery scans on LaRenna. One particular test had interesting results. I ran it twice just to be sure."

"What now?" LaRenna grabbed Krell's forearm, fully expecting to hear another dread infection had invaded her body.

"You have a condition that invades Autlach females from time to time. It's parasitic."

"Curable?" Krell picked up on the beginnings of a heightened link. LaRenna was frightened.

"The initial stage lasts around ten moon cycles in Autlach women. I suspect it will take about as long for you, too. The second stage usually lasts sixteen passes or so."

"That long?" It was so unfair, thought Krell. LaRenna had been through so much already. She deserved a little happiness.

I have happiness as long as I have you, Krell. Whatever this is, we'll face it together.

Krell nodded to LaRenna then looked at Tatra. "Is the condition life threatening?"

"Not usually," replied Tatra. It took every ounce of her control not to blurt out her findings. "And, Krell, unless I miss my mark, you're responsible for her condition."

"ME!" Krell's eyes grew large. "How could I be responsible? I'd never do anything to harm LaRenna!"

"There is no evidence to the contrary, so I believe you are responsible. Furthermore, it is my belief that your soul phase is what caused the condition."

"How's that?" LaRenna propped up very slowly on her elbows. She could sense Tatra holding back. Curiosity told her to probe for the truth, but moral tact told her otherwise. It wouldn't be ethical, not with a friend.

"Well," continued Tatra, "without the technicalities—"

LaRenna grinned at her. "You? Not technical? Since when?"

"It serves no purpose among you laypeople. Firman informed me of that recently." *And probably will again*, she added silently.

LaRenna stifled a giggle. She'd heard that thought without prying. "Go on, without the technicalities—"

"Without them, it's relatively simple. It seems in a soul phase there is a small level of genetic exchange. Basically, you each gain a little of the other."

"And?" prompted Krell.

"It appears, First Officer Middle, that some of your genetic material found its way into a critical part of LaRenna's, forcing a change in her body."

"Meaning?" Krell drummed her fingers on her chair.

"It's only a couple of days old, if that. Very little division has taken place, maybe to the size of pinhead. One of LaRenna's hormone levels is extremely elevated for a Taelach. In an Autlach female, the level would be only slightly elevated, not much of a sign, but in one of us any level is cause for alarm."

Krell gripped her seat. "Spit it out, Tatra. What's wrong with my wren bird?"

Tatra didn't have to finish. LaRenna suddenly realized what she was getting at. *Oh, what a glory-filled realization it was!* She squeezed her soul guardian's hand and looked up with a shining smile. "Don't you see what she's saying? When we soul phased in the Hiding Caves, you not only saved my life, you created one. Praise be to the Mother. I'm pregnant!"

Chapter Thirty-seven

You want to see life anew? Look into the eyes of your newborn child.

—LaRenna Krells

Malley's memorial service was simple and intimate. Her raisers, Dressa and Whellen, having recently renounced their Oath, each refused to attend the event if the other was present. Chandrey called their actions shallow, but LaRenna was relieved. Malley should be put to rest by those who knew her, not by those who had caused her lifelong pain.

Firman accompanied Krell to spell her from carrying LaRenna the entire three-kilometer hike, Krell resisting his assistance until he flat insisted on a turn. After all, he boasted, LaRenna was his sister. Tatra made up the rear of the small procession, fussing for them to be careful of her patient's ribs, foot, and for goodness' sake, treat her delicately—she was with child!

They stood at the Freedom Summit above the Training Grounds, facing the low rolling hills that grounded the nearby mountains. A light breeze had chased away the few remaining clouds, leaving a perfect morning for Malley to be laid to rest.

"Ready, wren bird?"

LaRenna nodded as Firman transferred her into Krell's loving arms. "Hold on!" she gasped when Krell pulled her close. "The mourning sash is digging into me. Would someone please adjust it?" Firman tugged the blue cloth back into place. "Thank you. I'm ready now. Tatra, the ash box, please."

Tatra passed her the intricately carved container. "Do you need another draw from the smoker before we begin? I know you're in pain that Krell and I can't entirely take away."

"After I'm finished. I want a clear head for this." LaRenna removed the box lid, held the container at arm's length, and looked to the three faces surrounding her. The rites were easier to speak with so many caring individuals present. Their sympathy and understanding proved comforting.

Let her go, LaRenna. Krell pushed the thought through their open channel. *It's time to send her home.* LaRenna nodded, sighed softly, and began to speak.

"Malley Alexa Whellen, those who care for you have gathered to say their farewells. Your colors of life have faded away as you were taken from us suddenly and painfully. We cry not for you, but for ourselves, for the loss and loneliness we must bear. You have gone and only your memory remains in our reach. I scatter your ashes to enrich the land so once again we can see your colors blossom. Your work here is done. I release you, Malley. Your spirit is free to fly to the stars. With the Mother Maker's help, we'll meet again someday."

Krell turned away from the breeze as LaRenna let the first handful of ashes sift through her fingers. They scattered over the hillside, landing mostly in a patch of pale yellow wildflowers in the valley below. LaRenna repeated the process until the box was emptied, each handful blowing to the same ribbon of color. Krell took the wooden box from her and tossed it down the slope. Now everything that was Malley could return to the ground and become new again.

LaRenna leaned into Krell's shoulder. "Did you see that?" Her whisper was resigned. "The ashes landed in the skirt nipper patch. They were Malley's favorite. I bet she planned it that way."

"I'm sure she did, Wren bird," replied Krell. "From now on when we see them, we'll all think of her." Krell turned toward Tatra, who held a lit smoker to LaRenna's mouth. LaRenna took two deep puffs then settled into the pain-free comfort Krell offered with it.

"Is two enough?" worried Firman as he pulled back the lighter. Even now, he managed to offer her a supportive if not comical smile.

"Yes, thank you." LaRenna looked at the flowers one last time. "No doubts, Malley. No regrets. No what ifs. The only thing that remains is the fact you loved me. You gave yourself for the life growing inside me. I will always love you for that. Peace be with you on your journey. We'll meet again someday. That's my oath to you." A single tear rolled down her face as she turned to her guardian. "Take me home, Krell. We've a life to build and a family to raise."

Chapter Thirty-eight

LaRenna and I decided to crew our own explorer vessel. Two more and we have a full complement.

—Krell Middle on the birth of the twelfth Krells child

An internal kick roused LaRenna from her night's sleep. Once again, Krell hogged the bed and covers, leaving her overly pregnant mate with a scant corner of each. LaRenna shoved Krell's sprawled leg from the top of hers and rolled on her side so she could sit upright. Movement made the pressure on her bladder overbearing but then again, she seemed to feel that way quite often the last couple of moon cycles. Krell stirred and reached to draw LaRenna close. Not finding her, she opened an eye. "You all right?"

"Yeah, nature calls."

"Again? That's the third time tonight."

"I might as well live in the bathing chamber these days." LaRenna pulled onto all fours, used a chair to maintain her balance, and stood. "Back in a minute." She padded across the cool floor to the chamber. "Make that two or three."

"Mmmhmm." Krell watched in amorous humor as she went. LaRenna's short legs and braced ankle paired with her heavy abdomen to create the effect of waddling. She slid the bathing chamber door shut then immediately back open.

"I do not waddle."

"Yes you do. It's adorable."

"Really!" LaRenna gave an incensed snort and shut the door again. A few seconds later, it slid back open. "Krell, come here please."

"Wren bird, it's the dead of night."

"Now, please." An urgency in her voice brought Krell bolting from the bed.

"What's wrong?"

LaRenna pointed to her feet. "My water broke!"

"No you don't!" Krell's eyes bounced from the floor to LaRenna. "Tatra says you're not due for another twenty-one days. The midwives aren't here yet. You can't have the baby now!"

"Well, it's not my idea!" cried LaRenna. "Talk to the child." She clutched the washbasin as an unexpected tightness formed across her stomach. "Get Tatra. Now! This isn't going to wait."

"Let me help you back to bed."

"Don't touch me!" LaRenna white-knuckled the basin with both hands until the contraction passed, leaving Krell standing lost by her side. "Dear Mother that hurt. I'm sorry, dearest, I just couldn't move."

Krell's eyes flashed blue sparks of helplessness and frustration. "Is it over? Can I touch you now?"

"Please."

She scooped LaRenna up and carried her toward the bed. Halfway there, another contraction began and her grip on Krell's arm became tight enough to leave marks.

"Ow! That's bare skin!" Krell deposited her on the bed and transferred a blanket to her laboring mate's shoulders. "I'm going for Tatra."

"Don't leave me."

"I'm just going to the next building." Krell slid on a tunic and leggings. "I'll be right back."

"Take me with you. We'll go together," LaRenna pleaded through her practiced breathing. "Please, Krell, I need you."

Krell sighed, wrapped the blanket snug about her, and scooped her up again. "So you do, Wren bird, so you do. Let's go." The main square was empty except for the sentry and she was leaning against one of the lighting poles, fast asleep. Krell made a mental note of the dereliction and kicked at the door of a neighboring apartment. "Carrying you is not at all easy right now."

"Really?" LaRenna huffed back, deep in another contraction. "I'll carry you without complaint if you'll give birth." The child pushed against its confines, poking tiny knees and elbows into her ribs and back. "Is labor always like this?"

"From what I've seen, yes. Who'd have thought the first birthing you would attend would be your own child's? Blast it! Tatra, open up!"

The door hatch hissed open and there stood Firman, dressed only in his leggings, standing in the dim glow of the room beyond. "Krell?"

She pushed past him to lay LaRenna on the front room's lounger. "Fancy seeing you here, Fir. As much as I would love to razz you right now, and I guarantee I will later, we need Tatra."

"I'm here. It's not time, is it?" Tatra appeared wearing only Firman's tunic. "How far apart are her pains?"

Krell's answer was almost drowned by LaRenna's sudden cry. "Close, and her water broke."

Tatra smoothed back LaRenna's unruly curls until the contraction eased. "How long have you been having them?"

"Not long. I woke up feeling as if I would burst if I didn't get to the facilities. The waters ruptured as soon as I got in there."

LaRenna patterned her breathing as the tightness began again. Tatra gently stroked her hair until it passed. The pains were quicker and more intense than she had been taught, LaRenna barely able to catch her breath between them.

"Better?" She patted LaRenna's hand. "Appears you slept through the initial stage, unusual but not unheard of. I believe you're in transition. We'd best get you to the birthing suite. Your raisers will be highly disappointed if you don't make use of it after all the effort they poured into its construction."

"I don't care where I have it!" moaned LaRenna through gritted teeth. She was being squeezed again only this time the pain radiated from her back. "Just get her out of me!"

"Krell, you and I'll take her to the med unit." Tatra ran back into the bedroom to slide on her skirt and slippers. She returned with Firman's boots and cloak. "Here, Firman, send a sentry to the Autlach settlement in the foothills and bring back their midwife, and hurry! She's close to delivering."

"My shirt, Tat. It's cold out."

Tatra rushed back to the bedroom and quickly changed tops. "Here, chilly man. Get going. Ready, Krell?"

"Yes." Krell reached down to pick up LaRenna, but was fiercely pushed away—both physically and mentally. "Don't touch me!" LaRenna clutched the back of the lounger, her knees drawn toward her chest as she struggled for air. "I'm not going . . . *ooh* . . . to be able to wait for . . . *Ow!* . . . the midwife or the birth suite. This child is coming NOW!"

"Change of plans, Firman." Tatra retook her place at LaRenna's head to support her patient's shaking torso. "Bring my emergency kit and some towels from the bed suite. Get that sentry going, then wake Belsas and Chandrey. They're about to become grandparents."

"We're not doing this in your front room!" cried Krell.

"We are," replied the healer. "And you're going to deliver it unless the midwife hurries up. You've done it before."

"Not my own child! This is different!"

"No, it's not." Firman dropped the medical kit and an armload of towels by Tatra's side. "It's merely a more personal experience. Back in a flash."

The entire compound sprang to life with Firman's courtyard ranting. It wasn't time to sleep! The first true Taelach child was being born.

Tatra laughed as his bellows reverberated throughout the compound. "I don't know who's more excited, Krell or Uncle Firman." LaRenna leaned against her, struggling through another back-breaking contraction. At her feet, Krell had pulled the blanket back and was making a quick internal exam.

"I can see the head!" She smiled up from between LaRenna's splayed legs. "The hair's Taelach white and there's lots of it!"

"She fully dilated?" Tatra was far more concerned about that than hair color.

"Yes, she is," said Krell. "Push whenever you're ready, love."

"How about now?" LaRenna groaned as she tried to force the infuriating presence from her body.

"Remember to breathe, wren bird."

"That's the least of my worries!" Sweat beaded on LaRenna's pale forehead. "I'm pushing out a damn ground melon!"

Tatra rubbed on her patient's taut stomach, trying to soothe away some of the pain with a phase. *No, LaRenna, it's just a baby. Autlach women have been doing this for hundreds of thousands of passes. If they can do it, Taelachs can, too, probably better.*

Belsas and Chandrey were still tying their loose robes about their waists when they burst into the apartment. "Why isn't she in the birthing suite?" Belsas moved to the side so Chandrey could take Tatra's place at LaRenna's head. The healer joined Krell for her own examination as the urge to push overwhelmed LaRenna again.

"Atta girl, wren bird!" encouraged Krell. "Count it out. One, two—"

All present lent their support by counting along. "Three, four—"

274

"FIVESIXSEVENEIGHTNINETEN!" LaRenna moaned. "It doesn't help!"

"There wasn't time to take her to the med unit, Grandmaster Belsas," said Tatra. "It happened too rapidly. The head crowned about the time they got this far."

"Tatra!" Krell jerked the healer's attention back to the immediate matter. "The head is in the canal. Is that what I think?"

"The cord!" Tatra reached to untangle the cord, but it was pulled too tightly around the infant's throat.

"Midwife's here." Firman's smile faded when he saw the despair wrenching across Tatra's slender face.

"Hurry up," begged Chandrey. "There's a problem." LaRenna wriggled in her arms while clutching the hand Krell extended.

Firman returned a few seconds later with the midwife bent across his shoulder. "Here she is!"

The midwife struggled out of his grasp and slid from her perch. "Put me down, young man, before I give you the spanking a spoiled child deserves. What could be so urgent that you need to abduct me in the dark of night?" She dropped her wrap when she saw what was happening. "Merciful heavens! The Taelach are finally breeding." Her hands were warm on LaRenna's quivering leg and her voice was unmistakably familiar. "Hello, young woman, we meet again."

"Nyla Smalls." LaRenna smiled weakly. "I was hoping I'd see you again some day. Never dreamed it would be like this."

"Me neither, child. Now let's see what we have here." Nyla examined her charge but looked unconcerned about the tightly wrapped cord. "I need the assistance of all three of you stronger types. One of you hold her upper body and the other two hold her legs. This baby needs air."

Krell took her position at LaRenna's head, while Belsas and Firman, faces turned respectfully away, each steadied a leg. "All right, mother." Nyla rubbed cleanser into her wrinkled palms. "Next contraction don't push. We must free the cord."

LaRenna took an apprehensive breath as the urge to push

275

resumed. Nyla looked straight at her as she inserted her hands to pull at the cord. LaRenna sobbed over the extra pressure that invaded her.

"I know it's painful, child, but we must, it's almost, yes, there it is. It's free!" Nyla wiped her hands on a towel. "I believe that strapping babe is ready to come out. Everyone except the father, no, guardian, needs to leave." Firman readily fled the room, but Belsas and Chandrey lingered, unwilling to go until Nyla asked them a second time. "Please, Grandmaster Taelach, you and your lady must leave. Things will go better if you wait in another place. This is a moment for the parents alone. My presence is medical only."

The elders left without further complaint. It wouldn't do to argue with the midwife. She appeared to have matters well in hand.

"It's time." Nyla gave LaRenna an experienced smile. "With the next one, you will push harder than you ever thought possible." She pointed to Tatra's emergency kit, motioning for the healer to spread it in front of her. She selected a small blade and doused it in cleanser.

LaRenna gasped when the pressure became acute. She had to get rid of it, the sooner the better. It was ripping her in half. Krell drew against her, supporting her by wrapping under LaRenna's arms as she prodded her for an open connection. "Let me in, wren bird." A nauseating wash of pain in Krell's groin and back signified the open channel. So this was what labor was like. No wonder most Autlach women opted for the relief of drugs.

"Are you linked?" Tatra watched Nyla intently, wondering what she intended to do with the blade. "Krell?"

"Mother help me," whispered Krell in a high pitch. "But this is intense."

"Inform me when you feel the start of another contraction." Nyla wished Autlach fathers could obtain the understanding Krell was. "Either of you." She was careful to keep the blade from LaRenna's sight. "Is the male who rushed outside the birth father?"

"No," Tatra replied before Krell managed to say something less than civil on the matter. "This child is pure Taelach. I'll explain how after this is over." Nyla's expression became puzzled, but she left the matter alone as LaRenna began to shake.

"Now?" asked Nyla, knife ready.

"NOW!" Krell could feel the pressure and sting of the cold blade as it sliced into LaRenna's undercarriage. The baby slid out of the birth canal to the shoulders. Nyla cleared the infant's nose and mouth, explaining her actions to Tatra as she worked. "When the child is this large"—she cleared the baby's eyes—"the cut keeps tearing to a minimum, reduces infection, and makes healing faster."

"I see," replied Tatra. "This is all so new."

"And almost over. All right, LaRenna, make this contraction your last. Deliver the shoulders and it will be finished. Help her, guardian. She's tired. This labor has been hard and fast."

Krell nodded and mustered her strength. *One more time, Wren bird. Let's bring our child into the world.* LaRenna remained silent but squeezed the arms cradling her. Together, they concentrated on the effort. There was a shot of squelching agony then a sudden release.

"The baby," whispered LaRenna. "Let us see her."

"Soon." Nyla knotted then cut the cord and rubbed the child with a towel, trying to stimulate a breathing response in the still, blue child. "Come on, cry for Nyla." She massaged the infant vigorously until it gasped, skin soon glowing the ruddy pink of new life as its whimper grew to an angry squall. "There we are." Nyla sighed. "Get mad and cry. It's healthy for you. Lets everyone know you've arrived."

"Let us see her," repeated Krell.

Nyla finished cleaning the wailing infant and wrapped it in a towel. "Soon." She stood silently over the child, gazing into her face.

"Please." LaRenna filled with the pain a few Autlach mothers felt when their Taelach children were ripped from them. "Is something wrong with her?"

277

"Nothing at all," replied Tatra, who was assisting in the delivery of the afterbirth. "Nothing at all." She took the infant from Nyla and turned to them. "She thinks you're impatient."

"The midwife?" queried Krell.

"No," cooed LaRenna as Tatra placed the infant in her arms, "our daughter thinks we're impatient." The new family cuddled on the lounger, Krell holding LaRenna and their child close. The infant ceased her crying, parted her pale blue eyes, and opened her mouth in a large, toothless yawn.

"Hello, young one," said Krell as the newborn's eyes fixated on her. "I'm your guardian parent, your sire, your gahrah. The beautiful lady holding you is your mother. Did you know you are the first true Taelach ever born? That makes you special. You're one of a kind, just like your mom."

LaRenna gazed at the little face that peered up at them. It was so similar to her own—round and glowing. Shades of Krell were present as well, evident every time the baby crinkled her forehead or raised her eyebrows in that peculiar manner all the Middle family seemed capable of. "Hello sweetheart," said her mother. "We've been waiting for you. Your gahrah is right. You're special. You're ours and we love you."

A new presence opened up in the mental link between the soul phasers, unexpected but soft and familiar in its touch. It didn't exactly express words, more like a stream of mental images depicting happiness, contentment, and love, even a slight amount of hunger. The infant blinked, her pudgy fist finding its way to her mouth, one mental picture projecting stronger than the rest. It was one of identity, self-awareness, a name—Jenza.

"Greetings, Jenza Mallen Krell," whispered Krell, unable to withhold the emotions that were already showering LaRenna's face. "The future is now and it's all yours. You've brought the Taelach full circle with your arrival. Welcome to the world."

Sarian People, Places, and Words

aerolaunch. Mode of transportation used by the Taelach and Autlach for long-distance travel.

Asabane Tackwell. Starnes Banes's father.

Autlach. Indigenous species to Saria Two, the second planet orbiting Sixty-One Cygni, short and stocky humanoids with dark features. Also called Aut for short.

bandit beast. Large, bison-like species native to and extinct on Saria Two but successfully reestablished by the Taelach on Saria Three.

battle braid. Taelach marker of battle victories and military rank worn in the hair.

Belsas Exzal. Taelach of All, life mate of Chandrey Belsas, guardian raiser of LaRenna Belsas.

bitterwine. Thick unsweetened berry wine.

blood marking. Archaic Taelach commitment ceremony; nuptials.

Brandoff Creiloff. Twin of Cance Creiloff, drug-addicted guardian and escapee from Trimar prison colony.

Cance Creiloff. Twin sister of Brandoff Creiloff, drug-addicted guardian, former Kimshee second officer in Silver Kinship, Chandrey Belsas's ex-life mate and escapee from the Taelach Trimar prison colony.

Chandrey Belsas. Raiser of LaRenna Belsas, life mate of Belsas Exzal, former life mate of Cance Creiloff.

crystal. Silicone substance found naturally on Saria Two, used for windows and containers; comparable to glass.

Death Stone. Marker used to record names of Autlachs buried in communal graves.

Farstar. Sixth planet in the Sarian system and location of the Trimar prison colony.

Firman Middle. Autlach brother of Krell Middle.

Firewall. First planet and uninhabitable world in Sarian solar system.

gahrah. Term of endearment Taelach daughters use for their guardian raiser.

grand master. Highest rank in the Silver Kinship military officer hierarchy.

guardian. Taelach who chooses to live in a more masculine role; butch.

healer. Autlach or Taelach physician.

Hiding Cave. Taelach stronghold containing items necessary for survival during times of trouble.

hunt. Outdated Autlach practice of capturing Taelachs for ritual execution or use as slaves.

Iralian commitment. A highly evolved reptilian species known for eating captives alive as a means of torture, originating in a star system near the Sarian system.

land-sculpting. Taelach process of terraforming (earth-shaping) a planet or moon in order to make it habitable.

Langus. Only moon of Saria Two and main agricultural resource for the Autlach.

LaRenna Belsas. True female daughter of Chandrey and Belsas Exzal, Silver Kinship Kimshee and junior officer apprenticed to First Officer Kimshee Krell Middle.

launch. Overland mode of transportation used by the Taelach and Autlach for short-distance travel.

life braid. Taelach marker of family and clan affiliation worn in the hair.

life mate. An oathed Taelach.

Kimshee. Silver Kinship military officers trained in diplomacy, Autlach customs, and advanced telepathy.

Krell Middle. Autlach-raised guardian Taelach, and First Officer Kimshee in Silver Kinship military.

Malley Whellen. Third officer engineer and LaRenna Belsas's roommate during officer training.

moon cycle. Thirty days on the Sarian calendar, comparable to one month.

Mother Maker. Taelach deity comparable to Gaia.

Myeflar. Moon of the planet Firewall, destroyed by the Iralian commitment during their initial invasion of the Sarian solar system.

pain phase. Lesser used of the two types of Taelach telepathic phases. It produces pain ranging from minor discomfort to death depending on the energy used by the originator.

Pass. Four hundred and twenty days completing the Sarian calendar, comparable to one year.

planetary launch. Mode of transportation used by the Taelach and Autlach for interplanetary travel.

pleasure phase. Taelach telepathic phase that creates sensations varying from enjoyable conversation to sexual ecstasy.

Prock. Native plant of Farstar; an addictive stimulant when inhaled.

Raskhallak. Popular Autlach deity that openly condemns the Taelach.

Saria. An uninhabited giant gas planet second closest to the sun in the Sarian star system, a collection of six planets and their respective moons orbiting Sixty-One Cygni; another name for the Sarian solar system.

Saria Two. Third planet orbiting Sixty-One Cygni, planet of origin for the Autlach and Taelach.

Saria Three. Fourth planet in the Sarian Star system land-sculpted by the Taelach and home to the Sarian High Counsel.

Saria Four. Fifth planet in the Sarian Star system terraformed by the Taelach and home to the Taelach military officers' Training Grounds.

Silver Kinship. Governing body of the Taelach.

Sixty-One Cygni. A yellow dwarf star in the Milky Way thought to be similar to Earth's sun.

soul phase. Deepest of Taelach pleasure phases used by long term couples for intimacy and healing.

Starnes Bane. Autlach owner of Waterlead Bar, son of Asabane Tackwell.

Strong's Disease. Disease of the nervous system common in elderly Autlachs; fatal if untreated.

Taelach. A subspecies of the Autlach who are all born female, pale-skinned, willowy in build, sterile and telepathic.

Talmshone. Spy for the Iralian commitment and co-conspirator with the Creiloff twins.

Tatra Wileyse. Taelach Healer and first officer in Silver Kinship.

Trazar Laiman. Autlach brother of LaRenna Belsas, mid-ranking Autlach enlisted military.

Trimar. Taelach prison colony located on Farstar.

true female. Taelach capable of childbearing.

Vartoch. Moon of Saria Three.

About the Author

Jeanne G'Fellers, her partner, and three children (two being those testy creatures called teenagers) live in Tennessee, where they share half an acre with two cats, a three-foot-long water dragon lizard, a dozen pampered Arbor Day trees and two gardens—one for herbs, the other for veggies. When not shuttling children or rescuing cats from the roof, Jeanne attends a local university where she also works as a graduate assistant.

No Sister of Mine is Jeanne's first novel.

Publications from
BELLA BOOKS, INC.
The best in contemporary lesbian fiction

P.O. Box 10543, Tallahassee, FL 32302
Phone: 800-729-4992
www.bellabooks.com

NO SISTER OF MINE by Jeanne G'Fellers. 240 pp. Telepathic women fight to coexist with a patriarchal society that wishes their eradication.　　ISBN 1-59493-017-1　$12.95

ON THE WINGS OF LOVE by Megan Carter. 240 pp. Stacie's reporting career is on the rocks. She has to interview bestselling author Cheryl, or else! ISBN 1-59493-027-9　$12.95

WICKED GOOD TIME by Diana Tremain Braund. 224 pp. Does Christina need Miki as a protector . . . or want her as a lover?　　ISBN 1-59493-031-7　$12.95

THOSE WHO WAIT by Peggy J. Herring. 240 pp. Two brillian sisters—in love with the same woman!　　ISBN 1-59493-032-5　$12.95

ABBY'S PASSION by Jackie Calhoun. 240 pp. Abby's bipolar sister helps turn her world upside down, so she must decide what's most important.　　ISBN 1-59493-014-7　$12.95

PICTURE PERFECT by Jane Vollbrecht. 240 pp. Kate is reintroduced to Casey, the daughter of an old friend. Can they withstand Kate's career? ISBN 1-59493-015-5　$12.95

PAPERBACK ROMANCE by Karin Kallmaker. 240 pp. Carolyn falls for tall, dark and . . . female . . . in this classic lesbian romance.　　ISBN 1-59493-033-3　$12.95

DAWN OF CHANGE by Gerri Hill. 240 pp. Susan ran away to find peace in remote Kings Canyon—then she met Shawn . . .　　ISBN 1-59493-011-2　$12.95

DOWN THE RABBIT HOLE by Lynne Jamneck. 240 pp. Is a killer holding a grudge against FBI Agent Samantha Skellar?　　ISBN 1-59493-012-0　$12.95

SEASONS OF THE HEART by Jackie Calhoun. 240 pp. Overwhelmed, Sara saw only one way out—leaving . . .　　ISBN 1-59493-030-9　$12.95

TURNING THE TABLES by Jessica Thomas. 240 pp. The 2nd Alex Peres Mystery. *From ghosties and ghoulies and long leggity beasties . . .*　　ISBN 1-59493-009-0　$12.95

FOR EVERY SEASON by Frankie Jones. 240 pp. Andi, who is investigating a 65-year-old murder, meets Janice, a charming district attorney . . .　　ISBN 1-59493-010-4　$12.95

LOVE ON THE LINE by Laura DeHart Young. 240 pp. Kay leaves a younger woman behind to go on a mission to Alaska . . . will she regret it?　　ISBN 1-59493-008-2　$12.95

UNDER THE SOUTHERN CROSS by Claire McNab. 200 pp. Lee, an American travel agent, goes down under and meets Australian Alex, and the sparks fly under the Southern Cross.　　ISBN 1-59493-029-5　$12.95

SUGAR by Karin Kallmaker. 240 pp. Three women want sugar from Sugar, who can't make up her mind. ISBN 1-59493-001-5 $12.95

FALL GUY by Claire McNab. 200 pp. 16th Detective Inspector Carol Ashton Mystery. ISBN 1-59493-000-7 $12.95

ONE SUMMER NIGHT by Gerri Hill. 232 pp. Johanna swore to never fall in love again—but then she met the charming Kelly . . . ISBN 1-59493-007-4 $12.95

TALK OF THE TOWN TOO by Saxon Bennett. 181 pp. Second in the series about wild and fun loving friends. ISBN 1-931513-77-5 $12.95

LOVE SPEAKS HER NAME by Laura DeHart Young. 170 pp. Love and friendship, desire and intrigue, spark this exciting sequel to *Forever and the Night*. ISBN 1-59493-002-3 $12.95

TO HAVE AND TO HOLD by Peggy J. Herring. 184 pp. By finally letting down her defenses, will Dorian be opening herself to a devastating betrayal? ISBN 1-59493-005-8 $12.95

WILD THINGS by Karin Kallmaker. 228 pp. Dutiful daughter Faith has met the perfect man. There's just one problem: she's in love with his sister. ISBN 1-931513-64-3 $12.95

SHARED WINDS by Kenna White. 216 pp. Can Emma rebuild more than just Lanny's marina? ISBN 1-59493-006-6 $12.95

THE UNKNOWN MILE by Jaime Clevenger. 253 pp. Kelly's world is getting more and more complicated every moment. ISBN 1-931513-57-0 $12.95

TREASURED PAST by Linda Hill. 189 pp. A shared passion for antiques leads to love. ISBN 1-59493-003-1 $12.95

SIERRA CITY by Gerri Hill. 284 pp. Chris and Jesse cannot deny their growing attraction . . . ISBN 1-931513-98-8 $12.95

ALL THE WRONG PLACES by Karin Kallmaker. 174 pp. Sex and the single girl—Brandy is looking for love and usually she finds it. Karin Kallmaker's first *After Dark* erotic novel. ISBN 1-931513-76-7 $12.95

WHEN THE CORPSE LIES A Motor City Thriller by Therese Szymanski. 328 pp. Butch bad-girl Brett Higgins is used to waking up next to beautiful women she hardly knows. Problem is, this one's dead. ISBN 1-931513-74-0 $12.95

GUARDED HEARTS by Hannah Rickard. 240 pp. Someone's reminding Alyssa about her secret past, and then she becomes the suspect in a series of burglaries. ISBN 1-931513-99-6 $12.95

ONCE MORE WITH FEELING by Peggy J. Herring. 184 pp. Lighthearted, loving, romantic adventure. ISBN 1-931513-60-0 $12.95

TANGLED AND DARK A Brenda Strange Mystery by Patty G. Henderson. 240 pp. When investigating a local death, Brenda finds two possible killers—one diagnosed with Multiple Personality Disorder. ISBN 1-931513-75-9 $12.95

WHITE LACE AND PROMISES by Peggy J. Herring. 240 pp. Maxine and Betina realize sex may not be the most important thing in their lives. ISBN 1-931513-73-2 $12.95

UNFORGETTABLE by Karin Kallmaker. 288 pp. Can Rett find love with the cheerleader who broke her heart so many years ago? ISBN 1-931513-63-5 $12.95

HIGHER GROUND by Saxon Bennett. 280 pp. A delightfully complex reflection of the successful, high society lives of a small group of women.   ISBN 1-931513-69-4 $12.95

LAST CALL A Detective Franco Mystery by Baxter Clare. 240 pp. Frank overlooks all else to try to solve a cold case of two murdered children . . .   ISBN 1-931513-70-8 $12.95

ONCE UPON A DYKE: NEW EXPLOITS OF FAIRY-TALE LESBIANS by Karin Kallmaker, Julia Watts, Barbara Johnson & Therese Szymanski. 320 pp. You've never read fairy tales like these before! From Bella After Dark.   ISBN 1-931513-71-6 $14.95

FINEST KIND OF LOVE by Diana Tremain Braund. 224 pp. Can Molly and Carolyn stop clashing long enough to see beyond their differences?   ISBN 1-931513-68-6 $12.95

DREAM LOVER by Lyn Denison. 188 pp. A soft, sensuous, romantic fantasy.
                                                          ISBN 1-931513-96-1 $12.95

NEVER SAY NEVER by Linda Hill. 224 pp. A classic love story . . . where rules aren't the only things broken.   ISBN 1-931513-67-8 $12.95

PAINTED MOON by Karin Kallmaker. 214 pp. Stranded together in a snowbound cabin, Jackie and Leah's lives will never be the same.   ISBN 1-931513-53-8 $12.95

WIZARD OF ISIS by Jean Stewart. 240 pp. Fifth in the exciting Isis series.
                                                          ISBN 1-931513-71-4 $12.95

WOMAN IN THE MIRROR by Jackie Calhoun. 216 pp. Josey learns to love again, while her niece is learning to love women for the first time.   ISBN 1-931513-78-3 $12.95

SUBSTITUTE FOR LOVE by Karin Kallmaker. 200 pp. When Holly and Reyna meet the combination adds up to pure passion. But what about tomorrow?   ISBN 1-931513-62-7 $12.95

GULF BREEZE by Gerri Hill. 288 pp. Could Carly really be the woman Pat has always been searching for?   ISBN 1-931513-97-X $12.95

THE TOMSTOWN INCIDENT by Penny Hayes. 184 pp. Caught between two worlds, Eloise must make a decision that will change her life forever.   ISBN 1-931513-56-2 $12.95

MAKING UP FOR LOST TIME by Karin Kallmaker. 240 pp. Discover delicious recipes for romance by the undisputed mistress.   ISBN 1-931513-61-9 $12.95

THE WAY LIFE SHOULD BE by Diana Tremain Braund. 173 pp. With which woman will Jennifer find the true meaning of love?   ISBN 1-931513-66-X $12.95

BACK TO BASICS: A BUTCH/FEMME ANTHOLOGY edited by Therese Szymanski—from Bella After Dark. 324 pp.   ISBN 1-931513-35-X $14.95

SURVIVAL OF LOVE by Frankie J. Jones. 236 pp. What will Jody do when she falls in love with her best friend's daughter?   ISBN 1-931513-55-4 $12.95

LESSONS IN MURDER by Claire McNab. 184 pp. 1st Detective Inspector Carol Ashton Mystery.   ISBN 1-931513-65-1 $12.95

DEATH BY DEATH by Claire McNab. 167 pp. 5th Denise Cleever Thriller.
                                                          ISBN 1-931513-34-1 $12.95

CAUGHT IN THE NET by Jessica Thomas. 188 pp. A wickedly observant story of mystery, danger, and love in Provincetown.   ISBN 1-931513-54-6 $12.95

DREAMS FOUND by Lyn Denison. Australian Riley embarks on a journey to meet her birth mother . . . and gains not just a family, but the love of her life.   ISBN 1-931513-58-9 $12.95

A MOMENT'S INDISCRETION by Peggy J. Herring. 154 pp. Jackie is torn between her better judgment and the overwhelming attraction she feels for Valerie.
ISBN 1-931513-59-7 $12.95

IN EVERY PORT by Karin Kallmaker. 224 pp. Jessica has a woman in every port. Will meeting Cat change all that?   ISBN 1-931513-36-8 $12.95

TOUCHWOOD by Karin Kallmaker. 240 pp. Rayann loves Louisa. Louisa loves Rayann. Can the decades between their ages keep them apart?   ISBN 1-931513-37-6 $12.95

WATERMARK by Karin Kallmaker. 248 pp. Teresa wants a future with a woman whose heart has been frozen by loss. Sequel to *Touchwood*.   ISBN 1-931513-38-4 $12.95

EMBRACE IN MOTION by Karin Kallmaker. 240 pp. Has Sarah found lust or love?
ISBN 1-931513-39-2 $12.95

ONE DEGREE OF SEPARATION by Karin Kallmaker. 232 pp. Sizzling small town romance between Marian, the town librarian, and the new girl from the big city.
ISBN 1-931513-30-9 $12.95

CRY HAVOC A Detective Franco Mystery by Baxter Clare. 240 pp. A dead hustler with a headless rooster in his lap sends Lt. L.A. Franco headfirst against Mother Love.
ISBN 1-931513931-7 $12.95

DISTANT THUNDER by Peggy J. Herring. 294 pp. Bankrobbing drifter Cordy awakens strange new feelings in Leo in this romantic tale set in the Old West.
ISBN 1-931513-28-7 $12.95

COP OUT by Claire McNab. 216 pp. 4th Detective Inspector Carol Ashton Mystery.
ISBN 1-931513-29-5 $12.95

BLOOD LINK by Claire McNab. 159 pp. 15th Detective Inspector Carol Ashton Mystery. Is Carol unwittingly playing into a deadly plan?   ISBN 1-931513-27-9 $12.95

TALK OF THE TOWN by Saxon Bennett. 239 pp. With enough beer, barbecue and B.S., anything is possible!   ISBN 1-931513-18-X $12.95

MAYBE NEXT TIME by Karin Kallmaker. 256 pp. Sabrina has everything she ever wanted—except Jorie.   ISBN 1-931513-26-0 $12.95

WHEN GOOD GIRLS GO BAD: A Motor City Thriller by Therese Szymanski. 230 pp. Brett, Randi, and Allie join forces to stop a serial killer.   ISBN 1-931513-11-2 $12.95

A DAY TOO LONG: A Helen Black Mystery by Pat Welch. 328 pp. This time Helen's fate is in her own hands.   ISBN 1-931513-22-8 $12.95

THE RED LINE OF YARMALD by Diana Rivers. 256 pp. The Hadra's only hope lies in a magical red line . . . climactic sequel to *Clouds of War*.   ISBN 1-931513-23-6 $12.95

OUTSIDE THE FLOCK by Jackie Calhoun. 224 pp. Jo embraces her new love and life.
ISBN 1-931513-13-9 $12.95

LEGACY OF LOVE by Marianne K. Martin. 224 pp. Read the whole Sage Bristo story.
ISBN 1-931513-15-5 $12.95

STREET RULES: A Detective Franco Mystery by Baxter Clare. 304 pp. Gritty, fast-paced mystery with compelling Detective L.A. Franco.   ISBN 1-931513-14-7 $12.95

RECOGNITION FACTOR: 4th Denise Cleever Thriller by Claire McNab. 176 pp. Denise Cleever tracks a notorious terrorist to America.   ISBN 1-931513-24-4 $12.95

NORA AND LIZ by Nancy Garden. 296 pp. Lesbian romance by the author of *Annie on My Mind*.   ISBN 1931513-20-1 $12.95

MIDAS TOUCH by Frankie J. Jones. 208 pp. Sandra had everything but love.
                                                          ISBN 1-931513-21-X $12.95

BEYOND ALL REASON by Peggy J. Herring. 240 pp. A romance hotter than Texas.
                                                          ISBN 1-9513-25-2 $12.95

ACCIDENTAL MURDER: 14th Detective Inspector Carol Ashton Mystery by Claire McNab. 208 pp. Carol Ashton tracks an elusive killer.   ISBN 1-931513-16-3 $12.95

SEEDS OF FIRE: Tunnel of Light Trilogy, Book 2 by Karin Kallmaker writing as Laura Adams. 274 pp. In Autumn's dreams no one is who they seem.   ISBN 1-931513-19-8 $12.95

DRIFTING AT THE BOTTOM OF THE WORLD by Auden Bailey. 288 pp. Beautifully written first novel set in Antarctica.   ISBN 1-931513-17-1 $12.95

CLOUDS OF WAR by Diana Rivers. 288 pp. Women unite to defend Zelindar!
                                                          ISBN 1-931513-12-0 $12.95

DEATHS OF JOCASTA: 2nd Micky Knight Mystery by J.M. Redmann. 408 pp. Sexy and intriguing Lambda Literary Award–nominated mystery.   ISBN 1-931513-10-4 $12.95

LOVE IN THE BALANCE by Marianne K. Martin. 256 pp. The classic lesbian love story, back in print!   ISBN 1-931513-08-2 $12.95

THE COMFORT OF STRANGERS by Peggy J. Herring. 272 pp. Lela's work was her passion . . . until now.   ISBN 1-931513-09-0 $12.95

WHEN EVIL CHANGES FACE: A Motor City Thriller by Therese Szymanski. 240 pp. Brett Higgins is back in another heart-pounding thriller.   ISBN 0-9677753-3-7 $11.95

CHICKEN by Paula Martinac. 208 pp. Lynn finds that the only thing harder than being in a lesbian relationship is ending one.   ISBN 1-931513-07-4 $11.95

TAMARACK CREEK by Jackie Calhoun. 208 pp. An intriguing story of love and danger.
                                                          ISBN 1-931513-06-6 $11.95

DEATH BY THE RIVERSIDE: 1st Micky Knight Mystery by J.M. Redmann. 320 pp. Finally back in print, the book that launched the Lambda Literary Award–winning Micky Knight mystery series.   ISBN 1-931513-05-8 $11.95

EIGHTH DAY: A Cassidy James Mystery by Kate Calloway. 272 pp. In the eighth installment of the Cassidy James mystery series, Cassidy goes undercover at a camp for troubled teens.   ISBN 1-931513-04-X $11.95

MIRRORS by Marianne K. Martin. 208 pp. Jean Carson and Shayna Bradley fight for a future together.   ISBN 1-931513-02-3 $11.95

THE ULTIMATE EXIT STRATEGY: A Virginia Kelly Mystery by Nikki Baker. 240 pp. The long-awaited return of the wickedly observant Virginia Kelly.
                                                          ISBN 1-931513-03-1 $11.95

FOREVER AND THE NIGHT by Laura DeHart Young. 224 pp. Desire and passion ignite the frozen Arctic in this exciting sequel to the classic romantic adventure *Love on the Line*.
                                                          ISBN 0-931513-00-7 $11.95

WINGED ISIS by Jean Stewart. 240 pp. The long-awaited sequel to *Warriors of Isis* and the fourth in the exciting Isis series.   ISBN 1-931513-01-5 $11.95

ROOM FOR LOVE by Frankie J. Jones. 192 pp. Jo and Beth must overcome the past in order to have a future together. ISBN 0-9677753-9-6 $11.95

THE QUESTION OF SABOTAGE by Bonnie J. Morris. 144 pp. A charming, sexy tale of romance, intrigue, and coming of age. ISBN 0-9677753-8-8 $11.95

SLEIGHT OF HAND by Karin Kallmaker writing as Laura Adams. 256 pp. A journey of passion, heartbreak, and triumph that reunites two women for a final chance at their destiny. ISBN 0-9677753-7-X $11.95

MOVING TARGETS: A Helen Black Mystery by Pat Welch. 240 pp. Helen must decide if getting to the bottom of a mystery is worth hitting bottom. ISBN 0-9677753-6-1 $11.95

CALM BEFORE THE STORM by Peggy J. Herring. 208 pp. Colonel Robicheaux retires from the military and comes out of the closet. ISBN 0-9677753-1-0 $11.95

OFF SEASON by Jackie Calhoun. 208 pp. Pam threatens Jenny and Rita's fledgling relationship. ISBN 0-9677753-0-2 $11.95

BOLD COAST LOVE by Diana Tremain Braund. 208 pp. Jackie Claymont fights for her reputation and the right to love the woman she chooses. ISBN 0-9677753-2-9 $11.95

THE WILD ONE by Lyn Denison. 176 pp. Rachel never expected that Quinn's wild yearnings would change her life forever. ISBN 0-9677753-4-5 $11.95

SWEET FIRE by Saxon Bennett. 224 pp. Welcome to Heroy—the town with more lesbians per capita than any other place on the planet! ISBN 0-9677753-5-3 $11.95